Mansions of Fire

Ken Berryhill

authorHOUSE®

AuthorHouse™
1663 Liberty Drive
Bloomington, IN 47403
www.authorhouse.com
Phone: 1-800-839-8640

First published by AuthorHouse 1/7/2010

ISBN: 978-1-4490-4293-6 (e)
ISBN: 978-1-4490-4291-2 (sc)
ISBN: 978-1-4490-4292-9 (hc)

Library of Congress Control Number: 2010900177

The views expressed in this novel are not held by the author, but are intended to emphasize the morals and values of another time and era. Any similarities found in the characters of this novel and any person, living or deceased, is purely coincidental.
Printed in the United States of America
Bloomington, Indiana
This book is printed on acid-free paper.

Contents

Chapter 1. Chateau Villa   1

Chapter 2. A Mentor Passes   11

Chapter 3. Saddle Business   20

Chapter 4. Rebellious Youth   27

Chapter 5. An Anxious Tryout   33

Chapter 6. Annual Horserace Society Ball   38

Chapter 7. The Railroads Decision   50

Chapter 8. The Chesser Family of Atlanta   58

Chapter 9. A First Horse Race   66

Chapter 10. A Promising New Career   78

Chapter 11. The Beginning of a New Life   88

Chapter 12. French Quarter Hotel   101

Chapter 13. Hurdle Jump Training   112

Chapter 14. A Secret Admirer   116

Chapter 15. News of Civil Strife   124

Chapter 16. A Future Beau   129

Chapter 17. Threat of Succession   138

Chapter 18. A Union Militia Activates   145

Chapter 19. A Sudden Departure   148

Chapter 20. Sins of Slavery   153

Chapter 21. A Tragic Accident   168

Chapter 22. A Timely Meeting   183

Chapter 23. Succession   195

Chapter 24. A Grieving Widower   206

Chapter 25. An Improvement   224

Chapter 26. A New Responsibility   247

Chapter 27. The Auction   264

Chapter 28. Unexpected Events   280

Chapter 29. First Days of Work   300

Chapter 30. The Great Race   321

Chapter 31. Puppy Love   338

Chapter 32. A Special Night   345

Chapter 33. Confrontations and Political Issues   377

Chapter 34. From the Front Lines to the Home Front   401

Chapter 35. Can A House Divided ... Stand?   407

Chapter 36. A Meeting of the Minds   419

Chapter 37. Mansions of Fire   438

Chapter 1
Chateau Villa

The stately, white plantation mansion home of the wealthy Fontenot rice crop family looked every bit of the opulence that would befit a king and his royal family. A carefully manicured lawn and landscape served to highlight the inlaid brick carriage drive at the front of the massive white mansion. High foliage hedges and strategically positioned weeping willow trees with Spanish moss graced the rolling grounds of the estate. Decorative iron gates divided the drive into two parts: the guest reception area, the second a passage to numerous stables and out buildings on the estate. The mansion, fondly named Chateau Villa, was indeed a superb example of French designed craftsmanship, the finished product of several years of careful estate planning.

Several prized race horses along with their caretakers were always at the brick stables. A small workout track situated behind the stables kept the horses in shape for high bet races near East New Orleans. To the far left and out of sight to the viewing eye were the ramshackle cottages of the manor slaves who worked in the rice fields. A lane dirt road led from the cottages to the edge of the fields. Adjacent to the mansion on the far right were the crop fields of rice with the road in parallel alignment.

Pierre Fontenot, the wealthiest man in the region, earned his fortune through hard work and dealing honestly in business, two principles his mother had engrained in his mind. His father had passed away on the voyage to the new land. As an only child Pierre was raised by his hard working and encouraging mother who didn't speak any English but insisted that young Pierre learn English to become successful in the new land. He had successfully built his rice empire from humble beginnings, first as a small time slave auctioneer, then later as a racehorse owner who consistently won small bet races, then by leasing land to local French rice farmers that were sharecroppers. Finally, a purchase of a huge tract of land, paid for in cash, was the result of years of savings and frugal living.

Apart from his huge rice farming manor the love of his life was his wife, Andrea, and their young sixteen-year-old daughter Gabrielle, an only child. Gabrielle was the light of his life, pudgy cute faced with dark almost black hair. She was the little pristine princess of the manor. He had met Andrea while negotiating a farm land lease deal seventeen years earlier. She was the sole daughter of a local French widower hotelier who had built and had involvement in many of New Orleans upscale hotel porches. Andrea had come from an up and coming local family. Her father had only become successful in recent years with his innovative hotel porch designs. Much of her early life had been spent in slightly below average to average surroundings in New Orleans.

Her marriage to Pierre had been late in life and matured fully, at least in the financial sense, only shortly before Gabrielle was born. After miscarrying once after Gabrielle's birth, Andrea was warned against having any more children. Both she and Pierre cherished

Gabrielle and waited on her every need, encouraging her desire to be a young aspiring socialite in the French population of the well to do.

Andrea still looked very young for being forty three; she was often mistaken for being ten to fifteen years younger. Pierre's mother, Anna, lived with them on the estate and kept up a separate floor of the manor to herself. She avoided any direct business transactions with her son but took an ambitious role in maintaining the interior of the estate. Still robust at age sixty nine she had a keen sense of detail for interior design; Pierre trusted her and was never disappointed with her exquisite purchases. She was the grand dame of the French well to do society and was well known for her tasty pastries and tea parties with other elderly French ladies of the rice farming and horse racing society circles.

Several well dressed colored house matrons served the Fontenot family well; Pierre had gone through great lengths to teach them French so that they could receive guests in their native tongue or in polished English. Being a Fontenot house matron was an honor among the coloreds. Anna herself had handpicked them after rigorous selection, when it was obvious that she and Andrea could not keep up with the maintenance of the mansion.

Pierre's natural ability to turn a profit in whatever he did was a gift that had been good to his family and himself. He never forgot those that helped him along the way and contributed generously in their times of need.

During a recent torrential rainstorm when many of the neighboring crop fields were lost, Pierre visited each and every of the affected rice farms and replaced their lost crop yield with outright cash. After all, they had in one way or another, contributed to his rice business success years earlier with free borrowed labor at planting and harvest time, which he could not afford at the time.

He often compensated family owners of horses that hardly ever won races. Horse racing was an expensive habit, and several losses in a row would bankrupt an up and coming racing enthusiast. Pierre wanted every player to have an equal chance, winning big at the races was no longer his financial security. His horses played a close second to his family. He owned several Arabian stallions as well as other well-groomed racehorses. His bricked building stables also boarded competitors horses. A hefty fee was charged for their housing and maintenance, their owners paid for the convenience of having a local quality stable instead of transporting their horses to as far away as another state.

A racehorse event was held every last Saturday of the month in East New Orleans. There were always huge turnouts for the wealthy horse owners and their wives, mostly because the women enjoyed catching up on juicy gossip and the men savored slapping each other on the back while sipping goblets of imported brandy, all the while boasting over what horse they would favor. Pierre, known as Perry, by those that knew him best, was a generous benefactor to lesser fortunate people and asked nothing in return for his monetary kindness.

Adjusting his collar and straightening his coat he approached the stable building to meet a local boy that wanted to be hired on as a stable hand. As he passed by the back of the mansion, he looked up to see his daughter waving and smiling brilliantly at him from a curtained window. He winked and waved back. Somehow Pierre thought that one day perhaps one of his better young hired hands could court Gabrielle, marrying the bosses daughter was an honored social norm and would be totally acceptable to him.

He had the sole responsibility of hiring outside of the mansion. Andrea and Anna took care of the domestic inside help. Approaching the stable, he noticed a tall, well-built, muscular young man waiting at the entrance of the main stable building.

"Pierre Fontenot," he greeted extending his hand.

"Charles Boyer sir," the young man answered as he shook hands with Pierre.

"Ah yes,…you are the eldest son of Francois Boyer of north New Orleans, I have heard about your stable skills, an` yes ah do board two horses of the Boyer family."

"Yes sir, two of our finest, my father brought them over here after our stable caught fire awhile back, one of the horses kicked over a lantern three of them were lost, but two were saved," he explained.

"Ah so, ah dreadful thing to hear, we all heard about it," Pierre responded.

"I'll work hard sir," Charles injected, "You won't be disappointed."

"Ah know you will, if not your father will hear about it, like I say….ah know you have excellent stable skills…so I don't see any reason why you can't hire on, you'll join the other boys on Monday."

"I'm much obliged, sir!" Charles responded.

"You'll help feed `em, brush em` and work em` out for the races," Pierre explained.

"My many thanks sir, "Charles again acknowledged, "It is quite an honor to work for the Fontenot family."

The two again shook hands and discussed race topics in general while Pierre walked him to the iron gates. Most of the time, Pierre spent more time asking questions and acquiring needed information prior to employing a new stable hand, but on this day, he was in a hurry, his elderly neighbor was ill and bedridden.

Walking back to the main stables he motioned with a head gesture to one of his chief stableman. The head gesture was a wordless understanding, he soon had prepared transportation. The stableman had known of his departure and was prepared with a polished buggy. Pierre mounted the buggy and was soon on his way. The wheels made a clickety clack sound as the buggy emerged onto the inlaid cobblestone drive and outward toward the road. His elderly neighbor had been an early mentor in many previous business deals. Pierre had learned a lot from him and never forgot his business prowess.

Arriving at the stately house a French speaking colored matron took his coat then escorted him to the upstairs bedroom. His elderly friend lay in a huge mahogany bed in a massive bedroom. His aged wife changed small white linen hand towels on his perspiring forehead and wiped his face.

"Philippe, my friend," Pierre said as he approached.

"Perry, so good to see you," she replied in a hoarse whisper, "Philippe has been like this since Thursday last, and his fever hasn't gone down. I have sent for the doctor."

Pierre could tell that his old friend knew he was there because of the movement of his eyes and a slight smile.

"I heard that he was bad off," Pierre replied, then, after a moments thought he added, "I have known him so long that ah feel like he is a part of my family."

"I have never seen him this sick," she replied in French.

Pierre just looked at her for a moment. He had almost forgotten, when excited or angry she would speak French, her native tongue.

"I will see to it that a doctor arrives to treat him," he replied in French, as well.

His elderly friend was very ill and had a high fever; his old feeble hands were crossed at the waist, outside of the quilts.

"This just happened last week, he complained of pain in the chest and nearly fell down several times," she explained, this time in English.

A colored maid entered the room to present a pitcher of cold water. As per cue she placed it on the dresser, and then just as quickly as she entered she turned about and left.

"Water will do him well," Pierre stated, "His fever might soon go away."

She continued to wipe his perspiring forehead and assured him that he would get better.

"You have your staff here to help you," Pierre stated, "The best I can do is summon a doctor that ah think is available today, no need to worry about his fee. Philippe is an old friend of mine and we go way back. I'll take care of it."

"That is very nice of you," she replied in French.

"Water will help, but he needs more than that, I'll be on my way now," Pierre said.

Pierre didn't personally know of another doctor, but his wife did. He knew that when he arrived home, Andrea would be sympathetic to the elderly man's immediate need for medical attention. She would have no issue with him offering financial help, and the doctor that she knew might be readily available.

"You have been very helpful, although he is weak and can not speak to you, I know that he knows that you are here," she assured, in mumbled French.

Pierre nodded, turned about, and then looked back one last time at his old friend.

"Thank you Perry," she said in French.

Arriving back at the manor he explained to his wife that Philippe was very ill with a high fever and that his summoned doctor had not arrived to tend to him.

"That poor man," Andrea replied, "So old and all, I know of a doctor that is at the Bellaire house bringing a baby, and he has been there for quite sometime, I know he should soon be done."

Gabrielle heard her father's voice and came bounding down the massive stairs.

"Papa!" she exclaimed.

"Gabrielle," he acknowledged, "How is my little princess today?"

Her gave her a big hug and looked her over.

"My, you are certainly beautiful and sweet," he said with a big smile.

"Is Mr. Philippe bad off sick?" she asked in French.

Andrea gave her a quick look because she had spoke in French, they had hired language tutors to perfect her English, and so asking in French was just her way of being a minor annoyance.

"Yes, he is," Pierre responded in English, "But he will be better soon, just as soon as I get a doctor to him."

"That is too bad," she replied switching back to English, "I know he will be better then."

Anna motioned for her to come into the kitchen area to assist with coating sugar on pastries. Gabrielle liked to sprinkle sugar; it was her favorite little job to help out.

"Grandma needs me," she said.

"Indeed she does," Pierre noticed, "I'll be looking forward to having some sugar coated pastries later."

Gabrielle went toward her grandmother and received a sieve of sugar to sprinkle on the awaiting hot pastries. The mansion's kitchen smelled like fresh dough and baked bread, Pierre turned back to Andrea.

"I know where the Bellaire place is, because Philippe is like family to us I will seek out a doctor for him, I'll be back in an hour or so."

He was in a daze as he realized, as he spoke the words, that he would probably never again see his friend alive. Andrea could see the sadness and shock in his eyes, and he looked into hers, he knew from her glazed over, numb stare that the feeling was mutual.

"He has always been so good to us," Andrea replied, as her voice trailed off because she was deep in though. Pierre gave her a minute to get herself together, expecting her to say something more. Finally, she said, "Go then, the doctor would be available by now, at best he will know where to go next."

Pierre looked back to see Gabrielle doing her little help out deed in the kitchen. Both of the colored kitchen matrons' helped as well. Anna smiled as they watched her delightfully sprinkle sugar on each, and then proceed to another.

"Beef roast tonight, along with rice and tomatoes," Andrea added.

"I will be back long before then," he added.

With that Pierre walked into what had become a cool day and got into the buggy to leave but not without waving to Gabrielle, who was peeking out from the kitchen window with a big smile. The cool autumn wind had rustled the treetops and caused leaves to fall onto the inlaid drive. He made a note to himself to have the drive swept when he came back. With a jiggle of the reins the horse picked up speed and headed onto the road.

Back in the kitchen, Andrea watched as Gabrielle sprinkled sugar on each of the lot of pastries that came from the huge hot spatula.

"Not too much!" she chastised, "Just a little on each one."

"Miss Andrea," a colored house matron said with folded hands, "Miss Gabrielles' tutor is in the vestibule, "May ah show him into the sitting room?"

"Gabrielle, it is time to wash your hands and get to your work," Andrea instructed.

"Yes mama," Gabrielle replied as she stepped away from the pasties.

Andrea had forgotten that this was the day of her tutors visit. The tutor was actually the local one room school teacher who also taught the children of the wealthy for extra income. He wasn't her only tutor, but one of three.

Hot fresh pastries and tea were immediately offered to him while he waited on Gabrielle to appear. He accepted the sweets and a julep with a wide grin. After a short time Gabrielle reappeared with her assigned work. She greeted the tutor with a slight curtsy, who was already in the sitting room.

The kitchen was busy now, two more cooks took over the sugar sprinkling, it was Gabrielle's job but she was painfully slow, although no one would ever say anything to that effect. She was the princess, they knew better. As a sixteen year old, she had almost made it look difficult; just to get attention.

Looking outward one of the house matrons noticed an ugly cloud formation in the sky and promptly began shuttering the windows.

"Oh my lands," he observed, "It's going be a comin' down mighty hard real soon!"

"Be sure to close the upstairs window shutters if you would," Andrea said, "It does look bad out there. I just hope Pierre makes it over there in time."

"Yes ma'am," came a curt reply.

The wind picked up and howled through a natural echo between the mansion and the stables. Several of the stablemen could be seen scurrying about getting the horses in from the feed bins, and other men shut the windows as quickly as they could. The tutors' horse and buggy was retrieved from the front of the mansion and taken to safety within the confines of the bricked stable building. The treetops bent with the ever increasing wind. Loose hay and debris could be seen hurling upward and onward. An even uglier darker overhead cloud appeared, and then settled as the wind slightly changed its course. A torrential rain poured down so fast that the stables couldn't be seen through the kitchen window, which one of the cooks quickly shuttered.

"It sho' is coming down hard!" one of the cooks replied.

"Good thing we got all the well water we needed," replied another, "We needed the rain, but my lands; if it don't stop them crops might be beat half to death!"

Chapter 2
A Mentor Passes

Although Pierre had not realized it, the original summoned doctor had arrived at Philippe's house shortly after he had left. The arrival was too late; the elderly respected man had passed away while his wife had tried valiantly to cool his raging fever. The doctor knew that he was gone when he arrived. He had been detained by the torrential rainstorm several miles away. Any antibiotic would not have worked anyway. The doctor put his medical tools away and closed his bag.

"He is gone," he said, "This fever is a wicked thing, but he fought as hard as anybody could have, his sweet soul will live on."

The elderly widow collapsed on the side of the bed with exhaustion. Opening the door the doctor signaled for several of the house maids to come and assist her because she had spent hours by the bedside waiting on him. He pulled a sheet and quilt up and forward to cover the lifeless body so that the housemaids would not be as afraid to enter the room.

"There was nothing more that could done, you did all you could," he said.

It was apparent to him that she more than likely did not hear him, as she was asleep with exhaustion. Standing there for a moment and not quite knowing what to do, he decided to lift her and place her on the sitting couch that she had the housemaids move there from the parlor after Philippe became sick.

"Yes suh?" said one of the housemaids as she stood in the bedroom doorway. It was obvious to the doctor that she knew that he had passed and was afraid to enter the room.

"The madam is asleep, having been very tired, "I need for you to send a messenger to Pierre Fontenot's house with the word of his passing," the doctor requested, "I will remain in the residence until she awakens."

"Right away sir!" she responded with a French accent as she scurried away.

Phillipes' funeral was attended by a multitude of mourners; Pierre had lost an old friend, a financial seer as well as an early mentor. He had looked at Philippe so much as a father that he scantly remembered. He was elderly and vulnerable to illness and fever. Pierre knew that he was gravely ill but didn't want to let on that that he knew. Pierre paid, out of pocket, for a special funeral carriage and gave the widow a nice settlement gift. After all, Phillipes financial advice had contributed to making the Fontenot family wealthy and a high ranking family among the French well to do. Out of respect for his friend, the next day Saturday, Pierre elected not to go to the horse races. He was in personal mourning he elected instead to visit the stables to check on the newly hired stable boy and receive any information that he could about the horses well being.

"The boy looks good to me," the stable supervisor said, "Comes to work when he is suppose to, does his job, always friendly and attentive to the horses, ah don't really have any complaints."

"That's good," Pierre added, "He comes from a good family so ah would expect as much."

The newly hired boy could be seen in the near distance helping the others with one of the priced race horses. Pierre watched him for a moment and envisioned that one of the best stablemen might be an excellent suitor for Gabrielle, but that was in the future.

"Next month is a big race from what ah hear," Pierre mentioned, "We'll have two horses there, and I expect that they will both be ready to run."

"Oh, they will be Mr. Fontenot you don't have to worry about that," the supervisor said, "All groomed and fit to run."

"Very good then, I'll leave you alone to your work," Pierre replied.

It had been awhile since Pierre had visited the back of the property, he had a large pond build back there even before the mansion had been completed. Wild geese and ducks made it their home, along with a variety of other wild life. The pond had been forsaken in recent years, there were more important matters to attend to, weeds were overgrown about the banks, wild reeds and honeysuckle had appeared where there had been none. The pond property just about came up to his back neighbors property line. It was on the other side of where the cottages were for the plantation slaves. The pond was isolated from its view; a grove of thick trees carefully hid it, as well as the natural landscape. Walking back up to the house he once again saw Gabrielle smiling and waving from an upstairs window. He smiled and waved back as he walked onward. The recent torrential rainstorm had not damaged the crops, and he was glad for that. Many people who bought his rice harvest would have been affected, as they sold their recently purchased crop from him to a broker, at an even higher margin.

Looking across the near horizon he could see the rows of coloreds working in the almost muddy fields. Farm wagons and field horses were nearby. The day was coming to a close; an orange sunset appeared in the horizon, the fields would be empty soon and twilight darkness was settling in. It would be another banner crop harvest year, maybe better than last year and the year before.

The family sat together at the huge mahogany dinner table. The table and eight matching chairs were custom designed by a local craftsman, a man that Andréa's father knew well. The gentleman, a man of great skill whose hands had calloused over the years from his diligent work, had crafted the table in a response to a request from Andréa's father. Her father had befriended the man many years before and watched his work evolve. He knew that his work was exceptional and Andrea would not be disappointed on her wedding day when her father presented the new couple with the gift, as he planned.

A white laced table clothe completely covered its surface, the scrolled and curved surfaces of the table and chairs were indeed a work of art. True to her father's expectations, Andrea had not been disappointed in the gift. In fact, as one of the most treasured possessions they had, it was card for accordingly. A delicately made lace tablecloth adorned the table top. It served to protect and preserve the intrigue engravings. This became especially important when Gabrielle entered the lives of her parents. As much as they doted on her, she, like all children, had made hundreds of messes at the table as a toddler as she grew.

Always a bit of a rebel, Gabrielle had enjoyed extra attention, whatever its nature, through out her life. Although she would never admit it, she occasionally carried out mischievous acts just to turn a few heads. She knew better and had never done anything malicious because although she was a handful, she possessed certain innocence as well. She never truly wanted to hurt anyone. Her parents were very well off; consequently she had been raised among the elite of society, people who only associated with other educated, well mannered individuals.

From the time she was young Gabrielle was taught to speak two languages. She was taught to say 'please' and 'thank you' sit up straight at the dinner table, always address elders with respect and not to say anything nasty when she felt angry. She had been reprimanded and disciplined by her father and mother when such actions were called for; never-the-less, she savored any opportunity to break one of the etiquette rules.

Wearing plain white aprons the colored kitchen matrons brought out enormous platters of steaming food. As per their custom they then stood against the dining room wall. Gabrielle playfully batted at the steam that arose from her plate, and then watched in amusement as the steam dissipated. Andrea glared at her. The piercing gaze of her eyes silently scolding her for her bad childish manners.

"It is so amusing to watch the steam," Gabrielle said in French, with the full knowledge that her mother would not like her speaking French at the dinner table. Andrea was patient because she knew very well that Gabrielle was feisty at sixteen, and determined to get a reaction out of her. Pierre returned thanks for the food in English. As always; the colored matrons bowed their heads during the prayer time.

It was a matter of respect for God. Pierre knew that only God could have brought him to the place he was at. He, his wife and Gabrielle lived in prosperity and had been richly blessed. Pierre tried to live out a life that would please God. He shared what he had and in that way he showed the needy God's love without preaching.

He didn't see God as a Sunday morning convenience. In his mind, the church was full of people who were pew warmers on Sunday and lived by the world the rest of the week. He thought there was way more to demonstrating true love and faith than two hours in a pew once a week. So although he wasn't much of a church attendee he tried to live out his life in a way that showed Christianity.

Gabrielle looked up and about and caught the scowling gaze on one of the matrons. She elected to bow her head as well. This time she had been caught peeking during meal prayer time. Although she would never confess it to anyone, Gabrielle, like many young women her age, questioned God. She was on a quest for answers to many deep questions, not all of which she fully understood. Some, she did not even know how to ask. Others, she did not dare to ask, for fear that she would be ostracized by the influential in high society, from whom she had been accepted. Deep down inside, Gabrielle thought that God was some far off entity that did not care for her personally. Sure, she had been taught differently, but the Bible was in her eyes just another book that the preacher opened every Sunday morning and nothing more. She thought if God cared and was all powerful, like they said, life would be all peaches and cream. There wouldn't be any sickness and suffering. There wouldn't be any death, or for that matter, any sin.

Despite her riches in the world Gabrielle sensed that there had to be more. Still, this whole idea that there was a God, well, she wasn't so sure of just yet. She had seen how cruel man could be to fellow man, and she had been hurt herself and she had carried that as sensitive feelings. Outwardly, she was all she had to be: well dressed, beautiful, smart, driven and adventurous. Inwardly she lacked any real sense of where she was heading in life, although she was expected to be a high achiever. She felt pressured to do what was expected, not who she was or what she wanted to do. There were times that she was so confused and upset that she didn't know what she wanted.

Afterwards, the matrons lifted the platter covers and even more steam rolled out, much to Gabrielles smiling delight, but this time she kept her hands to herself. Each first serving plate was attended to by the matrons, and second helpings were served independently. Supper was a family time for the Fontenots, not a time to discuss business and not a time for amusement. It was quiet time, a time to relax and enjoy a family dining setting.

But Gabrielle always some sort of distraction. In her own cute charming girlish way, something that she would do, or say, would get a scowl look from somebody, but never any verbal reprimands. She was the heir-to-be princess in the family, after all.

A huge roast was immediately sliced with a butcher's boning knife. Silver bowls of vegetables and rice were served to each member of the family. Gabrielle turned up her nose to steaming beets, but knew that she would have to eat them anyway. Anna was served her usual hot steaming teapot, with the first cup of tea being poured by the nearest kitchen matron standing next to her. Several lemon slices were placed nearby.

As usual the family ate in silence, as it was their usual custom. Only a few small comments from Pierre directed to his mother of brief local government policies interrupted the silence. Gabrielle could have cared less about what her father was saying about what the mayor thought or what was happening in the legislature, but her grandmother seemed to listen intently.

The deep dish banana pie that she saw in the kitchen looked delicious, but she knew there were still the rest of the beets to eat. She hated the beets but loved the pie. So, in one heaping portion, she crammed all of the beets into her mouth until beet juice ran down her chin. Her mother, totally horrified at her daughter's reaction, shot her a stare for her unfeminine like manner. Such dining habits were reserved for the stable hands, not for anyone of the Fontenot family.

Eventually, the banana pie was served on separate plates and was readily devoured; it was a favorite family dessert. Gabrielle savored every bite, eating hers slower than the others, but with the same level of enjoyment. Banana pie, although it was a family favorite only appeared on the family table when a special occasion deemed it appropriate.

Both Andrea and Andrea knew that, and they had a feeling that they knew what the special occasion might be this time. Mother and daughter glanced up at each other as they wiped their mouths on white table towels that were handed to them. The silent, knowing gaze of Andrea confirmed what Gabrielle had suspected as her mothers happy eyes became a sly grin. Finally, the trip that had long been discussed was perhaps at hand. Gabrielle knew that Andrea knew more than she what she was trying to communicate, but decided that is was of no matter, she was almost clueless.

At the end of the meal, Pierre stood and heartily announced, "We are going to New Orleans!"

Gabrielle leapt up from her seat, sending it toppling backwards. Andrea was too amused by her sudden reaction to scold her.

"Oh, Father!" she squealed in a child-like falsetto voice.

Pierre beamed as his heart was warmed by his daughter's joy. She ran to his arms for a hug.

"Yes honey, we are really going!" he replied.

He was eager to sign off on a huge parcel of rice and be paid for it accordingly. Twelve of the railroad rice cars had come from Fontenot farm, it had been a record breaking harvest year as last year he had eleven cars. Each of the major produce plantation farmers were there to collect on an agreed to price for their crop. Various produce harvests were available and weighed by the ton.

Andrea and Gabrielle waited by the passenger loading area while the Fontenot rice shipment was being weighed. Pierre finally appeared with a big smile and a bank draft for the seasons harvest sale.

Finally, the huge long freight train belched with steam as it pulled out of the depot in New Orleans then headed eastward. All of its cars were laden with rice and produce products from the region. Freight trains ran one stretch of the track, passenger trains ran on the other. Several miles down the track a switch funneled the two onto a common railroad track, with several miles in between.

"We did very well," Pierre said to his wife as they walked away.

"Well, good," she replied, "Every year gets better as we sell for more money."

Pierre helped Gabrielle get into the carriage that that brought them there, then assisted Andrea, after untying the horse from the hitching post he himself boarded and turned the carriage around. The wheels made a metallic clickety clack sound on the inlaid brick street as they headed toward the downtown district. Andrea looked back to see Gabrielle was just amazed at the sights of the city. Every passing building of interest to her got a big wide eyed smile.

"What's that mama?" she asked of the building to the right.

"It's a restaurant, more than likely they serve our rice in there, aren't those windows beautiful?" she noticed, "That's stained glass, all those pretty frames as well."

The numerous carriages, buggies and single rider horses filled the inlaid brick streets with traffic in both directions and from perpendicular streets. Two lanes of traffic went both ways. Well dressed city people walked down the wooden boardwalk in front of the businesses, children could be seen tagging along behind. Horses and carriages were parked and tied in front of watering troughs, some were being led away, and others had been there for awhile. Pierre tipped his hat to one of his buyers who had just passed by in a two seat buggy.

"Andre," he murmured to his wife, "He's goin' ta collect his dividends on the rice, he is too late, the train has left."

"I believe I met his wife once, at the races maybe six months ago, she was quite nice," Andrea responded.

Gabrielle, sitting in the back, took all of the sights in. It had been several years since she accompanied her parents on a rice shipment trip to New Orleans. She had not quite remembered all that she had seen. It had changed a lot in her eyes. She was overwhelmed with it all and sat mesmerized at the various tall decorative wood buildings, in her eyes they might as well be a mile high. Slightly pointing and smiling as she went she was truly transfixed with the city, it was so much different than the rice manor. Pierre and Andrea agreed that she and Gabrielle would shop for apparel.

Chapter 3
Saddle Business

He wasn't interested in going with them, but would return for them in three hours. Pierre had planned to visit one of his horse racing friends who had an idea for a newly styled racing saddle. A huge faced circular clock, by coincidence, faced the general area of the apparel shops that Andrea had wanted to visit.

"Three hours then," she said, "That will give us enough time."

Gabrielle was still so transfixed that she didn't hear her mother speak to her when the carriage stopped.

"Gabrielle, stop your daydreaming!" she admonished, "We are going dress shopping, Papa is going to visit a horse friend and will be back to get us in three hours."

"Yes mama," she replied in French, further taunting her mother, Andrea just rolled her eyes and slightly shook her head.

Pierre helped them both get out of the carriage, "Gabrielle, you listen to your mother, don't go wondering about, this is a big city!"

"Yes Papa," she replied in English this time, with a downward pout look.

Once they were situated on the boardwalk Pierre continued down the inlaid brick street.

"Ah, Perry!" said the saddle master, upon his arrival. "How good to see you, ah trust you did well at the sellers harvest market?"

"Very well, indeed," Pierre replied as he shook his hand, "It's been awhile Jacque, how have you been?

"I been keeping the stables in harnesses, a lot of saddle repair, but staying busy, a little of this and a little of that."

"Yes, we did very well," Pierre stated again, "You had said several weeks ago that you had a new saddle, thought ah would just come by and see for myself, if you don't mind."

"That's what they're all saying, very little bargaining this year, everybody got their asking price, ah yes, rightly so, ah did say that, come in the back and see for yourself."

Pierre followed him past the busy leather craftsman at their work tables, various sheets of cowhide could be seen hanging about, and they then went to a bigger secluded work area that was only Jacques.

"The new race saddle, finally!" Jacque said as he proudly pulled a cover away from his hidden creation.

"It's so different!" Pierre exclaimed with a wide grin of admiration, "It's lighter, leans forward, looks very good, very good work!"

"Well thank you. We tried it last week on a couple of runs, and the horse responded well, so we're anxious to win some races now," Jacque replied.

"To be fair, all of the horses have to run using the same saddle," Pierre reminded him, and he nodded as Pierre asked "How many are you going to make?"

"Well, Perry, that's going to be a problem. I can't keep up the way it is, and this saddle would require my best craftsmen. They are busy, as you can see. If I were to take on this new project, I would have to hire more men to take over what they are doing now and move them to working full-time on the saddle. Well, right now, this one that everyone is used to is the only one in existence, and to introduce something so different means taking a risk. Are you willing to risk it? It could mean the loss of money and your reputation," he replied.

"How many are you going to make?" Perry asked again, this time more directly and with firm conviction.

"I would think a hundred an` sixty this year alone, all things being right."

His voice sounded tense, almost uncertain and quieter than usual. Pierre could read between the lines. He sensed that his friend was financially strapped at the moment.

"Deliver this one to my stables," Pierre requested, "If it is everything you say it is, I'll provide the funding for production, provided you pay me back."

"I am not so sure that this will work out. It's a good product, but the jockeys are so used to the old saddles that I am unsure if this new one will go over as well as we think. What if it doesn't?"

"Then, you needn't pay me back, but I apparently have more faith in this saddle than you do. I think that once the jockeys start using it, everyone will want one," Pierre responded.

Just then, one of the nearby leather craftsmen shook his head and directed a silent glance at Jacque; he understood immediately. This was the unspoken cue to hide the saddle. An army cavalry officer had just entered, and they did not want anyone knowing about the new saddle yet.

Jacque immediately placed the cover over the new saddle and directed Pierre away from it for a moment. Pierre sensed the level of Jacque's intent to keep it secret for now in front of other customers. He thought that wise, so for the moment, he pretended to just be a common horseback riding, saddle buyer.

The officer removed his hat and looked about for the proprietor. His expression was serious. He was anxious to either place an order or purchase some things and knew what he wanted.

"May I assist you, sir?" one of the craftsmen finally asked uncomfortably.

"Perhaps you may," the officer responded, aware of the man's discomfort and trying to use a less-serious tone than he normally used in order to make the gentlemen more at ease, "I'm interested in saddles for the cavalry. We would need many, as I am sure you probably assumed. I wish to speak to the proprietor about a quote for a substantial order."

Not wanting to be rude to Pierre but still take care of his customer's request, Jacque stepped forward to address the need.

"I am Jacque Claude Barbot, the owner. How may I assist you, sir?"

The officer reached inside of his pocket and produced a ledger that described the cavalry's need for saddles.

"You read English?" the officer asked rather sarcastically.

"Of course, sir," Jacque replied as he slightly bowed, "I read, speak and write both English and French."

Pierre stayed in the background and pretended to look at another saddle, but he was listening to the conversation with interest and slight concern. He didn't show it, though. Pierre had nothing to worry about, though he didn't realize it. The officer had barely noticed him.

Jacque looked the order over. It was an order for two hundred and twenty one of the most common riding saddles that the cavalry used. Thankfully, there was nothing special about them. The order came complete with a delivery schedule requesting seventeen saddles per week until the order was complete. On the order, it stated that the task would commence in a month.

This was a very good business opportunity. However, the government had a habit of being slow to pay, much more so than regular public accounts. Jacque studied the terms, frowned thoughtfully, and then conferred with his lead leather craftsman over the delivery terms. It was a rigorous schedule, to say the least.

"We have made a few custom saddles for cavalry army officers in the past," Jacque finally said, after a few moments of rubbing his chin.

"I'm aware of that," the officer shot back, "I own one of them, and it has been comfortable. I thought about your business for this order, and if you want the order, I need a price for your services and a commitment to the schedule."

"When do you need your price," the lead leather craftsman asked in broken English.

"No later than the day after tomorrow," the officer replied, "Ah, one more thing. This is to be kept between us," he said in a lower tone of voice.

"Very well, sir, my lips are sealed" Jacque replied, "Please come see us again in a day or two. You shall have your price at that time. We have no problem with the schedule of seventeen a week. I will also respect your request to keep this confidential. That is always good business practice, anyway."

The response had just put Jacque in a bind. He wanted to fulfill the army's order for the saddles. Unfortunately, wealthy Pierre Fontenot was in the background inquiring about possible production for the new racing saddle.

"Payment is cash, once a month, or every fourth Friday," the officer replied.

The word cash raised the eyebrows of both Jacque and his lead leather craftsman, particularly if it was once a month. It would be a good contract. Jacque rubbed his chin some more and wryly smiled to himself as he thought of Pierre in the background inquiring about production costs that Jacque didn't presently have, the funds to cover production for the new racing saddle.

Especially if they were paid monthly, it would be a good contract. Jacque rubbed his chin some more and wryly smiled to himself as he thought of Pierre in the background. This would certainly provide him an excellent opportunity for him to make some extra money to help cover the costs of producing the new racing saddle.

"Perhaps I could look for a riding saddle for my six-year-old boy," the officer said, "He wants to start riding soon, so do you make such a saddle?"

"Oh yes!" Jacque replied, "We do make riding saddles for children. We have to, of course. Young ones have to get around too, and the horse is the main mode of transportation."

Before the officer could explain more about his son's experiences with horses or what he might want in a new saddle for the boy, the front door opened unexpectedly. Two frizzy-haired, bordello blondes with very low-cut dresses that showed quite a bit of their cleavage entered, and seeing the officer, seemed slightly annoyed.

"Why James!" one said looking dropped jawed at the officer, "How dare you leave us for so long? You said you would be right back!"

"We waited for such a long time. You said you wanted to play!" the other stated in passionate protest.

"This is New Orleans, not a northern city," the first one interrupted, "You said this saddle business wouldn't take very long. Shame on you for making us wait!"

"You Yankee boys just take too long!" the second interjected as she batted her eyes.

The cavalry officer turned red in the face, knowing that he had been totally humiliated by two bordello ladies of the evening. Looking quickly at Jacque, he turned about and left with them. Jacque smiled and chuckled to himself, and then to his lead leather craftsman. The seemingly serious-minded acquisition officer had other things on his mind.

"Jacque," the craftsman said uneasily, "Are you certain we can deliver seventeen saddles a week?" he asked in French.

"I think we can do it," he replied, in French as well.

Pierre finally emerged from his somewhat concealed location and laughed at what he had just witnessed between the officer and the ladies. He knew that adultery or even lust after another woman when a man was married was sin, and yet the whole scene struck him as funny.

"Ah," he exclaimed in English, "An army warrant officer that cheats on his wife!"

"I didn't know what to say, Pierre," Jacque said hesitantly, "The army offers good business. Seventeen saddles a week is unheard of, and we get paid in cash."

"Don't you worry about the racing saddle for right now," Pierre responded, "Let me take it for the racing ball, let me see if it is popular with the jockeys, from there, we can determine production needs and such."

"Are you sure?" Jacque inquired, not wanting to insult his wealthy friend.

"The military is planning something," Pierre explained, "I can assure you that there will be another order after this one, and you need to remain in good standing with them because they will pay you well and you need the money. They are training new cavalrymen for possible action that might involve retaliation for ruining Harper's Ferry."

Chapter 4
Rebellious Youth

"Papa, Papa!" Gabrielle exclaimed as he came into sight, "Mama bought me four beautiful dresses, oh, they are so beautiful, ah am so pleased!"

Pierre acknowledged her presence and smiled but gave his wife an inquisitive look. Andrea let out a sigh and rolled her eyes in response, apparel shopping with Gabrielle had been quite an experience.

"Well that's wonderful!" he responded, "I trust that you stayed with mama and didn't wonder off on your own?"

"She at least stayed with me," Andrea responded, "It took awhile!"

Pierre could see that she was annoyed. Gabrielle had taken too much time selecting her own clothing and Andrea had no time to buy anything for herself. The original plan was for both of them to buy in the time allotted. The new dresses were for the up and coming horse race social gala that only happened once a year. But now it was time to return to the manor, it would be getting dark soon in New Orleans. It would be a long ride back. He could tell that Andrea was continually annoyed with Gabrielle. Her demeanor wasn't the same; she wasn't her usual talk able self. She seemed distant, almost disappointed in the trip.

Gabrielle once again sat in the back of the carriage and clutched her prized purchases close to her, ever beaming all the while. She was in heaven. Normally Andrea would have made the dresses herself, but this year she elected to buy because the rice harvest had been so good and that meant that there was quite a bit of money to spend. Now she would be constrained time wise to make her own dress in time for the gala, or would have to use a previous one.

Finally, Andrea broke the silence as the carriage made its way to the outskirts of the city.

"I trust that Jacque and his family are well?"

Pierre could tell that she had settled down from the experience and more relaxed now.

"I suspect his family is fine, he didn't say anything to the contrary, Jacque has developed a new racing saddle which will be shipped to the manor and will be shown at the racing gala," he responded.

"Oh that's wonderful! He's very talented like that; I know it will do well."

"It looks very good, but all of the horses would have to run with it," Pierre stated.

Andrea looked back to see that Gabrielle had opened one of the boxes and was admiring her new dress.

"Gabrielle, if you don't mind, that can wait until we get to the manor," she admonished.

Gabrielle looked up startled; she didn't know that she had been watched, "Yes mama," she replied in French as she stuffed the dress back into the box. Andrea had gotten use to her little nuances. Any negative response would prompt Gabrielle to do it more. Instead she ignored it.

Late twilight had set in as Pierre pulled the carriage up to the front entrance of the manor, almost immediately a stable porter arrived to take the carriage and the horse to the stable. Pierre helped Andrea and Gabrielle out of the carriage, and then nodded for the porter to approach and take the carriage away. It had been a very profitable day for the rice harvest; the rice was over for the season now. There was little lead time between the rice harvest season and major horse racing events. Miss Prissy, the heavy set colored house matron, as she was known to all, heard them arrive and opened the massive mahogany double doors as they approached.

"Did yeas have a good time in the city?" she asked.

Andrea gave her a wry smile as she passed by but Gabrielle was beaming with delight as she clutched her apparel boxes. Pierre was proud as well. He did very well in the railroad rice resale market.

"Prissy," Andrea said as she entered the foyer, "I'm not feeling very well, if you could make some tea?"

"Right away madam!" she responded, as she scurried away.

Prissy was Andreas` personal pick to head up the colored house matrons, she kept the others in line very well and was the fastest of the group to learn basic French.

Andrea herself promoted her two years ago. Prissy never disappointed her.

Gabrielle immediately bounded up the massive stairs to try on and show her new dresses.

Pierre retreated to the study to work up some numbers for manufacturing the new saddle. The saddle looked promising, unlike anything he had ever seen, it as sure to be a hit at the horse racing ball. The annual festivity ball had actually started as a small social gathering of cigar smoking men and had evolved from that into its current collection of high stakes society families that formed a social dance, then, later, a formal ball. This would be the third year that an orchestra was hired to play, select colored house matrons from each of the families would be present to wait on tables and serve drinks. Miss Prissy would once again represent the Fontenot family. Pierre sat at his desk and mentally figured out the labor as well as the material to produce various quantities of the saddles.

"The madam has gone to sleep for the night," Miss Prissy stated, referring to Pierre's mother, "She was very tired."

"Just as well," Andrea replied, as she sat at the table and adjusted a dinner napkin on her lap. Miss Prissy then served her a saucer and poured tea from a silver pitcher.

"Thank you so much, Prissy," Andrea responded as the steam from the tea arose in front of her. Miss Prissy just curtly nodded and hesitated for a moment as her jaw dropped.

Gabrielle appeared at the top of the stairs in one of her new dresses and was walking down the massive stairs.

"My lands child!" Miss Prissy noticed, "That dress is just too low for you, you just can't be showing your bosom like that!"

Andrea also noticed the low cut dress; it was obvious to her that Gabrielle had done her own altering to make it fit the way she wanted.

Miss Prissy approached Gabrielle and pulled up the front of the dress to hide the cleavage that she deemed unfit to see.

"Why that's just scandalous!" Miss Prissy said as she tugged even harder.

"I'll do what I want!" Gabrielle hissed in French.

Gabrielle had altered the front of the dress so that it would not come up any further.

Miss Prissy looked upward and ahead at the top of the steps to see one of the colored house matrons quickly dart out of view, as she had assisted Gabrielle in the alteration.

"Well, you can wear it in the house, but not to the ball," Andrea stated, "No decent French girl would be seen dead looking like that!"

"You don't like it mama?" Gabrielle inquired, knowing full well that she didn't.

"It's too revealing and you know it," Andrea quickly replied.

"But mama," Gabrielle responded, "It's what I saw on the boardwalks in New Orleans. I'm prêt near grown up anyways!"

"Those ladies are grown, ah have no control over what they do, and the way they want to look, but ah do have control over you, you will not wear that to the ball, don't try that on any of the other dresses that we bought!" Andrea explained.

Gabrielle nonetheless turned around several times with her parasol and modeled the dress for the sheer sake of annoying her mother. Miss Prissy shot her a glare of contempt and would make it a point to speak with the matron that assisted her in altering the dress to make it much more low cut, exposing cleavage that she deemed unfit.

"Alright then mother," Gabrielle sighed, "I won't change the others."

Miss Prissy shook her head in disbelief that Gabrielle would even consider going out in a dress as such.

It suddenly occurred to Andrea that Gabrielle had noticed the wrong fashion statement in New Orleans. They had no choice but to pass by several bordellos, Gabrielle had noticed the low cut dresses and high fashions, but not noticed or appreciated other things about the seemingly beautiful ladies. She sullenly turned about and approached the stairs, whispering something under her breath as she went; Miss Prissy just stood there with arms folded and gave her a fixed scowl. For Gabrielle this was the first time attending the horse racing ball, there would be other young people there as well, but they all would sit with, and be with their parents.

"Are ye feeling better, Miss Andrea?" Miss Prissy asked as she attempted to pour more tea.

Andrea gave her a hand motion that she had enough tea for the time, "A little I suppose," she murmured.

Pierre reviewed his findings; the manufacturing payback for the new saddle was greater than what he had originally anticipated. All that was left now was to prove the new saddle on his proving track; that would be done readily enough tomorrow or the next day.

Satisfied with his findings he lit one of his favorite cigars and approached the huge curtained window in the study, the stable was quiet, only a few lantern reflections could be seen in several of the out buildings, the stablemen were getting ready to leave for the day. He would go to the bank tomorrow morning and deposit his bank draft for the rice harvest sale.

Chapter 5
An Anxious Tryout

After a few minor adjustments to the new saddle, the jockey gave the nod that he was ready for the run. Pierre nodded back and moved to a viewing position behind the split rail fence yet in front of them. Raising his starting pistol, he glanced one more time for the start. The jockey was ready.

At the sound of the gun's fire, the horse took off from the start with majestic speed and fluid agility. The horse's mane billowed in the wind, as it took all of the jockey's strength to keep the horse under control. With arms bouncing up and down and legs clutching the side of the horse, the jockey sensed the horse was moving faster than he ever had.

Pierre watched as the horse and rider disappeared in the horizon. He kept a close eye on the jockey. He was sitting further back than usual and crouched forward more. There was a better arch in his back, but it looked uncomfortable.

Finally, the practice run was over. The jockey directed the horse back to where Pierre was standing. The jockey felt very proud because he thought this had been his best run yet.

"A good run, I'd say!" the jockey said breathlessly.

"Very good" Pierre commended, "Excellent run. Are you comfortable with that saddle?"

"I have to admit that it is different. It takes a different stance, sir, to ride it," the jockey replied, "It does give more control, and just takes some getting use to, that's all."

"Very good, then. We'll do more practice runs tomorrow, on a different horse," Pierre said, "Good run, very well!"

Pierre looked over at the stable to notice that his new hire was preparing to receive the incoming horse. The horse would be brushed, fed, and then walked for a bit.

"If I can say, he's an excellent blue blood horse!" Charles said as he knew he was being observed.

"He ought to be. He cost enough!" Pierre replied.

The jockey dismounted and handed the horse over to others standing about. Charles, being new, would only assist in the duties. Others remarked about the new saddle. It was different, but the jockey was happy with it. Pierre was happy with the results of the day and his saddle looked like a promising prospect for the future of riding horses.

The following day, a different jockey and horse would try out the saddle. They didn't have much time for the trial runs; less time than what Pierre would have liked potential customers to have at the horseracing ball, which was coming up very soon.

None-the-less, several saddles would be presented and discussed. Still, the new saddle would take center attention because it was so radically different.

Pierre joined a discussion with his stablemen about the practice run, which they had witnessed as well. Opinions were favorable, and the horse reacted very well. Pierre smiled to himself, realizing that his product had gone over far better than he expected.

"We'll see what tomorrow brings," Pierre remarked as patted the horse on the mane.

"Have a good day, sir," his chief stableman said as Pierre was preparing to leave the stable area.

"Likewise," Pierre replied, "The new saddle looks good. The jockeys seem to like it. Let's just see what another horse will do with it."

His work at the stable was done for the day. He had accomplished all that he wanted to get done for the time being. There would be minor adjustments on his cost for manufacturing the saddle. Jacque would have to be consulted once again, but it wasn't a big issue.

Gabrielle again modeled another dress for her mother. It was a better fit, and one which was approved. This time, the modeled fit up was in Gabrielle's bedroom.

"But it binds me so, mother!" she objected as she tugged at the sides.

"The rest of the girls will be wearing about the same style of dress at the ball," Andrea commented, "I can let it out some if it is uncomfortable. It won't take much."

Andrea got her sewing basket and extracted her clothe chalk. A line was drawn at the area where Gabrielle said that it bound her. Gabrielle eased out of the new dress and put her other dress back on. Andrea handed the dress over to Miss Prissy, who was told to let the hem out some at the marked area.

"That should do it. You should be able to wear the dress when it is fixed. You will look so pretty and grown up," she commented.

"Will there be boys at the ball?" Gabrielle asked.

"Most certainly," Andrea replied, "Young sons of the owners and young jockeys."

"Should I wear this hat or that hat?" she asked as she directed her mother's attention to two slightly different hates.

"Well, we didn't buy a hat for you. That one best matches the color and style of the dress, and most of the girls will be wearing hats like that," Andrea replied. Gabrielle modeled it and received an immediate chuckle from Miss Prissy.

"That's wrong, child," Miss Prissy commented, "It tilts backward more and to the right. Here, let me help you."

Miss Prissy approached and gently repositioned Gabrielle's hat. Gabrielle stood before the full length mirror, admiring her hat. Turning about, she tried several rather seductive poses before she was satisfied that the hat would stay in place.

"You ain't going do that in front of those boys, are you?" Miss Prissy asked, half teasing her, "You can't just tease and tempt those boys by moving like that!"

"I just might!" Gabrielle stammered back, "I'll just see what they like!"

Another colored house matron appeared in the bedroom doorway, "Miss Andrea, Miss Atkinson is in the vestibule for Gabrielle's harp lesson."

Andrea glanced at Gabrielle for a reaction to the announcement. Gabrielle had taken lessons from Miss Atkinson since she was five. She loved to play the harp. Even at five, she would practice for hours, and it only seemed like minutes to her. It was as common to hear music in the house as it was to eat at the dinner table. Pierre had purchased several harps for her over the years, and she was so skilled that it was almost to the point that Gabrielle didn't need lessons anymore.

Gabrielle disdained several of her other tutors' lessons, but the harp lesson never felt like work because the harp was her first love. The whole household would stop to listen to her play most days, and this day would be no exception. It was a treat to all.

Miss Atkinson refused any offered pastries. She opted to work with Gabrielle on a variety of difficult classical arrangements. Removing the linen cover from the harp, Gabrielle immediately went about tuning it for several minutes. Each string was tried and tuned to perfection.

"Very good, Gabrielle," Miss Atkinson observed, "Lets play the minuet in C, and be mindful of the bass clefts," she said as she placed the sheet music in front of her.

Gabrielle played the minuet to perfection. Almost all of the colored matrons, as well as her mother, were nearby, yet out of sight, listening to her play.

Chapter 6
Annual Horserace Society Ball

The well dressed porter motioned for Pierre to bring the carriage up to the drive at the stately home of that year's sponsor of the horse racing ball. Pierre obliged him and, tugging gently at the horse's reins, directed the horse up the drive.

"Ah, Monsieur Fontenot!" announced the owner of the mansion, Jake Kelehey, a man in his mid-forties with brown, graying hair.

"A pleasure to see you, sir," Pierre replied as he extended his hand, smiling.

"I see that you brought the Misses and Gabrielle, as well. Welcome to the festivities!"

"It is a pleasure to be here, and thanks for inviting us," Gabrielle said as she smiled and curtsied. Although he said nothing, Pierre felt very proud that Gabrielle had been so polite. If only she was always so well mannered, perhaps life would be just a little easier, he thought.

Several colored porters helped them emerge from the carriage, and many in the crowd stepped forward to welcome them. Other well-dressed couples met them on the massive front porch as other carriages arrived. The reception was brief, but very formal. With no exceptions, the reception was a time when all the well-to-do, horseracing enthusiasts needed to act appropriate. Making their way into the reception, the Fontenot's beamed and briskly walked, greeting long-time friends that they had not seen in quite some time.

Looking about for anyone she knew, Gabrielle noticed several of her friends gathered in a corner and joined them. She immediately noticed that, as she had expected, the fashions, dresses and hats that they and others at the event wore were very similar. The hairstyles were impeccable, and some women had highlighted some features on their attire with diamonds and other fine gems.

"You look so good and so grown-up," noticed her friend Martha, who looked Gabrielle over with approval as she approached them.

"Oh, thank you," Gabrielle replied, "This is my first time here. I guess its part of growing up, and we are not children anymore. It's kind of exciting being here, but I think it's rather fancy. Not that I mind that, but it sure seems to be all business and no fun, really, at least for our parents."

"Well, there's a first time for everything. It's mine, too," Martha replied, "Some of the parents have let the kids come before. Mary was here last year, and Georgette was here two years ago. Oh look… there comes Mr. and Mrs. Boyer. Victoria is with them, as well."

"Some people's name really fit them. You know that her name means victory, don't you? Well, in this case, I don't think the name fits at all," Mary scoffed with a smirk, "She's had it easy all her life, and never had to overcome any real challenge. If some really tragic event happened, she would fall to pieces. Tori thinks she is just the queen," Mary murmured, speaking slightly under her breath, "That's just because she has a prize-winning racehorse named after her."

Victoria, better known as Tori to her friends, emerged from the carriage first. Her mother scowled because that was a slight violation of proper etiquette. But, she was young and still learning how to govern her properly as a woman of class in public, so her mother decided to not correct her right then and there. They would discuss the matter at home, in private.

As Tori came into the light more, so they all could see her more clearly, the other girls almost gasped at her appearance. Her low-cut, red, ankle length dress revealed much more cleavage than theirs. Her hat was tilted at a tempting angle, considered by several of them to be very unladylike. She only glanced at her friends as she passed by, smiling mischievously.

The crowd of girls glanced at one another in dumbstruck amazement, and then silently watched Tori to see what she would do. She knew that she was being observed, but Tori paid no attention to that. Georgette's jaw dropped at the slight of Tori as she strutted about with her parasol, obviously seeking attention from the unmarried, young men, who had their own reception area.

Seemingly oblivious to their daughter's behavior, although they weren't, Mr. and Mrs. Boyer were both graciously received by the awaiting reception line and joined them in small talk. There were handshakes, hugs and compliments all around.

Carriages arrived in what seemed liked an endless stream. The reception lasted for about an hour, until all the guests that had been on the list had arrived. Amazingly, everyone on the list had arrived. The list was double and triple checked to be sure that everyone that had been invited had actually shown up.

"Please join my wife and I, if you will," Mr. Kelehey announced, "The foyer and the guestroom are just right inside and to your right."

Several colored house matrons opened doors for the guests and smiled as each passed through. Some murmured thanks, while others just smiled and looked about. Andrea spotted Gabrielle and motioned for her to join them. Other parents, as well, now had their children with them.

Gabrielle approached her mother and exclaimed, "Mama, I had no idea it would be so beautiful and a busy here tonight!"

"Well, you are not a child anymore, Gabrielle, and I would rather have you get into the adult world slowly, with some guidance and explanations of what is right and wrong and expected and not… from me…" Gabrielle's mom responded, speaking slowly, seeming distracted.

Andrea was indeed distracted and concerned. She watched Tori, all the while hoping that Gabrielle better not follow Tori's example. Tori continued to flirt about with her parasol, and enjoyed the attention of the young men, who seemingly couldn't get enough of her. Gabrielle knew that her mother noticed. Tori's dress was not as revealing as the one that Gabrielle had altered. Somehow, Gabrielle was jealous; she wanted boys to notice her, as well.

Whether singular or as couples, all the guests were ushered beyond the foyer and the guest room, and then into a massive dining area. Low hung chandeliers, high, plush curtains and ornate wallpaper was featured in the beautiful dining area. Long, oak tables had been covered by tablecloths and fine china had been placed at each chair. The guests smiled in delighted surprise because the room was not what they had expected it to be. The Kelehey's, although fairly wealthy, weren't known for their ability to give guests in their home the best of everything, so this was a shocking surprise. They had gone all out to make this an eventful, enjoyable evening for their well-to-do guests.

"It's just beautiful," Andrea whispered to Gabrielle, "I know good and well that they had this room done over. Just look at how well polished and new everything looks."

A line of colored matrons stood in silence along the wall. They knew very well that they were expected to serve the meal and nothing more, nothing less. Each of the guests was assigned a seat according to seniority in the horseracing society's circle of the wealthy and respected. Chairs were pulled back for the guests as they all found their respective seats. Gabrielle watched the spectacle in silence, quite amazed at the elegance and the number of people together in one room. Almost immediately, a spoon clinked against a crystal glass, a cue that everyone needed to hush and an unspoken request for the audience's attention.

"For your pleasure," Mr. Kelehey announced, "My wife and I are proud to announce that we will soon be first time grandparents!"

The audience responded with a round of applause as the Kelehey's son, Michael, stood with his beautiful wife. They both smiled and nodded at the applause. Mrs. Kelehey then gave the nod to the matrons to bring out the first course of the feast, a hand-tossed salad with fruit garnish. Each crystal bowl was placed in front of the guests. Glasses of nectar, marmalade and coffee were also served.

When all the salads had been eaten, Mrs. Kelehey gave the nod for the next wave of food. In what was truly not even five minutes, three varieties of soups, biscuits and bread were served as the old bowls were removed. The main course was delivered next; twelve roast turkeys, steamed vegetables and wine were served. The matrons hand-sliced the turkeys, inquiring of each quest whether they wanted dark or light meat, and obliging the response with the expressed amount and color of meat.

Gabrielle and Mary didn't sit very far from Tori. They both noticed that she had more than enough male attention. Three young men were arguing over who would have the honor of cutting her meat. She finally said something, and the one in the middle of it all agreed to cut her turkey for her. Young, handsome, muscular men seemed to be clamoring for her smiling attention and southern charm.

Tori took it all in as she slightly batted her eyes and teased them about which choice of meat to eat. Actually, she didn't care one way or another. She just wanted whatever attention she could get. She was waiting to be talked into a choice by a wide smile and convincing manner.

The matrons didn't have to wait on her, so they just smiled and tried to ignore the fact she was, at least in their opinion, too immature and spoiled for such attention. They thought that she had a great deal of growing up to do before she was ready to attract the gazes of youthful men. That, however, did not change reality. She had all of the attention that she could ever want.

Somehow, in all the buzz of activity, Gabrielle's, Mary's and Georgette's eyes met. They were just amazed at the willing role that Tori was playing in the flirtation and the attention she was getting. They had to force themselves to remain silent.

To them, she was not acting appropriately, but what did they know? If the adults weren't saying anything, nothing would come of them speaking up. Besides, deep inside, they were jealous of her to an extent.

After the main course, four different types of puddings and pies were presented to the guests, once again presenting them with an array of choices. Tori had a difficult time making up her mind and had to be coaxed along by different men. Finally, she made her choice, and a beaming young man went off to fetch her dessert. The faces of the rest of the men fell as the selected one disappeared, and then reappeared with a huge piece of apple pie and a scoop of churned ice cream on the side.

Andrea was no blind fool. All of this attention hadn't escaped her notice. She could also see the jealousy in Gabrielle's eyes when their gazes met. Glaring silently in Tori's direction, then back at Gabrielle, she slightly shook her head and gave Gabrielle a condescending look to let her know that she disapproved of the manner in which Tori had gained this attention, if not the attention itself. She scowled, as well, as the low-cut dress that Tori was wearing.

"Now, let us get along with the rest of the festivities," Mr. Kelehey announced some time later, "If you didn't get enough to eat, shame on you," he mused. His comment triggered a slight chuckle from the guests, as there was enough food there to feed an army.

"Please join me in the guestroom for the recognition service and an overview of all of the new things that horseracing will have to offer. While we are there, this room will be cleared and prepared for the ball."

The guests arose and followed the matrons into an adjoining room, where plush chairs and couches awaited their arrival. Mr. Kelehey again stood before them and addressed them.

"In recognition of his contributions to the sport, I call upon Mr. Fontenot to present the awards."

The audience applauded as Pierre stood and made his way to the front. Gabrielle watched in wonder; she had not known that he had been asked to hand out the awards. This was Pierre's assigned duty. He had known about it for months and knew all of the deserving candidates, so he didn't need a script. A table had been previously prepared and the prizes were covered with linen.

"For outstanding ability for most races won last season, the award goes to owner, Mr. Boyer, and his horse Tori," Pierre announced.

The audience applauded wildly as Mr. Boyer arose to accept. Pierre gave him the prize, a beautifully polished, custom made sculpture of the head of his winning horse, Tori.

Turning to face the crowd, Mr. Boyer said, "I am most grateful to my wife for her countless hours of work, and for keeping us all fed. We all know that men have to eat in order to work and provide for our families. I also need to thank the jockey that has worked so hard with our winning horse and also helped make Tori what she is. She has come further than I ever dreamed she would. Finally, my daughter, Tori, is here today.

She has been a wonderful daughter, and I am so proud of the young lady that she has become. If any of you fine young men out there are looking for a wife," Mr. Boyer added after a momentary pause, "She'll make a fine wife for someone one day, and as hard as it is to believe, I think it will be sooner rather than later. We fathers all know how hard it is to see our children grow up. But I am very proud of her."

The men in the crowd chucked quietly. Tori felt her cheeks burn as she blushed. But truthfully, she knew deep in her heart that her parents wanted her to get married and have babies, and she knew she had to, but she wanted to be a flirting girl just a little longer. True, she was interested in boys, but so was everyone else her age. It didn't mean she wanted to get married in the very near future."

"I am so happy to have received this award today. I know it could have gone to anybody, because we all work hard. So, thank you to all that were involved in the selection process, in figuring out the figures, and everything else. I am honored," Mr. Boyer said as he bowed and sat down.

"For most races ran last season," Pierre continued, "The award goes to Rufus Stables owner, John Rufus and his horse."

Mr. Rufus arose and accepted his prize, a beautiful, mahogany plaque with an etching of his horse and the dates of the races. He thanked all of those that worked at his stables to make the horse ready for every race. As he had not expected the recognition, he had not prepared a speech, and he could think of nothing more to say, so he sat down amidst a nice round of applause.

Eventually, all of the various prizes were awarded. Pierre nodded to Mr. Kelehey, letting him know that he was done with his portion of the program. The audience gave Pierre a nice round of applause for his participation.

"Last but not least," Mr. Kelehey announced, "We have the latest things for next year."

Nobody had anticipated any surprises, and this had not been noted on the program. They knew they would hear about what was new in horseracing, but this was something to see. They had not known there would be anything new to see. Mr. Kelehey smiled knowingly. He nodded as several porters brought out a new, linen covered table. The men leaned forward to observe better.

"Now, now!" Mr. Kelehey teased, only half-heartedly scolding them because he was just as excited and curious himself. Once again, the audience chuckled quietly.

"Now, for your pleasure, the owners of the submitted items may come forward to answer any questions," he instructed.

A dozen men, including Pierre, arose and stood near the covered table. Mr. Kelehey withdrew the linen as the crowd gathered about in awe and surprise. Pierre's sponsored saddle attracted a lot of attention because it was radical in design and the jockey himself was on hand to answer questions. John Rufus joined the discussion. Obviously, Pierre and his jockey were being overwhelmed with questions regarding the availability and cost of the saddle.

A new and improved bit was also displayed. There were also new lotions available, which were said to treat cuts, scrapes and other wounds in and under the horses' fur more effectively. Additionally, lighter horse shoes, grooming brushes, and an array of other supplies were on display.

Some of the ladies elected not to look at the new things, while others at least glanced at the new gadgets. It did not take long for their fascination to wear off, though. To them, the racing was men's business. They opted, instead, to gather in their own group and entertain gossip. It didn't take long for the rumor mill to start.

Once again, Tori was overwhelmed with male attention, but this time, there were whispers about her and her scandalous dress and flirtatious demeanor. The men were vying to be the first to dance with her once the current proceedings were over with. They knew the ball would start shortly, as they could hear the orchestra in the next room tuning up and getting ready.

With her index finger pointing this way and that way and her mouth constantly moving Tori teased the young men without mercy. The ladies' mouths dropped as they witnessed the rather brash and abrupt method of getting attention for the first dance.

Gabrielle, Mary and Georgette sat transfixed at the rather unorthodox, unladylike behavior. They had no men approaching them for the first dance, and still, it didn't seem right to them.

After a time, the discussion at the item table was coming to a close. Mr. and Mrs. Kelehey stood near the crowd and announced that the orchestra was ready to play.

The younger people let out sounds of delight as they arose to be led into the other room. Andrea gave Gabrielle a nod to let her know that it was fine with her if she remained with her friends, but she really had an ulterior motive. Truthfully, although she didn't want Gabrielle interrupting or overhearing it, either, Andrea was involved with a gossip mill with their mothers and didn't want to let it go. As long as Gabrielle was kept busy with her friends, she would stay out of the way.

Just a few minutes later, the men all arose and took their wives by the arm as the doors swung open for the event. Gabrielle and her friends had all joined the mass of guests. Tori had no problem at all finding someone to escort her. Gabrielle, Mary and Georgette had no escorts at all. No one had even offered.

The well-dressed orchestra was seated in a corner. The room was abuzz with conversation. Everyone seemed to be having a wonderful evening. All of the tables and chairs had been removed, making the room they had dined in earlier that evening a huge dance hall. They didn't wait for a cue; the orchestra started playing a slow tempo waltz.

Husbands and wives paired together to join the dance. Soon, so many people were swirling and turning that there was hardly any room to walk between them. Andrea broke away from her group to accept Pierre's offer to dance the slow waltz with him. Watching from a distance, Gabrielle was quite surprised. She didn't know that her parents could waltz so well.

Tori had plenty of young gentlemen offering to dance with her. She made her choice and left the disappointed ones behind, with downcast faces. Gabrielle was asked several times to dance, but refused all the requests. She wasn't much of a dancer, and enjoyed just listening to the music.

One offer came from Charles Boyer, the stableman at the Fontenot's Stables. He had spent most of the night flirting with Tori.

Disgusted with the way he fawned over Tori, Gabrielle refused because she felt that she was just another dance on the rebound. Still another offer came from John Rufus's nephew. Although handsome, he, too, was one of the group that fawned over Tori and gave her undue attention.

The third one wasn't part of the group that had flirted with Tori, but Gabrielle didn't like him because he stuttered a lot. He was often picked on for that very reason. Others her age thought he was not too intelligent. She just didn't want to be seen in his presence.

Pierre was personally disappointed in Gabrielle because he had thought that she would start up a conversation and dance for while. He had hoped that a nice, local boy might take notice of her. He kept his thoughts to himself, however. There was always next year. Gabrielle would mature more and be more out-going. Being with two friends was certainly a start. Besides, Gabrielle's friends had no takers for the dance. For several hours, while Gabrielle chatted with her friends, various couples twirled on the dance floor, sat out for awhile, and rejoined. Time just seemed to fly by, and it was soon over.

Gaslight lamps illuminated the brick-inlaid street as Pierre directed the carriage back home. It was late, all of the businesses were closed, and the boardwalks were deserted.

"Oh, I just can't believe that Tori!" Andrea stated, "She is just shameless! Did you see the way those boys were just all over her? Why, last year she wasn't like that."

"She let it go to her head," Pierre responded, "That horse is the fastest in the county. Of course all the boys want to court her because of her father's successes and money, but I do agree. That was quite a display of affection."

"Why, you would think that she had just come from the red light district," Andrea added.

"Mama," Gabrielle asked, "What's the red light district?"

"Oh, never mind, Gabrielle," Andrea responded, "It's just a sin the way she looked and behaved. All of the rest of the ladies think as much, too."

"Gabrielle, I saw that Charles asked you to dance," Pierre stated.

"He did," she responded, "I just didn't like the way that he and the others were part of the group that fussed over Tori."

"Well, that's good," Andrea said firmly, "You just keep right on thinking like that."

Pierre turned the carriage intro the drive and was immediately approached by several porters from the stable, who offered assistance to them. Gabrielle was glad that she went to the event, but glad to get home, as well.

Chapter 7
The Railroads Decision

Cigar smoke billowed from Railroad Commissioner Jeremiah Peter's nostrils as he surveyed the railroad yard from his high trestle office. He had a lot on his mind. He saw that the railroad cars from Memphis and New Orleans were parked in the distance, and workers were scrambling to unhitch them. The orange glow of the sun reflected brilliantly off the tracks. It had been a busy day for all of his employees. Studying the horizon, he appeared to be searching for something and not finding it.

"Well," he said to his Deputy Commissioner, George Hood, "It's not getting any better. Good people are hard to come by these days. You know as well as I do that the board wants that job filled. I simply do not see that the men that applied are qualified."

"You are right about the desire of the board," came a fast response, "We are both under pressure to do something about this. The situation concerning New Orleans is of utmost concern. We must push westward from there to California."

Jeremiah approached a wall map of the region and studied it, as he thought that looking at the map might get the wheels in his head spinning and the map might have an answer that would jump out at him. In the back of his mind, he knew that would not happen, but he had no clue what else to do.

"I never thought it could be so hard to fill an opening. I thought about Phillip Rogers for it," Jeremiah mused, "Good man from Charleston. He helped us a lot here in Atlanta."

"Good man alright," George responded, "I know good and well that his wife is sick. They could really use the money. Doctors aren't cheap, and the doctor has had to come out a few times."

"Well, then it must be serious. People don't usually call the doctor right away, or at least not unless its life and death," Jeremiah replied, "Nobody can afford to do that, not with the cost of living and taxes the way that they are."

"I hear you, but it's pretty bad. I know he won't go without her, and she has been down and out for awhile now."

"Well, of course he won't. Nobody expects that. A man needs to take care of his wife and family if and when he has one. Nobody expects him to leave his wife alone when she is ill. That would be wrong," Jeremiah pointed out with conviction in his voice. He stroked his beard and thought some more.

"What about Adams?" George suggested.

"Adams? Nah, not enough education or experience for what we'd want from him," Jeremiah murmured.

"If education is what you want, coupled with experience, how about Smith?" George asked.

"Nah, he's made some bad decisions. He might be book smart, but life has not taught him too much in all his years, obviously," Jeremiah responded, "Doesn't think things through, and he's too quick to spend money that isn't his."

"Daniel Farley, then," George suggested. He could tell that Jeremiah was getting irritated. They had been over this time and time again with no results. They could not come to a decision about who to hire to fill the vacant position for deputy commissioner for New Orleans.

Jeremiah again looked out of the window and was amazed that the railroad cars were now gone. He smiled to himself, pleased with his workers' haste and precision. The rail yard workers had done a great job clearing the tracks.

"I know this is getting irritating and…sir, I want to reach a decision in this matter as badly as you do," George sighed.

"I am so disgusted and frustrated with how long this is taking that I could pitch myself from this window!" Jeremiah exclaimed as he briefly turned to face George. George was a bit shocked and unsure how to respond. Jeremiah was not normally so open about his feelings, though everyone knew he was emotional. He normally tried to keep his professional and personal life separate.

Turning and looking out the window again, he spotted the rail yard's superintendent, John Chesser, with his group of foremen. They were headed toward the pay office because it was payday. The men needed to be paid that day before they went home. John had known about the opening in New Orleans, but had not applied for it. Jeremiah really wished he would have. He was more than qualified.

Jeremiah was impressed with the rail yard because it always ran on schedule and looked good.

"What about John Chesser? Why didn't he apply?" Jeremiah asked.

"Chesser?" replied George, "Can't say I know much about him. I do know that he lives in Lawrenceville, Gwinnett County. He won a lot of land in a lottery from the state. If he didn't want to, he wouldn't have to work so much, but I think he likes to work. He's been with us about nine years now, I believe. He started as a switchman."

"A switchman," Jeremiah mused, "He got to where he is at today by starting out as a switchman?"

"Yes, sir, but doesn't the word of God say that he who is faithful in little will be faithful in much? Maybe God has chosen to bless him for that very reason. Maybe God is pleased with his work," George commented.

"I guess I wouldn't know about that. I am not God, am I? I am just a man who has done evil deeds, as we all have," Jeremiah said.

"No sir, you are just a man, as you say, and not God. Yes, sir, the word of God also says that we not good, but evil. I think it's in Genesis chapter six where it's first stated. It's a verse that says that all the thoughts of a man's heart are evil," George said.

"Oh, come on now. I did not come here to get preached at," Jeremiah said as he quickly added, "Chesser...what do you think of him filling the spot?"

"You certainly wouldn't consider him. Why, he didn't even apply, which means he isn't interested," George immediately replied.

"You don't know that for sure, do you? As long as we are quoting scripture, I seem to remember that there is also a verse in there somewhere that says that God alone can see the hearts of men. So, can you really know for sure why he didn't apply or if he is at all interested? Send a messenger. Call him up here," Jeremiah stated.

George opened the office door and whispered the request to an awaiting attendant. She disappeared as George shut the door again.

"Why Chesser? Why would you consider him?" he asked.

"Did you not just say that he who is faithful in little will be faithful if given more to oversee? Look at the yard," Jeremiah responded, "It has never looked better. Why, I remember how things were before him, and what it looked like, and you do too."

"Well, yes, he has done a good job with the yard, but what I remember the most is that, before him, the local whores would line up at the pay office, waiting for tha men to get paid. Some would have no money to bring home. Somehow, I don't see how, John took care of that in good time. To this day, there has been no more of that," he replied.

"Well, he is obviously a man with a solid work ethic and good morals. Perhaps it's time to see if he wants another promotion," Jeremiah said. Just then, a knock on the door ended their conversation.

"Ah, Chesser, that sure was fast," Jeremiah greeted as he opened the door and extended his hand. The two men shook hands as John entered the room.

"I got a message that you needed to see me, and I came right away, sir. What is your concern?" John asked.

"Thought maybe we would have a little talk," Jeremiah said, not wasting any time. He gestured toward George and said, "You know George here. Have a seat on that chair that's open. I have summoned you here for a reason."

"All of the men have been paid, sirs," John said, "The yard is ready for Monday morning's arrival of freight from Baton Rouge and Richmond."

"I'm sure it has all been done accordingly," George responded.

"John, the reason I brought you up here is that I want to know if you want the deputy commissioners job in New Orleans. None of the applicants are qualified in our opinions. You have proven to be a dependable worker. I believe you will do quite well," Jeremiah commented. John stared straight ahead for a moment, obviously in thoughtful silence.

"It would mean moving there, right? I don't mind this job or the folks here. I don't know what the family would think," he finally replied.

"It's a chance of a lifetime, Chesser," Jeremiah replied, "Should you refuse, you will never be asked to come up with the railroad again, and that would be a shame for such a fine worker. I know it's a big decision, but money can be worked out and details can be worked out."

"I can't give you an answer now," John responded, "True, it's a big step up for me, but I'm not concerned about the money. God has always been faithful to provide our every need," John said with a broad grin, "It's a family thing, so we will decide as a family. I will have to discuss it with Amanda and get back with you."

Jeremiah looked at George as though there should be a wordless understanding.

"When can you get back with us?" George asked.

"I need a week," John responded.

"Uh, Chesser," Jeremiah added quickly, "We prefer that you keep this to yourself for now. I really hope you'll take it, and I'll be disappointed if you don't, but I'll understand if you don't."

"So be it, then," John replied, "I won't say anything."

Jeremiah had an excellent candidate in front of him and he knew it. He didn't want to let him go without sweetening the pot some more. Something a little extra to help him make up his mind would be of immense benefit right then, especially since it looked like he wasn't so keen on the offer and would probably turn it down in the end without an extra push.

"Chesser, take the position… and we will set you up in a house that is just as good as or better than the one you have now. You can live there as long as you are employed by the railroad."

George raised his eyebrow slightly over that one. What fool could refuse a free house? Even he had not received an offer like that, and he had been with the railroad a lot longer than nine years. John's eyes widened a bit as his mind processed what he had just heard.

"Like I said," John said after a moment of silence, "I'll talk to Amanda."

"A week then," George added, "Say Monday after next?"

"Monday after next," John replied as he got up to leave.

"Been a pleasure, John," Jeremiah stated, "Think on it. I know it's a big choice that you have to make. Like I said, money and details can be worked out."

John shook hands with the both of them one more time. George led him to the door.

Jeremiah felt relieved that John seemed at least a little interested, but he didn't have a suitable candidate if John didn't take the job. He was completely counting on an acceptance.

"Why did you offer him a house?" George inquired when John had departed, "I never got anything like that."

Jeremiah relit his cigar as he said, "True, however, you are up for a raise, so I thought we'd talk about that as long as we are here. Fair is fair, I guess."

"I get paid well enough, but a house?" George shot back.

"I need him to take the job. If he doesn't," Jeremiah said, getting irritated with George, "I am out of qualified candidates, and I don't just want any old man off the street for this job!"

"Well, a house? I have worked for you for twice as long, almost! I never got a house! What?" George shot back.

"And do you wanna keep your job or lose it?" Jeremiah hissed so menacingly that George shut his mouth. Jeremiah sat back and sighed, frowning thoughtfully.

"Fine then," he said after a long and uncomfortable silence, "Here's the deal. I will give you a twenty per cent raise and, if you want it, a house."

"A twenty cent raise!" George exclaimed gleefully, almost as if he was a child at Christmas time.

"You heard me," Jeremiah replied.

"That would be wonderful. I thought for a minute there you were going to fire me!" George confessed.

"I am having a hard enough time finding one man to fill one empty position. I do not need to be looking for a second man to fill yours. And besides, you are a hard worker, too. You should have a raise… and the house if you really want it," Jeremiah said.

"I will certainly take the raise, and I will talk to my wife about the house," George responded.

Jeremiah laughed lightheartedly as he said, "First, you whine about me offering George a house, and then you aren't so sure that you even want one? I said you could have one if you want one."

"Well, sure, but I have to talk to my wife. She is one of those people that don't like change, so she might just want me to take the raise and forget about the house," George said.

"Oh, well, fine. Either way, you have the raise. You deserve it, anyway," Jeremiah said.

"Thank you, sir. I should get going now, too. See you tomorrow," George said as he turned to leave.

"See you tomorrow," Jeremiah said.

He wouldn't be leaving for another half hour because he had some paperwork to do.

Chapter 8
The Chesser Family of Atlanta

The Chesser children were just finishing some housework when John asked the children to leave the room.

"But I normally set the table. Don't you want me to do that tonight, papa?" Elizabeth asked.

"I will set the table if the need be as such, but supper won't be ready for a little while yet. You just run along and find something to do, like your father has asked," her mother responded, sensing that John had something important to discuss with her.

She also knew that he needed privacy to talk about the matter. Whatever it was, he didn't seem to want the kids knowing about it yet.

When the kids had left the room, John said, "The railroad has offered me a promotion. It would mean moving to New Orleans."

"What kind of promotion? Did they discuss money?" Amanda asked.

"No," John replied, "All they talked about was providing a better house for us. Unfortunately, they also said that if we refused, I would never be asked again to come up with the railroad. That means there would be no more promotions, and maybe I would even lose my job at some point. It sure sounded to me like Jeremiah wanted me to accept. It's a one time offer, but money was never discussed."

"I don't know what the children would think," she said, "But I suppose if this is the way things are meant to go—this is how they will go."

"Amanda," John said gently, "I have loved you since the day I met you. I couldn't be happier with you. We have worked hard and had more good times than bad. For twenty four years now, I have been by your side and you have been by mine. I love you because you are beautiful and you have a sweet spirit. You are the mother of our three beloved children, and they respect us and have become very well-rounded."

"Moving to New Orleans is a big decision. If we did, perhaps Thomas could stay and continue with what we have here."

"We still do have a lot of charges here, don't we? If he stayed here, it isn't like Thomas would starve. Remember a few years ago when I went to work with the railroad on basically a full time basis?" John asked.

"Oh, yes, I do. I also remember that's when we started renting out the fields to folks, and they would give us part of the crop in return for letting them use the field. We have fared well doing that. We have yet to go hungry," Amanda said happily.

"True, but that is also because God is faithful to provide our needs. I think Thomas could stay here if he wants to. He has a lot of friends here. He may not want to go. Elizabeth and Ben would go, for sure, but perhaps we should go down there first," John suggested, "Just being certain that this is the right thing for us. The railroad has never lied to me about anything and I have always gotten more than what I should have, but this is a big decision."

"New Orleans," she muttered, "French speaking people live there, you know. Not to say that it is bad or anything. My maternal grandpa was half French."

"The plan, the way I see it, is that they want to press on to California with the railroad lines. You know that gold was discovered there. Passenger and freight lines would be the next thing to get there. The single existing line that they already have running in there isn't enough," he explained.

"Well, let's talk about this some more. We have a week," she recommended, "Let's just keep this to ourselves until we have a plan worked out. If we decide to do this, then we'll tell the children."

"I can smell that beef roast now," John mused, "All the fixings, too, I suppose? Supper's pretty near ready."

"Sweet corn on the cob too, and churned butter to put all over it," she added.

"Butter beans too?" he asked, "As well as beets…. and taters too?"

"All of that, and more later," she replied with a smile and a slight wink.

"I'll go ring the bell for supper," he replied, "The kids can't be too far away."

Once seated at the table, they all bowed their head as Thomas, the oldest, offered thanks for the meal. Bowls and platters of food were passed around, and each had the opportunity to take a generous serving of each.

"Pop," Thomas mentioned, "I was at Hannigans Feed Store today. Chester and the rest of 'em were talking about slavery, claiming that there would be a new market set up in Gwinnett County. I heard them also say that, as they called us, 'them Chesser folks' were strange for not owning any slaves and having their land leased to folks that don't own slaves."

"Well," John replied, "So be it, then. Slavery is wrong, and the other reason I leased that land is because I have no time for it. God created good land like that to be used for planting and harvesting to provide for folks. Since I took that railroad job nine years ago, I just don't have any time for farming or tilling the ground anymore."

"Well, pop," Thomas continued, "What do you think of what the newspapers are writing about? I mean what happened at Harper's Ferry and states' rights over slavery?

"Each state has its own rights," Ben innocently added.

"I can't speak for what's going on over on the east coast," John answered, "That's a long ways away from here, but the politicians had better soon come to terms with states' rights."

Thomas was getting slightly annoyed. His father wasn't answering his question like he wanted; he wanted a direct response. Everybody who could afford to have slaves had them, but not the Chesser family, and they weren't poor white trash, either.

"Father," Thomas asked rather bluntly, "Is slavery a state's right?"

"The northern states don't have them," Elizabeth added, then sheepishly looked away because she knew that she had committed a slight breach of social etiquette. After all, political issues were best left to the men folk. Women had little voice in the political arena.

Her mother shot her a quick glare. Elizabeth had spoken out of turn. John ignored her comment, considering that she didn't know anything about slavery or states' rights, anyway. She was just trying to be one of the boys.

John was hard pressed for an answer. If he agreed that it was the state's right, then the north had no quarrel with the south, as far as the south was concerned; if he disagreed, then his own state, as well as the entire south, was wrong for claiming as such. Thomas wanted a direct answer and waited in patient silence.

"No, Thomas," John finally answered, "Slavery is wrong. Like I said earlier and will continue to say, it's not right for another human to own another, be it black or white."

"So," Thomas added, "You think that the states have no rights to own slaves?"

"But the Bible speaks of being bond or free," Ben interjected.

"Boys," John replied, "You asked of what I thought... and you got it. Slavery is wrong."

The Chessers had no slaves and no paid colored maids to their beckon call. It had been just them all of their lives. Hard work had paid off for them. Starting out as newlyweds twenty four years earlier they had so little that they lived with her mother for awhile, then a rented little house where Thomas was born, finally to the current farm house in Lawrenceville where the remaining two were conceived and born. John had been a successful farmer but was lured to the railroad during the off season. He started as a switchman, then various supervisory roles to his current position. The farm acreage was leased to slave holding farming tenants when John went full time with the railroad. The tenants gave them a generous portion of the harvest; it was a good arrangement for both.

Although Thomas listened to what his father had to say, he wasn't convinced that his father knew the truth on the matter. If slavery was wrong, then all the neighbors who owned slaves were wrong, as well as the entire county, state and south. It was difficult to understand because very few people thought that slavery was wrong. The only ones that didn't slavery were the abolitionists, who seemingly stirred up trouble just to make headlines in the news.

Ben was seeing a different side of his brother, a side that questioned family values that went against accepted social tradition. Thomas had always been the agreeable son, the respected one that never questioned authority. It was quite unlike him to inquire about states' rights regarding slavery.

The family didn't own slaves, but were prosperous and able to do as much if they wanted to. Perhaps Thomas was finally getting envious of the neighbors. They didn't work as hard as the Chesser family. Their field slaves did all of the planting and harvesting. It just didn't seem right to Thomas.

The Chesser family toiled like the slaves that the neighbors owned, but John's answer wasn't to buy slaves. He joined the railroad full time and leased the surrounding farmland to sharecroppers, who did indeed own slaves. Thomas had often wondered as to whether or not his father sold out to slavery by taking the railroad job, or was the new opportunity a further stepping stone for success?

Amanda could sense that the table discussion was going nowhere with Thomas. He was obviously not happy with his father's response to his question and had his own opinion.

Changing the subject a bit, Amanda looked at Thomas and asked, "Are you still sweet with Sarah Whitney?"

Thomas blushed a bit, then replied, "Yes mama, but its not what you think, and no, I ain't asked her to marry me or nothing like that."

"You might be thinking about that some time, young man of your age, twenty three, strong and all, and besides, she comes from a good family," she replied.

"Aw, now Amanda," John chided, "Don't go teasing the boy about getting` hitched, there's plenty of time for that."

"Well, before you know it Ben here will find a beau, as well," she continued.

"I don't know mama," Ben replied as he blushed, "I aint ready for nothin` like that, ah`m just happy to have my race horse. He's worth more than any girl!"

"You just keep right on thinking like that," John reminded, "There's plenty of time for having beaus and getting hitched, plenty of time."

"Are you going to renew the land lease with the Pruett's next year?" Thomas asked.

The harmless question put John in a tough spot. Considering the new railroad job in New Orleans he would have thought that Thomas would stay behind and supervise the farm. That there wouldn't be a lease next year for the land tenants. He didn't want to let on right now that he was considering the job in New Orleans.

"Well," he replied, "We'll see, they have been with us for seven years, we shall see."

Amanda gave John a slight inquisitive look. She knew as well that the question would be difficult to answer, if John said yes then Thomas would tell the Pruett's forthright to depend on the lease next year. If he said no then Thomas would really suspect something.

"I saw Cecil Pruett today as well," Thomas explained, "He was asking about it, about leasing for next year... that's why I asked of it."

"I'll decide soon," John replied, "There's still time."

The roast beef platter made another round and all of the meat and gravy was soon gone.

"Ben, can you finish the rest of those lima beans, there's just a little left," Amanda asked.

"Sure," Ben replied, "As well as the beets, love those beets."

"How is your race horse, Bunches, doing Ben?" Elizabeth asked.

Ben looked up in surprise. She was the quiet type, asking about his horse was unusual for her. She could have cared less about race horses.

"He's fine, sis," he responded as he chewed a mouthful of beets, "Going to run him this Sunday at O'Tooles track."

"Not a bad running horse Ben," Thomas added, "He's winning more races and doing better. Perhaps in the future you could hire a jockey to ride him, instead of yourself."

"Oh, it would take more then just a few races," John mentioned, "Those jockeys get good money for riding. Bunches has got a long way to go before then."

"Hopefully, he won't be past his prime when that happens pop," Ben said, "I've ridden him so long now that ah couldn't imagine anybody else. A jockey would weigh less though, Bunches could move faster."

"I can think of a colored jockey that could be available," John mentioned.

"We'll see pop," Ben replied, "Bunches can't rightly afford a jockey right now."

Chapter 9
A First Horse Race

The horse race held every other Sunday at O`Tooles Farm featured the areas good to fair horses, there was no prize money involved, it was all bragging rights. Neighbor ran against neighbor in an all fun event where other activities included apple bobbing, and games of horseshoes. The horse races were always the last event of the day.

Afterwards, the crowd enjoyed donated cakes and pies as well as apple cider and cold well water. This Sunday was Amanda's turn to donate a pie or a cake, most of the time it was two apple pies and a urn of whipped cream. It was a tradition for a long time, most of the time most of the participants appeared for the event. The Chesser family never missed an opportunity. The only exception was a rain out, when the event was cancelled. During the events, if the ladies weren't participating they were at best discussing the latest local gossip. There was always time to catch upon the latest news, true or not.

After helping his mother with some basic domestic chores Ben retreated to the old barn to brush Bunches for awhile. Sunday was a big day. It would be Bunches' first race with Ben riding. He had raced before with other riders, but this was the first time that Ben was old enough to ride and compete. Ben brushed Bunch's back and daydreamed about winning big. He got the feeling he was being watched as he worked.

Elizabeth watched Ben brush the horse then spoke up, "Ben, why is it that mama spoke of you and Thomas having beaus but not me?"

Ben thought about that and replied, "You're only twelve," he replied, "Couple of years from now she will say something about it, but until then, she won't," he replied.

Elizabeth's continued conversation was cut short by the sound of an approaching buggy along the old dirt road.

"It's Jesse McCarthy," Elizabeth said as the buggy came into view. Ben stopped brushing Bunches and looked up for a moment.

"Hey, Chesser!" came an exuberant, competitive shout from the dusty road, "I just heard from ol' man Walker that I'm gonna race ya Sunday. Just to let you know, I aim to run ya off the track. You ain't got no business runnin' against someone like me!"

"Is that so?" Ben replied.

"Yeah, it's so! White trash like you ain't gonna win against skilled horseman like me. You, some skill-less novice? Dream on. I have seen you ride, and a six-year-old could do better! " Jesse snarled as he jiggled the reins and took off in a powerful display of speed and clouds of dust.

"Ben, you ain't got no chance against him," Elizabeth stated, "He's won more races than anybody. Ol' man Walker did that on purpose so that he'll win and not you."

"Maybe so, but Gideon only had three hundred men. He was up against a million or something, and look at David. Folks said he had no chance against Goliath, and look what happened. He killed a giant with a slingshot," Ben replied as he fanned his dust caked face and added, "Besides, who is to say he will win and I will lose? I gotta try, if for no other reason than to say that I gave it a shot. With Jesse, it's all about winning, and he's so good at what he does that he has a big boast over it. He may go to church, but he doesn't acknowledge that everything he has in on loan from God. I gotta try 'cause he runs against the best horses in tha county."

"Jane Cooper likes you, Ben," Elizabeth abruptly stated, changing the subject.

"I don't care if she does or not," he replied, "I don't rightly like her, but I am no blind fool. I know she looks at me on Sundays, and she can just keep looking too!"

"That's no way to be," Elizabeth stammered as she turned about and left.

Ben had known for awhile that Jane Cooper had been eyeballing him. However, she was painfully shy and would not approach. That was all the better for him, because he had been gazing at her as well. He was almost just as shy, but she was the daughter of one of the church's elders and he didn't quite know how to start a conversation with her.

There were some distinct differences between Ben's family and hers. Her family possessed slaves and Ben's did not. Although they weren't despised for it for the most part, the other families in town all felt that they were a bit strange for not having a single slave. To Ben, who had grown up with a man that opposed enslavement, it was just normal. John Chesser didn't own slaves, and that was that. He didn't flaunt his reasons for not supporting slavery; he just didn't own slaves.

After church on the day of the race, Bens mother had her customary two apple pies and whipped cream ready. The family got into the carriage. Bunches was tied to the back of the carriage, trotting along the dusty road as the carriage made its way to O' Tooles Farm, about three miles away.

Many people had already arrived when the Chessers' finally pulled up and parked the wagon. Other families had already been busy setting up games. One family brought the horseshoes, another supplied the buckets and apples for the apple bobbing, and Amanda had her pies.

Ladies of the church were just getting started setting up the pie and cake tables when the Chessers' and a few other carriages arrived. Amanda immediately joined the other ladies of the church. Elizabeth joined her awaiting friends, John, Thomas and Ben headed for the stable at the start of the track.

"Now, remember what we talked about, Ben," John reminded, "Keep your head down, your back arched, and always look forward. You'll do fine."

"Just do everything that we did when we did the practice runs," Thomas added.

Ben noticed Jesse McCarthy in the next stall. He knew that John and Thomas were there and said nothing, but gave Ben a glaring look of contempt. Looking about, Ben also noticed a crowd of well-dressed church girls near the outer perimeter of the fence, waiting in anticipation for the race to begin.

Finally, the judges were walking to their places. There were a total of three, one at the start of the track and two others to witness the win at the end of the track. Looking about for another moment, Ben noticed Jane Cooper looking directly at him from the fence line. When their gazes met and he knew it, he looked away.

"Alright boys," the judge announced, "You both know the rules. There's no need to tell you something you already know. Line your horses up. We've got other races behind ya, and it looks like rain, so let's be quick about it."

Both riders mounted their saddles and the two horses were lined up evenly. The judge took his place at the starting line and looked about to signal the other judges that they were ready. Retrieving his pistol, he pointed it upwards and then looked at the two riders. After a moment he pulled the trigger and the horses took off with powerful speed.

Jesse pulled ahead of Ben. Both riders were low in the saddle and looked straight ahead as they raced in a full gallop. Ben took the lead briefly as he nudged Bunches onward with a small kick to the belly, and then Jesse did the same and pulled ahead. Back and forth the lead bounced, each rider desperately wanting to take the lead as they neared the finish line.

Choking clouds of dust followed the horses as they ran with all their strength. Bouncing up and down and maintaining control of his horse was all Ben could do. He had never run Bunches this fast before. Headed for the finish line with Jesse in the lead by two feet, Ben tried to give Bunches one final push. It was clear to him that Jesse was about to win, and Ben wasn't going to lose without at least trying to remedy the situation.

Finally, the two horses crossed the finish line in front of the two judges. Both horses were brought to a canter, and then a trot, then a slow walk, then stopped.

The race was much closer than what Jesse had wanted to admit because most of the time he would win by a wide margin. The mere thought of losing to a first time rider was humiliating, but at least he had won. Whatever the cost, and however close it was, he had won.

"Told you ah would win! I swear that I must be a prophet! Why even try? All you are gonna do is fail, and not even God can help you!" he snarled, "You ain't got no business out here."

"How dare you accuse God of failing to help me? How would you know what He did or didn't do? The Lord rebuke you on my behalf. I am going to let Him deal with you, and I hope He does so with more mercy and compassion than you have shown me," Ben said indignantly.

The horses approached the two judges, who had started walking towards them. Jesse had expected a lot of smiles, handshakes and compliments. Ben could tell just by their serious expressions that something was wrong.

"Uh…, Jesse," one of the judges said, "We've got a little problem here."

"Oh, and what would that be?" he responded.

The other judge spit a wad of tobacco on the ground and spoke, "We both saw you kick Ben's horse towards the end of the track, and you know the rules."

"It was an accident!" Jesse stammered, "You know I wouldn't do that on purpose! Besides, it was his fault! He got too close!"

"No Jesse, if it was an accident, why didn't you confess to us that you had done it when you reached the finish line?" The first judge inserted, "We don't see it like that. You know the rules, son. Now you have to suffer the consequences of your action. We both decided that there is no winner. The race is a draw. Next time, keep your feet to yourself."

"This isn't fair!" Jesses snarled, "Where's ol` man Walker?"

"Right over there," one of the judges said, "He saw the whole thing, as well."

Jesse looked in the direction the judge had pointed. Old man Walker sat on a bench, looking disapprovingly at Jesse and shaking his head. Jesse realized that indeed he had lost, and so his cheating had backfired.

"This isn't chariot and gladiator days," the judge said, "You have to ride like a gentleman."

"I'll get you next time!" Jesse snarled at Ben under his breath.

Ben said nothing, realizing that in a way, he had won. Perhaps the race had been a draw, but God had indeed helped Ben. He had revealed a deceitful action by allowing the judges to notice, and thus, declare that Jesse had 'won' in an unfair way and declare that nobody had won. That, Ben realized, could very possibly tarnish Jesse's reputation worse than losing to a novice competitor that had not raced before.

Both riders rode away to join the activities and to watch other the other boy's race. There was only one chance to win every other week, one race each, and one opportunity.

John and Thomas coached Ben and commented on his performance in the race. Ben had to admit to himself that he had done better than he had expected. He was actually very proud of himself.

"It was close alright. That kid should not have cheated like that. Many people saw it. You did well, and you made me proud," John said, "Next time, arch your back more and keep to the inside."

"Look straight ahead," Thomas recommended, "Keep your head down."

"I'll remember that next time," Ben replied.

He looked across the crowd to see Jane Cooper. This time, she gave him a smile for his efforts in the race. Her father was one of the two judges.

He had almost forgotten about that. Jane would have had a seat closer to the track because her father was a judge, so she would have seen the whole thing very clearly. Realizing that, Ben was all the more disappointed that he had not won. It had been such a close race. It was Jesse's fault that he lost, and Jesse had caused the race to be a draw.

Ben didn't feel that he owed Jane anything, but it was too late. Jane and several other girls approached.

"Hello, Ben," Jane said.

"Hello, Jane," Ben replied, "Beautiful weather we're having, ain't it?"

"Rightly it is, but I thought it might rain. Well, it hasn't yet," she said as she sheepishly smiled and asked, "Would you like to sample some of my mama's cherry pie?"

Ben looked about for a moment. She had caught him by surprise. Ben looked back to see John and Thomas smiling at him. John nodded, signaling that he would take care of Bunches while Ben ate pie with Jane.

"Sure Jane, I'll sample some pie."

Jane again shyly smiled. Both Ben and Jane sat at a nearby table, each with a heaping serving of cherry pie.

"I saw the race, Ben," she said, "You did very well against Jesse. Just look at him over there. He lost, and he thinks he is everything, anyway."

Ben looked over to see that Jesse had several girls with him. Laughing all the while, one girl was attempting to feed him a piece of Amanda's apple pie. Ben did not waste too much time looking at him.

"Thanks," Ben replied, "I did the best I could."

Ben had almost finished the pie and didn't quite know what to say to Jane. He liked her, and she liked him, but both of them were so terribly shy. He wondered how he would ease his way away from her.

"It took a lot to go up against Jesse," she commented.

"Well," he muttered, "I didn't have any choice in the matter. Ol' man Walker matched us up. I think he just wanted to see me lose, so I got stuck with Jesse."

"He wanted you to lose," she replied, "You didn't hear this from me, but I heard that there's money bet on these races. Even though nobody actually bets, some do. It's all kept on the quiet. I bet a lot of people were betting on Jesse, and nobody expected what happened to happen."

The revelation startled Ben. He had no idea that the races were bet on. To him, this was just a friendly social gathering of church folks. Ben was just amazed at her knowledge. He knew nothing about it. It was all news to him.

"Ya think?" he asked.

Jane said nothing as a new set of judges passed by them, within earshot.

"Yes," she revealed, as they moved out of earshot again, "My father is trying to put a stop to it, but all of the payoffs are done later, away from the track. That way, it's all done in secret."

"Yeah, I think there's a lot of money to be made," he replied, not knowing what else to say.

"You would have no idea on how much money is won and lost," she replied.

Finally, Ben caught Thomas looking at them from a distance. He was waving at Ben, trying to signal him to let him know that he wanted to start a horseshoe game. Ben politely excused himself, seeing his brother's unspoken request as a timely rescue.

"Well, Jane," Ben said, "The pie was very good. My compliments to your mother, but I can see that the boys want me to join them at the horseshoes."

"You don't have to be so shy with me, Ben," she said as he got up to leave.

That caught Ben completely by surprise. He had been trying to hide his sheepish discomfort, and thought that he was doing fairly well.

Unsure what to say, after a moment, Ben said, "I'll run Bunches again next week, maybe against Jesse again. I'll be back."

"I know you will, Ben," she replied.

Ben joined Thomas and several other boys from church, and they teamed together in pairs. Ben thought about what Jane had said about people placing bets on the horse races, and wondered if there was silent betting at horseshoes, as well. He doubted it, but didn't have any way to know for sure.

"A ringer!" Thomas said, "Can you beat that, Ben?"

Ben had been looking towards Jane. She had also been eyeballing him. He didn't even hear his brother.

"Hey Ben, pay attention here!" another young man said.

"Uh… sorry," he replied, as he hurled the horseshoe, not paying any attention to where he was throwing it. His aim was way off. He had made a fool of himself and felt embarrassed.

"Hey, Chesser!" Jesse shouted, "My grandmother can do better than that."

Ben blushed. Yes, he could have done better. He had let his mind wonder. He looked over at Jesse, who still had several girls with him. One had her arm around his neck. Jesse had called their attention to Ben when his turn had come. They were all entertained and laughed at his very bad aim.

He felt like crawling in a hole at that very moment. He did very well participating in his first horserace, but made himself look ridiculous in an event he did every weekend.

Still, Jane wouldn't keep her eyes off of him, and he could sense that. He knew he was being watched.

"C'mon, throw another," Thomas said, "You can do better than that."

Although he didn't get a ringer, he was much closer to the stake. After several games of horseshoes, he had forgotten all about his clumsiness and could now look over in Jane's direction and still concentrate on what he was doing. But the games were over now. The kids were done bobbing for apples. The men were done talking politics, and the ladies' gossip circles seemed to be winding down. That was just as well, because a slight misty rain begun to fall.

Ben found himself alone with his horse at the very moment he saw Jesse approaching him. With his usual, sly grin and threatening presence, he repositioned his hat and spit on the ground.

"Hey Chesser, I hope you ain't planning to run that nag next Sunday, 'cause I aim to run ya off tha track!" he snarled. Ben just looked up and gave him a wry smile.

"Besides, Chesser, that little elder's daughter friend of yours ain't nothing but a cheap, dime whore anyway. You must like those kinds of girls."

Ben was enraged at the comment. Actually, he had never felt such fury in all his life. He wanted to smack Jesse right in the mouth for saying something like that, but he didn't dare because he knew that he would be whipped. Jesse was much bigger and stronger.

Spitting on the ground again, he again commented, "Yep… a cheap dime whore. She'll open her legs for any man."

It was all he could do to contain himself, but Ben could clearly see now that Jesse was trying to pick a fight in front of the whole crowd. Seeing that Ben was leading his horse away and to the carriage, it became obvious to Jesse that Ben wasn't going to react. Jesse repositioned his hat again and looked back at Ben defiantly. He had expected a reaction and was disappointed and angry when he got nothing.

The rain began to pick up then and people ran for cover. Some sought shelter under the tress, and others, in their buggies, carriages and wagons. John and Thomas joined Ben in getting ready to go home. Several other families had already left. Amanda gathered her pie pans and knives. Elizabeth assisted her as the rain seemed to relent slightly.

Fortunately, the day's events weren't a total loss. Adults and kids were done for the day, so it was time to go home. The rain just seemed to hasten it along.

"That sky is gonna open up again," John said as he looked upward, "We can make it to the farm if we hurry it along."

Wagons and carriages quickly rolled away from the area as, apparently, others got the same idea. The roads were wet, but not muddy yet. The moisture was not enough to make everything a sloppy mess yet. It was just enough to keep the dust down, but not enough to make wheel ruts.

"You did very well at the race," Thomas mentioned to Ben, "Next time, Jesse will keep his feet to himself."

John added, "If you race next Sunday, you won't race Jesse. You'll race Rufus, the red-headed boy."

"Why?" Ben asked, "Why him and not Jesse? Rufus ain't never won any races. His horse is slow, and he doesn't know how to ride."

Ben had failed to realize that John had spoken to the judges and they had overruled old man Walker who was more than happy not to take another chance that Jesse might lose.

The big torrential rain that everybody thought was going to happen didn't happen after all. The sky cleared up after a second, short downpour, and the clouds moved away.

That night John took a bath and shaved to get ready for bed. In his mirror, he could see Amanda in her nightgown. Her long hair was down. He could clearly see two inches of cleavage. He didn't expect as much that night, but it was her way of signaling.

She held a single lit candle in a holder. Her face was dimly illuminated as she approached.

"Have you thought more about the New Orleans offer?" she asked, almost in a whisper.

"No, I haven't," he replied.

John was getting the message clearly now. She indeed wanted him to take it. What went on that night would just be a way of sealing the deal between them, a personal celebration of a new beginning somewhere else. John studied her for a moment and dried his face with a hand towel. Taking her by the hand, he led her down the hall and into their bedroom.

Chapter 10
A Promising New Career

Jeremiah waited in anticipation as he looked at the rail yard from his lofty, wide window. The day had finally come that John would come in and let his decision about the position and relocation to New Orleans be known. Neither John nor Jeremiah had slept well the night before. Jeremiah had spent most of the night tossing and turning because he knew from repeated requests from New Orleans leadership that the position desperately needed to be filled soon. A recent telegram he had received just three days before had indicated a dire need, due to a lack of local leadership.

John felt anxious for different reasons. How would the children handle the move? Would all go well in New Orleans? Would all that he had been promised really come to pass? Could he really do the job? Unable to sleep for the vast majority of the night, he had spent it in deep thought and awoke just as the sun was rising, feeling very refreshed.

Cigar smoke rolled from Jeremiah's nostrils as he again studied the employment proposal for John. All seemed as it should be. Now, it was just a matter of whether or not John would accept the offer, and then he had report to work as soon as he could. The commission had reviewed it and approved it, in spite of its obviously generous appearance. Several signatures provided affirmation that they indeed wanted somebody like John Chesser.

Still, Jeremiah was nervous. He didn't have a back-up candidate. He had none, so it was John Chesser or nobody. Waiting for an answer from him was almost as agonizing as waiting to hear if a loved one was going to live or die, or so it seemed. At last, an attendant opened the door slightly and announced that John Chesser was waiting outside.

"Well… show him in, by all means!" Jeremiah responded. John entered the room and shook hands with him.

"I trust everything is fair with you and your family, John?' Jeremiah asked, with the offer on his mind, "Take a chair at the table, if you would, and we'll have a talk."

"We're doing quite well. This is a big move for us, and it was a hard decision, but thank you for thinking of me. I would have never thought to ask me if I were you, sir, and I am honored," John replied.

"Well, you are not me, are you? Hot coffee or wine?" Jeremiah asked.

"Coffee would be good," John replied, "Nothing like railroad coffee!"

Jeremiah poured hot coffee from a previously prepared decanter. He was so tense, but tried to relax. John could tell he was apprehensive. He also saw the authorized forms on the table. He assumed they were the details of his employment opportunity.

"John, I have an offer for you, and I hope you take it, as I said before," he said as he quickly gazed at him. John pulled his chair up to the table and leaned forward slightly to better see and understand the proposal.

"The railroad has purchased an enormous country home from a widow in New Orleans. The telegram tells me that it is beautifully rennovated and empty at the present time. It is part of your offer, both the house and the grounds. That includes the out buildings, which includes a stable. They are all yours at no cost as long as you are employed with the railroad," Jeremiah explained.

With that said, he turned the offer right side up so that John could read it. "It is a very good offer John."

John studied the offer. Indeed it was a very good one; in fact, it seemed almost too good to be true. One detail caught his eye. It had not been mentioned previously, but there it was, in writing.

"Five hundred shares of stock as well?" he asked.

"Yes, and a hundred more after that, for every year you stay with the railroad," Jeremiah continued. He watched as Jeremiah's eyes brightened even more as he read the fine print. He was very happy with the money because it was a substantial amount more than what he presently made.

"I trust you have discussed this with Amanda?" Jeremiah asked. John ignored his question at first. Jeremiah watched him in silence as he finished reading the papers.

"I accept!" John responded jubilantly.

"Just sign right here," Jeremiah said as he pointed to a line, "I am so relieved to have finally found someone, and you are very qualified. We are all very pleased, John."

"Yes, Amanda and I did discuss this," John said, "She is all for it, and we didn't even know all the details when I told her. Maybe we all need a change. She will be very pleased with this offer. I know I am. The offer is better than what I thought it would be."

"Well, we all felt that you were the right man for the job, John. You are a good worker and I will miss you around here, but I am happy that you took this opportunity. I wish you all the best of luck, but you won't need it. You know what it is to work, and you will do quite well," Jeremiah said with confidence.

After signing the contract of promotion with the railroad, John shook hands with his soon-to-be former boss.

That evening both John and Amanda decided to tell the rest of the family after suppertime. The sooner they knew, the better off everyone would be. Amanda was very pleased. She thought the offer was outstanding. He had let the railroad know he wanted a week to think about things, so they had also had a week to work out the details of the offer, and it paid off. They really wanted him.

Again, being the eldest, Thomas bowed his head to offer thanks for the food.

Amanda had prepared fried chicken, a favorite of everyone's. In addition, hot mashed potatoes were heaped on plates; gravy was next, then peas, then green beans. Hands were kept busy, and the serving utensils hardly saw a dull moment.

"How was work today, pop?" Thomas asked, "Keeping ya busy?"

"Staying busy isn't the word for it," he replied, "There's a lot of freight comin' in, but not so much going out. Still, the crew always does a good job."

"I heard that Buddy Tyler asked Isabelle to marry him," Elizabeth injected. She had been waiting all day to announce that at the table.

"I'm not surprised," Thomas replied, "I just wonder why he waited so long."

Although Amanda knew, she wasn't going to say anything. She knew that their next door neighbor was about to have a shotgun wedding. It was common knowledge in the secret gossip circles.

"I'm certain that they will be happy," John said, sounding totally assured of himself.

"I heard that they are just going go to the Church of Christ gospel preacher and get married like that," Elizabeth continued.

It was obvious to Amanda that Elizabeth and the rest of them did not know the truth. They only saw that Buddy and Isabelle had been courting for almost six months.

There was more information about them, but Amanda wasn't about to say anything, as it wouldn't be prudent at the supper table. To John and Amanda, it really wasn't news. But neither of them could say anything. After all; it was just a parent's way of protecting information.

Ben expressed his dissatisfaction with having to race Rufus, the red headed boy, this Sunday. He believed he could do better than that for competitors.

"Look at it like this, Ben," John said, "You have to start somewhere. Old man Walker owns that horse that Jesse was riding, so he wanted him to win. But Rufus owns his own horse, whether he is slow or not. It will be good for both of you. You might be faster, and you will likely win, but he has more experience, and he might teach you a little something. It's a matter of competing against a rider with similar ability."

Ben felt a little better about it now. His father was telling him that his day would come when he could race with the better horses, but it wasn't just yet.

"You did very well against Jesse," Amanda mentioned, "All of the ladies that I sat with thought so, as well."

"But I didn't win," Ben replied, "I wanted to teach him a lesson. He thinks he's all that, and he's not."

"Well, look at it this way. Because of you, Jesse's cheating was exposed and he was disqualified. Who really can know whether or not Jesse has done that before? I think it says somewhere in the Bible—in Psalms or Proverbs, I believe—that the Lord honors those who walk uprightly before Him and exposes the sins of those who will not. He certainly exposed what Jesse did through a very distinct set of circumstances. You won in your own right, and you competed honestly. That is far more important than any recognition," Thomas replied, "Nobody has ever come that close to winning against Jesse. You did very well."

"Jesse is running scared now," John said, "He talks a lot, but he is afraid of losing."

The main course and all the other food had been eaten by then. Amanda motioned for Elizabeth to bring the dessert. There were smiles all around as peach cobbler was presented at the table. Two huge bowls of it were quickly devoured. Like the chicken, it was also a family favorite. Amanda had wondered when and how John would bring up the New Orleans offer. Suppertime was almost over. They had that it would be the best time to announce the move. John waited until the last spoonful of cobbler was almost finished before deciding to make the announcement.

"I have received and accepted a promotion with the railroad," he announced, "Your mother and I have discussed this and decided it is the best thing for me to continue. If I don't take it, I will never be asked to come up again."

"Aw, that's great father," Thomas said, "What are they going to have you doing?"

"Deputy Commissioner," Amanda added, beating John to the response.

"Really?" asked Ben, "That's really good, father!"

"What's a deputy commissioner?" Elizabeth asked.

"It's really important Elizabeth," Thomas replied, "It's like second in command of the entire yard and then some."

"The thing is," John continued, "It means moving to New Orleans. That's where the job is at, not here in Atlanta."

The table fell silent. Nobody had expected that. They all assumed that it meant staying in Atlanta.

"New Orleans?" Thomas asked with a blank stare.

"It's a wonderful opportunity," Amanda said, "Besides; the railroad is providing a house for us. It's a huge country mansion. It's part of the contract, so it comes at no cost to us."

"Is there horse racing?" Ben asked.

"The grounds include a stable," John added, "There is certainly horseracing there."

"What about the farm here?" Thomas asked.

"We'll have to work it all out," John replied, "There are a lot of open things to discuss."

John had the immediate feeling that Thomas didn't want to go. That was fine with him, because Thomas was old enough to stay behind. Besides, he was courting Sarah Whitney.

"Well when, pop? When do they want you to start?" Ben asked.

"Six weeks from now," Amanda answered, "Which means that we have to be down there and settled in that time."

Ben and Elizabeth suddenly realized that they would be going, but not Thomas. It was just a feeling that they had. They couldn't explain how they knew, but they knew. The feeling was so real and deep that they could not dismiss it. John expected him to stay behind and maintain the farm. He was the oldest, after all.

"Six weeks," Ben said, "There is a lot of work to do."

"It's a wonderful opportunity," Amanda said again.

"A chance of a lifetime to come up in the ranks with the railroad," John reaffirmed.

After the initial shock wore off, both Ben and Elizabeth felt better about it, but it would still be a big change. They had been born and raised in Atlanta. All of their friends were there, and they would miss them terribly. But, they would make new friends, and they could write their old ones. Moving somewhere else now was almost exciting and different. They were both abuzz with questions about the New Orleans area. John and Amanda answered as best they could.

The mood around the table had changed from very quiet to inquisitive. This was the reaction that John and Amanda had wanted. They wanted it to be a happy occasion for all.

Thomas excused himself from the table and went outside to finish some barnyard chores. Ben and Elizabeth were happy; they would experience something new and different. There would be a new, beautiful county house, and a new school, perhaps. Then, new friends, new things, and it was almost overwhelming to them. John and Amanda could hardly answer questions fast enough to please them.

It didn't take long for the word to get around in the rail yard that John was leaving because he had accepted the job in New Orleans. It was an unspoken rule that whenever anybody moved up with the railroad and left a vacated position that they assist with filling it, which meant being on hand to answer any questions that a new, interviewing candidate might have. John knew this because he had filled various positions with the railroad in his nine years as an employee, so he had answered questions and assisted in training in his replacement before.

The crew was unusually jovial on the first day that he showed up for work after accepting the promotion. Several of them had applied for his old job. They wanted a candidate from their own ranks, not someone from the outside, whom they did not know. They hated to see John leave, but like every one of them, he had come up from the bottom of the ranks.

There was a time when he had applied for the lowest paying job with the railroad and got it. From there, he had diligently worked his way up and earned the respect of his coworkers. Now, he had one of the most important jobs on the railroad, and had the full support of his crew. Now it was his turn to help the railroad's management select someone.

Of the entire crew, three had expressed an interest, and each of the three was qualified and had been there long enough to understand the needs of the yard. If management didn't like any of the three, they would select someone from other rail yards in other cities. John had been hired directly off of the Atlanta yard after several interviews.

John sat at the table with Jeremiah Peters. They were in the early process of screening candidates.

"Ellis Sanders," Jeremiah mentioned, "Is he any good? He relates well with the others?"

"Ellis is good. He does a good job, but he has a drinking problem. I am not so sure I would promote him because it could get worse if he has more stress and what have you," John responded.

"Raymond Yingling," Jeremiah mentioned, "How about him?"

"The trouble with Ray is that he never knows when to keep his mouth shut," John replied, "If you hire him, you might be sorry. He works hard, I have to give him credit there, and he has drive, but he is the kind of man that would spread rumors."

"Edward McCarthy," Jeremiah continued, "How about him?"

"Of the three, he would be my choice," John replied, "He is hard working, keeps his mouth to himself and is very well mannered, not like the other two."

Jeremiah wasn't in the mood to quibble over who to hire for the rail yard. Promoting John had been a task in and of itself. Looking at John he responded, "Alright then, Edward it is. Just keep it to yourself. I don't want any misgivings about this, so he will start the first day that you are gone."

"He'll be a good man for the yard," John stated matter-of-factly, "I never had a moment's worth of trouble out of him."

"Like I say, keep it to yourself," Jeremiah said again.

"As you might know, Edward and his wife have five sons. They are big on horseracing and such," John added, "Of course, that's not the reason why I would recommend him."

"I know," Jeremiah added, "His son, Jesse, does well on the track. I have heard of him."

Both John and Amanda weren't at all surprised when Thomas told them that he wasn't going to New Orleans with them. He was old enough to do what he wanted.

Amanda knew the real reason much more so than John did. Thomas wanted to be with his beau. They had been courting for quite awhile, and she thought they very well could be thinking marriage. John, perhaps, didn't see it like that.

Thomas had become quite independent in the last year. He wanted to do what he wanted to do. There had recently been a near quarrel with John and Thomas over states' rights, and his independence wasn't just evident at the supper table, either. Thomas disagreed with his father. They had almost come to raised voices over it in the barnyard on several occasions.

For Thomas it was a chance to oversee the family farm and perhaps get married in the near future; but, if nothing else, he wanted to see what he could do by himself. Having Thomas stay was an advantage. They wouldn't have to sell the family farm that they had worked long and hard over.

"I just can't do it, father," Thomas explained, "This is where I belong. I am happy here. This is my home. I can't stay a boy forever. I have to get out on my own. Before long, Ben will do the same, then Elizabeth, as they both come of age. I am of age to take care of things. Besides; you'll get a dividend wired to you every month."

"I wouldn't have taken this job if it weren't for coming up with the railroad," John replied, "To not take it would mean never being asked again."

"You'll do very well, father," Thomas added, "There's no need to worry about the old homestead here. I'm sure I can handle it."

"I wouldn't think anything less than that," Amanda said, "Of course, if you do get married, you will let us know."

"Oh, ma!" Thomas chuckled, "I haven't even thought about asking her father!"

"You will," John asserted, "All in good time!"

Chapter 11
The Beginning of a New Life

The Chesser family, without Thomas, all arrived at the New Orleans train depot as scheduled. Porters immediately went about unloading luggage, wagons, carriages and animals that various arriving passengers had brought with them.

The children looked about the strange city and suddenly felt very lonesome. It hit them like two dozen one hundred pound lead weights that they were now in a city where they knew nothing about the culture and nobody. Some odd combination of fear and anticipation washed over both of them, almost as if the fear itself were a vengeful cobra snake trying to choke the life out of them.

"I am not so sure that this will work out as well as we hoped," Ben whispered anxiously.

"Be anxious for nothing," Elizabeth thought as her eyes darted about, her mind racing as she went on, speaking barely audibly, "But in everything, with prayer and supplications, with thanksgiving, let your requests be made known unto God, and..." her voice abruptly faltered, as she suddenly blanked out the remainder of the verse.

"And the peace of God will guard your hearts and minds through Christ Jesus," Ben, who was right next to her, said aloud. With those words, the tension seemed to lift off their shoulders.

Their father looked back and said, "Come on, folks. We have to locate our luggage and get moving. I am not sure where it is, to be honest, but I am sure someone does."

"Uh, Mister Chesser," said a colored porter, "Right this way, if you would."

They all followed the porter to the third car from the back. It contained their packed carriage, luggage and personal effects. All of the animals were transported in a different rail car. The boardwalk was packed with recent arrivals, all trying to get unloaded and get on their way as soon as they could.

"Just look at how big this place is in comparison to the train depot in Atlanta," Elizabeth remarked.

"True, that, but what I can't get over is how many people there are that are here right now. The Atlanta depot, as far as I have seen, has never been this busy."

"Well, it is a bigger city, I think," Elizabeth commented.

"Yes, and it seems like the buildings are closer together, too," Ben pointed out as he gazed out a relatively large window.

"But there is one thing that is sort of the same. Look at the buildings. They are built a little different, but they are made of wood, like some many of the structures in Atlanta," Elizabeth commented.

"I can see that," Ben agreed, "That is why we better hope none of them ever catch fire. Wood makes for very good kindling, you know. If even one or two buildings went up in flames, soon the whole city would be up in flames."

"Oh, come now," Elizabeth said with an innocent smile, "Don't be so down. We just arrived here. Think about pleasant things. We have a bright future here."

"Listen to your sister, Ben," John called over his shoulder as they walked, "She knows of which she speaks. I like that positive attitude."

"Mister Anderson?" said another porter as they passed him. Each porter was seemingly assigned to one or two passengers according to the order in which they loaded. It was all very organized because a ledger of each family's belongings was kept, and later tallied, to be certain that everything and everyone was accounted for. Then, all the passengers followed their assigned porter and watched while other porters unloaded their luggage onto the arrival boardwalk.

"Mister and Misses Henley?" asked another.

The porters worked quickly and efficiently. The depot was starting to fill with departing passengers. Luggage and property that still needed to be sorted through and marked could be seen in a mammoth, organized pile to the right of the station. Animals were kept in a separate pen.

"Are you their new boss, pop?" Ben asked.

"No," replied John, "I control the cars in the yard and schedule the train repairs."

Ben watched as Bunches was removed from the car, followed by two other family horses. From a different car nearby, the carriage was next, and then the luggage. Other porters were busy hitching horses to harnesses and giving directions to people who weren't from the area.

"We're next," Amanda stated, "We'll let Bunches walk behind us as we go. He'll be fine."

Several railroad dignitaries and their wives appeared on the boardwalk to welcome John and meet his family. The entire welcoming committee beamed and shook with John first, then his wife and children. They'd brought several baskets of food and information about New Orleans.

"We are all pleased, John," said one, "You come highly recommended from Atlanta, and we are all proud that you and your family have elected to join us here."

"Well, we are all pleased to be here," Amanda replied.

Ben and Elizabeth continued to look about the depot; they could clearly see the downtown district and the town square.

"You'll like it here. There is a lot for young folks to do," a well-dressed lady said to them.

"It's different all right," Elizabeth said as she looked about.

"There is a carriage tour of the city meant for visitors," said another lady, "It leaves every two hours from the depot here."

The men spoke with John, providing directions to the stately house, furnishing stores, and local boarding stables.

"There's horseracing, too," said another, "It's real big here. A lot of prized runners that belong to the Rice Society racing group win big money."

"The Rice Society? What is that? A horse race?" John asked.

"The affluent local rice farmers," explained another. "They have more money than they know what to with, so they run the best and fastest horses."

Ben's ears perked up when speedy horses were mentioned. He wondered if there were many in New Orleans. He also wondered just exactly how big horseracing was. Perhaps he would have the chance to further develop his skills as a jockey there. He would be the first to admit that he was still very rough around the edges, but he hoped experience would take care of that.

"So tell me, John," asked the same man. "How many niggers did you bring with you?"

"None," John stated. "We don't own any."

"They're cheap down here…cheaper than they are in Atlanta," added another.

John and Amanda didn't want to pursue the conversation about slavery. They were new in town. Folks would find out soon enough about their feelings regarding slavery. They didn't need to get into a heated political debate or argument with anyone on their first day in a new place. That would not be a good start to a new life.

Still, they knew where they stood. Amanda fully supported John, even if Thomas did not. They did not support slavery. They didn't own any slaves, and never would. Nobody's insults could ever change that, either.

"It's been a long ride," John mentioned, "I know Amanda and the kids want to see the house and get settled in."

"Ah, that reminds me," one of the men said, "Here is a voucher to cover the cost for a month at a nice hotel until ya'll get settled in."

Another man stepped forward, "Here are directions to the house and to the hotel. The hotel will board your animals and store your belongings at no charge. Just sign the voucher when you check out."

"Oh, that is so nice!" Amanda replied.

"It's the least that the railroad can do. The workers at the hotel will also give you directions to the rail office," another lady responded.

"Well then, John," one of the men said, handing him a sheet of paper, "Here is my address. If you need anything, just have the hotel send a messenger over and I'll get it provided."

"Many thanks again," John responded, "This is more than we expected."

"We are just amazed," Amanda added, "Thank you from all of us."

Once again, it was smiles and handshakes all around as the welcoming committee handed over the baskets of food and information about New Orleans. The food baskets were a nice touch and well appreciated. It was thoughtful of the railroad's welcoming committee to put them together.

John took his seat in the carriage behind the reins. Amanda sat next to him, and Ben and Elizabeth sat in back. They all tried to relax, but they were so nervous and excited.

New Orleans seemed so different from Atlanta. Although the buildings were constructed mostly with wood, the layout of the buildings was different, and the streets' gas lamps were different. Even the inlaid stones in the streets were different. The businesses' and streets' names were in French, and very difficult to pronounce.

One thing, however, was reassuring. The people seemed nice enough. The railroad's reception committee had been completely unexpected. Several people in carriages smiled and waved as they passed by on the streets.

"Did you know any of those men in the welcoming committee?" Amanda asked John.

"The tall one with the beard was John Hintley, one of the chairmen. I saw him once in Atlanta, but the rest I've never seen before," he replied.

"Left here, on this street," Amanda said. She was looking at the map and directing the navigating. John turned the carriage left right where he was supposed to.

The landscape was changing now, from city properties to more rural. Several stately homes with acreage that was wide open, for the most part, could be seen off to the left and right. Gone were the hotels, the bakeries and the general stores. A few businesses could be seen, but it was mostly plantation properties now.

"We have a couple of miles to go yet, and then we turn left again," she remarked.

"Can we open the baskets?" Elizabeth asked, "I'm getting hungry."

"That would rightly be a good idea," John remarked, "We won't get to eat supper 'til later, when we get to the hotel."

"Lord Jesus, please bless this food to the nourishment of our bodies, keep us well, and help us adjust to life in this new place," Ben said, and they all said, "Amen!"

Elizabeth opened the first basket, finding jelly biscuits and salt pork. She immediately gave it to her mother, who took the first portion. While Amanda gave several samples to John, she also sampled several her self.

"Not bad," John remarked, "A little on the sweet side, but if this food is any reflection of what life in this city is like, it'll be fine."

"The French are known for their pastries, and obviously for good reason," Amanda stated, "These jelly rolls are just delicious!"

While John and Amanda munched on samples in the basket, Elizabeth opened the other one. This time, Ben took a keen interest because he was getting hungry just watching his folks eat.

"Let me see," he inquired.

"Fish, crackers and grapes," she said. Amanda traded baskets with her. Ben and Elizabeth munched on jelly rolls.

"Tastes spicy," John mentioned, "I think it's catfish with lots of breading and spices."

"You never know in New Orleans," Amanda added, "With the gulf right here, it could be anything, but it does tastes like catfish."

"Turn left at the next intersection here," Amanda instructed.

They all watched the landscape go by as John drove on. He struggled to eat and drive, but that was just a normal part of his life. He did not complain. They were surrounded by plantations now; there were no businesses in sight.

"Atlanta is nothing like this," Ben noticed, "These are all rice plantations."

The stone road had long disappeared, and the path narrowed somewhat and turned into hardened clay. Ben looked back at Bunches and reached to pet him on the nose.

"According to the map here, it's just around the bend, about a half mile ahead," Amanda said as she studied the map. The heavy covering provided by leaves and branches of the roadside trees arched upward and met at the top. It seemed as though someone had planted them like that years before, envisioning just what the Chesser family now saw.

A huge estate came into view. The country style home was designed the same as the plantation mansions back in Atlanta.

"Oh my!" Amanda gasped as her jaw fell and her eyes widened.

"That's our house?" Elizabeth exclaimed in total disbelief.

A beautiful mansion sat atop a towering, manicured grassy knoll. The drive was made of interlaced, inlaid tan brick, and several huge weeping willow trees graced the manicured front lawn.

"Not like back home, is it?" John asked, as he, too, was amazed. Amanda could not believe what she was looking at. She had envisioned something similar to what they had in Atlanta. This house was outright extravagant, with pillars supporting the roof, and French oak doors that opened inward, and many large windows.

"It's huge mother!" Ben gasped in surprise.

John pulled the carriage up to the entrance of the drive and stopped. For a moment, he just stared at the house. Although they had always lived comfortably, they had never lived as the wealthy did. They had just what they needed, no more, and no less. They had never had excess, but God had been faithful. Now it seemed as if they would have more than they dreamed of.

"Let's go have a look. This is our house as long as the railroad wants it to be," he said.

"Oh, oh, here!" Amanda exclaimed, "One of the ladies told me that the keys are at the bottom of one of the baskets."

Both Elizabeth and Amanda searched through both baskets. The keys were hidden under a cloth in the one that Elizabeth had.

"Here they are! There are three of them! Who has ever had three keys for a house? There's a front door and a back door, right? Why would you need a third key?" She asked as she turned them over to her father.

"Well now, lets just go take a look about then," John said.

The whole family was just astounded at the open massive pillared front porch. A huge double door was positioned in the middle of it. John tried several keys before he found the right one for the front door. Swinging both doors open, they entered a huge foyer with mirrors and a polished, mahogany floor. Beautiful ceiling high drapes graced each window. The wallpaper was flawless. The beige carpeting was plush and appeared new. There was not a mark or flaw anywhere.

Amanda's jaw dropped again as she took in the extent of the beautiful décor. It had been well taken care of. Someone had gone through great pains to maintain it. There was nothing cheap in the room. Everything there was well beyond what the Chesser family could have afforded on their budget in Atlanta.

"My word!" she gasped.

Even though the mansion was empty of furniture, it revealed that the previous owner was classy, with exquisite, fine tastes. As they walked through, they noticed the kitchen, an enormous family room with a massive, marble fireplace and bookcases with beautifully etched carvings along the east and west wall of the room

"The railroad bought this place," John remarked, "But it's what we call home."

"I am just amazed!" Amanda responded. "This is absolutely beautiful!"

"Can we see the bedrooms?" Ben asked.

"It's all upstairs, I would reckon," John replied.

A spiral, carpeted staircase was located between the huge family room and a vestibule to the right.

"Oh, this is so nice!" Elizabeth gasped, "Thomas doesn't know what he's missing."

Huge shelves could be seen tucked into the wall along the stair case; etched wood accents graced the windows.

"Beautiful! It's just beautiful!" Amanda said.

A huge upstairs hallway divided an open-walled sitting room and six bedrooms. There were three to the left and three to the right. Each bedroom featured beautiful wallpaper, painstakingly hand-carved woodwork in the doorframes and entries, and high windows with drawn shears and ceiling high curtains. A tour of each brought jaw dropping from them all once again, and exclamations of shock at the grandeur of appearance of the rooms themselves and the view from each.

"Beautiful flower garden out there. What do you think, John?" Amanda asked, "This one is ours, and look. It's bigger than the rest, and the view is wonderful."

"It looks good to me," he replied, "All of these rooms look like no one ever lived here. We know that someone has lived here."

"Do we have our pick of the bedrooms?" Elizabeth asked.

"I don't see why not. There are only four of us and six bedrooms. Amanda, do you have a preference? I don't. All the bedrooms are nice," John commented.

"I guess we could take the largest of the bedrooms, that one down the way a bit and to the right," Amanda said as she pointed to the third door on the right.

"That one is mine," Ben said as he pointed to the room across the way from what would be his parents' room and added, "It faces out to the barn and stable."

"I like that one," Elizabeth said as she pointed and remarked, "The one at the end of the hallway."

"That's all fine and dandy," John said beaming, "I guess we won't have to worry about where we will have houseguests stay when they are here."

"Oh, no," Amanda said chuckling, "There is more than enough space here." Frowning, she added, "It will cost a fortune to furnish this place. It's going take some time."

"Time is all we have," John replied.

"Can we look outside?" Ben asked.

"We certainly can," John replied, "Let's have a look at the grounds and the outbuildings."

All of them descended down the spiraled staircase and headed for the back door.

Behind the house, a beautiful white terrace was situated between two tall, weeping willow trees.

"Oh, it is just beautiful!" Amanda gasped.

"Isn't that a work of art?" John marveled, "Somebody put in a lot of time with that, building it, maintaining it and such don't you think?"

Ben was looking more for the outbuildings and the stable that he had heard about.

He wasn't interested in the terrace, although it was nice. It just wasn't his choice of things on their new property to admire. He started walking slowly to the back of the property. Soon, the others followed and joined him.

Several outbuildings were positioned behind the house, including a big barn and a stable building. They made their way to the barn and opened the huge doors. It was well kept and organized, already containing a few saddles and other equipment they would need that had been left behind for unknown reasons. The stable building was much bigger and nicer than the one that they had in Atlanta. Each stall was much cleaner, and there was even a little office out there, tucked away in the middle of the stalls.

"Isn't this better?" Ben asked, "Just look at that high ceiling and those big windows."

"It certainly is bigger," John added, "Lots of room here for horses. Maybe we can eventually get a fourth one."

Amanda and Elizabeth didn't really care about the barn and the outbuildings. Ben and John, on the other hand, because they were males, seemed very impressed. Elizabeth and Amanda just smiled and listened, tagging along while John and Ben carried on about how well built and kept the new barn was.

"What are those out there?" Ben asked.

"Well, son," John said, his face somber for the first time that day, "We won't have much use for those. Those buildings were where the slaves lived."

"They were all got sold when the place was sold," Amanda injected.

"Mama, why do people sell other people? God made all people equal, right? That's what we learned from pa," Elizabeth said.

"Yes, child, all people are made equal. That's what your papa and I believe. But not everyone believes that. Some people not only own slaves, but treat them like animals, ore even worse," Amanda said sadly.

"I once saw a colored boy, no older than maybe six, being whipped," John said, his eyes downcast.

"Pa, are you serious? Dear God in heaven, I hope you are joking, aren't you? A child? Beaten?" Elizabeth asked in horror, her face pale.

"Honey, I can't shield you from the truth forever, and it will be easier to hear coming from me. There are people out there—colored folks—that are beaten so badly they are scarred for life. There are some white folks that will not feed their colored folks enough. There are others who rape woman just to get them with child, and then start the baby working when they can barely walk and talk. Many coloreds are not literate, so those that are…are revered. The colored folks aren't allowed in schools. They aren't allowed to learn to read and write, so those that can read and write at all learned in secret," John explained.

"It is very wrong how those colored folks are treated," Amanda added.

"Isn't there anyone that doesn't like it…besides you and papa?" Elizabeth asked.

"Sure there is, but it has been a part of things so long that people are afraid of change, I think. But you don't like it, now that you know what you know, do you?" Amanda asked Elizabeth.

"No, mama, I think it's sad," Elizabeth responded. John smiled.

His eyes were sad as he thought about the little colored boy who had been whipped years before.

"What happened to all the slaves that were here?" Elizabeth asked her parents.

"The railroad wouldn't have bought them, so they were more than likely sold in local markets."

"Sold like eggs and milk?" Elizabeth asked.

"Yes, sweetheart, some folks are just so used to things being how they have been that they only see colored people as property. Rather cruel, humans selling humans," John mentioned.

"It's getting rather late, John," Amanda added, "How about if we head to the hotel? We still have to eat and get our baths."

"Alright then. Has everybody seen enough for the day? We can come back tomorrow."

"Let us come back tomorrow," Elizabeth suggested, her mind still trying to comprehend all that she had just heard. She didn't want to believe it, but she knew that her papa didn't lie. She said, "The house is so beautiful, and it's like a dream come true."

"Yeah, pop," Ben chimed in, "It really is. I like that stable."

"Alright then," John added, "Let's be on our way."

Chapter 12
French Quarter Hotel

"Ah, yes, you must be John Chesser, the deputy commissioner. This must be your family," commented a man with a large bald spot and a dark ring of hair on his head as they entered the hotel, "Party of Four," the consignor remarked at the front desk, "We are delighted to see you."

"How did you know that I was the deputy commissioner?" John asked.

"We know who you are, sir," he replied, "Funny how fast news travels when it's something of significance isn't it? You are most blessed with the La Rue St. Lazar mansion. It is very nice."

"Well, how did you know that?" Amanda asked.

"Ah madam, the fine staff at the French Quarter Hotel know all!" he replied, with an all-knowing smile.

"I am just amazed," John replied, "That's very good."

"Ah, Mr. Chesser, porters will maintain your carriage and horses. You need not worry. You will find that our hotel is exquisite and most comfortable for our honored guests, and you should count yourselves fortunate to be amongst them."

The consignor handed the awaiting porter three keys for three rooms. John wondered why there were three keys. As far as he knew, he had only one room.

"If you would, just sign the voucher, Mr. Chesser," he then requested. John signed the voucher, which made their stay at the hotel an expense the railroad would have to pay.

"The rooms are to the right and down the hallway, sir."

"I thought we only had one room reserved. That is really all we would have needed. We would have made do," John stated.

"Oh, come now. With the children and all, we thought it would be more comfortable to have two," the gentleman responded.

Amanda and Elizabeth looked about at the massive hotel lobby. It was every bit as exquisite and beautiful than she imagined it would be. Satin curtains graced the windows, and leather furnishings provided an area to sit and rest for weary travelers. Crystal chandeliers hung from the ceilings. This was far more than she had ever dreamed they would be given. Back in Atlanta, they would have never been able to afford to live so well, even for just a short time.

"Aren't those curtains just long and wonderful?" Amanda gasped.

"It is so nice here!" Elizabeth replied, "Will our house look as beautiful and nice?"

"Hopefully it will be, but this is so gorgeous. I am not sure that our house will be quite this nice, but we can sure try to make it this beautiful."

"We aren't rich, but if we get things done gradually, we should have a lovely house when it's all said and done.

But, whatever it ends up like, it will be our home," Amanda stated with a smile. John added, "Well, this is our home away from home for now. I really don't think it will be too bad. This is the nicest hotel that I've ever stayed at during my years with the railroad."

In a few moments, another uniformed porter brought their luggage to the front. He knew who John was. He just looked at him, smiling as he waited to be told what to do next.

"Ah, yes, I see that you have our things. Thank you, kindly, sir," John said as he noticed him, "Right this way if you would."

In a slight mix of words that occurred because they all started talking at once, the Chessers actually followed the porter to the rooms, and not the other way around. The consignor smiled at the slight breach of etiquette. Stopping at each room, the porter opened each door just wide enough to deliver the luggage to each room.

"Here you go," John mentioned as he handed a generous tip to the porter.

"Why thank you, sir…. indeed," he replied, "For your dining needs, our restaurant is open until nine tonight."

"We'll keep that in mind. I know we will take advantage of that, thanks. We are all hungry, I think," John replied. The porter turned about and disappeared down the hall.

"Let's get our luggage in order and go eat," John suggested "It's been a long day of travel without a nice, sit-down, hot meal, because that is something that the railroad doesn't have to offer."

"These rooms are just beautiful, John!" Amanda mentioned as she looked about.

"Well, it's our home until we get settled into the mansion," he responded.

"How did he know that it was the La Rue St. Lazar?" she inquired.

"I guess word gets about very quickly, like he said," he replied, "A lot of New Orleans' people work at the railroad in one office or another. They have been looking for a Deputy Commissioner for some time now, from what I understand."

"So when one was found, word got around quickly. I certainly think we made the right choice, John, and obvious Jeremiah wasn't lying to you when he said they really needed to fill this position, and they wanted you. Look at all they are doing for us," she noted.

"Exactly," he replied, "Couldn't have said it better myself."

"I agree, but I am hungry, so let's go eat," Elizabeth suggested as her stomach growled. It rumbled loud enough that they all heard it and chuckled. John took the keys to the room and shoved them in his pocket as they made their way towards the restaurant.

Ben was impressed with the restaurant with its fine furnishings, but the paintings on each wall really caught his eye. With almost life-like detail, each one showed vividly colorful depictions of a horserace. Looking about in amazement, Ben barely noticed the uniformed waiter give him a tall glass of water. While his mother and sister were involved in a discussion about the beautiful décor, his mind was miles away as he was awestruck by the skillfully painted horserace paintings.

"Wonderful…. aren't they?" John asked as he noticed Ben.

"Yes, they are, father," he replied, "May I get up and have a closer look at each one? I know what I want to have when the gentleman comes back and asks."

"Certainly," John replied, "Just be back for the ordering."

Ben got up and admired each painting in its hand-painted detail. Even the horses' manes were finely brushed, painted with care and precision. One painting caught his attention in particular; it was a beautiful, white horse rearing up on its hind legs. Another waiter, available at the moment, noticed that he stood before the paintings and approached for questions and comment.

"Are these actual horses that people own, or just pictures of horses that the painter imagined?" Ben asked the waiter, still studying the painting of the white horse.

"Ah, yes, they are real horses, indeed," he replied, "That white horse belongs to Monsieur Pierre Fontenot," he commented.

"Oh," replied Ben as he suddenly realized that he had been noticed looking at the paintings.

"Actually, the owners and jockeys do meet and dine here," the waiter continued.

"Really?" responded Ben, as a combination of wonder and excitement washed over him.

"Yes, horseracing is big here in New Orleans," the waiter explained, "There are many folks that enjoy it, and just as many folks that are raising the horses that race, and lots of jockeys, too. These are pictures of only a few. If we let everyone who wanted to be painted have a painting up there, we wouldn't have enough space. Only the best horses and finest jockeys can have their horses painted and mounted."

Ben felt very small when he thought about his horse, Bunches, who was just a local dirt road runner. That was as far as Bunches had come. But, still, Ben couldn't help but envision a painting of himself and Bunches on the wall.

"It's…all very nice, sir," Ben stammered, not knowing quite what else to say at the moment.

"Only the best can be on the wall," the waiter again reaffirmed, "All of these horses are either top winners or show horses."

John glanced over at Ben and the waiting. Sensing he was being watched, Ben obeyed his father's unspoken queue that it was time to sit down and order. He felt disappointed because he wanted the waiter to tell him more, but a second chance for admiring the paintings would just have to wait.

"Father, all of those paintings are of the finest local horses," Ben mentioned, as he sat down.

"I know, son," he replied, "They would have to be the best, or they wouldn't be there."

Amanda and Elizabeth had been so involved in their discussion that they didn't notice that Ben had actually got up to look at the paintings.

"Father," Elizabeth asked, "Can we take the city's tour carriage tomorrow?"

John looked at Amanda, who smiled a skeptical smile, knowing fully well that Elizabeth had an ulterior motive. It was obvious to Amanda and John after only a moment that Elizabeth wanted to see not only the city, but the quaint, French stores.

"Sure," he replied, "We can go. I know you want to see the stores, and it would be a good outing for us, providing us an opportunity to get to know the city."

Elizabeth smiled at her father's approval as she squealed, "Ohhhhh, I can hardly wait!"

Ben could have cared less about the décor or the quaint stores. His interest was in the horseracing activities and what the waiter had said.

"John, why don't you order for all of us?" Amanda requested.

He quickly understood her logic; she didn't want to be embarrassed for not knowing the menu, which was mostly in French.

"Well, us males are mighty hungry," He teased, "But I don't quite understand French."

Once their waiter appeared, ready to take the order, John looked about at the family. He didn't have to look far because all eyes were on him. They didn't care what they ate; they were all too hungry to care. John pointed to a selection on the menu with raised eye brows.

"Ah yes," the waiter explained, "Plump roast duck au jus, soup, with baked sweet potatoes, green beans, and roll bread, comes with a bottle of wine, as well sir."

John looked about for family approval. They didn't know what else they'd want, even though they all kind of knew what they thought they wanted when they came in, and no one objected. They were just too hungry.

"Sounds fine to us, sir," John stated.

"Very good, then," The waiter replied, "Would you like coffee, milk, water, or natural juices to drink?"

"Apple juice, please, if you have it!" Ben immediately piped up without a thought. It was his absolute favorite juice in the world.

"Milk, please," Amanda and Elizabeth said, almost in unison.

"And I will just have water," John stated. His throat was so dry that it felt like sandpaper. The waiter left to get them their drinks and turn the order in.

"Did you know, Amanda that our food is free for as long as we stay here?" John asked.

"No," she responded, "I didn't know that. How did you know that?"

"Its all part of my deal with the railroad," he explained, "It was in the contract I signed, so it's part of my deal that we got when I was offered the job."

"They must have really, really wanted you," Ben interjected. "I could get use to staying here."

John just smiled at Ben's comment and said, "Don't get too comfortable. We only have about two weeks to get the house ready and get moved in. We can't stay here for all eternity."

"Oh, I can't wait to go on the tour of the city tomorrow," Elizabeth said again, "Oh, I want to see all the fashion dress shops and the furnishings!"

"We will," Amanda replied. "You know, of course, that Ben will want to see the horseracing stables, so you can't have all of the time to yourself."

"Oh, I know, but like daddy said, we only have two weeks to buy things for the house and get settled in."

Ben's mind was miles away, as the paintings again attracted his attention. Again, he could not help but see Bunches on the wall. He knew it was not likely, but he couldn't help but dream.

"I don't think that Bunches will ever get on that wall," John chuckled, almost as if he knew what Ben was thinking.

"I don't think so either pop," Ben replied. "Those horses are the best. Why… Bunches is just an old, dirt road horse."

"But Bunches is a fast horse. I know that first race was disheartening for you, but you did your best, and that made me proud of you even if you didn't win. You never got a chance to race Jesse again, and that's too bad. I know you would have beaten him. That time, you would have won fairly, too. The judges would have made sure of that."

"Aw, thanks pop," Ben replied, "Bunches isn't much for show, either, though. Just look at those arched backs on those horses in the paintings."

"True," John replied, "But those are paintings. A good artist can do anything with a brush. They may not look exactly like that."

The waiter appeared with the drinks, soup and bread. Everyone leaned back as he carefully served each person.

"It all smells so good!" Amanda commented.

"I'm so hungry I could eat a horse!" John said, teasing Ben all in fun.

"I don't think they serve horse here pop," Ben shot back.

"We need to be thinking about schools for the both of you," Amanda mentioned.

"Aw, mama," Elizabeth sighed. "Who wants to think about school? I don't have much left, anyway. I am twelve. I can read and write and add and subtract and multiple and divide, and do basic ciphering and fractions, and of course I know history. George Washington was our first president, and the Declaration of Independence was signed in 1776. Isn't that enough?"

Ben just rolled his eyes at the thought of going to school. He had done all the schooling he really wanted to do. It just didn't fit his personal plan; he dreamed of horseracing.

"The more education you have, the better off you are. You are fortunate that your mother and I want you to finish school. Most kids only finish the first six grades, if that," John added.

"This bread is so good," Elizabeth commented, attempting and hoping to change the subject.

"Well, that good. We'll talk about school later," Amanda replied. "But, both of you need to continue where you left off in Atlanta."

Two waiters brought their order. When the lifted the lid, a steaming, roast duck was revealed under a sterling silver tray, complete with baked sweet potatoes. The waiters weren't done. While one removed used dinnerware and served side dishes, the other withdrew a long knife and cut the plump, roast duck. Looking about, and offering the cut, the waiter served each piece to each family member. Both waiters then slightly bowed and turned away.

"Oh my, look at that! What wonderful service!" Amanda gasped. "It looks so good!"

"Did you see that?" Elizabeth whispered in amazement, "They even cut our meat for us."

"It's a sign of an exquisite restaurant. It's part of their job. Very few do that, but here, because it is such a high-end restaurant, they do. They are expected to wait on the people like that," John replied.

In silence, the family savored the roast duck with all of the trimmings. It still wasn't as good as home cooking, but it was much better than eating a meal in the dining car on the train.

"What are we going to do with that bottle of wine?" Amanda asked.

"Let's take it with us," John replied, "It's sealed, so it will keep for a long time."

"I haven't had wine yet, papa," Elizabeth commented.

"No, honey, there will be plenty of time for that when you are older. You can wait," her father told his young daughter.

"What kind of wine is it, pa?" Elizabeth asked.

"Merlot," John muttered. "It's a dark wine."

"And as your father said," Amanda interjected in a stern tone, sensing that Elizabeth was interested in it, "You can wait until you are older to drink. There is enough time for that later. Besides, people get addicted to alcohol if they drink too much too soon in life."

"Drunkenness is a sin," Ben remarked.

"Yes, preacher boy. What do you want me to do? Get on my knees and repent because I wanted a taste of wine?" Elizabeth retorted, rolling her eyes.

"Hey, now, you both can just behave yourselves and be silent. Ben, you are right. Drunkenness is a sin. The Bible says so. Elizabeth, no, it is not a sin to want a taste of wine, but your mother is right. You are so very young, and you don't need one, so you won't get one. Now, both of you be nice to each other and be good. We are in public, so behave like it!" John ordered.

When their father used that tone of voice, Ben and Elizabeth knew that he meant business. They dared not say anything, so they ate in silence. After finishing the meal, two different waiters appeared. One brought out an unexpected pie for dessert; the other cleared away all of the used dinnerware.

"Oh my! We didn't order a pie! Are you sure this is for us?" Amanda gasped again.

"Compliments of some very happy people that now have a Railroad Commissioner, ma'am. Elderberry with churned cream," the waiter said in a heavy French accent.

John patted his stomach and said, "Oh Lord, it's a bit much, but I can see what I can do about it."

The waiters just smiled. From across the room, an elderly couple that had been married for over forty years also smiled across their table at one another. They didn't want the Chessers knowing, but they had paid for the pie. As usual, the waiter cut the pie into pieces and served each member on separate china plates.

"Oh, this is so good!" Elizabeth said, "It's so rich that it reminds me of Grandma's pies."

"Yes, indeed it does," John replied, "I can taste the walnuts and pecans, as well. This is a real treat, huh?"

"Indeed it is. Pecans are a big crop in this area," Amanda added.

"It's very good!" Ben said.

"What do you enjoy more, Ben, this delicious pie or those horse paintings?" John teased.

"At the moment, pop," he replied, "I would have to say the pie!"

Several more patrons entered the restaurant and were immediately seated by waiters. Without even asking, Ben perceived that they were horseracing people. He could tell just by how they dressed. Studying one man briefly, he recognized him as the owner of the white horse, Pierre Fontenot. The man spoke with another in a very heavy French accent, often switching back and forth between English and French.

Chapter 13
Hurdle Jump Training

"Very good, Gabrielle, very good indeed!" exclaimed her private, horseback riding instructor, Marcel Thouredeau as he added, "You are progressing very well! Truly, you are a natural. We will have you competing in no time, or at least attracting some attention from those eligible bachelors because you ride so very well!"

"Well, it isn't as if I haven't ridden a horse before. We are riding them pretty much from the day we are born," Gabrielle replied, "That's how you have to get around sometimes. If there's no carriage, but there's a horse, you have to get on and go if you want to go anywhere."

Marcel just smiled and shook his head. Gabrielle wasn't like most girls in a lot of ways. He almost felt sorry that she had been a girl, because she had so many talents, from what he had heard, and she certainly knew how to express herself. Unfortunately, though, she would eventually have to marry and settle into the role of the quiet, often forgotten housewife and mother. That is what women did.

That afternoon, Gabrielle had started with a low hurdle, just thirty six inches off the ground. She had succeeded in jumping it without falling off her horse about a dozen times, so Marcel had allowed her to raise the bar to thirty nine inches. Gabrielle had just finished the much larger jump with her white show horse, Samson when Marcel told her it was time to quit for the day. Turning the reins to the left, she approached him from the right.

"Things went very well, Gabrielle. I am so very impressed with your work. You must be practicing hard," Marcel stated with a broad grin of approval.

"It's all Samson," Gabrielle replied. "All of these weekday workouts are paying off."

"Nah!" he affirmed. "He responds well because he is comfortable with the way you handle him. I know you really enjoy it, too, Marcel said.

"I do. May I just jump him once more?" Gabrielle pleaded.

"No, let's not jump anymore today. He's tired and you might fall over the hurdle. I mean, you wouldn't, but he would, and then you would fall off, and he could possibly break a leg. That would be horrible."

"Alright then, we're done for the day. Two hours is enough. Has it really been that long? That didn't seem like two hours to me," she responded as she dismounted.

Marcel snapped his finger to signal the stable boy, letting him that she was done for the day. Samson would need to have the saddle removed and a walk around to cool off.   Later, he would be watered and fed. Charles, the relatively new stable boy, was nearby and responded to Marcel's queue.

"Yes sir?" he gasped as he came running over. "What may I do for you, sir?"

"Miss Gabrielle here is done with her lesson for the day. You know what to do with Samson here," Marcel noted. "See to it right away."

Momentarily, Charles froze. He had never been close to Samson before, because he wasn't his normally assigned horse, but he dared not ignore the cue or the instructions he was given. He didn't want to lose his job. Of particular interest to Charles was Gabrielle, and he had never stood that close to her. He knew he was being watched and felt uneasy. He swallowed hard and tried to hide it.

Gabrielle removed her riding hat. Her flowing, dark hair fell to her shoulders. With striking, hazel eyes and a pleasant, wide smile, she was outstandingly beautiful. She smiled, yet said nothing to Charles as she handed over the reins.

Though she didn't want him knowing, she had also noticed Charles. She liked his high cheek bones, pleasant smile, and dark hair that was parted in the middle, almost flowing to his shoulders. It was unusually long, but he was a quiet and hardworking boy. She saw nothing wrong with him.

She knew that her father had hired him, and that he was relatively new. He had already gained a reputation as an excellent stableman, and he had come from a local family. They were respected and known to be as hard-working as he was.

Charles walked Samson away feeling as if it had been his lucky day. He arrived at the scene immediately when Marcel needed someone, and it was just happenstance. He knew that Gabrielle was Pierre's daughter; he had seen her about the estate, but only from a distance. To be standing next to her was an opportunity that he never even imagined would ever come about. She was beautiful, and he felt like a clumsy fool in her presence.

"Very good day, Gabrielle," Marcel again acknowledged "Your father will be pleased.

Perhaps next week we can look at the barrel hurdles next week if Samson is up to it."

"He will be," she responded in French.

Gabrielle approached the mansion with her riding hat in hand. She wasn't really thinking about Samson or her lesson; rather, her mind whirled with thoughts of the handsome stable boy that just smiled to her and said nothing. Perhaps she would learn his name the next week. He wasn't Samson's usual handler, but there had to be a way. She determined in her own mind that she would learn his name and find out more information about him.

Chapter 14
A Secret Admirer

Gabrielle entered her well-kept massive room and made her way towards the bathroom. Her bath was ready, as usual, after her horse jumping lesson. Gabrielle didn't want to admit it, but riding Samson had made her legs sore. He was a powerful horse, and it was only the second time that she had ridden him. She walked with a slight limp and didn't want anyone to know of it.

Miss Prissy had several towels at her tub of hot water, along with imported, scented soaps and body oils. Behind a beautiful folding partition, Gabrielle sat in the hot water. It soothed and relaxed her. She liked to ride and jump horses, but it caused muscle aches. She hoped that with time, she would get strong enough that it wouldn't make her so sore.

Relaxing in the tub, she wondered about that new stable boy. He seemed so self-confident and polite. Once again, she told herself she would investigate him more. He didn't seem to be afraid to approach her, like most of the local boys were.

"Miss Gabrielle," whispered Miss Prissy from behind the folding blind. "Do you require assistance?"

"I'll be getting out soon, but no thank you," she replied.

"Very well, then," Miss Prissy replied quickly.

Gabrielle heard the door close as Miss Prissy exited she knew she was alone. Her bath time was private to her. Now that she was nearly an adult, she didn't want to be seen bathing. She was not helpless anymore. The days of being a little girl were over.

There was a time when the matrons fawned over her. They would laugh as they made a lot of bubbles and washed her face and back, but that was a long time ago. The best that they could do nowadays was to lay out her selected clothes, draw the bath and provide towels. That was all she wanted them to do, and even that seemed like a bit much some days.

After her bath, she dressed and retreated to her room to comb out her flowing hair. Looking out her window, in the direction of the stables, she could see the same stable boy walking Samson about, without his saddle. He seemed to handle Samson very well. A slight nudge of the reins brought an immediate reaction from Samson. The young man walked around the stable, coral, and back again with Samson repeatedly. Gabrielle watched the handsome young man as the horse was given a good wind down workout.

"Is there anything else, Miss Gabrielle?" Miss Prissy asked from her door.

At first, she ignored the request, preoccupied with the young man that she was watching out the window. Miss Prissy only waited for her response, well aware that she was keenly interested in something. The young man glanced in her direction, though he did not see that she was watching him because she hastily turned her eyes to the door.

"Certainly," she replied, "Who is that stable man working with Samson?"

Miss Prissy entered the room and quickly peered out of the window to see who she was watching.

"That's Charles Boyer," she replied, "New boy. He comes from a local, French family that has horses. They had a tragedy happen not so long ago. Their stable burned down and it was such a loss. Your father himself hired him."

"I see," Gabrielle responded.

"Why do you want to know about him?"

Gabrielle had to think fast and not be obvious about her real reason.

"He isn't Samson's usual trainer," she replied calmly, "I thought Samson was assigned to someone else."

Her response satisfied Miss Prissy. Samson was Gabrielle's horse, and it seemed logical enough that she had inquired about the young man out of concern for him. Gabrielle did not want Miss Prissy knowing the real reason she had asked. But then again, she was much older and not ignorant regarding the thinking of young ladies, having once been one her self, so Gabrielle knew it would just be a matter of time until she figured things out.

"I can't say that I know too much about the boy," Miss Prissy added, "He works hard and pleases your father and the other stable hands. Other than that, I don't know what rightly goes on out there, just like they don't know what goes on in the estate."

"There is something," Gabrielle recounted. "Could you brush my hair for me if you would? I tried, and it is very matted up and a real mess."

"Sure," she replied. "Just sit here in your favorite chair and I'll brush it."

"You think that's my favorite chair? Now what makes you think that?" Gabrielle teased.

"Oh, I don't know, maybe the fact that you got it years ago, and even when it was too big for you, you would crawl up into it, curl up and fall asleep. We always used to worry that you would fall out of this thing. You were so little, and it was so enormous. But your father bought this chair for you, and you have always loved it," Miss Prissy replied.

"It has been so comfortable," Gabrielle replied.

As she gently combed through Gabrielle's hair, Miss Prissy said, "You haven't asked me to brush your hair in a month of Sundays. I see that it's gotten long in the back. Do you want me to trim it some?"

"Oh, alright then," Gabrielle replied, "But only a little. Not too much, just where it's longer than the other places."

Miss Prissy noticed that Gabrielle's eyes remained towards the window. She was making things harder than they needed to be. Her head's movements didn't match Miss Prissy's requests for brushing and cutting longer hair strands shorter.

"Now, Miss Gabrielle, if you could turn your head to the right?" Miss Prissy requested. Hesitantly, Gabrielle did so. Now, all she wanted was to be done with this so that she could go back to watching the young man.

With a snip here and a snip there, a few inches of longer hair that had flowed down to Gabrielle's back fell to the carpet. Miss Prissy knew fully well that Gabrielle was preoccupied with something outside of that window. At every chance, her head would turn to the left and her eye gaze would follow. It didn't take Miss Prissy long to figure things out.

"Now Miss Gabrielle, I've been cutting your hair ever since you were almost a year old. I know good and well that you'd rather be looking outside of that window, and I know what you are looking at, as well!"

"What would that be?" Gabrielle asked innocently.

"That boy, Charles Boyer," Miss Prissy stated, "Ever since you noticed him, you've been asking questions. At first, I wanted to believe it was about Samson because you have not been interested in boys until recently, but now I know that it's not about Samson."

Gabrielle's face fell and she felt herself blushing. She had been caught swooning, and she had been too obvious about it. She had no excuse for it. A denial would be blatant deception.

"Hey, there's no shame in your feelings. This is all a part of growing up. I won't tell if you won't," Miss Prissy whispered. Gabrielle smiled sheepishly as she added, "Now, that's much better. Just keep your head straight."

Miss Prissy knew Gabrielle very well, well enough to know that if she knew she was caught in a situation, she would back down. She had beaten Gabrielle at her own game, although Gabrielle was a little young to know it yet. Gabrielle looked ahead and kept her head straight for the remaining duration of the brushing and trimming.

When Miss Prissy had finished trimming her hair, she brought two mirrors into the room so that Gabrielle could see both the front and the back of her head for comment.

"Very nice, Miss Prissy! Very nice indeed!" Gabrielle exclaimed.

"Like ah say," Miss Prissy recalled, "I've been cutting and brushing your long hair for a long time, so I've had lots of practice doing what I'm doing."

"And it does look very nice. Thank you for doing that for me. I think I will go downstairs now," Gabrielle said.

As she descended down the spiral staircase, she could hear her father and Marcel talking in the vestibule. Marcel always made it a point to meet with Pierre afterwards and discuss the day's horse jumping activities.

"Ah, Gabrielle!" Marcel exclaimed as she appeared.

Gabrielle wasn't exactly overjoyed to see him, but politely greeted him. She respected him as her teacher, but wasn't very fond of him as a person. She had come down the staircase at the wrong time. She had forgotten that Marcel liked to stop in, smoke a cigar, and chat with her father about his horses and their abilities.

"Pierre, next week Gabrielle here will master the barrel hurdles. She's getting quite good, you know," Marcel said.

Gabrielle just smiled through her uneasiness. She didn't want to say anything because she didn't want anyone knowing she was uncomfortable. To make the situation worse, she was still sore from the jumping lesson earlier in the day.

"Glad to hear that," Pierre responded, "Unfortunately, I wasn't able to see the jumping today, but Marcel, if you say it went well, I know it's true. You have taught some of the best horse jumpers in the county."

Cigar smoke poured from Marcel's nostrils as he thought for a moment and said with conviction, "Well thank you, Pierre. I can assure you that Gabrielle will be among them soon."

Gabrielle didn't know quite what to say. The comment had come completely unexpectedly. She didn't personally aspire to be one of the best horse jumpers in the county. Obviously, Marcel saw something in her that she did not. She just wanted to jump small hurdles for fun.

"Father," she asked, "May I take Samson out for riding this Saturday afternoon? No jumping…just riding about the grounds?"

"Why sure!" he replied.

"The French mark of a true and dedicated horsewoman!" Marcel exclaimed in French.

"Certainly, you may take him out. One of the stable boys will get him saddled and ready," Pierre explained, "Just remind me tomorrow and I'll see to it."

"Thank you, father," she replied.

"Where were we?" Marcel inquired, referring back to their previous conversation, "Ah yes, the next race roster is arriving in the telegraph office. If you have the time, Pierre, why don't we both go and get the roster? I believe it's my turn to go get it, anyway."

Pierre stepped forward and looked toward the kitchen to visually inquire if he had enough time to go there and be back in time for supper with the family. Andrea and three of the matrons were still busy cooking.

"Supper won't be for another hour or so. You'll have plenty of time if you go now," Andrea said, understanding his visual queue.

"Alright then Marcel… I'll go with you," he said.

"Good afternoon, ladies," Marcel said as he slightly bowed and tipped his hat.

Gabrielle was glad to see Marcel leave. Now she knew why he was such a hard, driven horse teacher. Sadly, it wasn't for the benefit of his students as much as it was for his own acclaim, but he was good, and he knew it.

Pierre and Marcel left through a side door in the vestibule. Gabrielle breathed a sigh of relief. She watched as they got into Marcel's buggy for the short ride to the telegraph office.

"Your hair looks very nice, Gabrielle. Did Miss Prissy trim it for you again? She always does a fine job," her mother noticed. Gabrielle liked the sudden attention and turned about a few times for her mother to more closely look at her beautifully brushed and trimmed hair.

"You really like it?" she asked.

"Miss Prissy does such good work!" Andrea said approvingly.

"Indeed, you look very nice," her grandmother mentioned as she sipped tea.

Gabrielle appreciated the nice comments on her hair much more so than comments on her horse jumping abilities. Moving about made her suddenly realize how sore she really was from jumping small hurdles.

"Would you like some tea, Gabrielle?" her grandmother asked, and leaning close so only Gabrielle could hear, she added, "You look sore and tired."

"Certainly," she replied.

Andrea was surprised because Gabrielle didn't usually want to sit with her grandmother and drink tea, but, unlike her grandmother, Gabrielle's mother didn't know that Gabrielle was so sore that she could hardly take another step. Miss Prissy came down the steps and joined the other matrons in the kitchen. Andrea left the kitchen to join her mother and daughter in having a cup of tea.

Miss Prissy and the other colored matrons busied themselves in the kitchen with supper preparations. Without saying a word about it to anyone, Miss Prissy watched to see if Gabrielle would look out of the window toward the stables, but she didn't. She was too sore to go notice Charles anymore.

After awhile, Marcel's buggy could be seen in the drive. Andrea watched as Pierre shook hands with Marcel, and then one of the stable porters could then be seen quickly arriving to assist him with getting out of the buggy.

"Supper won't be too long now," Miss Prissy whispered.

Chapter 15
News of Civil Strife

Pierre came in through the same vestibule door he had left out of and hung his hat in its usual place. The latest and greatest horserace roster had come through the telegraph just fine. So had something else and it was a matter of concern.

"I didn't think you'd be back for awhile longer," Andrea mentioned, "I know how long-winded Marcel can be sometimes. Sometimes he forgets himself."

"The office was busy," Pierre said, "They had the horserace roster waiting for us, but there were crowds of people…all in the street talking," Pierre stated in a troubled tone.

"Talking about what?" his mother asked.

"Are there new and faster horses running this time?" Andrea asked, hoping that his troubled expression was not over anything serious.

"No," Pierre replied, "It seems that a harbor in South Carolina called Fort Sumter has been attacked and destroyed by an army calling itself the Confederacy."

"Attacked? Was it destroyed?" Andrea asked.

"We all thought it was just talk," Pierre responded, "Oh, there have been words between the southern states and the northern states in the Senate over states' rights and all, but that's the way the politicians are. They just argue and bicker. That's nothing new. That's what they have always done, and we all know that, but this is more serious. This could really lead to something. They attacked the fort. It was attacked and destroyed early in the morning."

"Oh, my word! Lord, have mercy, no!" his mother said.

"Oh, they'll talk it out and get over it," Andrea reasoned, knowing deep inside that what she had said was just a fleeting hope, and truly not very likely, "It's just a few navy rebels losing their tempers. It'll pass."

"Hope so," Pierre responded, "That seems to be all we hear anymore, politicians from both sides arguing back and forth. We just don't hear much from our own representatives."

Pierre excused himself to go wash his hands for supper. While he was gone, the kitchen matrons set the table with jambalaya with rice and sweet tea. All of the colored matrons stood along the wall, as usual, to wait for him to return and give thanks for the food.

Still very sore and even more stiff than she had been hours earlier, Gabrielle was barely able to get herself to the table to enjoy her favorite dish. She truly did enjoy riding, and was upset that it had made her so sore. Well, she thought, her body would just have to get over the aches and pains and get used to riding more often. Rain, sleet or snow, she loved Samson, and nothing would stop her from riding him.

Pierre returned, and then looked about. Sensing that everyone was ready, he stood by his chair, bowed his head and offered thanks for the huge, steaming supper. Gabrielle hoped that her soreness would go away for a ride with Samson that Saturday. While she ate her meal, she daydreamed about the handsome, new stable boy, Charles Boyer. Perhaps he would help her mount and dismount and watch her ride.

She was so involved with fantasizing about the ride that she barely heard her parents discussing a far away place in South Carolina. They had been very careful not to discuss states' rights over slavery. They had not told their matrons what was being talked about in the Senate, so as far as they knew, the colored matrons knew nothing. If they discussed the issue within earshot of anyone colored, the colored matrons would hear what they said and would know of the real issue in the Senate.

"Oh Gabrielle!" her grandmother sighed happily, jolting Gabrielle out of her daydreaming, "You looked so good with Samson this afternoon. We all saw you jump the hurdles. It was all quite nice!"

"Why, thank you. He is a good horse. I enjoy riding him very much," Gabrielle replied. She was more thankful that the conversation had turned to her. That was better than listening to bits and pieces of what her parents thought about the attack on Fort Sumter. Maybe she should've cared, but the truth was that she didn't. She, too, wanted to believe that little or nothing would come out of what had happened.

"Indeed, Marcel is an excellent instructor," Pierre added, "Why, it wouldn't surprise me at all if Gabrielle was a champion hurdle jumper eventually. I believe she very well could be. He has trained some of the best."

Gabrielle rolled her eyes. How many times did she have to hear about becoming a champion? That wasn't what she wanted. Her mother shot her a glance that silently cautioned her to remain silent. The colored matrons removed the plates and brought two hot peach pies to the table.

"Oh, my word!" Andrea gasped, "I couldn't eat another bite if my life depended on it."

"Well, my life doesn't, so I'll have a huge piece, Miss Prissy, if you don't mind," Pierre said.

"Why certainly, sir," she responded as she placed an enormous helping in front of him. Gabrielle and her grandmother each had a small serving. They wished that they would have known this was coming, because they both would have saved more room. The dessert was a family favorite, but the jambalaya was very filling.

"Gabrielle," her father mentioned, "Would you like to try out that new saddle?"

Gabrielle looked at her father in delighted surprise. Her face lit up. He was making her an offer that she could scarcely believe she was hearing. Maybe he saw something in her that she did not. The only other folks that had the privilege of, as her father put it, 'trying out the new saddle' were jockeys.

Chuckling gleefully at Gabrielle's shining eyes, Pierre said, "I'll have one of the stablemen fit the new saddle onto Samson. Even though it's a racing saddle, it would suit you well for riding. Let me know what you think of it. Just because I am your father doesn't mean you can't be honest. I won't be offended if you don't like it, and if you don't like it, then the other one might be better."

"Oh thank you, father," she replied, "I remember that saddle. It was all the talk at the racing ball."

"Indeed, it was," He stated, and added, "It will soon go into production for the racing jockeys. I know it's something new and more costly, but it isn't that much more. Besides, it is getting good reviews from the jockeys that have used it, and to make the racing fair, everyone would need to ride on it."

The colored matrons, upon Miss Prissy's cue, cleared the table of the remaining, leftover dessert. Andrea had not had any, so she was glad there was some left. She planned to have some later, when she wasn't so full. Gabrielle had barely taken her last bite when her plate was whisked away.

After supper, Pierre excused himself to go on his late afternoon tour of the building and grounds. He personally oversaw the stables and the fields. In the twilight of the evening, he saw that it was all secure. The horses were in for the night. The stables were locked down.

The field slaves had a small campfire burning in the distance, by their cabins. Pierre listened as they sang spirituals, each male voice, usually in a deep baritone, ringing out in the evening's breeze. Each figure standing about the fire seemed to take turns singing lead. They were happy that the harvest season was over, but nonetheless, they couldn't leave. They sang of freedom and equality, and that was truly the yearning of their hearts.

Pierre enjoyed the singing and back up scat vocals, but didn't dare go any closer to the area. He enjoyed it, they could sing. They might have been slaves, but they sure could sing. He wanted to move closer, but knew that if he did they would stop. To them, singing was expression unlike any other. The freedom to sing was better than no freedom at all.

Somewhere deep inside him, Pierre's heart almost ached for them. This way of life—the one in which slaves worked the fields—was all he had ever known. But, for the first time he wondered: was it really the only way or the best way to do things? Was this what God had intended life to be for them?

He brushed those thoughts back in his mind as quickly as they had come. There was nothing he could do to change things. Slavery had been around for hundreds of years. If it wasn't God's will, then He could change it. Pierre had no power to change it. Besides, he treated his slaves much better than surrounding family plantations. They ate, lived, and slept better. Still, he could not give them what they sang of and desired the most, freedom and justice.

Chapter 16
A Future Beau

Gabrielle was delighted when the following Saturday arrived. She had recovered from her soreness and was ready to meet the new stable boy that she had daydreamed about. He too, had thought about her, but would never admit it. How could he help it? She was so young and attractive, and he was a young man with raging hormones.

As Gabrielle entered the stable, she wasn't disappointed. Charles stood with Samson, trying to relax. He had heard that Pierre's daughter would be arriving soon to ride Samson. He had brushed and fed Samson carefully for the event. He wanted to impress Gabrielle.

"I'm Charles Boyer," he said with a beaming smile when he saw her. Without missing a beat, he added, "Samson is ready to ride."

Gabrielle was nervous, too. She didn't quite know how to respond. It was as if she had temporarily lost all the manners that she had ever been taught. Although her soreness was gone, she felt weak in the knees.

"My name is Gabrielle," she responded after a moment, "Thank you much for getting Samson ready for me."

"You are most certainly welcome. Do you require assistance getting your foot into the stirrup?"

Gabrielle looked at the saddle, debating whether she would really need help. The stirrup was higher than the other saddle, and the saddle looked much different than when she had seen it last. She ignored his question and placed her left foot close to the stirrup, attempting to mount, but losing her balance and falling backwards onto Charles, who was standing behind her.

"Oh my!" he gasped.

"I'm so sorry!" she stammered. "That saddle isn't like the other one."

"Let me help you," he recommended. "Place your foot in and then lift yourself up and over. I will stay right here and make sure you don't fall. I think you can do it if you do as I said to," Charles said compassionately. Gabrielle did just as she told and quickly found herself in the new saddle.

"Will you be alright now, young lady?" Charles inquired.

"I do believe so. Thank you for your help. Oh...I'm so sorry that I fell into you like that," she said again, knowing full well that she had made a spectacle of herself.

"It's quite alright," he replied with a wide grin. "If I am not here when you get back, someone else will be. If there's not someone here to help you, just ask for Charles."

"Oh, thank you, sir! I don't quite know what I would have done had you not been there when I fell," Gabrielle confessed.

"Well, you may well have been seriously hurt, so it was a good thing that I was here. You wouldn't have needed to pull a muscle or hurt your back. You are quite the fine rider. It will take you places," Charles said confidently.

"Thank you, sir, that's what daddy seems to think, too. I just do it because I enjoy it," Gabrielle replied.

"Well, you do quite well," Charles said softly.

"Well, that may be the case, but I enjoy my harp more. I have played since I was small. Now I have had lessons so long that I almost don't need them anymore, but I like them so much that I haven't stopped. Besides, I like having those regular lessons. It gives me a time that I know is set aside for playing my instrument and keeping my skills sharp," Gabrielle said.

"Well, if you are half as good on that harp as you are on this horse, I am sure you do very well and fill the house with music," Charles said.

"Oh, yes, it has been filled with the sound of music for years now. I play the harp just to relax when I am worried or stressed, and of course when I am in lessons," Gabrielle informed him.

"Well, that sure is a terrific and productive way to deal with stress, and if it's something you enjoy, hey, that makes it better. You have a wonderful time riding. I better get back to work," Charles said as he flashed a grin.

"Nice meeting you," Gabrielle said, and added, "Maybe sometime, you can hear me play if you would like."

"Yes, it sure was nice meeting you, as well, and I would like that very much," Charles responded.

Gabrielle tugged at the reins and Samson walked forward and then turned to the right.

Immediately, Gabrielle noticed that the new saddle felt much better than the old one. Samson seemed to be more responsive to it. She was going to have a pleasant ride, but she hated the fact that she made a fool of herself in front of a stable boy that she had daydreamed about. He had been everything she had hoped for. He had a brilliant smile, soft voice, broad shoulders, and he was helpful and not overbearing.

Samson headed down the dirt road. Gabrielle looked back to see if Charles was watching. Indeed, he was standing by a split rail fence; he smiled and waved as she headed off into the road's horizon. She returned the wave and almost lost control of her stance in the saddle. This saddle didn't allow for a lot of body movement.

Looking slightly to the left, she noticed that a new family had moved into the Rue St. Lazar mansion. It had been vacant for almost six months. She was perplexed because she didn't see any occupied slave cabins or colored help maintaining the property. To her shock, the new occupants were outside doing it themselves.

In the distant, open field, she could see a young man riding a horse with an old saddle. Turning to the left to see better, she lost her balance and tumbled out of the saddle and onto the dirt road. The rider witnessed the event and quickly galloped to her location, by the side of the road. She was on her feet by then. Although she was not hurt, she looked quite the sight, all covered with dust and dirt.

"Were you hurt?" he asked, "That was a bad fall."

Trying to wipe the dust out of her eyes, she appeared confused and slightly dazed. He reached into his shirt pocket and offered her a handkerchief for her dusty face.

"Thank you very much. I'm fine," she responded almost breathlessly, "I don't know what happened."

Gabrielle was grateful for the handkerchief to clear her face and eyes of the dust from the road. Being a well-brought-up young lady, she felt compelled to introduce herself, as well. She wasn't far from home and this young man had been helpful in a time of need.

"Gabrielle Fontenot is my name," she responded.

"Well, I'm just glad you are fine. That all happened faster than I could blink. One minute, you were on that saddle and the next you were on the road!" he observed.

"I don't know how it happened," she sighed as she continued to wipe dust away from her face.

"Did you say Fontenot?" Ben asked, as he gave Samson a looking over.

"Gabrielle Fontenot," she repeated.

"I have seen that horse before," Ben mentioned, "He's in a painting in a restaurant in New Orleans. I know I have seen him before."

"Are you new?" Gabrielle asked, hoping to learn more about him.

"Yes, we recently moved here from Atlanta. My father is the new deputy railroad commissioner," he replied.

When Gabrielle had completely cleaned her face, she noticed that he looked similar, but not the same as, Charles. He had broad shoulders, and his hair was parted in the middle and flowed to his shoulders. He was more muscular, and he had a pleasant voice and beautiful eyes.

"From Atlanta," she murmured, "That's a long way away."

"Do you race that horse?" Ben asked.

"Oh… Samson? No, he's just for jumping and riding, but my father does own several racehorses," she replied.

"Well, I was wondering about horseracing here," Ben admitted out loud for the first time, "My horse, Bunches here, won several races back in Atlanta. I was thinking about running him in any races that might be coming up. Do you know of any?"

"Do you have a jockey?" she asked.

"No," he replied, "It's just him and I."

Gabrielle didn't want to hurt his feelings, but he was a little out of touch with the races in the area. They all featured uniformed jockeys, professionals. An owner would never ride his or her horse. That was simply unheard of.

"I'll ask around," she said, not wanting to disappoint him, "My father would know more, I think. But I would like to talk about horses with you more."

"Well, my name is Ben Chesser… and you know where I live."

Ben had actually committed a breach of social etiquette. It would not be proper for a lady to call on a man. Societal expectations were that it was always to be the other way around.

"You might have a chance one day to race that horse of yours. I have to admit that he is fast. You came to my aid quickly," Gabrielle said.

"Well, I have been riding horses since I was very small, and I am sixteen now, so that was awhile ago," Ben stated humbly.

"Well, Bunches is very pretty," Gabrielle said.

"Thank you. So is your horse. What his name?" Ben asked.

"This is Samson. I have just started hurdle jumping lessons with him. My daddy and grandmother seem to think I am very good and could do it in competitions," Gabrielle said with a small smirk.

"But you don't really want to, do you?" Ben asked.

"Not really, no. I mean, I guess I would just because I need to respect my father's wishes, but...I just like doing it. I don't do it for any other reason but the enjoyment of it. I am sorry if they are disappointed, but that's why I do it."

"There's nothing wrong with that, either," Ben replied, and Gabrielle smiled, and then asked, "Why don't you have coloreds working your place?"

Ben could tell that she was not asking to be malicious. Maybe she had never known anyone that did not own slaves. She simply seemed curious. Obviously, her family owned slaves. Ben looked down briefly, hoping she would not be upset when she learned the reason.

"My dad says slavery is wrong. We don't own slaves, and that might seem strange to you...I hope you aren't upset," Ben said slowly, choosing his words with care.

"We have slaves, but to me, it's fine that you don't. That is a different way to live and think, I must admit, but that's fine. Maybe slavery is wrong. I guess it is all that I have ever known...I mean, having coloreds around, but times change. You think slaves will always be slaves?" Gabrielle asked.

"Gee, I guess I don't know. There have been slaves in this country for a long time, and that would be so different to not have slaves, even though I have no slaves. It seems like everyone has at least a few. What I mean is, I think that that's what we expect in general. There are very few free coloreds. The colored people are the slaves, and the whites are the free folks that rule them," Ben replied.

"Papa treats our slaves well," Gabrielle replied, and blushed slightly as she added, "This morning, my colored servant, Miss Prissy, helped me with my hair. It was all matted, so she brushed it out and cut it. I think I am a too old to have a colored brushing my hair—but…"

"If I had such long hair, I would need help, too!" Ben chimed in. Gabrielle giggled softly.

"Well," she replied, "I should get going. Samson needs his workout. I live about three- quarters of a mile down the road. Should you want to talk about horse jumping, you'll now know where I live, as well."

"Ok, that sounds fine. Perhaps some day I will see you. Are you sure that you are doing alright? You won't fall off again, will you?" Ben asked with gentle concern.

"Oh, no, I will be fine," Gabrielle responded confidently. Remembering what Charles had told her, she put her left foot in the stirrup first and swung her weight up and around.

"Nice meeting you, Gabrielle," Ben said with a wide smile.

"Nice meeting you as well, Ben," she replied.

With that, she turned Samson about. She elected not to ride on the road anymore, but decided to return to the plantation to ride on the open grounds. At the cobblestone drive, she nudged the reins and Samson turned to the left. Quickly gazing over toward the stable area, she realized that Charles was no longer standing where she had last seen him.

Riding onward, she passed the stables and headed to the open areas. She eased Samson into a slow, graceful trot, nothing fast. Sitting tall in the saddle, she was able to see the ancient pond ahead. She had known of it, but not stopped or been there since she was a little girl. It was overgrown with weeds and brush. She hardly remembered it. Several ducks scampered away as Samson trotted slowly by the edge.

Turning him about, she headed back to the stables. The pond would have to wait for another time. Charles wasn't there. An older, grizzled stableman took Samson after she dismounted and led him away. He said nothing, but she knew that if thoughts could speak, he would likely say that she was just a spoiled little rich girl who had everything at her beckon call.

"Oh my lands! Gabrielle!" Miss Prissy exclaimed as she entered the house, "What happened to you?"

"Oh, I just wasn't use to the new saddle and took a spill, but you won't tell father of any of it, will you? He would never let me ride in that saddle again, and I really like how it feels."

"Oh, I reckon not. I won't say a thing. You are old enough now that your father doesn't have to know everything. If he sees you like that, though, he will figure it out. He is no fool. Let's get you a bath drawn. Look at all of that dust in your ears and nose. It looks like you been a rolling in the dirt."

Miss Prissy drew a bath for Gabrielle, laid out her clothes and waited behind the folding blind while Gabrielle took a bath.

"Miss Prissy," Gabrielle asked, "What do you know of the new people in the La Rue St. Lazar mansion?"

"I didn't even know that there were new folks living in there," she responded, "I heard that the old widow that lived there couldn't keep up with it anymore. The place was sold to the railroad, from what I heard."

"That makes sense," Gabrielle said under her breath.

"Why do you ask?" Miss Prissy inquired. Gabrielle had to think quickly. She didn't want to let on that she had actually met Ben. She only wanted Miss Prissy to know that she knew someone now lived there.

"Oh, I just saw a carriage in the drive, and people working outside," she replied.

"Well, its news to me," Miss Prissy added, "I know nothing about any new folks living there. It must have just happened recently."

"If I can ask, Miss Prissy," Gabrielle inquired, "What's all this talk about a place called Fort Sumter?"

"Oh, Gabrielle, it's just men folk talk, that's all. There ain't nothing that's going come of it. Don't worry your pretty little head."

Her answer satisfied Gabrielle. Based on what she had half listened to at the dinner table, it seemed like more than just men folks' talk and politics, but Miss Prissy's answer reassured Gabrielle.

"May I have my towels please?" Gabrielle requested.

Chapter 17
Threat of Succession

Amanda quickly closed the sitting room shutters as a violent, unexpected downpour fell from the night's sky. Elizabeth ran upstairs to do the same. She remembered that she left her shutters open in her bedroom. John and Ben had been sitting out on the front porch discussing horseracing. An abrupt shift in the wind caused the torrential downpour to cascade towards them.

"Let's get on in the house before we get soaked," John said.

"That sounds like a fine idea. Just feel that wind. I may be young, but I am no fool," Ben stated, "We're going to drown out here!"

Amanda finished setting the table. Supper was later than usual that night because she and Elizabeth had been to the city and were delayed getting back. Elizabeth could see that she could use some help. She lit more candles and joined her mother. The family usually dined during the daylight hours, but they had gotten back late and the storm's dark clouds had hidden any sun light that was left in the day. Only a dim hue of light from the outside filtered into the room as they both worked quickly and efficiently to provide a hot meal of corn on the cob, baked chicken, beans, and rice.

"Calling all hungry folks! Dinner is served! Come and get it unless you wanna eat in the dark, and I sure don't!" Amanda shouted.

John and Ben entered the dark dining room quicker than usual. They, as well, wanted to take advantage of the day's last light. John gave thanks for the food, and as the usual, the platters and bowls hardly saw a dull moment as they were passed around the table. There was no talking while the food was being passed. They were all too hungry at the moment, and there would always be time for talking, if even in the darkness. It was easier to talk under the cover of darkness than it was to eat.

They all sat in relative darkness. The dining room was lit by only several narrow candles and the stream of light that seemed to be growing dimmer by the second. The storm had come unexpectedly, so they were not prepared with an arsenal of candles. The food disappeared just as quickly, if not as easily. The darkness had little effect on hungry stomachs.

Ben explained that earlier in the day he had met a girl named Gabrielle, the daughter of a man whose painting he had seen in the restaurant in New Orleans. Posing with the man in the painting was a majestic, white horse that Ben now knew was called Samson. When John asked Ben how he and the girl had met, Ben said that he had come to her aid when she had a spill near the front of the house. John smiled and nodded with approval. His son had handled the situation just as any young man should have, and John praised his actions. Ben accepted his father's remarks with a smile, and added that she was skillful in hurdle jumping.

"Was she hurt when she fell?" Amanda asked.

"No," Ben replied, "She just got all dirty. Thank heaven for that! I would have hated to have to explain that accident to her family. I think she must have had a guardian angel."

"Well, everyone has guardian angels that come to their aid sometimes, I think. God works in mysterious ways. Maybe you and Gabrielle...is that what you said her name was? Maybe you were supposed to meet. You want to race here. Maybe she can help make that happen," John said hopefully.

"Oh, now, papa, don't put the cart before the horse! We have just met!" Ben exclaimed.

"Well, I would bet that you two talked horses and racing," Elizabeth chimed in.

"Well, sure we did. Horses are something we have in common. But just because we talked about that doesn't mean she will help me get started in racing here," Ben replied.

"You said her name was Gabrielle?" John asked again.

"Yeah, father, she said her name was Gabrielle Fontenot," Ben replied.

"What'd you think of her? Was she a spoiled little rich girl?" Elizabeth asked.

"Now, Elizabeth, judge not lest you also be judged, don't assume that she is spoiled just because she has money. Job had money, and he was a man of God, not a man of the world or with a worldly mindset," Amanda said.

"Not all rich people are snobs, or spoiled or selfish. She seemed very quiet and confident," Ben told Elizabeth.

"I remember that painting, Ben," John recounted, "Uh, Pierre Fontenot, isn't it?"

"I believe so. She's his daughter," Ben replied.

"She was riding that big white horse?" Elizabeth asked.

"Sure was," Ben responded, "She said that they live just up the road about three- quarters of a mile."

"We have all seen the place," Amanda mentioned, "Never knew who lived there though."

"Oh father, before I forget, there's something I should tell you. Before we went to the city, a preacher man from the Church of Christ named Robert come calling and wanted to speak to the head of the household," Elizabeth mentioned.

"A preacher man from a Church of Christ wanted to speak with me?" John inquired.

"We told him you were at work, and to come back some other time," Amanda added.

"Did you find what you wanted in the city?" John asked.

"Well, John, we did and we didn't. We did find that there is a cartage company that will take anything you buy and bring it home for you," Amanda answered.

John chuckled out loud, "So all you need to do then is spend the money and someone else brings anything heavy home for you?"

"You know what else, daddy?" Elizabeth added. "The horses are former racehorses that have been put out to pasture, because they're too old to race anymore."

"Is that right?" Ben asked.

"Sure enough," Elizabeth recounted, "The man told me himself."

"Well, Ben, when Bunches is too old to race, there is always something else for him to do," Amanda added.

"Never thought about that," Ben replied.

The rain continued to pour; several lightning strikes lit the night sky in the horizon.

"Did you see that one?" Elizabeth asked. But Ben did not hear the question. He was off in his own thoughts.

Ben didn't want to let on that he was very impressed by Gabrielle. She seemed very intelligent and well rounded. She was beautiful, with her long, flowing hair, beautiful smile and pleasant demeanor. She seemingly was quite the catch. Her presence just next door, really, had not left his mind since she left on the towering, beautiful white horse called Samson.

He would have to see her again. He would have to get to know her. She was different. Unlike other girls he had known back home, she seemed very mature. There was something about her that made him feel at ease, and he thought that perhaps it was the common interest they shared in horses. Perhaps it was that she inquired about his family's presence in the La Rue St. Lazar mansion. His mind wandered off on an imaginative tangent. He barely heard his father ask him if he had closed the shutters in the barn.

"Ben?" John asked again, "Did you close the shutters?"

"Uh, yes, I did," Ben replied, snapping back to reality, "Sorry, I had to think twice on that one. I couldn't remember if I did or not."

Ben had covered himself nicely, he believed, for letting his mind wander. If only for a few seconds of not responding to his father's question when he had asked it the first time, it was well worth it. Gabrielle was worth every bit of the split second delay that he had to cover his thoughts of her.

"Well," John said, "We got an interesting telegraph at the office today. Most of the time, the telegraphs inform us of schedule or freight changes… but this one said that Fort Sumter in South Carolina was destroyed, in kind, for northern aggression over states' rights in dealing with slave issues."

"Slaves, a state's right?" Amanda asked.

"That's what they're saying. The telegram went on to say that South Carolina is threatening to pull out of the Union."

"Is that right?" Amanda responded.

"That's what it said, but I am not so sure that I believe it," her husband responded, "You don't know what to believe anymore," John added, "The newspapers, even back in Atlanta, always wrote of state's right this and state's rights that. I wish the politicians would agree to something, like what's a state's right and what isn't."

"Maybe it'll be just like the storm and blow over," Amanda said.

"I pray that you are right, but I doubt it," John said, as he glanced at his children. To his relief, they did not seem to be listening attentively. They could care less what state had what rights, or what was right for each state.

Later that night, Ben had trouble sleeping. His mind raced back over the events of the day. What if he had not been riding Bunches that day? He had almost waited until later in the day. What if he had not been at the location where he could see Gabrielle fall off her horse and unto the dusty, hot road?

Ben did not allow those thoughts to come for too long before dismissing them. Things had not transpired like that, anyway. Fortunately, he had been there when she needed him. He felt lucky to have met her, and wanted to see her again. He knew that she would never knock on the front door. He would have to go to her. He would need a good reason to visit, other than just a cordial gentlemen's call. It couldn't be obvious that his real motive was because he wanted to court her, or was considering it. He would have to devise a plan to meet her again. She seemed very interested in horses and knowledgeable about them, as well. Maybe, he thought, he could use that somehow, but how? How could he not be obvious and incorporate her love of horses into his plan?

Perhaps he could watch the estate and wait for her to go outside, and then hurry to meet her on a yet-to-be-determined in his mind pretext. Perhaps it could happen that way, perhaps not. It was just too much to think on right then. Something would have to be devised. She wasn't spoken for, that was for sure. She had no suitor, or they would be riding together.

Tossing and turning in his bed, he thought of various ways that a so-called 'chance encounter' could happen, premeditating on what he would say to make it look like it wasn't planned, how he would act, and what questions he would ask of her. She knew that he was new to the area; perhaps an innocent question, asking directions to somewhere, could lead to further discussion.

The rain continued to pour down in torrential sheets. Looking out of his window, he could see only darkness and hear the tree branches as they were being tossed by the wind. Normally, he enjoyed allowing his mind to get engrossed in watching storms, but this night he simply didn't care. Gabrielle was unlike any girl he had seen before. He was a spell-bound regular home spun boy. What else could he envision himself?

Well, he just happened to be in the right place at the right time for the right circumstance to happen. Perhaps she was sleepless with infatuation and gazing out her window, too. Perhaps she wanted to know more about him, as well. There was no way to tell right then and there, but he could dream, couldn't he?

The only thing that he knew for sure was that the torrential rain was pouring three- quarters of a mile up the road, as well. The beautiful painting in the restaurant came back to him. The huge, powerful horse called Samson with his proud owner, Pierre Fontenot, wasn't all there was to the story. The painting had not depicted Gabrielle at all, and to him, she was far more stunning than the horse or her father, so the painting had omitted the best part of Samson's world. How could he be so lucky? Who was he that he would have the privilege of accidentally meeting the beautiful daughter of a wealthy Frenchman? Best of all, she was a daughter that was friendly and a horseracing enthusiast, as well.

Exhausted, Ben rolled over and shut his eyes. He could think more about her in the morning. He was very tired, and his mind was being clouded over because of his fatigue.

Chapter 18
A Union Militia Activates

One day later in the week, Pierre found himself with Marcel in the stables once again. Marcel had come by with an old work mare that needed to be fitted with new shoes. Her hooves were split and would soon be infected if she wasn't fitted with new shoes for her work in the fields.

"Ah, Pierre, have you thought more about making that racing saddle more available to the jockeys?" Marcel asked.

"Well, it seems to have gone over quite well, I would say. I am in the process of making it available on a more wide-spread scale as we speak," Pierre responded.

"That is very good news, and I am sure I am not the only one that will think so," Marcel replied.

Both Pierre and Marcel watched as the stableman tapped the last nail into place. The mare completely cooperated, which was unusual; most didn't.

"There! As good as new!" the stableman proudly proclaimed. Marcel himself lifted the mare's foot to closely inspect the work. He found that it was flawless.

"Ah, perfect," he replied, "What do I owe you Pierre?"

In the back of his mind, Marcel knew that Pierre wouldn't take any money. It was just a polite thing to ask among friends. Besides, Marcel didn't want to appear to just take for granted that it was free, even though he knew that he would mostly likely not be asked to pay.

"Nothing, Marcel. You are good to Gabrielle, and I appreciate it. As good as you are at teaching her how to handle those hurdles, I wouldn't dream of charging you anything," he replied.

"I appreciate that," Marcel responded in French.

The skilled stableman didn't speak French. Pierre realized that Marcel wanted to speak in French to avoid the stableman's understanding of the conversation. Again, this time in French, Marcel asked if there was further interest in the racing saddle. Following his cue to speak in French, Pierre explained that he hadn't thought much about it because the saddle maker was busy with work for the cavalry's men. The racing saddle would have to wait for now, Pierre said. His friend, the saddle maker, Jacque, was just too busy delivering seventeen saddles a week, and understandable so.

"Seventeen a week?" gasped Marcel. "That's unheard of!"

Marcel had breached his own logic because he had responded in English. Pierre paid no attention to it. He could see Marcel's surprise. He had just simply lost himself at the moment.

"That's a lot of saddles, an' I can see Jacque's need to fulfill such a request. He is a businessman, after all. He needs money. Unfortunately, one cannot live without it," Pierre continued in French, not missing a beat.

"His profit is greater with the army than with racing saddles," Marcel added, switching back to French.

"Well," Pierre stated, also in French, "I'll just bet that after this order they'll be another, then another, because that's how the military does business. Once they have someone doing what they want, they won't let them go. Besides, Jacque has made special saddles for them in the recent past."

"Ah, guaranteed repeat business," Marcel exclaimed. "Perhaps he needs to hire more help and increase his business!"

The stable hand wondered what in the world they were talking about. The one sentence he had understood only bewildered him. But he knew better than to ask any questions if he wanted to keep his job. Both Pierre and Marcel walked away from the stable building with Marcel holding the rein of his old mare.

"I think there's more to it than that," Pierre explained, "I have seen the military at the wharfs an' at the boardwalk. They camp there, out and away from anyone or anything, in the open fields, watching the activity of the incoming frigates. There's something going on that I can't quite put my finger on."

"It's all politics!" Marcel responded in disgust, "They just want to be seen, Pierre. No worries. They are just a bunch of men, barely not boys, that think they know how to use a cannon. I've got to get this old mare back to the field, but I do appreciate the help with her."

"Well, I owe to you whatever you might need," Pierre answered, "Gabrielle is coming along very well with the hurdle lessons. That's only because you are the skilled teacher that you are."

Marcel just smiled as he received the compliment. A man like Pierre Fontenot rarely recognized skill. Pierre watched as Marcel turned right at the end of the cobblestone drive, disappearing into the horizon of the clear afternoon.

Chapter 19
A Sudden Departure

Pierre turned about abruptly. A sudden, desperate, piercing scream could be heard from the Chateau Villa mansion. It took him only a second to figure out that it was Miss Prissy's devastated wail that he had heard. He hesitated for a moment, the blood seemingly frozen in his veins. Then, his numb legs were catapulting him towards the massive porch. Miss Prissy had a habit of using shrill vocal emphasis, but this was different. It almost made him heartsick just hearing her.

Opening the huge, mahogany double doors, he saw several of the colored matrons scurrying about, obviously upset. Without him even asking about the matter at hand, one of the matrons quickly told him, "Miss Prissy found Anna in her bedroom! She was just laying there on the floor, not a breathin', sir! Oh, Lord, no, this can't be!"

It took him a minute to process what he had just heard. He felt his eyes widen with shock and concern, and then he felt his mouth go dry. Words came to mind, but he could not put them together to form a thought into a sentence. He quickly bounded up the massive staircase. He never went into his mother's bedroom without permission. This time, though, was different. He ran directly toward it and froze in the doorway. He saw Miss Prissy kneeling down by his mother, who was indeed lying lifeless on the carpet.

"My Lord!" he exclaimed, "What happened?"

For a moment, Miss Prissy could not speak; she just stared at him. He looked at her with compassion, but also expected an answer. Miss Prissy tried to swallow her tears, with only a small degree of success. She'd settled down a bit, and her screaming had stopped, but she was now sobbing uncontrollably, tears ran down her cheeks.

"I—ah…come up here to see if Miss Anna wanted her tea," she gasped between stifled sobs, "Because she usually takes her tea this time in the afternoon, and when I opened the door, this is what I saw!"

Miss Prissy moved a short distance away to let Pierre view the grim scene before him. He fought back his own emotions. He just knew that she was dead, though he had to be sure. If she was, he couldn't show his feelings. He was a man, and men didn't cry in front of anyone. He would have to save his tears until later, when he could cry in private.

Pierre approached the body slowly. Anna lay huddled, her arms up to her chest. Her lips were blue, and there was no reaction when Pierre spoke to her or slightly shook her. His heart, it seemed, had been crushed.

Miss Prissy again stared at her, crying uncontrollably. Several of the other colored matrons appeared in the doorway. Somehow, Pierre's presence made them feel better about viewing the ghastly scene. They had never seen a dead body before. Pierre knew that his mother was gone. There was no mistake about it; a slightly blue pallor covered her cheeks.

"Miss Andrea and… and… and… Gabrielle is in New Orleans," a colored matron sobbed as she turned away.

The gravity of that aspect of the situation suddenly hit Pierre like another ton of bricks. How would he tell them—especially Gabrielle—that Anna was gone? How would Gabrielle, who had not yet experienced the death of anyone very close to her, take it? He knew he had to tell them. He suddenly wished that things could be different.

Pierre had recalled that they were out shopping. Earlier that morning, they had invited Anna to go along. She usually would go with them, but that morning she said she didn't feel well and wanted to rest. She had immediately added, after turning down the invite, that she would go the next time.

In a last ditch effort to deny to himself and others what he knew to be true, Pierre placed his ear against his mother's chest. He heard no heartbeat. There was no breath and no movement, and then he knew beyond a doubt that she was gone.

"She's gone," he whispered so quietly that they all had to struggle to read his lips.   Raising his voice to a level that was again easily heard he said, "Go on and leave now. There was nothing that anybody could do. It was just her time, I guess. We all have to die someday."

Miss Prissy and the others quietly obeyed, but continued the sobbing and crying as they disappeared down the stairs. Pierre kneeled down by his mother's lifeless body and quietly began to sob himself.

"You know, mom," he said quietly in her ear as if she could really hear him, "You were one brave woman. I know that you loved me, and I loved you. I know that you knew that. I just wish we could have both said it and heard it one more time. You know, when we came over on that ship from France and you lost papa, had I been in your place, I would have wanted to die too. I would have given up. But not you," he said with conviction as he sat back on his heels and held her hand.

His voice shaking, he continued, "You were a tough old bird. You knew that you had to on for those of us that loved you, and because of you, we made it here. Then, much to my displeasure I might add, you made me learn English. It got to a point where I spoke English as well as those that had been born in the 'New Country' as we called it. But you knew what you were talking about, mama," he said as he started to choke up badly, "And…I am glad…that you made…me… do…what you…made me do. You must have known best, even when I thought you were my worst enemy. I thank you for making me go to school and learn. I am where I am today because of you…and God. I love you, mama. Sleep well until you sing with the angels," Pierre said through wrenching sobs.

After about a half an hour of sitting by his mother's limp, cold body in a daze, Pierre heard the door open and close downstairs. Then he heard Gabrielle chatting gleefully. He felt a knot of dread in his stomach. He really didn't want to tell his wife and daughter right then, but he thought he had better. The sooner he got that over with, he decided, the better.

"Gabrielle, come upstairs, please," he called down to her. He tried to hide his emotion, but Andrea could tell right away that something was very wrong. So could Gabrielle. Obediently, she inched her way up the steps, dreading whatever her father had to say. Something told her it was very bad.

The door to her grandmother's bedroom was ajar, and Gabrielle headed towards it. She expected to see the doctor, perhaps. Instead, she gazed in horror at the sight of death. Her father was still kneeling on the floor. His mother's lifeless form lay crumpled on the floor, her skin glossy and blue.

"She's gone, Gabrielle. Jesus took your grandma home!" Pierre heard himself say, though he had expected to say some long and comforting remark.

"No, daddy! It can't be true! It can't! It just can't be!" Gabrielle shrieked in anguish. Pierre went to her and pulled her to him. He silently brushed away a tear from his own cheek as his baby girl, now a young woman, started crying on his shoulder.

"I…I…should have….had more tea with her….and…asked more about the past. I should have…gotten to know more about…her… and…spent more time with…her! She…was….my grandma. I could have treated her better!" Gabrielle sobbed regretfully into her papa's shoulder as he compassionately held her.

"You treated her fine. She knew that you loved her," Pierre whispered, trying to console her.

"I should have had more tea with her!" Gabrielle repeated.

"She did like her tea, yes, and she loved it when anyone would join her. Old age is lonely. She had lost so many of her friends and family members. She just loved any company at all. But she also knew and understood that you were young. She would want you to go on and be young. You are old young once," Pierre stated.

"I feel old! Oh, Lord, I feel so old! Daddy, one day that will be me lying on the floor! One day, someone will find me dead! And what have I done with my life? Will anybody care when I am gone? What do riches do? What have I done for anyone that will make them remember me?" Gabrielle asked, as she suddenly didn't feel so young. She was suddenly confronted with the fact that she, too, would die one day. It horrified her.

Chapter 20
Sins of Slavery

The cobblestone streets around the French Quarter bustled with carriage and buggy traffic. Along the boardwalk's curbs, other empty ones were parked while their owners were out on business or doing some shopping. The sidewalks were crowded with pedestrians of every kind, from finely dressed gentlemen and ladies to those wearing the more common attire of everyday working people.

Several boys could be seen trying to get a kite into the lofty breeze. They ran, coaxing it along against the wind. Bonneted young girls could be seen with their mothers, sitting on the shaded wood benches to get relief from the blazing sun. More hearty girls played with their dolls in the town square, while their mothers stood nearby in a small gossip circle.

It was a hot day, so many stopped to get a free drink of water in front of the sundry store. It proved to be clever advertising, as many of the same customers that would stop for a drink would see something in the window that caught their interest.

John and Ben had come to town to purchase a list of items
that they needed back at the house. On it was a box of nails, a new
Sunday necktie, flour, sugar and, lastly, darning needles for Amanda.
They had quite a list; at least to them, it was rather lengthy. Neither of
them liked to shop. But, they worked in focused haste, and now they
had only one thing to get.

"We better not forget mama's darning needles," Ben mentioned as
he wiped perspiration his forehead with a handkerchief, "She'll be fit
to be tied if we forget."

"Hell hath no fury like a woman without darning needles," his
father mused, though he meant it only in good nature. As the buggy
traveled along the cobblestone street, John spotted an opening and
pulled to the right. Stopping the buggy, he tied the reins to the
hitching post next to the sundry store.

Almost immediately a huge, prominently placed poster in the
window of the store caught Ben's attention. It advertised a horse race
the following Saturday night. Directions were given for a local farm,
where the race would be held. Local competitors were listed with their
horses and a history of their wins and losses. Ben looked longingly at
the poster.

"What are you thinking about? About horse racing again?" John
teased.

"Ain't no sin in it, is there?" Ben answered.

"No, I reckon not," he replied. "A horse like Bunches can't run in
that kind of race," John explained, rather matter-of-factly.

"Well," Ben responded defiantly, "I don't see why he couldn't. Just
because you don't believe that he can run doesn't mean God didn't
make him a runner!"

"Oh, come now, son..." John began, but Ben cut him off with the
declaration, "I don't care what you say! You believe what you want,
but I believe Bunches can run in any race that any other well trained

horse can. I have worked Bunches hard and long, and he deserves that chance! I am going to try my darnedest to see that he gets it!"

"That there is a race for mounted jockeys and thoroughbreds. It's a different race all together, Ben. You keep thinking that you are back in Atlanta, where bareback racing is common. This is not Atlanta, and the racing scene here is different. Those riders are highly paid jockeys."

"Really?" Ben asked doubtfully, as he studied the poster a bit longer.

He found that his father was indeed correct, and his spirit was crushed. He fought back an awful lump in his throat. How he yearned to be on the track again, and he wondered if he and Bunches would have that chance ever again.

"Take my word for it, son. You are not going to be able to run in this race. We can go if you want, but only as spectators. But, hey, I do indeed believe that you will run with Bunches again, and you have to start somewhere, so this would be a good start. How about it?" John replied.

"Aw, thanks pop!" Ben answered with elation.

They approached the little store, not much more than a booth, where a gentleman sold the darning needles. John handed the water ladle to Ben, who quickly swallowed the whole ladle and then another.

"Let's get on in and get your mother those darning needles," John reminded him as he scanned a wall, "I think that's the last of it then."

The proprietor smiled to himself, thinking that he had tempted another customer with the water. But smile as he will they would have bought the darning needles anyway. Amanda had bent her other ones, and she had been rather lost without them.

After they had all they needed, Ben and John started walking towards their carriage. John smiled and waved to several people who worked in various positions at the railroad yard. Another buggy occupant had seen them turn their buggy about and go. He wanted their hitching spot.

"We're always in a hurry," John mused to himself.

"Yeah, well, life isn't as simple as it used to be, you know," Ben replied.

"Oh, sweet Jesus, have mercy on us all! Isn't that the truth! Life gets more and more difficult with every year. It only seems to get faster and more stressful," John sighed.

As they moved forward along the cobblestone street, the traffic suddenly almost came to a halt. Ben leaned out of the carriage slightly, so that he could see around those in front of them. Four dilapidated, open wagons full of filthy black slaves were crossing the intersection; several young boys shouted insults and hurled fistfuls of dirt in their direction.

"That there is a sin! All men, no matter what their color, are created beautifully, fearfully and wonderfully created by God to serve Him and carry out His plans for them," John said under his breath.

"But not all folks are Christians, pa," Ben replied.

"I know that, son, and we need to respect those that are not Christians. Sometimes the best way to reach people with Jesus' love is to be Jesus to them. We can share Christ through the way we love. That is powerful to any person. God doesn't force Himself on anyone, and people will reject Him. But, God loves them even when they don't love Him in return. The truth is, Ben, that all people will hear the truth at some point in their lives. That truth is simple. It is that God is the I AM, who sent His Son in flesh, to live amongst us, to minister to the hurting and the sick, to heal them, and ultimately to die on a cross and rise again and ascend into heaven. He died so that all men could come to know the Father as He did, and what they do with that open invitation of peace and forgiveness by the blood of Jesus is their choice," John said.

"Throwing handfuls of dirt at them like that is a sin?" Ben asked.

"Yes, son. That is not love. That is pure hate and ignorance that makes them do that. God hates nobody. I can promise you that He takes no pleasure in what they are doing right now," John said.

"That's not the worst of it, is it?" Ben asked.

"No," John replied, "That wagon full of coloreds is on the way to the auction block. Families will be separated. It is sad, but in a few hours, they will all be sold and have new owners."

"Really?" Ben replied, rather surprised. John suddenly realized that this was the first time that Ben was seeing the slave trade in action this close. He had never really allowed Ben to see it, because it could sometimes be brutal. Ben watched, transfixed, his face filled with horror and sorrow. He squinted against the sunlight to read a poorly written, painted sign on the last wagon as it passed through. John noticed him doing it and gave him a slight hand motion in an attempt to get him to not to pay any attention to what he was seeing.

"That sign says 'Farm Niggers' Pa," Ben whispered.

"I know that," John responded with a heavy heart, "They will all soon be working so hard that they will ache to their bones. Must be rich future owners waiting to buy them. The slave wagons don't usually come this far up in the French Quarter. This shipment is mostly for people with powerful money, I'll bet. The owners are waiting for the wagons to arrive, I bet, and you better believe that they brought fistfuls of money, too," John explained.

"But people aren't pawns that can just be thrown around like garbage! God made them, Papa!" Ben objected. The zeal in his words turned a few heads in their direction. Neither Ben nor John noticed.

"I am glad that you can see that. It took me a lot longer to realize how wrong slavery really is. You have wisdom beyond your years," John said with hushed conviction, "It's too bad that so many people see the coloreds as property. That's what wealthy plantation owners think about them, and they are about ready to change hands."

"I don't remember ever seeing all of this back in Atlanta," Ben said.

"I tried to keep you children away from this sort of thing back in Atlanta. You were so young and I didn't need you exposed to this sort of thing, or so I thought. But you have to grow up sometime," John said.

"This isn't right at all. Selling people is a sin, an' they are people. They're not animals or farm niggers."

Ben's attention was diverted momentarily to the right when he heard the sound of a carriage clacking along and a horse that quietly neighed. The carriage was almost along side their buggy. Gazing further back, he thought he was seeing things in the glaring sun that nearly blinded him.

Gabrielle Fontenot sat with an older woman in the back of the carriage. Ben assumed that she was her mother. A much older, well-dressed man sat in front and had control of the reins. At first glace, the man looked a lot like the gentleman that Ben had seen in the fancy restaurant, but his head was turned to the right, so Ben could not see his face. When he turned to look Ben's way, almost instantly, Ben recognized him from the picture. Indeed, he was Pierre Fontenot.

But Pierre was not whom Ben was most interested in. He stared wonderingly at Gabrielle. He had almost forgotten how beautiful she was, and now she looked even more striking in a gorgeous, white sun dress. The handle of a sun parasol rested on her right shoulder, but Ben could clearly see that it was her.

He wanted to wave, smile, or greet her in some manner; unfortunately, this wasn't the time or place. She looked different, a far cry from the dusty-faced, embarrassed girl that had fallen off of her big, white horse.

Ben barely heard his father talking about a trip to the horse races the next Saturday night. John said that he knew exactly where the farm was, and would be more than willing to take him if he chose to go. Their buggy pulled ahead of Gabrielle's carriage, and he dared not look back. John chuckled silently to himself, suddenly aware that Ben had been gazing at an attractive young lady.

"Hey, you!" Ben heard a female voice chirp from above just seconds later, "The handsome one! Yeah, you there!"

Ben sensed somehow that she was shouting at him. He looked up at the building, his gaze moving higher and higher, until it reached the third story. Several women were leaning over the banister, gazing at the passers-by and street traffic.

"C'mon on up here and see me, honey! My name is Louisa Lovejoy!" she exclaimed, even louder this time. Ben noticed that the young lady's attire revealed more than half of her breasts. It absolutely shocked and disgusted him.

"Oh, what nice big shoulders you have. I'll bet you could go for a long time!" A different lady in the group said.

"Don't be shy," another said, with a big smile, "It won't cost ya much!"

Eventually, several ladies on the balcony joined Louisa as they smiled and blew kisses to Ben, who ignored then all the while. Ben turned flush red and looked straight ahead.

Certain that Ben was now ignoring them, the first lady said, "Aw, c'mon honey! I bet you can teach us a few things!"

"That's another sin," his father said as the buggy moved forward and away from the building. "I am glad that you think the way you do, son. I must have done some things right in bringing you up the way I did. You had enough sense to not give into them. Well done. Pay no attention to them. Those are the types of ladies that I had to run out of the rail yard in Atlanta on pay day. You know better than to pay attention to them, anyway."

Ben was perplexed. He sort of knew what they wanted because he wasn't stupid, but never had he been approached like that. Sure, he knew he wasn't a bad looking boy, but he didn't understand why they would tempt and taunt him like that, so openly in public.

Buggy and carriage traffic moved along at a faster pace now; they were getting away from the French Quarter. The humid, hot day was finally coming to a close. For Ben, it had been a very good day, on the whole. He discovered a local horse race and got to see Gabrielle again, if only for a moment.

The horizon started to turn colors, taking on orange and yellow hues as more familiar surroundings appeared. Eventually, the cobblestone street turned to a packed, dirt road, and traffic became scarce. A distance of approximately four miles remained until Ben and John would be home.

Minutes later, as the last traces of daylight faded, an eerie feeling blanketed the very air. Ben could feel it, as could John. Something wasn't right, but neither of them dared say anything.

Suddenly, as if out of nowhere, four heavy set men appeared out of the shadows. Neither Ben nor John could see their faces, and they were petrified. One man was armed with a sharp knife. Its blade glowed in the moonlight. He held the blade to Ben's throat and the second man tied his arms and legs with a thick rope so quickly that Ben did not realize what was happening. Then, a second man kicked him over onto the road.

Ben fell to his knees and winced in anguish as the rope cut off the circulation to his hands and feet. John leapt from the buggy and tried to defend them, but the two men quickly overpowered him. They bound and gagged him, then beat both John and Ben until their rib cages and muscles throbbed from the blows.

"We don't like you Georgia people coming down here and talking about the way we race our horses," one of the men hissed hatefully as he pointed at John.

"We don't take too kindly to strangers," the other responded, "We don't have a whole lot of compassion, maybe you boys ought to know that," the second said as he spit on the ground.

"In the future you won't be reading our posters and thinking about bringing competition in here, we control the race track and what we say goes," another said.

"Well, kick them in the head. They will be knocked out, wake up with pain and with a little luck, forget all of this," the third man suggested.

That is exactly what they did. Ignoring both Ben's and John's pure terror, each took a few turns with a foot blow to their left temples with his right foot.

The last thought John thought before he was knocked out was, "Lord, please help my son to live, and please protect Amanda and let me live so I can see my children get married and see my grandkids."

Ben's last glimpse of reality had been his father's saddened, angry, pained expression. Then, he thought, "Jesus, please keep my mom safe, and don't let them hurt us anymore. Please let us live."

The four burly thugs silently went through what little was in the wagon. In the end, all they got for their crime was seventy-seven cents and the bag of sugar. But, they had enjoyed the fear that he had caused Ben and John to feel. It was, to them, pure joy. The four men left John and Ben on the road, thinking that in the very least; they would wake up and now know that they were not to bring any horses to the race track.

Several hours passed. The buggy did not move, and not one soul passed by on the road where John and James lay, beaten to the point of unconsciousness.

Amanda sent Elizabeth to bed at ten that night. At midnight, unable to stay awake any longer, Amanda fell asleep. Around two, she awoke and found that John was not home yet. Panic began to rise up within her.

Amanda stayed awake the rest of the night. At dawn, she hastily put on her shoes, scribbled Elizabeth a note letting her know that she had gone and would hopefully return in a couple hours and left the house in a mad dash. Although it did not seem that she ran that far, Amanda ran the three miles or so to the buggy in just twenty minutes. The minutes seemed like hours.

"Oh, God, no!" Amanda shrieked when she saw them lying on the road.

She bolted towards, struggled for what seemed like forever to untie them, and put her ear to their chests, first to Ben's and then to John's. They both were breathing and had a pulse. She tried to calm down, telling herself that it could have been worse.

Ben groaned when Amanda put her head on his chest. Then he said, "Mama, is that you?"

Having heard him speak, she gave him a big smile. That was a relief. Whatever had happened, she could deal with it when they were both feeling stronger. At least they were alive.

"Baby, what happened? Look at you!" Amanda exclaimed, "Who did this?"

"Me? Where am I? Mama, what happened? Ouch, mama, my side hurts!" Ben wailed, "My side hurts! Mama, I don't know what happened. What happened?" Ben asked.

"Oh, Lord, now what?" Amanda asked frantically. She then asked, "Ben can you squeeze my hands?"

Ben took her hands in his and squeezed. She then slapped his leg gently and asked, "Did you feel that?"

"Yes, mama, I did. I am fine, I think. I feel like someone has beaten me and left me for dead. Where is papa?" Ben asked.

"He's right next to you. He is not awake yet. I think someone must have knocked you both out. Do you remember anything at all? Anything?" Amanda asked.

His head pounding like someone was hammering a nail into it, Ben tried to think. He just couldn't. All he could feel or think about was the pain. Amanda looked at him with concern, and then said, "Maybe in time you will remember. Right now we should get you home and get your father in somewhere safe with you."

Amanda tried to lift Ben, but couldn't. She tried three more times and still failed. Finally, she knelt down next to him and, sobbing, cried, "Lord Jesus, send a man to help us!"

Then, she had no choice but to sit and wait. Ben faded in and out of realty. She watched them both, praying for them and hoping that they would eventually remember what had happened. Whoever had done this needed to be punished?

A half hour passed. Then a carriage appeared. Amanda's eyes widened as he got closer. Could it be?

Seeing her peril, he sped up. Yes, she could now clearly see that she was not imagining anything. He was indeed a doctor. She praised God, realizing that in His wisdom, He had provided her with even more than what she had asked for.

"Thank you, Jesus," she whispered as the doctor approached. He parked the buggy at the side of the road, grabbed his medical bag and practically jumped from the carriage.

"I don't know what happened! I just found them like this. Oh, please, help!" Amanda gasped.

"Now, calm down, ma'am. It looks like they were assaulted, but you could be dealing with worse. I believe they were just knocked out. Just let me look them over. You are lucky that I happened by, and that I have my bag. I just had a call that I had finished."

Amanda didn't exactly know what to say. She didn't believe it had been luck. She finally said, "I believe you were an answer to prayer."

The doctor said nothing. After about ten minutes, he said, "Believe what you want, but whatever the reason, you are one fortunate lady. This must be your husband and son, I assume."

"Yes," Amanda responded quietly.

"Well, they both are lucky. Their pupils look good, and their reflexes are responsive. That should mean that as far as I can tell, they are alright. I mean, they both have concussions, and mighty bad ones, I think, but I believe they will be fine. They aren't paralyzed. You got lucky, all they need now is rest and warmth and food, and you will need to watch them carefully," the doctor said, "If anything new develops, let me know and I will come as soon as I can."

He handed Amanda his name and address on a small sheet of paper. Then, he helped her hoist Ben and John into the carriage. He waved farewell to them then, informing Amanda that John should awake soon. Still shaken, Amanda took the reins and slowly, carefully, drove home.

Elizabeth was up and about when they arrived. She gasped and immediately knew that something was very wrong when she saw her mother driving. She dashed outside to personally investigate the concern.

"Elizabeth, help me get your father and brother inside. Something terrible has happened. I am not sure what, but they were apparently beaten!" Amanda proclaimed in a hurry. Elizabeth rushed over to help. As quickly as they could, Elizabeth and Amanda moved first John, and then Ben, inside. John was the most difficult because he was not conscious at all. Ben groaned again as Amanda and Elizabeth carried him in.

"It's alright, Ben, you are home now. You will be all better soon," Elizabeth said, trying to sound more sure of that than she actually was. Ben just whispered, "Fine," in response.

Over the course of the next few days, both John and Ben fully recovered. Amanda had totally forgotten about the items that John and Ben had purchased in town. They just sat in the back of the buggy for several days while Amanda and Elizabeth took care of Ben and John.

Slowly, as the two of them regained their strength, the memories of that night came back. Thankfully, they seemed to have no life-changing, lasting effects from the incident. Amanda was grateful for that, but still insisted that they report what happened to the sheriff.

So, a little over a week after it had all happened, she and Ben and John all traveled to town to report what had occurred. They had no trouble at all finding the sheriff's office. It was clearly marked, a large, wooden building almost in the center of town. They parked their carriage, entered, and for the next hour, repeated the details of what had happened to the sheriff so many times that they thought he was testing them. They thought that he believed that they were lying.

When he said he had all that he needed, they got up to leave. He shook their hands and stated, "I will investigate this case the best I can, but with so little information about the suspects, there is not a really great chance I will ever find them."

"I just feel better now that we have reported it. I would have brought it to your attention sooner, but my husband and son were weak. I wanted them to get their strength back before we came," Amanda replied.

"I can understand that. I will do my best for you," the sheriff replied.

"Well, if you don't ever find him, God knows who he is. One way or another, he will be punished. He shouldn't be able to do this to anyone again," Ben said.

A month after their tragic encounter, Amanda announced excitedly, "I got a letter from Thomas today. He and Sarah Whitney got married. Can you believe that?"

"I am not really surprised," John stated, and then added. "I wonder why he waited until we left to make up his mind."

Amanda reached for the top shelf of the fireplace mantle, where she had placed the letter, and gave it to her husband. John read part of it silently, sometimes reading out loud.

"Jesse McCarthy was a witness. Now, that's different. I didn't think that either of them liked him much. Things must have changed," he muttered to himself.

"Isn't that something?" she replied.

"They have our old bedroom, as well," he continued.

"Other than that sounds like the old place hasn't changed any," she added. John finished reading the letter, refolded it, and put it back on the mantle.

"Well, well, we have a new daughter-in-law!" he said.

"I guess so. Well, she's a sweet girl, and I expect that they will be very happy," Amanda said with a smile.

"I expect so. Well, that's exciting news. Did anything else happen today that I should know of?" John asked.

"Well, there is something I forgot to mention that I just remembered today. The day that you had your incident on the road, the preacher's daughter came by while you were both gone and invited Elizabeth and I to a ladies social supper this Saturday night," Amanda explained, "Thought maybe we would go."

"Oh," John replied, "I almost forgot about that Church of Christ preacher man that sometimes comes around. So they are having a ladies social supper, hm? Well, that's thoughtful, anyway."

"I kind of thought we would go. They have two twin daughters Elizabeth's age, and she needs to find new friends. This seemed like a good way to do that," she replied.

Ben's presence in the rear door prompted John to think of the horse races on the same night.

"Well Ben, your mother and sister have a ladies church social circle to go to this Saturday night. Can you think of anything we could go to?"

Ben smiled and then replied, "The horse races!"

"Ben," his mother said, "You have a new sister-in-law. Thomas and Sarah got married."

"When?" he asked, appearing surprised, "When did this happen?"

"About two weeks ago," she replied, "Guess what else? Jesse McCarthy was a witness to it all."

"Jesse was?" Be replied, even more surprised.

"Well, I don't think I ever said so to any of you, but Jesse's father took over my old job at the railroad," John explained. "Maybe Jesse thinks he owes us something now."

"I didn't know he took your old job," Amanda replied with a surprised look on her face. "I guess I always knew that you and the folks at the railroad would take care of that, so I never even gave it a second thought as to who would."

"Well, in any event, you may go to that social with my full blessing, if that counts for anything," John replied.

"Well, thanks," Amanda replied, "What is this about horses racing?"

"When we were in New Orleans we saw a poster for a horserace not far from there. Well, since you both are going to a ladies church social that same night, I thought Ben and I would go to the races," John explained.

"Alright then, fair enough, but no betting!" Amanda replied.

"No betting, just watching," he assured her.

Amanda just smiled. Things were beginning to feel half-way normal again.

Ben stopped in at Bunches' stall and petted him on the nose, it was too bad that he couldn't run the race with the others, but his father was right. Bunches was just a dirt road racer. Sometimes bareback as well, he wasn't in the same league as highly paid jockeys and expensive racing saddles. It didn't stop Ben from imagining that he was a crowd pleasing winner, the standing ovation kind of crowd, with a wreath of roses around his neck. The crowds would stand and cheer whenever Bunches appeared on the track.

Chapter 21
A Tragic Accident

Several awaiting attendants motioned to each buggy and carriage, making certain that they knew to stop and hitch up at a certain location; they were forming a series of hitching lines. John pulled ahead, as directed, and then stopped the buggy.

"I'll take it from here, if you will," the attendant said as he re-adjusted his hat, "Just follow the crowd. You know that they're all goin` to the same place. There are lots of folks here today since it's free. They usually cost, you know."

John and Ben got out of the buggy; John gave the attendant several coins from his pocket as a tip.

"Aww, thank you sir!" he replied, "Just ask for James when you come back out here."

"Thanks, and maybe we'll see you later, then," Ben said. Turning to his father he said, "Let's hurry, look at all these people. I guess in a big city like this, I should have expected as such, but still. We had better get ourselves a couple of good seats before they all disappear," Ben stated, his voice almost musical with glee.

"Let's sit high, up there," John suggested, as he pointed to two vacant seats way up in the stands.

Ben had thought that the race would be attended by all men, but he quickly figured out that it was family night. He watched as people arrived as families. Fathers and mothers held hands with young children. Older sons and daughters, fat and thin, young and old, all dressed slightly different, but most were betting spectators.

The wagering windows were swamped with people willing to part with their money, or double it, or triple it. The few remaining seats were filling fast. The well-dressed horse owners conferred with their handlers and jockeys. Final instructions were critical, and all the participating jockeys believed that they had a winning horse.

The buzzing voices of the masses of people filled their ears. Ben sat mesmerized at all of it. He had never seen anything like this. This race was nothing like the ones he had seen back in Atlanta, where a race was called just by two riders getting up on their saddles.

"See what I mean, Ben?" John asked, "I wasn't trying to discourage you. You need to keep your dream of racing in your heart, but I just happen to be older than you, and I knew that you would react this way because I remember what it was like for me the first time I saw a huge gathering like this. It was a shock, to say the least. Bunches just wouldn't quite fit here. Besides, I wouldn't doubt if those four men are in the crowd."

"You know what, papa? You are right, and I am sorry I fought with you. But, God knows the desires of my heart, right? So, I can dream, can't I? I want to race in the big races," Ben said, "But that will take practice. Bunches wouldn't do well here yet. I was just thinking that. Look at those horses! Their coats shine like nothing I ever saw before, and look at those jockeys, all in uniforms!"

"Live and learn, Ben. I just knew it wasn't time for you to do this just yet. I definitely think you need to try to get here, though," his father replied.

"Live and learn, and I have much to learn," Ben answered.

"Wisdom will come with age, my boy, and if you allow God to help you," John said compassionately. Ben just smiled.

After a while, the betting windows were void of bettors and it was time to sit down and enjoy the race. John knew that a lot of money would be made and lost. A handsomely man appeared in the middle of the track and held his arms high. The crowd settled down.

"Ladies and gentlemen!" he shouted. "Welcome. Take your seats, if you will!"

Several small crowds of standing families quickly found seats. They weren't their choice of seats, but they had arrived late, and the wagering window was now closed. The well-dressed man walked up and down a straight line in the huge oval, exclaiming the same instructions as Ben had used back in Atlanta in the races as he went.

When the crowd was seated, a huge, horizontal double door opened. The crowd cheered and applauded as the first horse appeared with his owner. The jockey sat confidently in the saddle. Another horse followed right behind, then another. At a certain point in the track's oval, the horses did a fancy fox trot step to please the crowd, and received a very positive response. This was not yet the actually race. The jockeys and horses were simply being presented to the crowd.

Ben watched in fascination, and suddenly, a familiar owner's face was seen on the track. It was Pierre Fontenot, and he was leading the sixth horse from the front. If he was there, perhaps Gabrielle would be there, too. Ben scanned the crowd to see if he could see her, but there were so many people around him that it would take awhile.

Finally, on the extreme left on the opposite side of the oval track, he could see her sitting with the same lady he had seen in the carriage several days before He assumed that it was her mother. The last horse made its rounds, as usual, and the crowd applauded warmly.

While the parade of race horses was taking place, the starting gate was being prepared for the line up. The crowd fell into silence as the horses were being aligned. Last minute details were given to the jockeys. The starting judge, with his pistol in hand, stood on his podium and looked at the starting gate, then gazed at the crowd. Raising his arm high with pistol pointed upward, he looked one more time to be sure, and found that the starting gate was ready.

When he pulled the trigger, the gates quickly opened and the horses darted forward. All eight came charging out of the starting gate; almost immediately, two horses lurched forward and took the lead. Ben watched, transfixed, as the jockeys' stance and movements were unlike anything he had ever seen. They moved slowly and gracefully in the saddle. It was so different from what he had been accustomed to.

The crowd roared as they started down the straightway. The same two horses were still in the lead, but another was very close behind. Ben looked over at Gabrielle to see if she was watching as well, because her horse was in the lead. Both she and her mother were clapping and cheering for their family's racehorse to overtake the two leaders. Ben could tell that the third horse was the Fontenot horse because he had remembered the jockeys' shirt color.

As they progressed around the oval bend and toward the other side, the Fontenot's horse seemed to catch up to the leaders and was now a very close second. The crowd screamed and applauded as, from their angle, they could see the race better, and especially those that sat closer to the oval track.

Suddenly and without warning, a horse from the rear collided with the Fontenot's horse. Both horse and jockeys went tumbling end for end. They were left in a cloud of dust. Portions of the crowd screamed in horror as they watched the terrible accident unfold. Others gasped, and still others fell utterly silent.

The jockeys slowly got up and dusted themselves off. One jockey was stumbling about on one leg, but neither of them seemed to care too much about themselves. They tried to tend to their horses. One of the horses got up, looking very startled. The crowd seemed to breathe at least a partial sigh of relief, but their joy was short lived. After five minutes of repeated, valiant efforts, the Fontenot's horse couldn't get up.

Ben watched as Pierre Fontenot himself ran out onto the track. His jockey was the one that was stumbling about on one leg. The horse remained unable to stand, just lying on the track. Pierre approached him and tried to calm him by stroking him and quietly speaking to him. It was apparent that his leg was broken.

The crowd tried to go on with the race as if nothing had happened, and the jockeys, too, had to. Most of the viewers half-heartedly cheered for the winner that was about to finish. Others were subdued because of what they had seen and the realization that their horse wasn't going to win.

Other people appeared on the track now. The jockey put both of his arms around two attendants and hobbled away. Still, the horse could not get up. Pierre looked at one of his favorite racehorses and struggled not to start weeping like a little child. First, he had lost his mother, and now this. The horse's femur was broken, and the horse would have to be put down.

Ben looked over at Gabrielle and her mother. They were both standing and had sorrowful expressions on their faces. It was obvious to Ben, and obviously to them, too, that the horse would have to be put down. It would never race again.

"That horse has had it," John said. "I think that jockey has a broken leg, as well."

"Did you see what happened?" Ben asked.

"It looked to me like the horse in back leaped forward too far, but I am not sure. It all happened so fast," John replied, "That sure was a terrible accident to see, but things like this unfortunately do happen. You can never tell what may happen in racing. Well, you know that. You always have to be careful and look out for the horse behind."

"I have seen accidents before, but they have never been this bad. I wouldn't have expected something so tragic to happen on a track like this, where professionals race," Ben remarked.

"Well, sometimes even experienced riders have things happen to them or their horse," John replied.

The owner of the other horse, which seemed to be fine, appeared to take him away. The lead rope in hand, he went over to the jockey. The distraught jockey was still shaking, but he was overjoyed that his horse seemed alright.

"It was his fault," John muttered. "He probably gave the wrong signal to the horse."

"Well, at least the other horse seems alright. It is bad enough that one of the horses will have to be put down. That's Gabrielle's father's horse, papa. You remember that girl I was telling you about? Remember the girl that fell off her horse the other day that I helped?" Ben asked.

"Ah, yes. I do recall you mentioning that at the table a ways back," John replied, "So that horse belongs to the girl's family, you say?" John asked.

"Yes, papa, poor Gabrielle must be so worried. I am pretty sure that the poor horse will have to be put down, and that other horse won't finish the race. Do the people that bet on them get their money back?" Ben asked.

"No, Ben, they don't. It all goes back to the owner of the track," John responded.

Ben looked toward the other side to see if Gabrielle was still there; she wasn't, and neither was her mother. Looking down to the track, he could see that they had just arrived at the edge. From a distance, he could see that Gabrielle was hugging her father, who was obviously in terrible distress. Several men arrived on the track to take the fallen horse away.

"You want to stay for another race?" John asked soberly.

"Certainly," Ben answered. "We can't do anything for that poor horse, anyway, besides pray. It shouldn't be allowed to wreck our time together, as awful as it is. Hopefully this time all of the horses will finish."

Ben had an uneasy feeling in the pit of his stomach. He was fairly certain that the Fontenot's weren't going to run a horse in the next race. Perhaps that was for the best, since they were all so worried and heartbroken. More then likely, they'd only brought the one horse.

Once the fallen horse had been removed from the track, all of the men standing about, and their families, including Gabrielle and her mother, left. Someone else had taken their seats in the stands because they were done for the day, but perhaps there would be another time.

Unbeknownst to Ben or any of the other spectators, the fallen, injured racehorse was taken back to Chateau Villa. Gabrielle fought back both grief and anger as they all left. Pierre had a special stall made available, away from the other horses, where the once prized racer could be cared for, and hopefully recover, without unnecessary interference.

Once he was in the stall, Gabrielle kneeled down and petted him on the nose, stroked his neck and massaged his ears.

"Oh please don't put him away, father!" she pleaded, "He'll get better! I just know it. Let me take care of him. If nothing else, he can be just a farm horse."

Pierre rubbed his chin as he held a lit lantern high and pondered his daughter's plea. Others were gathered around. Everybody was in a subdued mood.

"There'll never be another Cajun King. He was one of my first horses, but we have to think of him now, and that leg looks bad. I wonder how bad his pain is," he said.

Marcel, who had been Cajun King's trainer, arrived after hearing of the unfortunate event from a messenger. He knew that the horse was one of Pierre's favorites, and because Pierre Fontenot was a prominent man and a close friend, he came quickly to the stables when he was told that his services were needed. He wouldn't have done this for anybody else.

Marcel joined the circle of bystanders at the stall without any greeting or conversation. This wasn't a time to be jovial. Pierre held the lantern low now so Marcel could assess the injuries. Marcel knelt down and took Gabrielle's place. Looking at the broken leg, Marcel mumbled something and then looked up at Pierre.

"Do you want to save him?" he asked in French.

"Oh please father, if there is any chance at all, save him!" Gabrielle pleaded.

"He might recover. It's a small chance, and there is risk of infection, but I can repair the leg, but his racing days are over," Marcel said. Pierre looked at Gabrielle, who was sobbing now, then looked back at Marcel.

"What would it take?" he asked in English.

"Bring me two boards and rope," Marcel asked, "I'll do a splint. I can't make any promises, and you'll have to watch him. You also need to know that this won't be cheap. When it's all said and done, it could cost you a small fortune in loss of future revenue. We are talking well into the triple digits, if not quadruple digits. He won't make you anymore money, and you need to know that, too. When this is all said and done, if it works, all he will be good for is slow pasture riding or plowing. It's up to you, Pierre."

"Oh please, father!" Gabrielle pleaded, "Let Mr. Marcel try and help him. I'll work with Cajun King, even though he won't race again. He'll get better."

Pierre was in a difficult situation. Prior to this night, he had put racehorses down because of old age, but never as a result of injury.

Pierre really did not want to put him down, but had to ask himself if Cajun King was suffering greatly, or if was worth putting him through the recovery. Cajun King had once been a winner and was easy to work with, so he was certainly worth trying to save. He wanted to please Gabrielle, as well; it would look bad if he refused to hear and grant the request of a sobbing daughter.

"Do it then! Do what you have to do to try and help him. I don't care about the cost," he commanded in French. Several of the nearby stablemen scurried about to find two boards and rope.

Gabrielle wiped her tears away and hugged her father, promising again, "I'll work with him, father."

Marcel accepted the two boards and rope that were handed to him, and immediately set to work. Cajun King jerked about, then settled down as Marcel set the broken femur and placed the straightened leg into a splint. Once that had been done, they all stared down at the horse, which was in pain, but seemed to be content.

"Pierre, this wouldn't have happened if he would have been wearing that new racing saddle," Marcel explained, in French.

"I know," Pierre replied.

"Was the jockey injured?" Marcel asked in English.

"He has a bruised leg, but he'll be fine," Pierre said, "For him, it was just a bad spill. Cajun King took the worst of it."

Gabrielle had never seen a bad spill before. She hoped that she never would have to. Now she had, and to have it happen to Cajun King, a one-time prized, Fontenot racehorse was emotionally devastating for her.

Once back inside of the mansion a few minutes later, Miss Prissy put her arm around Gabrielle and assured her that everything would work out.

"It was such a bad accident," Gabrielle sniffled, "I hope Cajun King will get better.

He has been with us since he was a colt."

"Things happen, Gabrielle," Miss Prissy said gently as she handed her a cup of tea in what had been her grandmother's favorite teacup and continued, "I don't know what to say. Maybe it would help you to get a bath. Let's do that. I will fill you a bath and you can sit and soak and think. You smell, anyway, and you'll feel better after that bath," she suggested.

"I bet I do smell like that old barn, don't I?" she chuckled, still wiping away her tears.

Andrea appeared and patted Gabrielle on the shoulder, "He'll be just fine, no need to worry about it. We all saw what happened. It all happened so fast."

Gabrielle finished her tea and took Miss Prissys' advice, deciding to take a long, hot bath. Andrea drank a half of cup of hot tea, then wondered into the sitting room. Pierre was looking out of the curtains, pondering the decision of saving Cajun King. If he had his way, the suffering horse would have been destroyed, but he didn't want to disappoint Gabrielle in front of the others.

While all the events unfolded back at the mansion, back at the track, to Ben, the next race wasn't as exciting, although the crowd cheered and applauded. He kept thinking of what had occurred, of the fallen horse and of Gabrielle. It just didn't seem the same. His heart wasn't in it. Still, when the second race had ended, both Ben and his father sat through yet another race, this one, a race between the horses that were losers in previous races.

It was obvious to Ben that the track was trying to set an elimination ledger. The best of the best, the second best and the third best horses would appear on the next week's roster. But Ben didn't know if he would return; the accident had happened, casting a dark cloud over the whole afternoon.

"Well, I've had enough if you have," John mentioned as he yawned.

"I suppose it's time to go home now," Ben sighed. "It'll get dark before we get back, that's for sure."

Crowds of people could be seen leaving through the old wooden gates. Ben and John just sat in the stands for awhile so the masses of people could pass and they would not get caught up in it all. Ben thought of the attack that had happened to them recently under the cover of darkness and felt chills go down his spine. He said a silent, brief prayer asking God to protect them, and then felt a deep peace wash over him.

"Let's go find our buggy now," John suggested.

It was apparent that most of the crowd had passed through the gates. Ben could not get his mind off of Gabrielle. He hadn't seen her leave, but rather quickly, she was gone. He daydreamed of his beauty, her soft voice and her shiny hair. He just had to see her again.

When they left, it was fairly dark. John then realized that he had forgotten to get lantern oil for the buggy's lanterns, but there was nothing he could do just then. He would just have to drive carefully. It never occurred to Ben that his father had forgotten to get lantern oil for the buggy. He did not notice it because his mind was somewhere else.

The porch lantern was still on when they pulled into the driveway. Amanda was still up and about, but Elizabeth had gone to bed. Amanda had waited for her husband and son to come home, not knowing exactly when they would be home. It was a quarter to ten when they pulled up. John unlatched the horse from the buggy and Ben took him into the barn and put him in his stall. Then, John and Ben entered the house together.

"Here," Amanda said when she saw them, "Both of you sit down and eat. You must be hungry. I made roast chicken with potatoes and greens."

When Amanda had served the hot food, Ben acknowledged his father's non-verbal cue and offered thanks for the food.

"How was it?" Amanda asked when he had finished praying, "Was it good?" She asked. "Did yea's have a good time?"

"Well Amanda," John answered, "We had as good of a time as you can under the circumstances."

"What's that mean, John? What happened?" Amanda inquired.

"We saw a bad accident on the track, and looks like one of the horses will need to be put down as a result of it."

"Oh my," she gasped. "Was it really that bad? Is there truly absolutely nothing anyone can do?"

"I am afraid not. I am sorry to say that, but it's the truth. The poor man that owns that horse seemed beside himself. I could see that even from a distance," John said, his eyes downcast. Ben dared not tell his mother just then that he knew that the owner of the doomed horse lived just up the road about three-quarters of a mile.

"How was your time at the ladies church social?" John asked.

"It was quite nice. We had tea and jambalaya," she replied. "They talked a lot about a quilting circle, jam and jelly making. I also got to learn more about this house, and the neighbors. We aren't the only ones that moved across the country, practically. Some of those ladies are railroad wives, so they are not from the area, either."

"Oh?" John asked, "What about the house? All I know is that the railroad bought it and that it is called La Rue St. Lazar."

"Well," she replied, "An older, wealthy French couple owned it. The old man passed away in the house and the widow couldn't keep it up anymore, so she sold it to the railroad for a lot of money."

"Somebody died here?" Ben asked, as she took a bite of chicken.

"Yes, in our bedroom, no less," she replied.

"They kept the old place up really well," John added. "It looks as though it was never lived in."

"Well," Amanda continued, "They did very little themselves. They had a small army of slaves. One lady told me that many of them are buried in the back garden. A sickness came around a long time ago, a killing fever."

"Is that what killed the old man, too?" John asked.

"It could have been. They said he had a really high fever first, and then he had this nasty cough, and I guess he started coughing up blood and then he died. What an awful way to die," Amanda said softly.

"What about the neighbors?" Ben asked, rather discreetly.

"Well," she explained. "I don't know much about them yet, but here's what I know. The way it was said to me, the county's richest rice plantation is just right up the road, about three-quarters of a mile. I can't quite recall all of what I was told, but their family name is the Fontenot's, I believe," she said, "They own that huge mansion, and they have a daughter Gabrielle, an only child."

Ben already knew all of what he had just heard, and his father knew that he knew. But neither of them said anything. It did cross John's mind that perhaps Ben was smitten with Gabrielle, but he quickly dismissed the notion. Ben barely knew Gabrielle, and besides, he wasn't interested in girls yet, was he?

I'll have to stop by sometime and introduce myself," John said, "It's nice to have rich neighbors."

"Oh, now John, you know that the Lord looks at our hearts. You can have all the money in the world on this side and still spend eternity in torment. That isn't God's will, of course, but there are people that seem to have it all together on the outside, and yet they are falling apart inside. I would rather be poor and know who Jesus is and what He can do in and through me," Amanda said with conviction. She then added, "Don't get too excited about having rich neighbors. He's the only one. The rest of them around here live in comfort and a few are rather wealthy, but not as rich as him."

"Where are the railroad families from?" John asked.

"All over," she replied matter-of-factly, "They come from Cincinnati, Ohio, New York City, Memphis, Tennessee, and even Minneapolis, in the Minnesota territory. Can you imagine coming into a state in the union from one of the territories? What a change even that would be. They all come from just a variety of places."

"Most of the men that I work with are from here," John explained.

"Well, anyway," she continued, "We had a good time at the ladies church social. Of course, the preacher stopped by and shook all of our hands and invited us to go to church. I told him that we use to go to the Church of Christ in Lawrenceville."

"Interesting facts about the house," John quipped, "The railroad leased out all of the surrounding land around the estate. Not our land, of course, but everything around it. Come spring, it'll all be tilled by the slaves, kind of like what we had in Atlanta, but closer to home. That bothers me some, but there's nothing I can do but pray."

"Papa, God alone can change a heart. I know you think slavery is wrong, and I agree, but all we can do is pray. That has power, pa, even more power than the president," Ben said. Amanda smiled as Ben turned to her and said, "That's mighty good chicken, mama," Ben said. "I hope when I get married that my wife bakes breaded chicken as good as you, or I'll be coming home to get some."

"Oh, thank you," she responded, "But your Grandma Chesser made the best chicken anybody could ever want."

John smiled a sad smile as he thought back on his mother's cooking. Even though she was gone now, she was indeed an excellent cook and baker.

Around the time that Ben and John were finishing dinner, Andrea approached Pierre. He was aware of her presence, but said nothing in that the moment. Andrea looked about to determine if they were alone. Gabrielle had already gone to bed, and none of the house matrons were in sight. Good, she thought, because she had something to say.

"Pierre," she said softly, "There is no question about it; I'm going to have a baby."

Pierre's jaw dropped as he heard what she said. He was dumbfounded. He looked at her and studied her face. He didn't know how to react. He hadn't even noticed anything different about her that would indicate that she was pregnant.

"Oh… my word!" he exclaimed, "Are you sure?"

"It's been three months," she answered looking down at her abdomen, "I'm getting bigger."

"Oh, my word!" Pierre gasped, still not knowing how to react.

"I figured it was time to say something to you," she said quietly, "I have not felt well lately," she added.

"Oh, I am so pleased!" he replied with a wide smile.

"You and me both, I suppose," She said timidly.

"You don't sound so sure. What's wrong?" Pierre asked.

"Nothing…just…oh, Lord, a baby at my age," she murmured.

"Oh, that's wonderful," Pierre responded as he hugged her, "Oh, I can't wait!"

"We will have to tell everyone soon," Andrea suggested, "I'm gonna start showing, and they will know. It's been sixteen years since we had Gabrielle. Maybe it'll be a boy this time?"

The thought of a boy hadn't occurred to Pierre. He loved his precious daughter dearly. Still, a male heir to the family estate would be wonderful. Besides, he had secretly always wanted a son, too.

"Oh Andrea!" he said in French, "I'm so pleased! Just think: we'll have a nursery made, you'll have the entire staff to help you, and it won't be like it was when you had Gabrielle, when you had to take care of her by yourself."

Andrea started to cry happy tears. She hadn't been sure how he would react. When he reacted so positively, she relaxed some and even felt more at ease with the situation herself. Pierre stood there in the dim darkness and held her for a long time.

Chapter 22
A Timely Meeting

Ben patted Bunches on the nose and rubbed his ears for a bit, as was his usual custom before a ride. Then, hurling the saddle quickly on his back, he quickly centered it to just the point where he wanted it, then secured it; after that came the canteen.

"Good boy!" Ben exclaimed, "Let's go riding, Bunches, and then you can have some nice hay when we get back."

Ben elected to take a different route than usual this time, because he was getting tired of riding on the property and a longer ride down the road would be good. Climbing up into the saddle, he envisioned himself as a winning jockey. Vividly, he imagined that Bunches had actually won that race at the track. He imagined that all money was on him, and the crowd roared with excitement.

"C'mon boy!" he exclaimed as he jiggled the reins. The horse obeyed, quickly strutting forward, out of the stable and unto the drive. Turning left out of the drive, he headed down the road. It was a hot day, and Ben adjusted his hat to cover the glare of the sun.

Bunches took off in a full gallop unexpectedly. Ben had all he could do to stay in the saddle, and the wind whipped his hair and shirt without mercy.

"Whoa now, boy!" Ben said as he pulled back on the reins, the horse slowed, then stopped as Ben had directed.

From a distance, to the left, Ben could see Gabrielle on a small track with a limping horse. She was walking next to it, coaxing it along. He watched in fascination as she worked the horse very slowly. He recognized it as the same horse that had fallen in the race awhile back.

Joy washed up within him at the sight of the horse. He was glad that it was still living. He thought it would have been put down, but was elated that it had not. It was an absolutely gorgeous horse.

Bunches wanted to run, but Ben had wanted to wait and watch. They did for a little bit, but finally, Ben said, "Oh, fine then! I suppose I didn't take ya out of the stable just to stand here in the hot sun!"

Whipping the reins, the horse took off like before. Again, it was all Ben could do to stay in the saddle. Bunches was fast, naturally, so he wanted to run fast. He ran past the Fontenot's estate and made a turn to the right. Adrenaline rushed through Ben's veins as it was a fast and furious ride.

Ben spotted a break in the road out of the corner of his eye and tugged the reins back to slow Bunches down. The horse obliged, then turned around, and once again, took off in a dust cloud of fury. Nearing the Fontenot's estate again, Ben pulled the reins to slow Bunches down again. He wanted to take a look at Gabrielle again.

She wasn't at the location where he had last seen her. She was further ahead on the road and slightly in the ditch, in the mud. Ben watched as she coaxed the horse without progress. This situation was different from any situation Ben had been in. The horse had stumbled off of the track and become stuck in the mud, which had accumulated in a low lying part of the ground as a result of a recent rainstorm. Gabrielle was trying to help him, as she pulled desperately on the reins.

Ben looked over to see if any stablemen had noticed this very awkward scene and found that they had not. She was all alone. Looking forward and backward, he saw no one that could help her. She was just a young and attractive female with her horse stuck in the mud.

Ben was a young, muscular man. He saw a prime opportunity to make use of himself. Seizing a chance to finally meet her again, he made a quick decision. He would have Bunches jump the low fence and he come to her aid.

"C'mon boy!" he said as he pulled the reins far to the left and said, "You better jump this little fence!"

Bunches followed Ben's lead and trotted way out into an empty field on the opposite side.

"Haw boy, haw!" Ben yelled as he lashed with the reins.

Bunches immediately obeyed and galloped at full speed toward the fence. Ben closed his eyes and held on tight as Bunches jumped the fence, then slowed to a trot. Riding over to Gabrielle, he stopped and tipped his hat. Gabrielle wiped the perspiration away from her face, and then took a second look at Ben.

"I can help you with that, if you would allow me, please?" he said, as he surveyed the muddy scene.

"Do I know you?" she asked.

"Yes," Ben replied, "You fell off of your white horse in front of my house awhile back. I'm Ben Chesser. I live in the La Rue St. Lazar place."

"Oh…oh I remember it all now!" she recalled, "I'm Gabrielle."

She wouldn't have needed to tell him who she was. He just smiled. He remembered her very well. He dismounted and removed his canteen from his saddle horn.

"You look like you could use a long drink of well water," he observed as he handed it to her.

"Oh my!" she exclaimed. "That's very nice of you, and yes, I'd love some!"

"Powerfully hot out here," Ben said as she drank from the canteen, "You look like you're a field hand out here the way you are sweating!"

Gabrielle ignored him as she took long swallows of the refreshing, cold well water.

"Oh thank you!" she replied with a big smile, "Cajun King here was injured in a race. I asked my father not to put him down, so I was out here walking him because I said I would help him while he recovers. The leg isn't healed totally yet, but he has to start using it and encouraging him to do what he can or he will never get better."

"I know that he was hurt pretty badly. I was almost sure that he would be put down," Ben replied, "My father and I were at the races and saw it all. It was a bad spill for both horses."

"You were!" she exclaimed, "So you like racing horses, too?"

"Sure do," he replied, "I ride every chance I get, and go to races, as well."

Gabrielle discreetly looked him over. He was handsome, had broad shoulders, strong arms and a gentle, compassionate demeanor about him. He seemed genuinely concerned, and it wasn't the first time that he had come to her rescue in a time of need.

The stable boy, Charles, was also handsome. She had admired him from afar, but he was evasive and quiet and didn't seem interested in doing anything more than what he had to do to please Pierre. She wanted a man that would go the extra mile for her when he needed to. Ben had certainly done that.

"I think you are sweet. You hardly know me, and you have now come to my aid twice. I really appreciate this," she said, "I should have known better than to come out here without anybody to help me, but the stablemen gave up on Cajun King."

"Forget what that stableman says. I'll help ya with him," he replied, "He ain`t done for just yet."

"Oh….. I really appreciate this!" she exclaimed again, this time with more emphasis.

"Here," Ben said, "Just tug on the rein a little. If you pull from the front, I'll push on his hind, and that way, he'll come out of the mud. It will take a little bit of work, though, but we can do it with God's help."

"I am mad at God right now. He took my grandma, and now he caused Cajun King to break his leg doing the only thing he is good at. As far as I am concerned, God can just go away," Gabrielle said bitterly.

"You don't really mean that. That is just your pain talking. Believe me; God knows how deeply you hurt. He will help us with this. You just watch, and I will bet you that we will get him out of this mess," Ben said with a gentle smile.

"How could a loving God allow so much suffering in this world if He supposedly has all the power to fix it?" Gabrielle asked.

"Well, honestly, I can't answer that, but I do know that Satan causes pain and God heals it. You shouldn't blame God for all that you are going through right now, but if you do, He still loves you. He has big shoulders that you can cry on when you are ready, but until then, go ahead and be angry. Anger is not the sin. It is what you do with that anger that can be a sin. You can even be angry at God if you really want to. He is a big God. He can take it," Ben said, speaking slowly and picking his words with great care.

Gabrielle pulled and tugged on the rein while Ben pushed on the horse's left, hind end. They had to be extra careful so they did not do any further damage to his leg. The whole time that they worked, Ben silently prayed that God would use this event to minister to

Gabrielle's hurt somehow. A little progress was made, slowly but surely. The horse seemed to sense what they were doing.

"A little more now," Ben suggested, "He's almost out."

Gabrielle pulled and tugged on the rein. From her angle, she couldn't see that Ben was making progress, so she stepped around the side to see more clearly. Ben pushed on the horse with all his might; the leg gave way and was now out of the mud. Ben lost his balance and pitched forward. The horse moved in an instant. Gabrielle was standing right there, and lost her balance as well.

The horse was finally free, but both Ben and Gabrielle slipped in the mud. Attempting not to fall, they both tried to save themselves by spreading their feet apart a little and using their arms, but instead, they fell forward onto each other and backwards onto the mud. Ben landed on top of Gabrielle. They were both covered with mud.

"Oh my!" Ben exclaimed, "I'm so sorry," he said as he lifted himself up, and then helped her up out of the mud.

"Were you hurt?" she asked.

"No," he replied, his face still covered in mud, "Were you?"

"It was my own fault. I should have just kept pulling on the reins and not let you come around," she said as she flung mud from her fingers.

"Oh, no, you didn't ask me to come to your aid. I came because I wanted to help you. It was my choice. Nobody is to blame. Things like this just happen sometimes. It's life," Ben replied.

They both looked at each other. A snicker turned into a smile, and a smile into a laugh. They laughed at the situation and at each other. They both looked as though they had been in a mud slinging contest.

"You can't go home looking like that!" she commented, as she attempted to wipe mud fragments from her face, "C'mon up to the house and get cleaned up."

Ben looked at her and looked away at the stately mansion. He thought of how ridiculous he looked, horrified by the thought of what Gabrielle's father might think if he saw Ben in such a state. Unfortunately, Ben also knew that Gabrielle was right. He simply could not go home covered in mud. Besides, now he would get to see the inside of her mansion.

"Sure it's alright?" he asked.

"Well, if it wasn't for me, you wouldn't be here, and certainly you wouldn't be covered in mud. One good turn deserves another, so c'mon. Nobody will say anything," she said.

Both horses just stood there, waiting to be led away. Pierre just happened to look across the way to the track and saw Gabrielle, caked with mud, walking along side a young man, who was also covered in mud. Both were leading their horses by the reins.

When they met, he just looked at her with amused eyes and a bewildered look. She described the situation, stating that she had managed to get Cajun King stuck in the mud and Ben, who happened to be riding on the road, came to her rescue. They had freed the horse, but they both fell into the mud. Pierre just smiled, then laughed and said something in French to her. She replied back in French, with a beaming, muddy smile.

"Pierre Fontenot," Pierre greeted as he extended a hand to Ben.

Ben wiped his hand on his trousers and replied, "Ben Chesser, sir!"

To Ben, it has like shaking the hand of a king. This chance made falling in the mud worth every second. Pierre looked shorter than what Ben had originally thought, but he seemed very kind. Gabrielle looked a lot like him.

"My thanks to you. You are quite the gentleman!" Pierre said with a French accent, "But you will have to forgive me, as I have a guest waiting on me. My staff will take care of your every need."

"My pleasure, sir!" Ben replied. Pierre glanced at Gabrielle, then tuned about to go receive his guest.

"What did your father say to you in French?" Ben asked, "If I can ask?"

Gabrielle looked to the villa, and then looked back at him, and said, "He said you are our dinner guest tomorrow night and that he is impressed with what you did."

"How did he know what I did?" Ben asked, "He wasn't out there with us."

Gabrielle handed the reins of her horse to Charles, who happened to be standing near the stable door. Then, turning back to Ben, she added, "No he wasn't, but he saw the whole thing. He saw you jumping the fence, talking to me, helping me, and he even saw the both of us falling in the mud. He didn't come to my aid because he wanted to see what you would do. He said only a gentleman would do something like that."

Ben hadn't known that they were being watched. To him, he wasn't doing anything any decent person wouldn't do. To Gabrielle, he had been a hero, a gentleman, and somebody there in a time of need. To her, it was just happenstance; he just happened to be riding down the road. To him, it was part of God's divine plan. One minute he saw Gabrielle, the next he didn't. When he did see her again, she needed assistance and there was no one else.

"Gabrielle, I appreciate your father's offer for the staff to help me, but home isn't very far away. I will just go home, but I will take him up on that dinner offer tomorrow night," Ben said.

Miss Prissy emerged from the huge, mahogany doors. She had been watching them approach from the stable's drive.

Gabrielle smiled, and then said, "Six o'clock then. Are you sure you don't want to get cleaned up?"

"I'm fine," he replied.

"Oh my lands!" Miss Prissy exclaimed, "Just look at you, Gabrielle!"

"I must go," she whispered.

Ben mounted his horse and then looked back. The mansion was beautiful, and it was unlike anything that he had ever seen. Pausing at the road, he looked back to see a heavyset, colored woman leading Gabrielle into the doors.

"C'mon boy," he said as he jiggled the reins, "You did good! You did real good!"

His presence hadn't gone unnoticed. Ben even dared to believe that perhaps God was opening a door or two for him. Maybe he would eventually get to race Bunches on the big track. Even better, perhaps he would marry Gabrielle.

Charles glared through a window in the stable building. Both he and Pierre had seen the whole thing. He was about to go out and help Gabrielle when a horse came bounding over the fence instead. He had waited too long. To make the disappointment in himself even worse, he wanted to get to know Gabrielle better and he got the feeling that Pierre wanted him to, as well.

He knew that a new family had moved into the La Rue St. Lazar place down the road. More than likely, that's where the rider was heading. Charles had not seen him before and assumed that he lived there. He was disgusted with himself; it could have been him falling into the mud with Gabrielle, instead of someone else that was a stranger to Chateau Villa. He would just have to redeem his personal credibility. He had been looking at Gabrielle and knew that she stole glances at him, but he was painfully shy and never found the right moment to pursue it further, until today when he was just too slow in responding.

Elizabeth laughed hysterically when she saw her brother coming up the drive; it looked as though he had been in a mud slinging contest.

"Did you fall off?" she mused, "Did you fall into tha mud?"

"I fell into the mud, but I didn't fall off," he replied.

With bewilderment all over her face, Elizabeth just stared at him. Amanda just happened to open the front door and saw him approach. For a moment, she had to blink back disbelief. Ben dismounted and, in an attempt to shake off some of the dirt, shook himself like a wet dog.

"My goodness," his mother finally said, "I haven't seen you that dirty since you were two years old a playin' in the dirt. What in tha world happened to you?"

"Well," he replied, "I helped that Fontenot girl get her horse out of the mud. You do remember that accident that we told you about after we came back from the races the other day, don't you? Well, the horse wasn't put down after all. Gabrielle begged her father to let her try to help him, so that's what she was doing. She was just walking him around to help him get stronger, and they got stuck in the mud. I then happened by, and being the gentleman that I am, I helped. The horse got out fine, but we both fell in the mud together."

Amanda laughed until tears fell down her cheeks, "You look quite tha sight!"

"It was worth it," he replied, "I met her father and got invited to dinner tomorrow night."

"You did?" Amanda replied in delight, "Well, good for you! I'll be…it must have been quite a sight if both of ye's fell in the mud."

"Yeah, it was, but so goes life. She's a sweet girl. I'm gonna put Bunches away now and get a bath," he replied.

"Good boy! See? Even mama is happy," he said as he removed the saddle, "I know ah said I'd give ye something, so let's go get it."

Ben rewarded his horse with a lot of hay and water and pats on the neck. He wanted to give him a carrot or two, but they didn't have any in the house. Oh, well, Bunches was content with the hay and fresh water. After giving him hay and water, Ben brushed out his coat and made it shine. As he brushed out Bunches, he wondered what

Gabrielle was doing. Although Ben didn't know it, Gabrielle was also thinking about him.

Not even a mile down the road, Gabrielle scrubbed herself with freshly made perfumed colored lye soap. It felt kind of rough on her skin. It also smelled very strong.

"Why'd you have to make this darn soap so strong this time?" Gabrielle whined.

"Well, you're just lucky that it was made last fall. Whether or not you have money, Miss Gabrielle, making soap is a time consuming chore. I don't like it, but it's one of those necessary things we all must do. I don't see that anybody but you will be using that soap once you get through with it, at least not if they can help it. But, we don't waste anything either. My word, you sure are filthy!" Miss Prissy exclaimed as she sat behind the folding blind, "I knew you'd be in here when I saw you out there with that horse, so I got the bath ready a long time ago."

"We have a dinner guest tomorrow night," Gabrielle said, "Father invited him."

"I was about to ask you: who was that boy that was with you? He looked mighty strong," Miss Prissy asked.

"Ben Chesser," she replied, "He lives in the La Rue St. Lazar mansion."

"Well, I'll be. I didn't know that anybody new was in there. It was awfully nice that he helped you like that. That really shows that he has character. Most boys wouldn't do a thing; they would just laugh at you."

Gabrielle paused and thought about that for a moment. Charles could have helped her. He saw her take Cajun King out, and he wasn't busy. It would have been perfectly fine with Pierre if he had stopped what he was doing and assisted her with a walk around the track.

"I think you are right. Most boys would not do a thing. Ben obviously has a heart," Gabrielle said.

"Well," Miss Prissy responded, "I'll make sure that we have a feast tomorrow night. You will want to impress him. What time did you tell him?"

"Six o'clock," Gabrielle replied, "An` seeing that he was so nice to me and father himself invited him… I'm gonna look like a queen!"

"Oh, now don't you go and over-do it now, Miss Gabrielle," Miss Prissy added, "You might scare him off!"

"Oh, I could wear that dress that I altered couldn't I?"

"No Miss Gabrielle, it wouldn't be fitting. You are a young woman raised up to be well-mannered and educated, a woman of class and honor. Everyone expects as much from you. You are no tramp for men," Miss Prissy explained.

"I think I will wear that dress anyway!" she teased.

"You sure think you can show your bosom, don't you? Well, nobody other than your husband and the woman that gave birth to you should ever see them and you are old enough now to know that only your husband, whomever he will be, should see you in any state such as that dress puts you in! " Miss Prissy responded sternly.

Chapter 23
Succession

Amanda could hear John come home from work; Ben heard, as well, and ran out to assist him with the horse.

"I had a trying day today, son, a trying day," he forlornly stated.

"What happened? Did you have to fire somebody?" Ben asked, half teasing.

"No," John replied, "It would take a lot for me to fire anybody. We heard some trying news, that's all."

"Oh, papa, I sure am sorry to hear that," Ben said, knowing that he could say nothing to really help the situation, but realizing, also, that his father could always use a reminder. "Mama's got supper almost ready," Ben said as he removed his father's horse's saddle.

"Your ma has always been a fine cook. Well then," John added, "Let's get on in the house and get to it then."

Ben was in an unusually good mood that night. Leaving the horse alone in the barn with plenty of hay and water, he shut the door, whistling. He had never been invited to dinner before, and to think Gabrielle was the most beautiful girl he had ever seen just made it that much better. To be asked by her father was the most perfect thing that he could think of. After all, if he wanted to eventually marry Gabrielle, he would have to ask her father. That was what was expected.

John looked like he had a lot on his mind as they sat down. To Amanda he didn't seem like his usual self; none-the-less, both she and Elizabeth served the hot food on the table. It was one of John's favorite suppers. Taking the cue from his father Ben offered thanks for the food.

As Ben prayed, John's heart did indeed fill with gratitude toward God. John knew that God understood that he had just had a rough day, and the fact that Amanda had prepared one of his favorite meals was at least a small blessing. John smiled to himself.

Still, Amanda knew that there was something on John's mind, but she wouldn't pry to get it out. He had a habit of telling her eventually if she waited for him to do so. This time John surprised her and told them all.

"We received a telegram today in the office," he explained, "This states' right issue has caused South Carolina to secede from the country. Word has it that other states will follow."

"They just up and divided from the country?" Amanda asked, "Can they do that?"

"Well," John continued, "They have whether it's right or not. I am not sure what will happen. What I do know is that having the other states doing the same thing will divide the railroad. Word has it that any seceding southern state will charge the railroad a high tariff for coming through their state."

"How can they do that?" Ben asked. "It's all railroad property."

"We all think that the railroad will divide into two and have a northern and southern half," John explained. "This secession thing will split the railroad…. because of the commerce. There is no law that says it won't happen."

"Oh Lord!" Amanda gasped, "What do you suppose will happen?"

"It's too early to tell right now. This could get serious. We should definitely pray about it. Most of the share holders do live in the north," He went on.

"What does secession mean?" Elizabeth asked.

"It means that South Carolina has decided to become their own nation," Amanda answered, "If others do the same, then… they will no longer be considered the United States. They will be whatever they elect to call themselves."

"Oh," she replied, "Like New South Carolina?"

"No, Lizzy," Ben explained, "All of the states that leave will have their own government and their own laws. I would guess that would mean that they would make laws that mean that they can keep their slaves."

"Oh," she thought out loud, "It's like there would be two countries, then."

"Elizabeth, yes, I suppose so. It's sad but true. The saddest part is that states' rights over slavery are really that it's all about," John recounted, "Hopefully, things can be worked out so that it won't be so hard on the railroad and the shareholders, not to mention the slaves."

"Well that's not good news at all," Amanda commented at the right moment, "People could lose their jobs and their homes over this."

"Well, we don't have much to worry about," John said, "It's the people who haven't been there awhile that might think about going back to farming. I know we have only been here a short time, but I worked my way up the ranks to get where I am now. I have worked with the railroad for nine years, and I plan to keep working for them."

"Ben got invited over to the Fontenot's house for supper tomorrow night!" Elizabeth blurted out.

"You did what?' John asked in surprise as he looked at Ben. Ben was a little uncomfortable that his younger sister had just blurted it all out, but she was like that. Hardly anything was kept a secret with her because she had a difficult time keeping things to herself.

"Well," Ben explained, rather sheepishly, "I helped their daughter get her horse out of the mud today and her father asked me to dinner."

Ben felt awkward. All eyes were on him, and everybody seemingly wanted a better explanation than just that. But there really wasn't one. He had told them all there was to tell.

"A stuck horse for a meal with Pierre Fontenot," John said as he laughed heartily, "That beats everything."

"They both fell in the mud together!" Elizabeth retorted again, "On top of each other, too!"

Once again John gave Ben an inquisitive look, one that silently demanded an explanation. Ben shot his sister a quick look of contempt, knowing that it sounded worse than what it was. She just looked back at him with pure innocence.

"Well," Ben quickly explained grouchily, "I was helping her when we both slipped in the mud and fell down. We didn't think anyone was watching, but as it turned out, her father saw everything."

What he had just heard from Elizabeth now made better sense to John. He just smiled as he once again reminded himself that Elizabeth had a way of just blurting out illogical bits of information that made no sense at first, because she only told partial stories. He was hoping that she would grow out of it soon, because it sometimes caused problems for her.

"Oh, that will be fun for Ben, Elizabeth, but let's not jump to any conclusions too fast. It's just a fathers way of showing appreciation," Amanda added, "It was nice of Ben to help her and nice of Mr. Fontenot to invite him, as well."

"They were both covered in mud!" Elizabeth blurted out again.

This time, Elizabeth over played it and she no longer had an audience. The shock value was gone now, and she knew it. She remained silent for the rest of the meal.

John's face was contorted with worry. Between Elizabeth's habitual loose tongue and what was going on at work, he could not stop his mind from racing. The fact that he did not know what would happen to the railroad made him especially anxious. Moving to New Orleans had nothing to do with it. After all, Atlanta was in the south, as well.

Splitting the railroad between the states would ruin the value of railroad stock; it would be a commerce disaster. The more John thought about it, the more he realized he could do little or nothing, and the more tense he became.

The conversation at the supper table needed a change of subject. Amanda provided just that as she told humorous things about the ladies that she had met at the church social. It was the first time that day that John started to relax and not be tense. It was nice just to sit back and smile or laugh over a funny situation.

The next afternoon, Ben made certain that every hair on his head appeared in place, that he didn't knick his face while shaving with the straight razor, and that his bow tie was straight. He then went and stood before his father, seeking approval, to be sure that no detail was left unaddressed. His mother had ironed his finest Sunday shirt and he had spent a great deal of time polishing his boots. Even his kid sister Elizabeth admitted that he looked like a new man, all dressed up and having somewhere important to go. His father had let him borrow the buggy for the day and it was cleaned out and washed down.

"It's about time that you get going Ben," Amanda noticed as she looked at the clock and realized it was twenty to six, "It's gonna take you a little bit to get over there."

"I know ma. Boy, am I nervous! I just want this to go well. Do I look like I'm good enough for a sweet and pretty girl?" he asked.

"You look just fine," she admired, "If it were the other way around, and I were her father, I'd be glad to have you sit down at my table!"

With one last look in the mirror, Ben turned about and wryly smiled at the both of them. They smiled back reassuringly. He then headed out the door and took his place in the driver's seat of the buggy.

"Our baby boy is off to see a girl," His mother said in wonder and disbelief.

"They grow up fast," his father responded.

"Elizabeth will be next, and then the house will be empty. What will we do then?" Amanda wailed forlornly.

"Hon, we will cross that bridge when we come to it. Don't you go crying just yet. We have to enjoy the time we have left with the children," John responded.

"And teach them what we can. God commands us as parents to 'raise up a child in the way he should go, so that when he is old, he will not turn from it.' John, do you think we did that?" Amanda asked.

"We did our best. That is all God expects, honey. We can't be perfect. Isn't that what is most important?" John asked.

"Yes, it is…but what if he is not comfortable? What if this ends up being a painful experience for him?" Amanda asked.

"Oh, honey, don't you worry. God will take care of him," John reassured her.

Less than fifteen minutes later, completely unaware of his mother's worry, Ben pulled into Gabrielle's drive. He brushed himself off, smiled to himself and then made his way to the door. Seconds after he had politely knocked, Gabrielle's father himself opened the door.

"Ben Chesser, so glad you could come. Please come in," Pierre said, and Ben entered.

"If you would like to have a seat at the table," Pierre stated cordially, "We are about to serve dinner. We have prepared ham, mashed potatoes with ham gravy, green beans, corn, and fresh bread, with cherry pie for afterwards, so save room. There's milk, water or red merlot wine to drink. What would you like?"

"Milk, please, sir," Ben replied politely as he sat down. Miss Prissy dashed off to get him a glass.

"Hello, Ben, thank you for coming," Gabrielle greeted with a broad grin as she glided down the stairs.

Ben's mouth dropped at her stunning appearance. She wore a beige satin gown that fell to her ankles. A string of pearls graced her neck.

"Well, don't you look lovely, Miss Gabrielle," Ben commented. She just blushed, grinned and joined him at the table.

As Gabrielle, her mother and father and Ben ate, they all exchanged small talk. Most of it was about racing or horses. Pierre also asked Ben many questions, and was surprised to learn that his father did not own slaves. That bothered him, but he tried to ignore that difference of opinion for the time they had together. Everyone was entitled to their opinions, after all.

As usual, Miss Prissy and the kitchen matrons stood along the wall and waited for a chance to serve the table. There had never been a young male dinner guest before.

"Father, maybe you should tell Ben about your new saddle," Gabrielle suggested as they were finishing the last of the main courses of their meal.

"Gabrielle, hush about that. I don't want anyone knowing about it just yet," Pierre said quietly. After a moment's thought, he turned to Ben and asked, "If I tell you about the saddle she is referring to, will you swear not to tell a soul just yet?"

"I swear, sir," Ben said.

"Well, then," Pierre said, as he lowered his voice and began to explain to Ben about the new saddle. He was speaking so softly and choosing his words with such care that Ben had to listen intently. He did not take his eyes off him until Pierre said, "Tomorrow, I am going into town to talk to a friend about the saddle."

Most of the time Pierre would have one of his stablemen drive him to New Orleans, but this time he drove himself. He arose quite early in the morning to prepare and was in the horse barn by seven, about an hour and a half later. Charles was on duty and loaded the saddle in the back of the buggy and then covered it with a stable blanket. Pierre didn't want to take a chance on any passer-by traffic noticing it. After three attempts to cover the saddle, it was obvious that Charles just wasn't getting it, so Pierre did it himself. Charles backed away and shuffled off to continue what he was doing. Pierre gave him a long stare down and wondered at that moment whether he had made the right decision hiring him. The saddle weighed heavily on his mind. He knew he had a promising product that could alter racing for the better. It was sure to bring top winnings, so perhaps Jacque could be somehow persuaded to start production.

Pierre's satisfaction with Charles was starting to wane, and Charles knew it. First, he had failed to come to Gabrielle's aid when he knew full and well that she needed assistance, he was too slow to react to Andréa's fall, and now there was his careless effort of covering the saddle when he also knew how important it was. When he hired

Charles, Pierre had thought that perhaps he would be a suitor. He was strong, handsome and came from a local horse family. His recent attitudes of being withdrawn and indifferent to detail, however, concerned Pierre. He had expected a longer-lasting continuation of what he had first observed when Charles had been hired on.

New Orleans was abuzz with talk of the secession of South Carolina from United States. The boardwalk crowds couldn't talk enough about the abolition movement and states' rights to maintain the practice of slavery. The majority of the public felt the northern states were wrong. To them, it seemed that there was no need to try to impose a nationwide policy banning slavery, and they were property, not citizens. Few felt that South Carolina was wrong for creating their own government; after all, they were a sovereign state, and each state had their own laws and had every right to defend them.

Jacque now knew that the huge order of saddles wasn't just coincidence. Pierre had been correct; they were planning something and knew something that the public didn't know. None-the-less, making saddles for the cavalrymen provided better financial security than making racing saddles. The government paid cash. Also, the demand for the production of racing saddles could easily fluctuate, based on the whims of the owners and the jockeys.

Still, Pierre was growing impatient. He had introduced the saddles at the racing ball and sparked much interest from deep-pocketed owners and experienced jockeys. His own jockey had test-ridden the saddle on several fast horses at different times and always had the same result. He stated that he was more easily able to control the horse, the saddle had better comfort and the horse ran faster.

But the testing was long completed now. Pierre's jockey had to give the prototype back; the saddle wasn't his and it was time to return it to Jacque. Pierre knew that it was time to have a discussion with Jacque to discuss manufacturing the saddle somehow.

He could see his friend's point of view, but this had to be done at some point. Pierre did understand that he ran a business and had to choose, daily, whether he wanted a stable income, which the military's contract with him provided or to risk investment in a saddle that could fail.

Nobody but Pierre and Jacque, and now Ben, knew about the saddle's alterations or how they could change the face of horseracing for the better. Pierre wanted to keep it that way a bit longer.

As Pierre rode along on the busy street he thought of the young man that had come to dinner who had a better attitude and was more congenial than Charles. Unfortunately, although Ben was very polite, Pierre had several issues about him. He didn't come from a local, blue-blood, rice affluent, horseracing family. He had his family's attitude about abolition.

Pierre could respect Ben's view of slavery without agreeing with it. Still, Pierre believed that he had found a better match for Gabrielle in Charles, whose beliefs were more in line with what he had wanted. Pierre knew that Gabrielle had noticed both, but recently, had shown more interest in Ben, although in the past, he had noticed her paying attention to Charles.

Pierre had a lot on his mind as he drove the buggy to the leather shop. He knew the time was fast approaching when his daughter would need to settle down. All he wanted was for her to be happy.

As usual, Jacque and his leather craftsmen were busy making saddles for the cavalrymen when Pierre came in the shop. They had divided the duties among the men based on the skill and ability of each and it worked well.

Jacque knew the purpose of Pierre's visit. He knew that he wanted to inquire about the racing saddles, and Jacque had concluded that it was just too much to take on right then. Jacque himself rarely got involved with the manufacturing process, but this was different; his hands worked just as quickly as someone else's.

"Pierre," he said in French, "I do not know what to tell you. We are so busy right now. I haven't even had time to sit down."

Jacque didn't miss a beat as he spoke. Pierre had to almost walk along side him to keep up with his pace because Jacque didn't let his visit interfere with the process.

"You could hire more folks on," Pierre suggested, "Look at these men. They are older, with experience, so they expect to be paid more. You could hire younger men that work for less money."

"Pierre, if you can find a young man or two that would be willing to work in this shop and learn the leather trade, I'd be more than happy to think about it, but until then we can't take the racing saddles. The business with the military is just too good right now," he replied, this time in English.

Pierre could tell that he wasn't going to have an audience with Jacque, he was busy and so were all of his craftsmen. It frustrated him. Pierre himself had brought the racing saddle in from the buggy and placed it where he would remember it when he left, but Jacque would still see that he had carried it in. Jacque nodded to show that he had noticed and that he was appreciative of the effort.

"Find one or two young men," Pierre muttered to himself, as he turned away. Turning back again, he asked, "Alright then, Jacque, perhaps I could buy some leather oil?"

"A gallon and a half, as usual?" he asked in French

"That would suit me just fine," Pierre responded, "If you don't mind?"

"Not at all, now, that I can do," Jacque responded. He stopped what he was doing and started to fill Pierre's order for oil.

Chapter 24
A Grieving Widower

A Fontenot stableman from the villa quickly dashed in the door. He was all breathless as his eyes darted about until saw Pierre waiting on his order.

"Monsieur!" he exclaimed in French, "I have been asked to find you. You must come quickly. Your wife is very ill. The doctor is with her. Gabrielle and Miss Prissy sent me. They said that you would be here. You must come home quickly!"

"The doctor is with her?" Pierre responded in French.

His first concern was for his wife, and then he wondered if he would lose his unborn child.

"You must come quickly. I got here as fast as ah could!" the stableman responded.

That didn't answer his question, but Pierre could sense the urgency in the matter, so he did not repeat himself. His mind flooding with questions, Pierre bolted out of the rear door and untied the horse as fast as he could. The stableman was right behind him.

The buggy and horse took off as fast as Pierre snapped the reins. Clouds of dirt and dust followed as Pierre raced passed others at the intersection. Only then did he realize that he had left the stableman behind in his panic. By then, the young man had already started home on his own horse.

With a straightaway up ahead, the horse ran with wondrous speed. All that Pierre could do was struggle to stay in his seat, but his mind was in a blur. He cracked the reins and the horse sped up somewhat. The stableman and his horse were nowhere near. Pierre had a commanding lead as he surged forward at every intersection without stopping. It never even occurred to him that what he was doing was not very safe and could get him in trouble. The horse dodged several near collisions as he ran in front of other slower moving carriages and wagons of hay.

Arriving at the villa's cobblestone driveway, he noticed that the doctor's buggy was ahead of his, and blocked the way. Then, his concern really escalated; apparently, the doctor was in such a hurry that he didn't park the buggy properly. Charles stood nearby, at the stable house entrance and watched as Pierre immediately jumped down from his seat and ran towards the front door of the mansion.

Pierre did not bother to do anything properly, either. He just left the horse and buggy parked lopsidedly in front of the house, behind the doctor's buggy. Charles decided he would take care of that. Miss Prissy met Pierre. As she opened the door, she was almost hysterical with emotion.

"What happened?" Pierre screamed at her, "Don't just stand there! Get a hold of yourself and tell me!"

Miss Prissy wheezed and gasped and spit and choked before she came to her senses.

"Miss Andrea, Miss Andrea!" she gasped as she pointed backwards, "She…she… has trouble and I summoned the doctor. He came right away, 'cause he was over at the other house a looking after a sick chil'."

Pierre, normally so calm and business-like, lost patience with her and pushed past, entering the huge foyer. She was too emotional to take it personally. The scene was one of absolute grief. Several colored matrons stood along the wall crying and murmuring about Miss Andrea.

"Would someone tell me what the hell happened!" he shouted in an enraged voice.

He almost never swore. He hated swearing because it sounded uneducated, in his opinion; however, he was so emotional that he hadn't even realized he swore. An answer to his colorful inquiry didn't elude Pierre very long.

The doctor, who had heard him shouting all the way upstairs, appeared in a bloody apron. He had shut the bedroom door as he descended down the stairs.

"What happened to Andrea?" Pierre continued to shout.

"Pierre, just follow me!" the doctor said as he continued down the stairs and into the study. He didn't have to be told where to go. He knew the layout of the house very well because he was friends with Pierre and had been at the house several times. Pierre took off after him and closed the door behind them.

"Pierre, you need to know that Andrea is gone," the doctor explained when they were alone, "So is the baby. I couldn't stop the bleeding. She had a slight fall and bled to death. From what I know, she was standing on a small footstool when she fell. Miss Prissy heard a loud noise upstairs and went to see what happened. Miss Andrea lay on the floor in blood, and by the time I got here, it was just too late. I am so sorry. It is at times like this when I hate this job. I did what I could, and she died. Sometimes, God's will is so hard to understand. She was at least four months along."

"Oh, God!" Pierre murmured in anguish as he grabbed his head with both of his hands, "Oh, God!"

"I'm so sorry, Pierre," the doctor continued. "I did all I could. I know there's nothing I can say to ease your pain, and I am truly sorry."

"Oh, God!" Pierre murmured again as he sank into a chair, "I can't believe this!"

"I'm so sorry," the doctor continued, as he put his hand on his shoulder, "its best if you don't go up there right now. It's a mess, and this is hard enough on you. I will clean it up. I was just on my way to find one you. I asked one of the coloreds you have where you were, and they said that you would be at the saddle shop. I told that young man of yours to go get you. He didn't move quickly enough, so I told one of the other, older ones to go find you."

"Oh!" Pierre sobbed, "It hurts so badly. My heart is so broken! Why does there have to be so much pain and loss in this world? I hate death! It takes everyone away from you that you love! Where is Gabrielle?"

"She is out with her harp tutor looking at a new harp. It is by the grace of God, I think, that she wasn't here when it happened. This will all be hard enough on her as it is. But now she'll need to know. We need to get her home, as well," the doctor said.

"Is there a way to keep this a secret from her? I mean about the baby and all?" Pierre asked. He was so grief stricken that he could almost feel his heart hurting in his chest as he added, "I will tell her eventually."

"I can do that for you, Pierre," the doctor responded. "Nobody will know."

Pierre and Andrea had planned to announce the expected birth that night. He thought about all that they had been through in the years that they had been married. Suddenly, the realization that she was gone hit him full force. He knew that he had to go on for Gabrielle's sake, but he didn't know how he would.

"Mama! Papa! I'm home, and look what I have!" Gabrielle sang out as she and her tutor entered the mansion.

When Pierre heard her, the knots in his stomach only tightened. Hadn't someone been sent to find her and her tutor? Indeed; unfortunately, they had barely missed each other. Gabrielle and her tutor had no idea what had transpired. Pierre was very disappointed; he had told one of his head stablemen to send Charles to seek Gabrielle. Charles knew her buggy and was told exactly where to go to find her. It didn't take Gabrielle long to figure out that something was seriously wrong. When she entered the foyer, she saw several colored folks leaning against walls, looking sickly. Their eyes were red as if they had been crying. Neither her father nor mother were anywhere in sight. It was then that she became aware that even the air felt eerie.

"I think I better leave now," her tutor said uneasily, and silently stepped out.

Gabrielle barely heard her because she was acutely aware that something was very wrong.

"What has happened?" she asked in a voice so quiet that it was barely above a whisper.

A colored woman standing near her tried to find the words, but they seemed to be caught in her throat. Then, as if she knew she was needed, Miss Prissy appeared. Gabrielle could tell just by looking at her that whatever had occurred was awful.

Miss Prissy's face was pasty from weeping and she was hunched over slightly, as if she was carrying a load of dead weight on her back. She looked drained, and her eyes still had tears in the corners.

"Miss Prissy…" Gabrielle began, but Miss Prissy only said, "Your father is in the sitting room, looking out the window. You need to go see him. Please do not go upstairs."

Bewildered, Gabrielle obeyed. She did not yet know the doctor was there, cleaning up her mother's blood. Pierre had put his buggy in the barn, next to his wives. He didn't want Gabrielle to panic when she saw it, so that meant that she couldn't see it. Pierre had made sure that she wouldn't, and she hadn't.

The next thing Miss Prissy heard was Gabrielle's heart wrenching screams. Pierre watched his daughter throw herself on the floor, something she hadn't done in probably a decade. Then, she started to wail so loudly and heartbreakingly that Pierre didn't know quite how to comfort her.

He knelt beside her on the floor and rubbed her back. The rhythmic movements of his warm hand provided at least minimal comfort, but that didn't change the fact that Gabrielle had lost her mother. She felt very alone all of the sudden. It was almost as if her very soul had been shattered and orphaned, all in the same instant.

Alone in their rooms that night, long after the doctor had left, both Pierre and Andrea talked and sometimes cried. Pierre had not slept alone in over seventeen years. The bed seemed awfully enormous and empty. He shivered, realizing only then that he had become accustomed to having Andrea's warm body next to him to keep him warm.

Andrea's death had a profound emotional impact on Gabrielle, much more so than her grandmother's death. It had happened so suddenly and without warning. One day, her mother was there to offer advice and encouragement and teach her about life, and the next, she was gone. Suddenly, she was alone and vulnerable, with no older female to lean on. She was now the queen, not the princess, of the manor, a role that she hadn't wanted to have for many more years.

She felt guilty because her mother had been altering a neck line on one the dresses that Gabrielle had sensually altered, or so her father said when she had asked why and how she had fallen. Gabrielle believed that if she hadn't been doing that, the whole thing would not have happened.

The girl that had been the day before her mother's tragic accident no longer existed. As one day turned to two, three and four, then a week, she found that she no longer had a real interest in her wardrobe; it didn't seem so attractive anymore. Several closets of both domestic and expensive imported dresses, as well as shoes and parasols, now seemed meaningless. It seemed too unreal to have the apparel there, but not her mother.

At times, not even playing her new harp eased her deep, internal yearning for just one more conversation or hug from her mother. It seemed like everywhere she looked, she found reminders of their times together. Whether it was a scent she smelled, the sight of something that Andrea loved, or a phrase that was spoken, she was constantly aware of her mother's absence. She just wanted to be outside, not in the mansion, and to be away from it all and not have to look at any of it.

Miss Prissy sensed a change in her, and chose not to interfere with her riding horses, or just spending hours sitting under the huge tree with its huge white swing. In the back of her mind, Gabrielle always sensed that there was more to the story than what she knew, but she had already been through enough. If knowing the whole truth would cause her more heartache, she didn't want to know it at that point.

Pierre noticed the change as well, although he felt guilty for not completely coming out with the truth. He and his daughter never really talked about their feelings. Each knew that the other was handling their grief the best they could, and that was left at that. For all he knew, Gabrielle thought that it was due to her mother's natural cycle.

But she did have more common sense than that, didn't she? She knew from experience that women didn't bleed to death over that didn't she? He knew she probably did, but whatever she believed about the situation seemed alright for the time being. He would tell her the truth someday, but not today. She was young, and she was still in the healing process, and it would take a long time. She was suddenly thrust into a role that she had not been accustomed to. Her mother and her grandmother before her had been the decision makers and ladies that were a part of the society circles and Gabrielle wasn't drawn to that. She didn't know how to handle the staff as her mother had. She didn't know how to be firm, and yet not aloof, in her approach to the black people. But, life was going to force her to learn.

Gabrielle had always thought they treated their colored workers better than most slave masters. They were fed decently and, most of the time, treated with respect. They were an important part of the staff, because without them, the mansion wouldn't look the way it did.

Miss Prissy and the household staff seemed different now that Amanda and Anna were both gone. They were not the same jovial, up-beat dedicated staff that she had seen in the past. They were worried that without Anna and Andrea, their jobs would be in jeopardy; after all, both of them had hired all of them, handpicking them from the field shanties. Miss Prissy had risen above that to become the head matron of the household.

Along with everything else that had changed in Gabrielle's life, Charles no longer looked attractive to her. At one time, she could see nothing else. He had scarcely even noticed when Amanda passed.

The new boy, Ben Chesser, looked better in her eyes. His family had attended the funeral for her mother, and mourned the loss as deeply as anybody else seemed to. Gabrielle was impressed with his family; his mother and father were friendly, unlike the snobbish, New Orleans society people that she had come to know from their constant visits to the villa. Ben's sister was a delight. She was a little young to be good friends with just yet, but still a delight to be with.

Sadly, Pierre felt different about the Chesser family. He was all for slavery, whatever the cost. They had no slaves and no ambition to own any. Although John Chesser didn't flaunt his feelings about slavery, Pierre perceived him as an abolitionist, a man that might perhaps turn on his own southern government if the trouble with the north continued.

His attitude about Ben was amicable, however; Ben worked hard and always had a pleasant attitude. Still, Pierre dreamed that Gabrielle would marry an affluent, slave holding gentlemen, and they would take over the Chateau one day and raise a family there. Ben Chesser didn't fit that need. In Pierre's eyes, he just wasn't good enough.

After Andrea's death, Pierre became more distant and lost interest in many of the things that he had enjoyed and even endeared before. The new racing saddle only seemed a passing fancy now. To make matters worse, Jacque had no time to deal with him. The Chateau grounds were always taken care of, whether he was directly involved or not, so Pierre became very listless and lacked any real drive or focus. In the past, he hadn't invested much time in making sure the house and grounds were taken care of, and now he took even less time out of his life for that. Without Andrea, he was lost. She had been an influential cornerstone in his life. It had been years since he was alone.

He had grown to disdain Charles, but kept him on the staff payroll as a favor to his father. Charles had lack luster ambition when he was called upon to summon Pierre when Andrea had fallen and was in dire need. Pierre needed someone to blame for her death. Had Charles moved faster, Pierre told himself that Andrea might have lived. Of course, Charles didn't know that it was a family emergency and he was just too slow to react.

Gabrielle felt at ease walking her horse, Cajun King, and riding Samson. Almost as if it was some sort of small gift of comfort from a God that Gabrielle was both mad at and didn't want to believe in, intended, she thought, ease her hurt a little, Cajun King had miraculously recovered. Although Cajun King's leg had healed, he would never race again.

It was a tragic end to a promising career, but Gabrielle was glad he had lived. She just had to get out of the mansion, and being with her horses gave her that chance. She also had much time to reflect on life, deciding that she would try harder not to worry about frivolous things like money, clothes and what others thought. That, of course, would be easier said then done at her age.

One afternoon, she was riding Samson when he decided to visit the pond, a place where she had once caught butterflies as a child. It was overgrown with weeds because she had outgrown any real interest in it, so Pierre saw no need to keep it on the maintenance agenda. It was tranquil there, so she liked it. She appreciated it differently now that she wasn't a child, but it provided her with a place to be quiet and listen to the ducks and the geese that were always nearby.

Gabrielle and Ben had become friends. He would visit on Charles' day off and assist her with Cajun King. Although Ben had seen the horrible accident and truly felt sorry for the horse, his real intention was to be with Gabrielle. Even Cajun King sensed that, but he also liked Ben. Ben almost always brought him a handful of hay or a carrot.

Ben felt comfortable around Gabrielle. She was quiet and confident, and she had a way of putting him at ease like no other girl back home had ever been able to. Granted, he knew girls in Atlanta that he had thought about courting, but never too seriously. If he would have stayed in Atlanta, then he may have courted Sarah, the elder's daughter, but she wasn't there, and Gabrielle was.

Gabrielle enjoyed riding Samson, but just at a trot, nothing fast. Ben would slowly run along side and make sure that she didn't loose her balance and fall off. At least that was his excuse for sticking close to her. The real reason, though, was because she always looked so beautifully natural in how she rode any horse, but especially Samson.

Afterward, when she was through riding; Ben would remove the saddle and feed the horse. Then, they would just walk the grounds.

That was the time that Ben looked forward to most. He'd have a chance to be alone with Gabrielle, holding hands, walking about the forsaken pond. Gabrielle would laugh with delight as the ducks and the geese would fly up and away. It seemed almost as though they were making room for them or giving them a welcoming.

When she realized that they would be visiting the pond more regularly, she had secretly prepared a huge log seat for them to sit on behind the foliage, away from prying eyes. It was perfect because it couldn't even be seen from her bedroom window. It was a natural place to sit and talk, as though that nature had provided a welcoming seat, and all that Gabrielle did was to clear away fallen leaves.

Ben was the only boy that she felt relaxed enough to talk to and just be herself. She had even cried in front of him and expressed her feelings about death, life and God. Although she did not know it, Ben prayed for her every night, asking God to show her that He loved her and bless her and help her through the pain that weighed so heavily on her heart.

Ben was fascinated with her. He held her hand as she spoke of her father arriving from France and the difficult times that they once had. Ben almost thought that his feelings about Gabrielle were just like that, nothing more. Still, this was a new beginning, something that he had never experienced before, just like her father had never been to the new land before he had come. Ben could not deny his feelings. He knew it was a whole new arena that he could explore and learn from and about, but also knew that he wanted to do so with a certain level of caution. Ben held her hand as she spoke of the Chateau's history, growing up there, Miss Prissy, her harp lessons and all that was involved of coming of age in the French well-to-do society. Ben discussed his past as well, speaking of Atlanta, of growing up in a local farming family, of his father's involvement in the railroad and eventually, giving up the farm to work at the railroad.

To Gabrielle, his simple and different way of thinking was fascinating. She appreciated him much more than the French, hand-carved frieze work and the twin, imported, marble mantels, the huge Baccarat chandeliers and the ornate mirrors that Chateau Villa had to offer. The exquisite décor and all of its finery seemed so far away to her because she had something more meaningful now. The richness of it all seemed so unimportant. Unlike almost everyone else in her world, he was common, down-to-earth and easy to talk to. He offered something that her father couldn't. With him, she felt a sense of belonging and a heightened awareness of all that was in the world.

Ben listened to her as he held her hand. For him, as well, the conversation was intriguing, and he was in awe of her and her description of her life before him. He didn't know how he existed without her. He was enthralled. Sitting closer now, he put his arm around her and gave her a comforting hug. He wanted her to know that he cared for her even though he knew that she wasn't aspiring to be a part of the French well-to-do society.

Her father's expectations of her didn't match her own desires. She wanted something else. She saw that Ben both knew and respected that, and she understood his hug. It was reassuring. She had never been hugged liked that before.

Reaching around him with her other arm, she wrapped it around his shoulder and pulled him closer. Locked in a tender embrace, he put his cheek gently onto hers and pulled her even closer. His face felt warm and soft to her, and to him, her face felt angelic. For a while, they just sat in silence.

The setting sun's rays reflected in the water, casting an orange glow in the twilight hours. Before they knew it, the sun had set. Ben slightly turned his face and pressed his lips on hers, and she did not fight him. It all felt so divine, so comforting, and so reassuring. She sensed his mutual feelings of enjoyment and puppy love and nudged him closer. What passed between them was a wonderful feeling, a true feeling of intimacy. The world around them didn't matter. In those moments, it was just them, communicating without words.

"I have to get going on home or someone with come looking for me," Gabrielle said softly as he withdrew from his embrace.

"But I will see you again sometime soon, won't I? Like…say next week?" Ben asked, her eyes still shining.

"Yes, you will, I promise. I wouldn't miss it for all the money in the world. Is Saturday fine with you?" Gabrielle asked.

"I believe that should be fine. I will somehow find a way to let you know if it's not," Ben whispered back, "See you then. I am looking forward to it. I promise I will be here. I will be thinking about you until then. Remember, Gabrielle, God loves you even more than I do," Ben said without even thinking.

Gabrielle scowled. She knew that he knew how she felt about God, and she also knew that he meant no disrespect by it. He had said it so naturally that he hadn't even realized he had said it until after it slipped out. Deep down, though, she could even start to feel that her heart was softening toward God again. Had it really been His fault that her mother and grandmother had died, or was He really as loving as Ben had said?

As they parted ways, she couldn't help but think that maybe God was a loving God after all. Maybe that was why He had put Ben in her life, or was Ben in her world just by chance? Did God really have a divine purpose and plan for her and everyone else? Was there really a Heaven? If there was, he put her in it.

As she entered the foyer once again, she could smell supper cooking. Miss Prissy smiled at Gabrielle and was surprised when Gabrielle flashed her weak, small smile in response. It was the first time in weeks that anyone had seen her smile.

"Miss Prissy, do you think that mama is an angel now?" Gabrielle asked, much to Miss Prissy's, shock and even her own.

John had just finished up resolving some scheduling issues and was getting ready to leave for the day. Looking down from the tower, the yard appeared to be organized. The trains were loaded and aligned for the next day's departures.

He still had a lot on his mind about South Carolina's secession and the possibility that the railroad might split into two halves. It was all the talk around the yard. What if more states succeeded? Then what would happen? How would the railroad continue to serve the rails across both the north and the south?

He noticed that there seemed to be a confrontation of some kind occurring at the side of the yard, near the building where the men washed up before going home for the night. Two men, both with a crowd behind them, were loudly arguing about something. He could not hear their words clearly from the window. Deciding that he had better get involved, he bolted from the office and headed down the stairs.

As soon as he was outside he could tell that the fight had quickly escalated, becoming worse than what he had witnessed from the window. The disagreement had turned into a brawl between the two men, each lashing out at the other with round house swings and body jabs. The crowd roared and cheered them on; each man now appeared to be battered and bloody.

"Does anyone want to tell me what in the world is going on here?" John shouted as he approached.

"A friendly disagreement, sir!" A man on one side answered. The two men, who by then had heard him, stopped their fight. One had a bloody nose. It appeared to be broken down the middle. The other had a gash in his palm that was bleeding badly.

"If this is a friendly brawl, I would hate to see a nasty one," he replied, "This will be a place of peace and unity. There won't be any fighting in my rail yard. Do ye's both understand that?" he demanded in a tone that scared both the men into complete silence.

"Aw, now Mr. Chesser," another responded, "Those boys are feuding over railroad rights to have nigger replacements. Why don't you just leave 'em alone?"

"I don't care what it was over! If you boys are going to fight, do it somewhere else. There won't be any fighting in my rail yard!" John snapped sharply, anger coursing through his veins.

"Well then," one of the bloodied combatants responded, "If you know the truth, then why don't you tell us?"

"The truth about what? What in the world are you talking about?" John asked.

"Seeing that Hiram here doesn't understand it, I decided to teach him a lesson or two. A little education doesn't hurt now and then," he replied.

"To hell with both of you and your nigger freight!" Hiram said, "The hell with the railroad, too! John Chesser, you wouldn't know how to run a company if Jesus Himself gave you an instruction book! I quit! The Confederacy needs me more than the railroad does!"

"Tha truth about what?" John asked again, ignoring the insult to Jesus. That was God's matter. He could deal with Hiram regarding what he had said. John just hoped that God would have a bit of mercy on the man.

"Well, Mr. Chesser, word has it that the railroad is going to hire niggers to replace us freight boys. Well, old Hiram seemed to think that any nigger can work just as good as a white man can. We all know that's a damn lie!"

"There ain't gonna be no replacing anybody in the yards," John replied, "Yeah, I've heard the rumor too, but that's all it is. It's a story that somebody made up to start trouble on the rail yard and get you boys all fussed up! Apparently, it worked. Now, come on. I am an honest man that has been where you are. Do you think I would do that with telling you first?" John asked. His question was followed by dead silence.

"There ain't gonna be no replacements if the railroad splits in two?" a voice in the crowd asked.

"No," John firmly stated, "Ain't nobody gonna lose their job or be replaced with colored people. As far as Hiram is concerned, everybody has a right to their own opinion on things. Ultimately, God alone is our judge, so let him think what he wants. What in the world are you doing fighting like this? You are acting like a couple of school boys. You are lucky that I am a man of compassion, or you would both be losing your jobs right now for fighting like this. You both should have come to me first if you wanted an answer."

"I am still quitting! I said I am, and I mean it!" Hiram barked as he stomped off the property.

"Maybe you should have told us first!" the man from the crowd replied.

He did have a point. They should have been told more about what was going on.

The railroad fight taught John a good lesson. He realized that he had not been communicating with the crews like he could have been. The two men were perhaps not even comfortable approaching him. They had fought over something that could have easily have been worked out, but Hiram had quit over it. John had never lost a man over political issues before. When he had lost a worker, it had always been over family or health, not political upheaval or a difference in political opinions. He took it personally, though he tried not to. The man from the crowd was right, and as a matter of fact, John had been there for awhile, and he didn't even know the man's name.

John assumed everybody was happy, but obviously, they weren't. Unbeknownst to him, there had been trouble brewing in the rail yards over the thought that jobs would be lost to coloreds if the railroad split. To him, the railroad was like the country; it was coming apart on issues that were based on states' rights and opinions.

The railroad fight was a wake up call for him. If he wanted to maintain unity, he had better get involved, so that he could quell uprisings and cool tempers before they turned ugly. Losing Hiram was devastating; it was like South Carolina quitting the United States. It just didn't seem right, and things could have been talked out.

Of utmost concern was the unity and contentment of the other workers. John was horrified as he suddenly felt that others could walk away from their jobs if issues weren't settled. But Hiram was Hiram; he was temperamental and liked to start confrontations among the crew. John realized that had been too mild mannered, too laid back in his approach toward them. He already had his mind made up. Things would be different in the rail yard from then on.

But John didn't want to take his trouble home. He climbed in his buggy and started home, determined to put the fight behind him. The situation with Hiram was forgotten for the time being. Perhaps his decision to quit had been a good one. He was gone, and so was the trouble that he had stirred up.

After the experience with Hiram, John regularly visited the yards, smoked cigars with the crew and made it a point to learn all of their names and some of their children's names. The tide was starting to turn. Morale was better; laughter could be heard from the wash building instead of yelling and insults.

One day there was no laughter. Everyone had somber faces because Louisiana joined the Confederacy and seceded from the Union. The possibility of the railroad splitting in two to appease both governments now seemed all too much a reality. Nobody wanted that to happen, but they all believed it would.

There was nothing that John could do about the political upheaval in the country, just as there was nothing that anybody could do. The country was practically split in two over slavery and sovereign independence. The men were afraid of being replaced. Many had been there most of their lives and didn't know anything else.

There had been frequent visits by both Union and Confederate officers, both for freight and passenger service. Relationships between them were workable at this time. It just didn't seem like a time for civil strife. The colored porters quit the railroad in droves. They were afraid of being pressed into service in other roles, like loading gunpowder. There had been rumors that they would be forced into such risky service if they stayed. Others felt that they had nothing to worry about and only reacted the way they had out of fear and peer pressure. None-the-less, they weren't taking any chances. They didn't want to fight for a country that enslaved them. Let the white porters load gunpowder for the Confederacy.

Chapter 25
An Improvement

Several weeks passed. True to family tradition, the colored matrons continued to make huge dinners at the Chateau. Miss Prissy and her staff were always busy in the kitchen. The only family members at the table were Pierre and Gabrielle, and it was different without Anna and Andrea. Pierre said his table grace in English as usual, and the wall was still full of standing matrons in their aprons. When Pierre concluded the offering for the food, the matrons would go about placing hot platters on the table, dishing up plates and pouring drinks.

Andrea's passing didn't affect Pierre's appetite any. He paid good money to employ the kitchen staff and was never disappointed with the cuisine. On the other hand, Gabrielle ate less than usual and took longer to finish. Pierre assumed that it was because of her mother's passing; she was still grieving.

Miss Prissy thought it would cheer Gabrielle up to have a favorite meal, so she planned one without saying a word to anyone. Much to the chagrin of Miss Prissy, Gabrielle barely touched her rice. Instead, she rolled it around in the fork and hardly ate. Pierre noticed that, as well, and it really worried him. Rice, red beans, and pork were among her favorite dishes.

"Aw, now Miss Gabrielle," Miss Prissy chided, "Have some more. You love this food. Here, have some tea as well. You look as thin as a rail."

Gabrielle rolled her eyes slightly, quietly exhaled, and ate some more. Things, she felt, would never be the same. Would this double loss she had endured in such a short period of time ever stop hurting so bad? And did God really love her? She had been silently asking herself that repeatedly for weeks. It seemed that nobody really understood what was going on inside her head and heart. Did God?

Without a word, Gabrielle took some more rice and forced herself to eat it. She really wasn't hungry, and she wasn't acting normal. She had heaped two scoops unto her plate without anyone's help. Pierre didn't mind Miss Prissy's admonishment. It seemed to work. Although she was acting odd, she was indeed eating better. But Miss Prissy couldn't do it all; he had to provide some motivation as well.

But what could he say or do? Pierre had to think about that for a minute. Then it hit him! He could talk about the new saddle! So, that's exactly what he did. She perked up some when he mentioned the racing saddle that never got into production,

"Well, it's a very good saddle. I have had nothing but positive remarks about it. But there's always something that can be better, even if something is really well do. Do you have any suggestions on what could be different?" Pierre asked.

"I do, father. The stirrups are too high for me. If they could be lower, I wouldn't need any assistance to ride Samson. I think you should change that, or make it so they can be adjusted somehow," she recommended.

"Adjusted, hey? That's something new that I had not thought of. So be it then," he replied, "I'll make certain that the alteration happens tomorrow."

Gabrielle seemed to slightly smile and perk up some then. Even being asked to make a little suggestion like that made her feel useful and important. She decided then that maybe she needed to start asking deep questions and try to find out who she really was. She knew she didn't want to be who her father expected her to be. He wanted her to be a part of the wealthy circles, and do what all wealthy women did. He wanted her to join quilting groups and gossip circles, have children and a husband and stay at home and cook and clean and take care of the mansion. Although she knew she was expected to do just that, that wasn't what she wanted. So, then she had to figure out exactly what it was that she did desire, and as of that moment, she had no real idea.

"Father," she added after a few minutes of silence, during which all of this was going through her mind, "Is it possible that the pond can be made to look beautiful again, like it was when I was a little girl and caught butterflies there?"

Pierre had never expected to hear anything like that from his daughter, but it seemed like a reasonable request. All that would take was a little time and work. Anything from her made Pierre feel better, because it was better than her melancholy. No, he decided her request wasn't so difficult to fulfill. He had a golden opportunity now; it was now up to him to do something to help her feel better.

"Certainly, I can make that happen. We can make it as beautiful as you want it!" Pierre chimed with a large grin.

"Could we have inlaid stepping stones and sculptured bushes and maybe a nice, white picket fence with vines and stone benches, too?" she requested.

"Well, now! You sure do wanna fix it up, don't you? We certainly can," he replied, "We'll make it beautiful, just like you want!" he replied in French.

Gabrielle was slightly taken back that he answered her in French, but it made no difference to her. She wanted a beautiful pond area, and he had said yes. Maybe in giving her someplace to go and be alone she would be happy. She wondered about that. But, whatever the reason, she would soon have the pond to herself again, and it would be beautiful.

Gabrielle finished the rest of her meal with a lighter heart than she had had in months. Pierre could sense that she was happy, and it made his heart soar. Miss Prissy's matrons served a cherry strudel and hot tea for dessert. The dessert was Anna Fontenot's favorite, and for a minute, Pierre and Gabrielle shot each other pained expressions.

Then, Miss Prissy crept out of the kitchen and whispered in Gabrielle's ear, "You once asked me if your grandma is an angel now. I did some talking to God about that one, and this is His way of letting you know that she's in His hands now. He says that He loves you and He wants to move in your heart and heal the hurt you feel, but He also says He'll wait for you. When you are ready, all you have to do is ask and He will help you. He also said that He wants you to enjoy this cherry strudel, and He says that if you want some in Heaven, it'll be even better there."

Gabrielle felt her heart jump and skip a beat. It sure seemed that she had indeed been talking to God. How else would she have known to say that God really did love her? Gabrielle felt even better then, just knowing that her grandmother was an angel, and she also thought that meant her mother was, too. She smiled to herself, realizing she now had two guardian angels. Her piece of cherry strudel quickly disappeared.

Afterwards, the table was cleared as usual. Gabrielle nodded to her father, silently asking if she could be excused, and he nodded back. He thought to himself that although she mostly resembled him, she had the mannerisms of her mother; she was coming of age and wanted nice things. Gone were the days of being a little girl, playing on the muddy banks or chasing butterflies with her mother.

It was twilight now. Gabrielle went into the study and looked out of the window, gazing toward the pond area. It would be beautiful. She would see to that. She was almost ashamed to take Ben there because it was so pitifully overgrown and neglected, but unfortunately, the only place where they could be alone. Pierre just wanted to do it because he wanted to see her happy and full of life again. But to Gabrielle, in her mind she could see it as if it was already a beautiful area to be alone with Ben, away from the interior pomp of the Chateau.

"We'll visit the pond tomorrow," Pierre mentioned when he entered the room and saw her looking forlornly out of the window, "You just tell me how you want it… and that's the way it will be!"

"Thank you father," she replied as she turned about, "It really does have potential to be beautiful. It's just that it's such a forgotten area of the estate."

Pierre had to admit to himself that she was indeed correct. It did have potential to be beautiful. He knew because he had seen it that way, but right then, it was forsaken and forgotten. As she had grown up and lost interest in the pond, he had ignored the area, as horse racing and slave dealing took up most of this time.

"Well," he replied, "It has been forgotten. That will soon change. It will be what you want it to be."

"I sure hope so. Daddy, do you think God loves me?" Gabrielle asked.

The question caught him off guard. Pierre had always tried to show Gabrielle that God did indeed love both of them. He also knew, though, that she had a rebellious streak and he hated to admit it, but he sensed that she was resisting God's truths. But all he could do—all he had done—was pray for her. The rest was in God's hands.

"Gabrielle, of course God loves you. Why would you doubt that? Is it because your mother passed?" Pierre asked compassionately.

Pierre thought about how pretty the pond would look when it was done. He allowed himself to believe, at least a little bit, that perhaps that was how their lives would be again someday. It would cost money to clean up the pond, but that was unimportant. To Pierre, it was a chance to please Gabrielle, and at the same time, help her get over her mother's passing. Gabrielle felt better about it already. She opened the shutter wider and continued to gaze from the window.

"It's starting to rain," she noticed, "Didn't think it was going to rain today."

Pierre approached her and saw for himself. It wasn't much if a rain, just a gentle sprinkling in the evening.

"Let me close this for you. Tomorrow, we will go to the pond and you can tell me what you want. Don't worry about how much it costs. I just want you to be happy with the pond."

"I will be," she replied, "I will be."

"Are you still walking Cajun King?" he asked.

"Some. He is really improving, so he doesn't need as much attention now as he did even a couple months ago. He walks fine, but I don't ride him. He's just a villa pet now," she replied.

"Well, that's good," Pierre responded, "He'll live a natural life, but he will never race again. Fortunately, he seems to be getting better. You realize he should have died or had to be put down, don't you? You know that it's a miracle that he didn't have to be, don't you? I can't explain why we didn't have to put him down."

"I never doubted him. I just knew he would recover if he was given a chance, but I have thought about the fact that maybe God did have a hand in it, yes. Have you thought about replacing him?" she asked.

"No, Gabrielle, I haven't thought about it very seriously. He is my favorite horse, and maybe I just can't yet accept the fact that he won't race again, but I think…I think everything has changed for me. Since your mother passed, I haven't been to the races much. Oh, there are stables about that I can buy another race horse from, but Cajun King was a great racer in his day, and maybe he still is."

Gabrielle hadn't noticed that until he said it; indeed he hadn't shown much interest in racing since her mother's death. Perhaps she could help him by showing more interest. Perhaps there could be a winning Fontenot race horse in the racing circuit. Anything was better than listening to Tori brag about her champion horse, and there hadn't been a winning Fontenot horse in a long time.

True to his word, the following morning after breakfast, Pierre suggested to Gabrielle that they tour the pond area to determine the renovations that she would want done. Gabrielle was delighted, and together they walked about the small wooded forest and the overgrown foliage that surrounded the pond. The ducks and the geese meandered away as the both of them walked about, observing what was there and discussing possible changes as they went along.

"Father," she noticed, "If we could have sculptured bushes along this row," she said as she gestured to an area near the banks of the south side of the pond, "It sure would look lovely, and we could do away with those old dying plants?"

"It would look gorgeous there; Gabrielle, along with inlaid stones and perhaps a gate could be added to the fence right here. What do you think?"

"That would be nice!" she replied.

Pierre couldn't help but notice how Gabrielle was becoming more like her mother. She wanted nice things and spared little expense to get them. He listened to her suggestions as they walked along the perimeter, finding that she had some very good ones indeed. She didn't let on that from that far corner of their property, she could see

Ben in the distance riding his horse in the huge pasture area of the La Rue St. Lazar estate.

"Could we have some huge rocks brought in and placed on the banks, father?" Gabrielle requested.

"Certainly could, and where would you like them?" he responded.

"One there and two or three over there," she explained as she pointed to the east and west.

"We can do all of that," Pierre said.

"Oh, that is just wonderful. Thank you, papa, this means a lot to me. It's mighty hot today," Gabrielle said as she looked skyward at the relentlessly hot sun.

"We best get on back inside," he explained, "I'll make the pond area beautiful again. Don't worry about that. It will be just like we discussed, with the work starting today," he explained.

"I do appreciate all of it, father," she replied.

"Oh, it's the least I can do. To me, if it helps you get back to being your old self again, it will be worth every penny. I know your mama's death really broke your heart, but she would want you to move on and be all that you can be in all that you do," Pierre said.

Gabrielle looked into the horizon to see that Ben was still riding his horse back and forth across the pasture.

"Father, what will happen to the racing saddle?" she asked.

"Oh, I don't really know for sure," he responded, "Jacque doesn't seem to have the time for it. There's some kind of preparation going on in the military, and they placed a big order for saddles. Jacque has to fill that. Perhaps I'll have to wait until his military contract expires before I can do anything with it."

"What's the military planning?" Gabrielle asked.

"I don't really know. I think only the people involved with whatever it is really know. I just hope it's nothing to awful, like a war," Pierre replied.

"Oh, daddy, you don't think they are planning to fight and kill each other, do you?" Gabrielle asked, "That would be awful."

"It would be, but why did you ask about the saddle?" Pierre inquired.

"I was just wondering where you were on it, as far as when you thought it would be selling to the public," she replied.

"Oh, come now," Pierre coaxed gently, "I know there is another reason. Why do you ask about the saddle? Is it because you like it and want to use it?" he asked, "I'll have it altered to fit your leg size, and that way you won't fall off."

"Actually," Gabrielle confessed hesitantly, "I was wondering if you would mind if Ben tries the saddle on his horse before the alteration?" she asked.

"Oh, that boy, Ben Chesser," Pierre mused, "Actually, Gabrielle, I don't have anything against their family personally. It's just that… they are abolitionists, and they are outsiders to New Orleans. Everyone here has slaves, and they won't ever have any. If he wants to try it, I have no problem with that, but you and he come from different backgrounds."

"Are you saying that we can't be friends because of that? Are you saying that what he believes makes you dislike him? Is that any different than treating someone unjustly because they own no slaves? Is it not the law of this land that all men are created equal? Was that not the very foundation for the reason you came here with your mother?" she asked in French.

He could see pain, anger and defiance in her gaze as she stopped and stared at him. Never had she asked such things of him before. Where did her way of thinking, which was apparently so deep and radically different from his, originate from? Looking into her eyes, he could see that she had thought through and believed in what she was saying, and it almost scared him.

"I'm generous to all of the neighbors except those outside Chesser people," he replied. "They are not one of us, and the only reason that he is here at all is because his father is employed with the railroad, otherwise I think he would prefer to live somewhere else."

"But Ben says that they like it here," she replied.

"What he thinks and what he does are two different things, Gabrielle."

"What do you mean, father?" she asked, her expression inquisitive.

"He and his family aren't one of us, and I'm not the only one that thinks as much, either," Pierre replied firmly.

"You mean of affluence and French origin?"

"That's part of it, but not all. They are different people, Gabrielle, outsiders. They have no place here. I worked hard for my money all these years, working the land and going to the races. Those people and others like them make money the easy way with railroad stocks and bonds. It's a fast living, one of which ah`m not accustomed to."

Although Pierre's opinion of the interloping Chesser family wasn't very high, he had told his daughter enough already. Gabrielle said nothing, but frowned as if she was deep in thought. He was afraid that if he told her more she would see Ben just out of spite and he didn't want that.

Gabrielle had done a decent job keeping her relationship with Ben a secret from her father. Although he sensed that she liked him, he had no clue what Gabrielle's real motive was for wanting the pond to look nice. He had no clue that she and Ben were spending time there. And he certainly did not know that his daughter was starting to love Ben.

As they walked about the banks of the pond, neither Gabrielle nor her father had the slightest clue that Ben Chesser, the new boy in town whom Gabrielle had just spotted from the distance, was not just out for a joyride on his horse. No, that particular day, he was a young man on a mission. He was on his way to the race track, aiming to fulfill his dream. He wanted to have a chance to race on the big track with the professional jockeys.

"Well, uh, do you have any representation son?" asked Jean Fournier, the bearded, burly manager of the horse race track, as he jotted down Ben's information.

"Well, no," Ben answered, "It's always been just me and my horse at dirt road races."

The manager then looked up and gave Ben a completely shocked, bewildered look, then said, "Well, uh, what is your horse's name?"

"Bunches," Ben replied, "I've always called him Bunches."

Almost completely mystified, the manager looked Ben over and then looked at the horse. Never before had an unknown jockey made such a request as the one this boy was making.

"Bunches, huh?" he smiled.

"Yes sir. I brought him here from Atlanta, and he won several races there, sir."

"Son, let me tell you something about horseracing here. We here in New Orleans take this racing seriously. We don't race on country roads… and we most certainly won't present a horse looking like that!"

"Well, I don't understand sir," Ben replied, "He's always been good enough before."

"A race horse should always be groomed and ready for show. This horse here that you call 'Bunches' just isn't ready to show, much less ready to run," the manager explained.

"But he's fast sir!" Ben added.

"If you race this horse the way he is now, you'll lose a lot of money, my son," he explained.

"Well, how so sir?" Ben asked.

"Folks won't bet on newcomers," Jean explained, "You have to let the people see the horse at the stables and walk the horse and have it all well groomed, and you haven't done any of that!"

"You just can't bring a horse it here and race?" Ben asked, rather dumbfounded.

"You have a lot to learn, son," he further explained, "This ain't Atlanta. We do things differently here. If you want to race this horse, then you'll have to do what I tell ya, or you can't run at all. You know how many jockeys and owners come in here? There are just too many owners that think that they have the next winner. It takes more than wanting to win. It takes a willingness to push yourself and the horse to want to win."

"Well, what do I need to do, then?" Ben asked.

"First, groom the horse, and then get rid of that old saddle. Winners have shiny, newer saddles. Nobody runs those anymore. Then shoe him, bring him to the stables and show him around, but don't ride him," he explained.

"If I do all these things, do you think he has a chance?" Ben asked.

"All horses have the same chance," the manager explained, "But I wish ah had a cigar for every boy like you that comes in here looking for a race. Granted, most of them aren't total strangers to this city like you. I have to admit that it was rather bold of you to do what you did, being not from here and all. But if I had a cigar for every dreamer like you that comes in here, I'd have a tobacco farm by now!"

"So it's up to the owner?' Ben muttered.

The experienced manager could tell that Ben wasn't experienced in how big races worked. Just like his horse had yet to be proven, so Ben himself was still inexperienced. But the manager saw something in Ben that made him want to find out more. He had seen a lot of boys come and go, but Ben's mindset was different, determined, focused and driven.

"Take him home and brush him, fit him with new shoes, and bring him back tomorrow," the manager instructed, "I might have a saddle that you can borrow, but the thing is, son, you can't ride him. It's nothing personal, but a jockey will have to ride him."

"A jockey will have to ride him?" Ben answered dumbfounded.

"That's the way it is if you want to race here, son," he explained, "This ain't no back country dirt road. This is a track where folks with money win and lose a fortune."

Ben took Bunches away. He knew the conversation was over, and there was nothing else to say or explain. The stable manager watched as Ben walked Bunches out to the cobblestone street, mounted him and turned right, out of view. He was just one of many boys who appeared out of nowhere thinking that his horse was a winner, but still, he could see something in his eyes that told him this boy was different somehow.

Perhaps this boy would be back, and then again, perhaps he wouldn't. Ben had waited for six weeks to see the manager, though he had never known that Ben had been there many times to see him. Each time, he was turned away because the manager was just to busy to see him.

He didn't get the thing that he wanted, but at least he hadn't been told no. He had expected the manager to be more aggressive about Bunches and enlist him for the next race. It didn't happen like that. The manager had turned the conversation completely around. Bunches had a ways to go before he would be considered. Ben had a lot to think about as he made his way down various cobblestone streets, past quaint shops and various businesses.

Street traffic was heavy for that time of day. He stopped at a trough to let Bunches have a drink of water. Perhaps Gabrielle could help him. The race track's manager hadn't given him the satisfaction that he wanted, and he knew that Bunches was better than all of that. He would take the chance of going to see her. He knew that she was at home, perhaps out walking her now pet horse, Cajun King. He became more eager now. The cobblestone road was open and Bunches seemed ready to run.

"Haw boy!" Ben shouted as he snapped the reins.

The horse broke into a full gallop. Ben leaned into him and worked with him. At least now, he had better control of himself and the horse when they were in a gallop.

"We'll teach 'em!" he yelled. "We'll teach 'em all!"

Around a long winding curve and past the bakery they bounded. The horse continued to race onward. Suddenly, Ben realized there was military men blocking the road up ahead and pulled back on the reins, then stopped.

"You're in a mighty hurry, ain't ya boy?" asked a Confederate army cavalryman as he approached.

"Must have lost my way," Ben replied, almost breathless from riding.

"Well you cain't come down this way, an' tell your friends not to come down here, either. This ain't no race track here, so you just turn right around and head the other way."

Ben could not believe what he was seeing and hearing. How would he go see Gabrielle again, and what were these men blocking the way for? Ben wanted to ask, but dared not say a word unless he was spoken to. After several moments, Ben caught his breath.

"What's your name, boy?" another soldier asked.

"Ben Chesser," he responded.

"My brother works for John Chesser at the railroad, you any kin?" the first one asked.

"He's my father, sir," Ben replied.

"Ah, yes. The railroad gave John and all of ye's the La Rue St. Lazar place," he muttered. Clearing his throat and speaking with clarity, the man said, "You get on out of here now and don't come down this way anymore."

Ben didn't respond, but pulled the reins hard to the left and Bunches quickly responded. As he left, he noticed several bordello women mixed in with the soldiers, drinking and laughing.

Ben had to think of another way to reach Gabrielle's house. He took an alternate, back road that would eventually lead to the Chateau. It was the long way around, but he couldn't go back to where he had been. Rows of black slaves could be seen in the distant fields. Work wagons weren't parked too far away.

"C'mon boy!" he yelled as he snapped the reins again

Once again, Bunches took off in a shot. The dirt road was comfortable to him.

Ben coaxed him along faster and faster down the long, country, dirt road straightaway.

Slowing down now at the intersection ahead, he turned left and kept up the run. Ben smiled as he realized that Bunches could hardly be slowed down. Eventually, the dirt road gave way to a cobblestone street. He turned right at the general goods store.

The Chateau wasn't far ahead. Both Ben and his horse were breathless again from riding hard. Decreasing his speed to a slow trot now, he could see the back side of the Fontenot's mansion ahead. Perhaps Gabrielle would be outside.

He raked his fingers through his hair and readjusted his hat to try to look more presentable in case she was. Riding past the estate from the road, he didn't see her at first, although he looked far and wide across the horizon. He smiled to himself when he finally spotted her near the back pond area, close to the split-rail fence. She appeared to be looking over the pond area; to Ben, it looked different than the last time that he had seen it.

"Any fishing allowed here?" he teased.

Looking back and around her sunbonnet, she didn't immediately recognize him in the glare of the sun. Holding her hand up to her forehead, she shielded her vision from the subduing heat of the evening.

"No fishing, Ben! No horse racing, either!" she teased back.

Ben approached and got off of the horse. Looking about, he noticed a lot of landscape alterations around the pond area. Although Gabrielle didn't want to admit it to him, she was renovating the pond area for him. The workmen had gone home for the night; the landscaping changes were obvious and starting to take shape.

Ben touched her fingertips with his and gazed about. They were alone, hidden away in the heavy foliage of the brush and reeds. Gabrielle took his hand and directed him to sit down on the same old log where they had previously sat.

Putting his arm around her waist was much easier this time because she was ready for that type of hug. Ben removed his hat, set it down next to him on the log, and placed his cheek next to hers. She felt soft and moist and warm, and it felt good again. Pulling her closer now, he closed his eyes then placed his lips onto hers. She placed her hand behind his head to draw then closer, into a locked embrace.

A cool evening breeze passed by. Leaves swayed in the wind, the breeze felt comforting to both of them. Sitting there in the tranquil of the evening, Ben just couldn't help but think how beautiful she was once again. Gabrielle was lost in her need to be wanted and desired. Nothing else mattered when she was with Ben, and he was so gentle, so understanding.

She slid her hand from behind his head, moving it to waist level; he, in turn, moved his hand slowly to her right side, placing it under her right breast. Turning his head, he became more aggressive now, more eager. She sensed his feelings, and she, in turn, kissed him harder, abandoning all gentleness. But she was distracted. She could hear noise in the leaves, as though someone was approaching from the stable house area.

"Ben," she whispered, "I do hear somebody or something."

Ben slowly but surely pulled away from her and stood up and moved away, believing he heard it as well. By now, it was undeniable. Someone was coming in their direction. It was just too late for him to leave on his horse, so he would just have to act innocent. The footsteps came closer, and then a shadowy figure emerged from the trees.

"It's Charles, the stable boy," she whispered. "If you want to see me again, you better talk about your horse or something different, 'cause he'll go right to my father with this, if he thinks it's anything more than just talk. I know he will!"

Ben nodded that he understood her concern. Charles approached from the trees and saw Gabrielle at first, but not Ben.

"You want some company?" he asked, "I could give you all the company that you will ever need!"

"What are you doing out here, Charles? Don't you have stable work to do?" Gabrielle asked coldly. She didn't like him much, and wanted to get rid of him.

"Oh, I do," he replied, "But I'd rather do what you wanted me to do."

Gabrielle was taken back by that. He had never been that forward before, but he saw an opportunity and thought perhaps he could take advantage of it.

Suddenly, Bunches neighed and Charles turned about to find both a horse and a man standing not far from the pond's edge. Taken by surprise, he looked at Gabrielle and looked at the stranger again. He was sweating and looked tired. It was obvious that he had just arrived, or so they wanted Charles to believe.

"This ain't the way to the stables," Charles said, thinking that he had lost his way and followed him there from a different direction.

"I do beg your pardon, then, I must have made an error," Ben replied, thinking quickly.

"Do you have business here with that horse?" Charles asked.

"Well, yes," Ben quickly said, "I was at the racing stable earlier, and the manager told me to groom and shoe the horse if I expected him to race."

"We do that here," Charles replied without missing a beat.

"I'm very sorry I came in at the wrong gate," Ben explained, "If you could direct me to the barn?"

Charles saw no harm in the stranger's presence. He had obviously lost his way on the big plantation. Ben quickly looked at Gabrielle. He could tell that she was quite satisfied with the way he handled that situation. Best of all, he hadn't lied. He had been at the race track speaking with the manager, and his horse did need shoeing. He hadn't planned on having it done right away, but it had to be done anyway, so his excuse was an excellent cover up.

"Charles, why don't you take him to the stables?" Gabrielle asked.

Charles was devastated. He had waited all this time for a chance to be alone with Gabrielle and talk with her, and now a lost, wandering stranger had ruined all of it. If he wanted to look like a gentleman, he would do what she had asked, and he knew it.

Being alone with Gabrielle was a cherished thought to him, but there would be another time. To Ben, it was all rather disappointing. He had been interrupted, and it just didn't seem right.

"You're out here quite a bit," Charles said to Gabrielle, "I'll be back another time, then."

Ben followed Charles back to the stables. He could easily shoe and groom his own horse, and to have a stableman do it, especially one from the Chateau Villa's stable, was going to be expensive. Perhaps he would think up an excuse really quick.

"I'm mighty tired from riding and do pardon me for saying so, but I'd rather bring him back another day," Ben said.

"Suit yourself," Charles replied.

Not wanting to look completely rude, Ben asked for a tour of the stables and promised to come back with the horse soon. Gabrielle was now worried. Charles had let it slip that he knew that she was out there by the pond quite a bit. How could he know unless he was watching her as she passed by the stable building? She would make it a point to guard herself from being caught alone out there. She didn't care for his up-front, aggressive attitude. She had never seen that in him before and didn't like what she saw at all.

Ben mounted his horse and trotted down the cobblestone drive, glad in one way and yet disappointed in another. He had been with Gabrielle, if only for a moment, it seemed.

He thought about what she had said, expressing her apparent fear that Charles would tell her father. Perhaps she was afraid of her father, but perhaps she was ashamed of their affectionate relationship, or perhaps Charles was watching her to report her daily activities to her father, as well. It was just too far reaching for Ben to think on, but one thing was for sure: Gabrielle wanted to keep it a secret. Ben respected her for that.

As he arrived home, he knew that he was late for supper, and it was a strictly enforced family rule that everyone needed be on time for the evening event. He removed the saddle and led his horse to the water and the hay trough in the barn.

"We'll show 'em Bunches! You ain't just another horse!"

"Talking to yourself?" asked his father from a far darkened corner.

Very surprised and embarrassed that he had been caught talking to his horse, he turned away and then looked back again. John was just looking at him.

"We all do it from time to time," John said, "Supper ain't quite ready. I thought you'd be coming home soon enough. We all did. You aren't usually one to be late You must have had a reason. May I ask what it was?"

"Yeah," Ben responded, "I was at the race horse stables and finally talked to the manager. I have been waiting pretty near six weeks to get in and talk to him."

John sighed and slowly said, "We've had this discussion before, Ben. If you are still thinking about running Bunches at the race track, I would rethink it."

"But why, father?" Ben asked.

"Ben, folks around here have powerful money and they don't like to lose. I'm not saying that Bunches is a loser, but you need to consider what's involved with being new. The folks around here have no idea who you are, or who Bunches is. They won't want to just take a chance on a newcomer. You have to prove yourself first."

"The manager of the stables asked me if I have any representation. What did he mean by that?" Ben asked.

"That's what I'm talking about, Ben. You are use to small races. Well, these aren't small. He wants to know if you have a manager. He knows good and well that you cain't make it on your own. Big time money is won and lost on that track, and it isn't like Atlanta where you can just challenge anybody on a country road."

"I didn't expect to do as much," Ben responded.

This conversation was not the type that John wanted to be having with Ben at that moment. He had hoped that when he did see his son, the conversation would be on a lighter note. John knew that Ben wanted to race, and he also knew that he eventually would. It was his passion; John knew that, and was not trying to discourage him from pursuing his dream. Trying to change the subject to something even more sensitive, John looked away, and then looked back to Ben.

"Son, you know where I stand on slavery. I feel that it's wrong, and the country is coming apart over it. Those rich Fontenot people in that beautiful mansion have an army of slaves, and on my way home tonight I saw Pierre Fontenot bidding on slaves for resale. He had quite a crowd around him. He makes a lot of money doing that.

It doesn't take much to figure out where a lot of his money comes from."

"What does that have to do with me?" Ben asked.

"We aren't like that, Ben. You need to be careful with being friends with that girl. You need to know that they won't have anything to do with us because of my views on slavery. Oh, I know that what we did when his wife passed away was respectful and kind, but behind all that, on his part, is a cold shoulder and indifference. It's nothing personal. They just don't agree with how I feel. It's difficult trying to blend in here. People don't understand us just because we are white they expect us to be slave owners," John explained.

Ben could sense something foreboding in the conversation then. He had a dreadful feeling that his father didn't want him to see Gabrielle anymore. He was feeling crushed, defeated, and caught in the middle of a dangerous, intimate, relationship. He wanted to just tell his father that he loved Gabrielle and would continue to see her, and he knew that Pierre and John were not ever going to get along. That had nothing to do with Gabrielle, or with him.

Ben and his father walked out of the barn together, toward the back door of the huge, rear porch. It was not quite twilight yet, but darker than when he was with Gabrielle.

Looking across the road, into the horizon, he glanced twice and quickly looked away. Standing near the back door of the huge La Rue St. Lazar mansion, he could see a clear view of the exact spot where he and Gabrielle had been. It wasn't hidden. Anybody that was standing in this exact spot could easily see them there, hugging and kissing.

He felt humiliated as the thought occurred to him that perhaps his father had seen them there. It seemed to make sense to him that he may have. His father had never discussed her before, but now he was open and frank about her. Something had prompted him to be laying in wait for Ben to come home and speak with him like that. They had engaged in a discussion about the horse before, but never about 'that girl,' as John had put it.

Everything seemed normal when Ben and John entered the house, but Ben could not get the possibility that his father may have seen something off of his mind. As usual, Amanda had a huge supper prepared. Elizabeth helped her get it all onto the table.

"We're just a little late this evening," Amanda explained, "Hope this smoked pork tastes alright. We had to wait a long time at the smokehouse. I thought Elizabeth here was going to pitch a fit waiting."

Elizabeth just blushed and turned away. True, she was getting impatient with the butcher, but all the time that they had spent there meant less time at the exquisite dress shop. Raw meat stank, too, and dresses were so pretty. Elizabeth was glad that she wasn't a butcher. All she wanted to do the whole time they had been there was leave and go look at dresses.

Amanda finished setting most of the table herself. She hadn't meant to embarrass her daughter in re-telling the story of what had occurred, but it just happened that way. She suspected that Elizabeth had a secret beau because she was all too caught up with looking nice and wearing clean, attractive sun dresses complete with a parasol.

Elizabeth got over it and seated herself at the table. John and Ben returned from the wash basin and dried their hands on a hand towel. Upon being silently asked to do so by his father's glance, Ben said grace over the meal and they all started eating. Ben sensed that his mother knew that John had met him the barn and worse yet, perhaps she knew about him and Gabrielle. Perhaps it was her that had seen them and alerted her husband to it. That was just a feeling that he had, although he could prove nothing. But his mother seemed to be in a livelier mood than usual, so perhaps Ben was just imagining things. Still, his father's remarks about Gabrielle had caught him off guard.

Later, as he lay in bed, he thought about the day and the time that he had with Gabrielle. He decided that, if indeed their little hiding spot was discovered, they would just have to find another. He would need to talk to Gabrielle about finding a new spot. He knew that she would.

His father's words didn't bother him at all. He knew Gabrielle, and his father did not. Gabrielle had nothing to do with slavery. Her father was the one that bought and sold slaves, not her.

Perhaps he would part with some money and have the Chateau Villa's stablemen shoe and groom Bunches. If anything, it would give him an excuse to see Gabrielle again.

He could arrive supposedly under the pretext of inquiring about a manager. If he didn't have what it took to race his horse by himself, perhaps someone at the Chateau Villa could help him; someone such as Gabrielle.

Chapter 26
A New Responsibility

Ben's plans were slightly changed the next morning at the breakfast table.

"Ben, would you like a job?" His father asked. The question seemed a bit out of the blue, but Ben was old enough.

"I guess I am at the age where I should think about getting one," Ben stated, "Did you have anything specific in mind?"

"Well, yes, as a mater of fact, I did. How about working for the railroad? I am sure we could let you do something if you are interested, but that would also mean less time with Bunches," John responded.

"Well, what would I be doing?" Ben inquired, surprised by this turn of events.

"Working at the depot, you would be loading and unloading incoming and departing trains," his father responded.

"You need something to do, Ben, and there have been a lot of depot resignations at the railroad. I think you should do this, if my opinion counts. Farming isn't for you, just like it wasn't for us," his mother explained.

"Well, why are the men quitting?" Ben asked.

"Well," John responded as he glanced at his wife, "There has been talk of the railroad splitting in two, one half going to the north and the other going to the south. They are worried about that and are running scared because of it."

"I see. So, it's just like you were saying in the barn, then. The railroad, as well as the country, is dividing?" Ben asked with concern.

"I don't know for sure. Nobody knows for sure. But, we are all scared about it, and lots of men are quitting. We need the help if you want to work. You would be paid well, you don't have to work more than thirty-five hours a week, and the experience would do you good. Besides, if you ever needed to travel, the tickets would be dirt cheap. You have holidays off, and you can even take short vacations if you want," John said.

"What about Bunches?" Ben asked, "He's use to get worked out everyday."

"He'll be just fine," John explained.

A non-farming job looked very good to Ben. He knew it was more secure. Besides, he could use some money, and the pay was good.

"Why don't you think on it, Ben?" John said, "We could sure use you over there. There are some other local boys that will be working there. They are not making the money that you'll make, but they are local boys. You've seem 'em about town."

"That's fair, father," he replied, "I'll just think on it, then."

"Can you take care of the back property today, Ben?" His mother asked.

"Sure mama," he replied, as he finished his breakfast.

Elizabeth went on about her business, helping her mother with general household chores.

"Well," John teased, "I don't think that the railroad can live without me, so I'm off and running."

Amanda followed her husband outside to the back area. John mounted his awaiting horse and gave her a kiss for the day, as was their custom. Both Ben and Elizabeth knew that they did that and dared not venture towards them during that time.

Ben pushed his chair in close to the table and went on about finishing his business, as he had some tall foliage to cut down on the back property. Looking out of the window towards the back, he sighed at the thought of his task. It seemed like a great challenge to him.

"It won't be all that much," Amanda stated as she entered the room and noticed him gazing out.

"I know. But, it just seems like that, though. I'll get after it," he replied.

Ben knew that he had a huge task in front of him, and that his mother was just saying that it wasn't so big to make him feel better. It was a job that he meant to do for weeks, but he'd never gotten around to it. Having his mother remind him of it was almost humiliating.

"It's not gonna get done if you just stand there!" Elizabeth taunted.

Ben just gave her a dirty look as he headed out of the back door.

Over the next couple days, Gabrielle's sinking feeling that Charles was watching her and perhaps even reporting back to her father on her villa whereabouts increased in intensity. She would find a way to get around it. Finding a way to visit the pond without being noticed, with Ben, and get back to the mansion was a personal mission for her. But Charles had appeared at the pond for a reason, and at the wrong time. She didn't care for him sneaking up on her like that, as well as his rather forward comments.

"That pond sure is looking good, Miss Gabrielle!" Miss Prissy stated one afternoon, "Why, I can see most of it from Miss Anna's former window."

"Oh, it's just that it's a part of the villa and it hasn't been taken care of in so long," Gabrielle responded, "It's just nice to see something different. I remember catching butterflies out there, and it was so well-kept then. I just want to remember it like that."

Gabrielle tucked her observation away in the back of her mind. She wondered if it really was as striking as Miss Prissy said it was when you looked at it from the window. She would visit her late mothers' bed room and see for herself without saying as much. If the area where they were could be seen from that angle, she would change it to hide it from view.

"Will you be out there today, Miss Gabrielle? If you are planning to go out there, don't stay out there for too long. That heat is almost unbearable. We have already had enough deaths in this family recently. I don't need you having sunstroke on top of everything else. I'll have some cold lemonade made for you when you come in," Miss Prissy said.

"I just might go out there for awhile," Gabrielle replied.

Of utmost concern to Gabrielle was to inspect the pond area from the window, and then she would plan, go outside and speak with the workmen about any further improvements.

"We'll have a hot bath ready for you when you come in, as well," Juneau, a colored matron stated. She had a plate of cookies and Gabrielle took one.

"Aw, now c'mon honey child, eat some more," Miss Prissy said, "You don't eat enough to feed a bird."

"It ain't tha same without mama," Gabrielle lamented.

Miss Prissy turned away at her comment; it was true, though. Life wasn't the same at the villa. In any event, Gabrielle was happy with the progress on the pond. It was starting to take shape, and everyone thought that it was a tribute to her mother. She would just let them think that. It was better to allow them to believe that than to tell anyone the truth. She had seemingly expressed interest in it shortly after her mother passed, but to Gabrielle, it wasn't a memorial.

Making her way to her mother's bedroom, she peered out of the window and could see that only a portion of the pond could be seen. Thankfully, the area where she and Ben had been sitting could barely be seen, but it was visible. It was visible enough to observe that there were two people sitting on that log, but not to see what they were doing.

Much to her relief, from the window, Gabrielle could also see that from Charles' prospective, he was able to see little. Miss Prissy's innocent observation had proven true to a small extent. Gabrielle would make sure that the area in question would be hidden by tall foliage, neatly planted to match the landscaping ideas that she previously had in mind.

She had entered and exited her late mother's bedroom without arousing suspicion. That was important. Miss Prissy would immediately know that she had been in there, and that would cause her to ask many questions. Gabrielle did not want to have to answer any questions.

"Juneau, I think ah will go out to the pond area. I think those workmen need to be told a thing or two," Gabrielle said as she laced up her riding boots, "While I'm out there, I'll ride Samson for awhile. I know that it's hot out there, so I wont be out there too long."

"Oh, alright then," she replied, "I'll have a bath ready for ya when ye come back."

Miss Prissy assured her, as well, that she would have lemonade made, once again warning her not to stay out in the hot sun as long as she had on previous days.

Gabrielle opened the massive doors, entering what felt like a steam bath outside. It was only mid morning, but it was a very humid day already. As she headed for the stables, the stablemen saw her coming and knew that she wanted to ride Samson. They didn't have to be told which horse to get ready for her.

"Give us just a little bit, Miss Gabrielle. I'll have Charles go get him from the stall and get him saddled up and ready," one of the men said.

The thought of seeing Charles again didn't exactly appeal to her at this particular moment. She didn't even want him to know that she was going riding. She thought that he might actually be planning to do something to her, but she didn't want to allow herself to believe that. Fortunately, she didn't plan on stopping at the pond for too long.

Looking across the horizon, beyond several out buildings, she could see the workmen squaring a fence line that she had requested earlier. She looked over the area that she wanted concealed better and figured out the final details in her mind.

Waiting for what seemed like an eternity in the cool shade of the stable, her horse was finally brought around from the side of the stable building. Charles tugged at the reins to make the horse stop right near Gabrielle at the main opening to the area where the stable and outbuildings were.

"Here you go," He said, "He's all ready. I gave him some water so he will be good for awhile."

"Thank you, Charles. I won't be out long," she replied as she threw her leg up and over the saddle.

"Anytime, Gabrielle, anytime," Charles sneered as she glanced at him; then she turned away.

She didn't particularly care for his parting comment. It wasn't the words that scared her, but his tone. She knew all too well what his intentions were, and they were just a little beyond being cordial.

She headed out to the pond area to inspect the progress up close. She found that since the last time she was there, they had made substantial progress.

"Top of the morning!" greeted the crew foreman.

"Good morning to you, as well, Caleb. I've come out here to see if you wouldn't mind a few alterations in the landscaping you are doing, although I must say that you are doing well."

"What's on your mind, Miss Gabrielle? What can we help you with today?" He replied. Gabrielle dismounted and walked over to where he was standing.

"Let me show you," She explained, "It won't be much, and the rest of it looks so good. Your crew is doing such a fine job here. It's starting to look beautiful."

Having said that, she walked over to the log where she and Ben normally sat.

"I'd like thick bushes on both sides of this log," She said, "Please make certain that they conceal this location from view. Perhaps a small tree behind it, as well. Maybe an apple tree?" Gabrielle suggested.

"An apple tree is not small, but I think it would blend in well, if my opinion matters,

an apple tree it is, then. Some of those trees really make nice apples, and dozens of them. You will be able to enjoy fresh apples every year," Caleb responded.

Satisfied that she had adequately expressed what she wanted, she once again complimented them on their improvement efforts and got back on her horse. It was a very hot day, so she wouldn't stay out too long, but she wanted to give Samson a workout. Nudging the reins, the horse moved forward, quickly picking up speed until he had reached a slow trot. They moved away from the pond area and towards the drive.

Charles gave her a slight chuckle and a wink as she passed by the stables. She pretended not to see that as she headed toward the road. Turning right, she continued onward, almost into a full gallop now. Samson was ready to run, but they were moving into the wind. She had all she could do to stay in the saddle. The wind was trying to force her off balance.

She was coming up to the edge of the La Rue St. Lazar mansion now. Ben lived there, and she found it difficult to resist the urge to knock on his door and see if he was home. Her desire to see him only increased when she remembered the time when she had fallen off of her horse and he had come to her aid.

Slowing the horse down, she looked over to the right. She was suddenly very glad she had not knocked at the door. She saw him with a sickle, hard at work, cutting down tall reeds.

"Well now!" she called out, "Doesn't that beat all? There's a white man doing a black man's work," she teased.

"Ah, come on now. The color of your skin and mine doesn't make us any better or worse than any colored man," Ben said with a smile. He didn't mind her slight off-beat humor, as she knew that they didn't own any slaves.

Wiping his forehead with his forearm wasn't exactly the most gentlemanly thing that he could do at that moment, but it was the only thing that he could think of. He was sweating profusely in the hot sun, but she, too, was a sight for sore eyes. Her arrival there was an absolute surprise.

"Perhaps you are a damsel in distress?" he joked.

"Depends on what kind of distress you may have in mind," she teased back.

"As long as you don't fall off of that horse, I think we'll get along just fine," he teased back, again.

Dismounting, she took Samson and led him away from the road, hiding him behind a small grove of tall, wild reeds. Gabrielle didn't mind at all that he was sweaty; after all, it was a hot day. Looking about, Ben saw that they were completely shielded from anybody's vision. The area was too far to see from the La Rue St. Lazar mansion, and the foliage was too dense to allow anyone to see anything from the road.

"I'm glad to see you," she said softly, "I'm so sorry that Charles disturbed us the last time, when we were at the pond. I have made recent improvements to the pond."

"You have? Why?" Ben asked.

"Well, papa thinks I asked to have it made nice there again as a memorial to my mother. We'll just let him think that. It isn't hurting either of us. But you and I both know that's not the truth," Gabrielle said with a mischievous laugh.

"Who is that Charles? I have seen him before, and wondered who he was," Ben responded.

"Oh, he's just the stable boy. There's something about him that isn't right. He gives me a bad feeling. I can't place my finger on what exactly it is about him that makes me so sure he doesn't have my best interests at heart, but something isn't right," Gabrielle said.

"Well, you have a good head on your shoulders. You need to trust your instincts," Ben advised.

"My instincts tell me that he is bad and wants to hurt me," Gabrielle admitted.

"Does your father know that?" Ben asked.

"If I told him, he would ask a lot of questions, and I really have no evidence. It's just a foreboding gut feeling I have. Besides, he likes me, but I don't like him at all. I like you," Gabrielle said quietly.

With that, Gabrielle reached her hand toward him and he pulled her closer to him. Together, they stepped backwards and deliberately fell into the tall reeds. It was easier for Ben this time. She had extended her hand to him in a sensual, ready gesture, and he could sense that feeling in her.

Gabrielle had never felt this way before. It was exciting to her. Ben placed his nose close to her neck and inhaled her sweet fragrance; there was nothing that he could think of that compared to it. Closing his eyes, he savored that precious touch and fragrance, if only for a moment.

Gabrielle's heart began to race. Was this the right thing to do? Oh, yes, it was. It had to be. It felt so right, so natural and exhilarating. Her senses overwhelmed, she surrendered to her emotions and let perfect peace wash over her.

Moving his head toward hers, he briefly scanned her beautiful face. Her eyes were closed. She was ready for his love. Placing his lips on hers, he pulled her closer now, in a locked embrace. She placed her fingers behind his head and pulled him even closer than what they had been. Rolling over and over in the hot, parched, tall reeds they moved about with carefree abandonment.

It felt so good to Ben to be carefree, so unobstructed, and so firm but gentle at the same time. Gabrielle felt powerless to evade him, and she didn't really want to. She had never felt this way before. She sensed the sweat from his body and didn't mind it at all as he reached toward her side, placing his hand under her right breast.

Breaking the passionate kiss, she repeatedly kissed his neck, until she had circled it in kisses from front to back. It felt so good to be alone with him and not worry about being seen or being interrupted. Moving his hand slightly upwards, he held her breast. It was soft and warm and tender.

She didn't mind at all, moving more freely so that he could have better control because it felt so good. He kissed her with more fervor and passion now, even more aggressively than before, and it felt so good to be free. From his chin and then to his neck, Ben held his head up while she kissed and nudged him in the throat area. She was receptive as he pulled her towards him at the waist area. It felt so good there, so natural. Communicating without words, they rolled over and over and could not seemingly get enough of each other's love.

In a moment her fingers, along with her long, well-cared-for finger nails, slid under his shirt and stroked his back, gentle at first and then more aggressively. Now he was on top of her. He closed his eyes and looked ever skyward. It felt so good to be touched like that that he could hardly take it.

Kissing her more passionately, he copied her idea and kissed her neck from the front to the back. She, in turn, closed her eyes and craned her neck so that he could have better control. It felt so good to her; she had never experienced anything like this before. It was so secret and so private to be with him like this. It was so wonderful that nothing else mattered. Like most girls her age, she was only thinking of what was happening at that moment, not any possible consequences to her actions.

Turning on their sides now, she gently raked her fingernails across his stomach and upward toward his sweaty, hairy, chest. He unbuttoned his shirt to give her more freedom with him. To him, too, it felt so good to be touched like that. She now did two things; she kissed him and massaged his chest at the same time, mostly together, then alternately. At the moment, she was in control, and he loved every minute of it. Her fingers felt so sensual on his skin and so soothing to the touch, stirring within him a feeling of absolutely heavenly freedom. He couldn't have imagined anything feeling this good at all, but this was very real indeed.

Lost in the moment, he gently raked his fingers through her hair again, all the while kissing her more gently, and then more aggressively. She responded with the same eagerness, a wanting, and a driving passion, that feeling that desired to satisfy him. Not at all caring and experimenting with their passions, they continued to kiss and hold and hug and touch in the sweltering, humid heat. It was a wonderful and endearing feeling, a very personal secret.

Ben gently rolled away from her and onto his back. The sweltering heat was becoming overwhelming. Somehow the tall reeds felt even hotter. He had never been so happy in all his life. It almost felt as though he had just released an untamed animal that had been penned up in him for years.

"Was that all too much for you? Are you feeling well?" she whispered.

"Oh," he gasped, "Suddenly I'm so hot that I can't stand it much longer!"

Ben staggered to his knees and then his feet as he looked down at her. She was outstandingly beautiful, even in the tall reeds of the hot day. She looked at him with concern.

"I'm sorry Ben. It was my fault for keeping you so long," she stated guiltily.

Her hair flowed to the left and right, and down to her waist. Her flashing eyes told of lust for him. She slightly bit her lower lip in anticipation of what he was going to do next. It was an enticing gesture, a tempting gesture that he could not respond to right at that moment. She was ready for more, but he wasn't at the moment.

Almost gasping for breath now, Ben bent over and rested his hands on his knees to breathe better. He was coming around now. She hadn't been in the hot sun most of the morning, either, like he had. He had needed to help his father fix some planks in the barn's roof that were starting to weaken and leak. He had hoped that she would understand that he was done for the time being.

She sat straight up and brushed away the reeds' debris from her shoulders and hips. Then, standing up completely, she in a moment realized how exhausted he was. He was sweating and looked a bit flushed. His eyes twinkled wearily. His legs and arms were limp.

"I didn't mean to keep you out here this long, Ben," she again said, almost apologetic this time.

"Oh, Gabrielle, don't worry about it. I willingly did what I did. It was my choice, and I can handle the results of my actions. It isn't like you made me do what I did with you. I enjoyed myself. It was so free, natural and good. I hope you felt the same way. I'll be fine," he replied.

"I enjoyed myself very much. I know I have never felt anything like that in all my life. It was so beautiful that I almost cried," Gabrielle confessed.

Brushing herself off with her hands, she suddenly thought of the irony in it all. She had been, just an hour earlier, making requests of the workmen who were preparing the pond area for them. In the end, it would serve as an expensive, personal secret retreat. Now, here in the wild reeds of this hot day, they hugged and kissed and held one another without being noticed.

"I'm feeing better now, Gabrielle, so why don't we just sit here and talk for a little bit?"

"Alright, Ben," she replied, "But I can't be too long. Miss Prissy, and worse, my papa, may wonder where I am and come looking for me. Miss Prissy worries about me, especially since my mother passed."

"Does she take care of you now?" Ben asked.

"I am old enough to mostly take care of what I need to do. Those matrons still cook for us, and they do a fine job of it. Daddy likes what they make," Gabrielle stated.

"I have never had coloreds. My papa is very much against slavery. We get mistreated wherever we go because of that," Ben admitted sadly.

"How do you feel about it?" Gabrielle asked him.

"I think every person is a human being and deserves to have the same rights, whatever the color of their skin is," Ben replied.

"As far as I have ever seen, papa treats our coloreds well. I know not all masters do. But doesn't the Bible say something about slaves obeying their masters, or something like that?" Gabrielle asked.

"Yes, I do believe so. But it also says that God created man in His own image, with free will. That free will has been taken away when a person becomes enslaved. Also, the Israelites were slaves for hundreds of years, but God eventually led them into the promise land. Does that show you that He likes slavery?" Ben asked.

Gabrielle looked down for a minute, and then responded, "I suppose not. Does that mean all the slave masters that ever have had slaves are going to hell?"

The question caught Ben by surprise. How could she have drawn that conclusion from what he had said? Well, somehow she had. It didn't really matter how.

"Oh, no Gabrielle, of course not!" Ben exclaimed.

"I was just wondering how you felt about that," Gabrielle replied.

"God never changes," Ben replied.

"Everything changes," Gabrielle said firmly.

"You're right, Gabrielle," Ben said, his voice so sure that it cut right to Gabrielle's core.

"You really do care about me, don't you, Ben Chesser? And you not only care about me, but you care about my heart, too, don't you?" she asked.

"I care about you, yes, and I know that you are hurting right now, and I also know that God alone can help you to truly heal," Ben said softly.

"It is mighty hot out here!" Ben observed as he wiped his forehead on his sleeve.

"I didn't mean to keep you all this time, Ben, I really didn't," she said as she gave him a reassuring hug. What she didn't realize was that Ben had been glad to stay. She was such a sweet girl, and he had been happy to talk with her about her well-being. He could tell that she was searching for something she had not found as of yet.

"This New Orleans sun sure is different from the sun in Atlanta," he said as he looked upward. Gabrielle laughed and playfully nudged him in the side.

"The sun is the sun no matter where it's at," she giggled.

"I've got something to tell you, Gabrielle," Ben said, "My father wants me to work for the railroad, at the depot, loading and unloading passengers' belongings for arriving and departing train passengers."

"Nothing wrong with that," she replied, "A lot of boys got jobs there, but working the depot wouldn't be at all bad."

"He wants me to start Monday," Ben replied, "Thing is, I had hoped to get my horse in a race as soon as I could, but with working I won't have time to work with him during the week."

Gabrielle thought about that one long and hard. Ben was in a tight spot. He was getting to the age where he would need to start to work; however, he wanted to race, and working would interfere.

"Well," she replied, "Don't give up just yet. Let me see what I can do. I might be able to help you out, if you want."

"Oh Gabrielle, that's awfully nice of you, and I would be more than happy to pay for any training that you might have to offer," He said.

"I think your horse has a chance," She stated, "He's fast. I've seen him run."

"Well, the man at the race stables told me that I would need a manager," Ben replied as he wiped his face again and added, "I don't have one."

"Well," she thought out loud, "He is right. All of the horses have owners and managers and jockeys, so you do have a ways to go, but your horse still has to run in front of them and look good," she observed.

"Do you think I have a good chance at running him at the track, all things considered?" Ben asked.

"You have an excellent chance. Yours is the same as everybody else, Ben. Remember… all of the owners and the jockeys had to start somewhere," she replied.

Her confidence made Ben crack a broad grin that was much deeper than his skin.

"Will I see you again before I have to go to work?' he asked.

His question wasn't immediately answered. Instead, she responded with a hug and a kiss on the lips, then said, "If you want to see me again… you know where ah live."

"That is something I do know," he replied, as he kissed her back.

"I have to go, Ben," she said as she nudged her cheek against his, "You look like you're ready to pass out from lack of cool water."

"I am just a little warm and thirsty, but I promise you that I will take care of that when I get home. I'll be fine," he replied, "Can't wait to see you again."

Gabrielle again brushed off the remaining debris from her shoulders and turned and smiled back at him as she stepped away from their hidden recluse in the tall reeds.

Ben watched as she disappeared from view, not moving. He heard her mount her horse, and then heard the horse slowly trot toward the road. He wanted to see her off, but he didn't dare. He was afraid that he would be seen, that they would be caught in the reeds, and there would be no explanation for it.

He didn't mind if there was reed debris all over him. His family knew that whenever he left for as long as he had, he would come back covered in mud or dirt or something else. The same was not true of Gabrielle, though. She was always expected to stay as prim and proper as possible.

He had been out there the better part of the morning working the sickle. They had never gone that far before, and it was unexpected. They most certainly were not planning on doing what they had done. It just happened, and it was more than what he had anticipated. It was more than a passionate drive that he had for her, and he now knew that she had the same feelings for him.

The rest of the day, Gabrielle went about business as usual. Miss Prissy did notice that she seemed to be unusually upbeat. She hadn't seen Gabrielle so happy in months. For over three hours that afternoon, Gabrielle played her harp, serenading everyone with one classical piece after another.

Chapter 27
The Auction

A huge crowd of well-dressed businessmen assembled in front of the town square. They were waiting in anticipation for the arrival of the slave wagons that would soon come. Today was going to be a big money making day for those selling slaves at a premium; whole groups would be purchased and resold at a substantial profit.

"Damn near two o'clock," a businessman wearing his Sunday finest and shiny, leather shoes muttered to himself as he looked at his watch. He impatiently added, "They said two o'clock, and I got money to spend!"

"Cool off, Harrison," his friend advised, "We're all out here together. I know it's hot, which is the real reason you are so cranky. You aint the only one that's hot, so take a drink of water and you'll feel better."

More late buggies and carriages were arriving for the sale. The swelling crowd was getting restless now. They could see that the wagons were late, and it was going to be an auction where the prices would soar higher than average. They all wanted this done when it was supposed to be. If they were going to spend thousands, was it so much to ask that the sales occur when they were supposed to?

A cloud of cigar and pipe smoke almost hung overhead. The windless, hot day was starting to wear on the patience of the slave brokers. Any murmuring about the weather stopped when Pierre Fontenot arrived. Most of the time he was one of the first ones there, but on this day, he was one of the last to arrive. Heads nodded in cordial greeting as he stepped away from his buggy.

He nodded back and remarked, "This weather sure is hotter than hell out here! Let's get this over with!"

"Well, we all feel that way," a gentleman responded as he sighed heavily.

"Won't be long now," he announced, "I saw the wagons about a half a mile away. There's nine of 'em, all loaded down... today's gonna be a good day, my friends!"

Pierre's observation relaxed most of them. If he said it was going to be a good auction day, it was. Handkerchiefs wiped foreheads and the water ladle was not idle for too long between uses. It seemed like an eternity passed as the large crowd waited under the blazing, merciless sun.

"Here they come!" yelled a voice from the crowd.

Heads turned to get a first look at the so-called 'merchandise' up for auction. Each person would be inspected before the auction, and the ones that appeared to be in better health would be auctioned off first. Then, the ones that were skinny or otherwise looked sickly would be sold second, until the whole lot was auctioned off. Without a second thought on the part of the new owners, mothers, fathers and children would be forcibly separated, sometimes as soon as the previous owners believed that the child was old enough to survive without a mother or father.

Each wagon stopped at a designated area. Young boys pulled down the side gates to the old, creaky wagons. The crowd waited even longer as each slave was placed into a first group to be looked at, and then the second one to be sold. Money was already flashing overhead in anticipation of a fast sale. Some buyers waved their money at the group that they wanted to bid on. None of the soon-to-enslaved colored people even wanted to look at the whites that would soon be their masters.

"Alright, alright!" the auctioneer bellowed as he held his arms high, "It's hot out here and we all know it is! We have to do this as quickly and as organized as we can, so just keep your money to yourselves until we get them all grouped."

When he had said that, each male and female slave was pulled away from the wagon and visually inspected, then separated according to height, weight and general appearance. Those that resisted had the blunt end of a rifle shoved into their back, but care was taken not to injure them because the wagon master made a percentage of the sale, and he in turn paid his helpers.

"These are salable coloreds! Get them out here!" the auctioneer yelled, "We ain't got all day!"

Pierre had his eye on several, but he would have to wait for a chance to bid just like everyone else. Finally, the first group was ready for the auction block. A tall, muscular black male stood before the crowd. He was the first and looked to be the strongest and healthiest of the whole group. But everyone there had taken advantage of the fact that harvest had concluded, so peak season for selling and buying slaves was over. The male would have fetched four or five times what they would pay that day just a few weeks earlier.

The crowd morale had greatly improved; perspiring faces ignored the handkerchiefs. It was time to make some money. The auctioneer held his gavel high as was his custom. Once the crowd settled down he commenced the bidding.

"We'll start at two hundred here!" he shouted.

"Two fifty!" yelled a voice from the crowd.

"Three hundred here!" shrieked an old man.

"Three hundred fifty!" yelled the first bidder again.

"Four hundred and twenty dollars!" hollered a boy that looked to be about twenty.

"Four hundred and forty!" yelled the first bidder again.

"Five hundred," Stated a man near the auctioneer.

"Six hundred," Another almost immediately stated, his friends looking at him like he had gone insane.

"Eight hundred!" bellowed the first bidder once again.

"Eight hundred fifty!" a new voice chimed in.

"Nine hundred twenty-five!" yelled the fist bidder again.

"One thousand, two hundred dollars!" screamed a voice, and everyone fell silent in shock.

"Going once! Going twice!" the auctioneer shouted.

"Fifteen hundred!" Pierre Fontenot shouted, "Got the cash right here!"

"Sixteen hundred!" another shouted in retaliation, "And I've got cash too!"

Pierre let it go. The other man wanted the slave more. All Pierre wanted was to buy a good, strong healthy one to tale care of the pond area, year round. But, there were others in the group who were just as strong.

"Going once, going twice!" the auctioneer shouted, "Sold to Jacque, the saddle maker for sixteen hundred."

Jacque looked over and gave Pierre a contemptible look of triumph. He had won, and it wasn't like Pierre to back off of a bid, but Pierre knew what he wanted that slave for. He wanted him to do all of the heavy work involved in making saddles for the cavalry. Fine, let Jacque have his way. There would be more slaves to buy; if not that day, then some other time.

After some thought, Pierre reasoned that Jacque would keep
his newly purchased slave for a time and then resell him. Pierre was
almost certain he would have a chance at this slave again. He didn't
mind losing to Jacque, because the faster the government's saddles
were done, the sooner the new racing saddle could be manufactured.
Pierre could see right through Jacque's logic.

Another one was brought up to the block. He appeared to be just
as healthy. He looked resolutely out at the crowd. If this was how
things had to be, he determined within himself to make the best of it.
He stood as tall as he could, his shoulders back. Although not as tall
as the first, he looked to be every bit as strong.

"Three hundred! Do I hear three fifty?!" the auctioneer shouted.
A well-dressed, bearded man waved to him for the bid. Another man
outbid him, and then another. The bidding came to a halt at seven
hundred and fifty dollars.

"Last call now!" the auctioneer yelled at the crowd, "Going once,
going twice, sold for seven hundred and fifty cash!"

Money changed hands quickly as each slave was presented to the
crowd and auctioned off. The bidding was fast, quicker than usual,
and eventually all of the wagons were empty. The wagon master
smiled as he accepted his handful of cash for the day's proceeds.

But there was another auction behind this one, that one an
auction for slaves that had already been used and were no longer
needed. It was an opportunity for the owners to get there money back
during non-harvest time; they could always purchase different ones
later if they ended up needing more slaves. The auctioneer nodded
that he was ready, and those that had slaves for sale brought them up
front for inspection.

Most plantations' owners were reselling. Slaves were expensive
to maintain during the off season. Pierre always thought it was
resourceful to keep his because he ended up saving money and
actually getting somewhat attached to them. Colored people though

they were, they were still people that had needs and emotions. He didn't trade his away like others did.

Older used slaves were sold in lots of three to five, for the same price as a colored person that had never been sold. Some of the ones that had not been well cared for looked gaunt and weak. It was obvious that quite a few had been whipped. Pierre almost felt bad for some of them, especially the children. Later, the next time they were sold, they would be purchased in another town as so-called 'new slaves.'

Black slave women that had never been to the auction before screamed as their children were pried forcibly from their arms. They had been assured earlier that they would be sold together. The children were petrified at the thought of being alone, but neither the mothers nor the children could do anything.

"Baby! No, don't take him! He's only four! Dear Lord, have mercy! Please don't take him!" one woman shrieked as her young son clung to her neck. Her back had been aching from supporting his weight so long. Now, she would give anything to hold him and never let go.

The child panicked and held onto his mother as if his life depended on staying with her. He screamed as a fully grown man yanked them apart with brute force. His mother crumpled in the dirt, weeping and silently praying in her shattered heart. Through tear blurred vision, she caught one last glimpse of her son, who was reaching in vain for her and screaming. The auctioneer was getting impatient in the heat of the day. These were the last of it and then it would be time to go home.

"Slap tha hell out of that nigger bitch!" he yelled, "We aint got all day!"

Two men took the grief stricken mother aside and beat her. Though they beat her until she had bruises on her face, arms and even her chest, the physical pain they inflicted on her was nothing compared to her aching heart. Though she prayed she was mistaken, she knew she may never see her son again. Their separation seemed so senseless and heartless to her. How would a four-year-old take care of himself?

The major buyers were getting impatient. They would buy slaves in bulk and re-sell them to slave brokers, who in turn, re-sold them in different towns and cities. Contributing to the crowd's impatience was the fact that the sun was unbearably hot and the slave wagons had been late as it was.

Trying to be protective of their children and women that they loved, black men shouted, arguing to keep their families together. Unfortunately, it was useless. Several men, as well as women, were knocked to the ground and tied with ropes to keep them from resisting. Men anguished and women screamed as their children were herded to the auction block.

"Please... Master Simpson!" one slave woman begged and pleaded in broken English, "You promised we would be sold as a family. Keep your promise to us!"

The man, wanted to appease the crowd and deny that he said just that just spit on her and turned away. She trembled and cried while her young daughter was taken away.

"Mama, be strong for me! Be strong! I will see you again! If not before then, I will see you in glory land!" The skinny but strong little girl yelled as she caught one final glimpse of her mother's tear streaked face.

"I love you, baby! Jesus loves you, too!" her mother muttered as her lips formed the words. She could not believe this tragedy was unfolding, but it was, and there was nothing she could do. At that point, she had to take her daughter's final words to heart. She had to be strong and believe that they would see each other again one day.

"Alright! Alright!" the auctioneer shouted as he wiped his forehead, "Let's get on with it!"

"Are these field niggers or house niggers?" a voice from the crowd yelled.

"They are what you want them to be!" the auctioneer responded.

Black women continued to yell, scream and cry as their children were successfully bid on and sold to new, white owners. Many of them would later be re-sold to a broker. Each colored child was introduced with their approximate age. From two years to sixteen years old, herds of poorly dressed black children were introduced and auctioned away. They were not allowed to go back to their anguishing parents, who were next up on the block.

The toddler-age children tried to reach back to their parents and were led away, kicking and screaming just as fervently as their parents. They had no idea what was happening to them. There would be nobody there for them to tell them they were property, though they would soon figure out that someone else owned them now. After the purchase, several of the new, white owners took a leather belt to the toddlers to get them to submit and to stop yelling and crying.

As it was, Ben and his father had been nearby in a buggy, after becoming trapped in the traffic of double and triple parked carriages and wagons near the town square.

The cobblestone streets were congested with slave-buying plantation owners.

John had been on his way to take Ben to the railroad depot to introduce him to his new job and responsibilities, but it wasn't going to happen today. It was just too hot and the streets were congested with slave buyers.

"That there is a sin, son," John mumbled to Ben, so that nobody could hear him, "Selling those people like that is the reason why the country is coming apart."

Ben said nothing as he sat, transfixed in horror by what he was witnessing. Pierre Fontenot himself had successfully purchased a male slave. Ben's heart broke at what he had seen occur next. Pierre had whipped him and put a horse's bit in his mouth as he begged to stay with his woman and three children.

"I know what you're looking at," John said, "That's Pierre Fontenot there. I'd know him anywhere, and look at that poor black man bleeding at the mouth like that. That's what happens when you stick a horse's bit in someone's mouth just for wanting to see his kids grow up. That's terrible!"

"I know father. Was his desire so wrong? Shouldn't he have the right to see his children grow up? Didn't God create those little children just like He created me and Elizabeth? How would you feel if we were just taken from you like that?" Ben quietly replied.

"It's wrong what people do, son, but God still loves even those slave masters. I saw a scene very much like this when I was half your age that you are now. I remembered it. I never saw slavery the same. I just couldn't. This is the reason why we don't have slaves. They are people, Ben, God's creations, just like you said, and they are treated like animals. This is the very thing that we tried to keep you kids away from in Atlanta. Witnessing something like this is awful, but now we happened upon it and you have seen it and know why I'm against all of this. Just look at those men beating those black children like that. I have to wonder how they can live with themselves. But the Bible does that the heart of man is dark and wicked. We are seeing that right before our eyes. There ought to be a law against that. Those poor children are being beaten like animals. Just look at that," John said compassionately.

Ben didn't want to look anymore. He turned away, wishing he had never seen anything. This scene would not leave his mind for a very long time, if it ever did.

If John could have told him anything right then, he would have said that Ben would never forget this day. He knew how he felt, and he knew that Ben shared many of his views, including his feelings on slavery. It was painful for Ben to see the brutal beatings and hear the anguished screams.

"Sin sure has an ugly face, doesn't it son?" John asked.

"Yes, sir. Lord have mercy on those coloreds," Ben responded.

"He will. He made them and loves them, too. Now, let's get out of here before we run into more evil that is the result of sin," John suggested.

"Well, the world is full of sin," Ben replied.

"Hey you!" a female's voice shouted from a porch balcony, "C'mon up here and see me. It won't cost ya much….I'm fast and good."

"Oh, no, not this again," Ben sighed, speaking barely above a whisper.

"Sin is sin, and she's being used by Satan to tempt you. I know you won't do that," John responded softly.

Ben looked up at the buildings balcony to see a buxomly frizzy haired bordello woman calling to him. It was not the same woman that had tried seducing him before, but he thought she had been with her on the balcony that day. He believed that he had seen her before.

"C'mon Sugar!" she beckoned, "You ain`t gonna buy any niggers today. They're all sold now. You're just too late, so c'mon up here and spent your money on me!"

Ben ignored her and looked ahead again, and found that he was just in time to see Pierre tie his newly purchased slave in the back of a wagon. The slave auction was now over. Ben had never been so relieved to see something end in all his life. His heart was still so heavy that it almost felt like he was being crushed.

Carriages, wagons and buggies pulled away, many with slaves of all ages in them. Street traffic was beginning to move forward again. Ben looked to the right to see the auctioneer with a huge pile of money and the slave wagon master standing there waiting for his cut.

"Damned shame," John muttered, "Those poor people!"

"It just isn't right, papa. God made them, too, just like He made us, and we hate them and mistreat them just because of the color of their skin? Is that good? Is that right? I think not," Ben said.

"I don't think so, either, but we will talk about this later. If we talk about this too loud in public, we could be beaten, like before, or have our home destroyed," John said, "We've had enough losses."

Ben looked up at the girl on the balcony. She had been trying to coax him up there the whole time, and he had been ignoring her. Actually, he knew that deep down inside, she probably was just looking for approval and love. She probably also needed the money that she made. Ben felt bad for her. He knew that she would never find real love or peace in what she was doing.

"Aw, c'mon honey, don't leave me like this!" the bordello woman yelled to Ben as they drove away, "Don't be bashful. Why don't the both of ye's come up here? I will be quick and then you can go."

Both John and Ben said nothing, but looked forward. The traffic was moving better up ahead. By that time, they both really wanted to get out of there. They had seen enough suffering at the auction, and then had an encounter that saddened them and made them uncomfortable.

"Ah didn't get what I wanted to get done accomplished today," John mentioned, "I wanted to drive down to the depot and get you your new uniforms for work and make sure we have the right sizes on hand, and enough of them. Then, I thought maybe we could start training. We still have tomorrow, I suppose."

"Uniforms, huh? Oh, yeah, I guess that everyone wears one. I became so use to seeing you in it at the railroad that I didn't pay that much mind. How many do I get?" Ben asked.

"Oh, you get several outfits, but you don't wear them home. They always stay there."

Glancing back to where the auction had been, Ben noticed the last old, creaky wagons pulling away from the auction site. Those, Ben supposed, were the wagons that would go to another city and sell the slaves again. It all seemed very inhumane to him. He didn't want to watch, but from a distance, he could not help hearing everything. He tried not to look, but could not help it; his gaze was almost transfixed again.

Colored children saw their mothers and screamed for them, their arms outstretched. Men saw their women and reached out; women saw their men and wailed all the more. It was painful to watch, heart wrenching, actually. Obviously, the black slave people had been lied to. They were assured that they would be sold together so that they could stay together.

Pierre's new purchase didn't see anybody he cared for. He was alone, and he just sat listlessly in the back of the old wagon and said nothing. To Ben it sounded like the whole world was wailing and crying. The emotion was overwhelming. He wanted to cry himself, or at least whip and beat some of the white men that had beaten some of the black children.

"Such a shame," John said when they got out of earshot of other people.

They were now on the outskirts of town, almost to the dirt road. Only a half mile remained and they would come to the end of the cobblestone streets. Finally, it was safe to talk about what he had just seen.

"Let's not come this way when they have an auction again," Ben suggested, "That all just made me so mad that I wanted to beat those white men the way they were beating those coloreds. They were so heartless about it that they didn't even spare the children! What did those children ever do to deserve to be taken from their parents and beaten?" Ben asked.

"Well, son, I am actually glad that you feel that strongly about it. You should be sad about it. It should be painful to see, and you should be angry about it. It isn't right, and it never will be. Your anger is justified," John said firmly.

"I don't care to see and hear all of that ever again," Ben responded.

"Perhaps now you can see the problems that slavery creates, it's wrong Ben, and now you can see that for yourself."

The traffic came to a stop at the next intersection. A regiment of Confederate cavalrymen and three cannons passed by, and the riders sat proudly in their saddles. They tipped their hats and waved to the adoring crowds of men and children.

"Don't wave, Ben," John whispered. He wouldn't have needed to say anything, because Ben had no desire to wave. These were men that were fighting to keep the slaves enslaved, and after what he had just witnessed, he despised slavery. He wanted the slaves freed.

One of the soldiers looked at Ben for a bit longer than the others in the crowd. He knew he had seen him before. It took a second, but he placed him. He had seen him when he was lost, and he was riding fast. Ben pretended that he didn't see the soldier, even though he indeed had remembered him.

"This local regiment is from the area," John whispered again, "More than likely; they are on their way to join up with other regiments to form a huge army company."

The crowds waved, shouted greetings and wished the Confederate regulars well as the last of them passed by the intersection. Ben noticed that Pierre's old slave wagon wasn't too far ahead. His new purchase just sat in the back, his left arm and leg tied with a rope to the side of the wagon.

"That man there," John nodded with his head, "That's Pierre Fontenot. He seems to think that a man, regardless of the color of his skin, can be bought and sold, just like a horse or another common animal."

"I know, father," Ben replied, "I know who he is. I helped his daughter get her horse out of the mud awhile back and he invited me over for dinner, remember?"

"Oh, yes, that's right. Her father has met you. Well, rest assured that now that he knows where I stand on the issue of slavery, just like most everyone in this town, he assumes that you feel the same way and doesn't like you," John said.

"I do feel the same as you do about slavery, pa. Now that I have seen how cruelly those slaves were treated, I understand completely why you feel the way you feel, and I feel the same," Ben stated.

"Well, that's good that you feel that way. You should. Any Christian should hate the injustice that is found in the way that slaves are treated, and I am glad that you saw what you saw today. I believe it opened your eyes to truths that you had not seen before. You don't need to be getting too friendly with his daughter. Pierre is not doing good things, and an apple never falls too far from the tree. There are plenty of other girls to choose from, Ben, nice church girls, just like in Atlanta," John suggested, "You're getting up to the point where you will be picking out a beau and courtin' soon and you can do better than Gabrielle Fontenot."

Ben wondered just how much he knew about Gabrielle and her family. He thought back to the area at La Rue St. Lazar and mentally tried to envision how much of the pond area could be seen from a different vantage point. Perhaps he was just imagining it all. Just because he saw it clearly in his mind didn't mean that they could in reality.

He pretended not to hear his father's comment about Gabrielle. His father didn't know her, and he didn't want to. She had a sweet, searching spirit, and was truly nothing like her father. She wanted nothing to do with slavery, so in Ben's eyes, there was nothing wrong with her.

Ben knew that Gabrielle could have her choice of many young suitors and many would stand in line for her hand, but she had chosen him. As far as the church girls were concerned, many spoke to him after church but showed no other interest beyond just social talk. He wanted more. He would need more in the relationship.

"I noticed that Brother Zachary's daughter likes you a lot," John smiled and playfully nudged his son in the side, "Ruby Lee really likes you!"

Ben wasn't interested in the discussion, but sought to appease his father. He didn't want to raise any concerns. In his heart he already knew that he loved Gabrielle.

He also knew that his father would not approve, and neither would hers. Still, that did not change the fact that they loved each other and would perhaps marry. For the time being, though, Ben had to play along with his father.

"Ya think?" he responded, as he rolled his eyes in the opposite direction, away from his father.

He couldn't care less for Ruby Lee. She was immature and she was kind of loud and not very ladylike.

"I don't think anything, I know. He's a good man, and she's a sweet girl. He works hard. Why, you know he owns that sundry store. It could be you and her get hitched, you never know. There could be two or three other stores just like it in New Orleans," he mused.

To Ben, if money was an object, not love, he could easily marry Gabrielle and be worth twenty sundry stores. He didn't care if he had a secret admirer at church or not.

He wasn't about to two time Gabrielle for a chance at Ruby Lee.

"Old Zachary's a widower and she's his only child. He could be looking for a good, local son-in-law," John mused more.

Ben was surprised at his father. He apparently had too much time to think. He had been thinking too far ahead, daydreaming all the while about things that would never happen. Marriage was too far away, and besides, Ben loved Gabrielle.

"Yeah, Ben" his father continued, "Her father will be making big money soon. This Confederate army is gonna need supplies, and where else would they go but to a sundry store?"

To Ben it looked as though his father was stuck in his daydreaming and conversation about this church girl, and wouldn't let it go. Ben was getting bored with it all. He had to change the subject.

"So father," Ben asked, "What will I be doing at my first day at the train depot?"

"Oh, the first day and even the first week, not much will be expected of you. You will just sweep tha platform and generally help out, like help the other porters… that kind of thing," He replied.

"Then I will help load and unload the baggage?" Ben asked.

"Yes, in due time," he replied.

Ben had successfully changed the subject, moving the conversation away from the church girl. He was very relieved. His father continued to ramble on about Ben's new responsibilities at the depot, but Ben wasn't listening. He noticed that Pierre's old wagon turned right. It was obvious to him that he was taking a short cut back to the Chateau. He said nothing as the old wagon disappeared in a line of street traffic.

"So, when is pay day?" Ben asked.

"Every Friday afternoon," His father replied, "The railroad pay master usually gets there about one o'clock. It's his second stop. He comes to the terminal first."

Ben had no way to be certain of his father's logic, though in the back of his mind, he suspected that the real motivation for offering him a job at the depot was to keep him away from Gabrielle Fontenot. His father believed that he would be would be too tired and worn out to even think about her, much less talk about her. He loved his horse and local racing activities, and John wanted to keep it like that. What he didn't know was that Ben also loved Gabrielle just as much, and would find time for her.

Chapter 28
Unexpected Events

Hearing someone rapping insistently, Elizabeth was the first to arrive at the door. They rarely had visitors, and this visitor was knocking louder than usual. Opening the door, she saw a man that she had never seen before. He had a beautiful black upholstered buggy parked in the drive and was dressed like a true, southern gentleman.

Tipping his hat, he stated, "I do beg your pardon, miss, but I'm Jean Fournier, the manager of the race track. I was wondering if Ben Chesser was here. I do have some racing business to discuss with him."

Amanda approached the door, hearing the sound of a strange man's voice and overhearing his introduction. Opening the door wider now, she introduced herself as Ben's mother and invited him in.

"Have a seat if you'd like. Would you like some tea? It's awfully hot out there," she stated.

"Certainly, madam," he replied, as he also accepted the invitation to sit down in the foyer.

Amanda disappeared and reappeared a moment later with a cup of tea. She had made a fresh pot just minutes before the unexpected guest arrived. The man smiled as he sipped at the glass of tea; it was a welcome relief from the heat of the day.

"I'll go get Ben," Elizabeth stated, "He's just out back."

"So," Amanda said, "You manage the racing stables? My son had mentioned briefly to us that he had been trying to see you for weeks and finally got to see you the other night, after quite some time. He loves to race, and he really wants a chance to race here. His father thinks he is not going to get that chance, but maybe you believe differently."

"Yeah? Well, sometimes persistence pays off. Indeed madam, I do own the stables. I've been at it twenty four years now," Jean replied.

Elizabeth raced to the barn as fast as her legs would carry her. Upon hearing that the racing stables' manager was waiting for him, Ben wiped his sweaty forehead on his sleeve and raked his hair with his fingers. Ben dashed past her and headed for the back door as Elizabeth remarked, "You better hurry up!"

"Ah, Ben!" Jean said as he stood up and extended his hand, "You remember me, Jean Fournier, manager of the racing stables."

"Why, certainly I do sir!" Ben replied as he shook hands with him, "Been a month and a half or so, but yes, I do remember visiting with you."

"Ben," the man explained as he sat down, "We had one of our owners up and join the Confederate regiment. We usually have nine horses on the circuit, but with him gone, it is down to eight. Well, we can't have eight. There has to be nine, so I was wondering if you would be interested in running your horse in next Saturday's race. It's a third card race. The catch is that a jockey would have to ride him, though. That's the rules, Mr. Chesser."

Ben looked at his mother with amazement. He couldn't believe his luck. She knew that this was his dream. He knew that racing was one of the desires of his heart, and that he had prayed for the opportunity to race on the big track. This seemed to be a true answer to his prayers. Her look and nod told him that it was fine with her.

"Well, sir, I'm just surprised!" he almost gasped.

"Does that mean you'll do it?" Jean asked.

"Why, sure, and I will do my best not to disappoint anyone," Ben cried ecstatically, beaming.

"Mr. Chesser, should your horse win, you, as an owner, would only get one third of the winnings. The money is split three ways between the track, the jockey and you. We each get a third."

"Well, one third is better than nothing!" Ben replied.

"Is he trained to run strong?" Jean asked.

"He's very fast, sir," Ben responded quickly and with confidence.

"Was wondering, then, if you wouldn't mind if our jockey rode him several days before the race and worked to get the signals straight with him?"

"Oh, no, not at all. He ain't ever had another man ride him, so yes, that would be good," Ben responded.

"Very good then, Mr. Chesser. I'll send a man over here Wednesday to get him. You can have him back right after the race," Jean informed him.

"Well, sir, I'm just very pleased that my horse will race after all. I've been looking forward to this for such a long time!" Ben responded with an awe and surprise.

"Just one last thing," Jean added. "Actually, two things. First I'll need your horse's name and your manager's name."

"My horse's name is Bunches, and I don't have a manager, sir," Ben replied.

"I can't be the manager…and neither can you. It has to be someone that more or less supervises you, makes sure that the horse is fed and worked out for tha race, or races should your horse win," he explained.

"His father, then," Amanda stated proudly, thinking quickly so they would not lose this golden opportunity, "He would make a good manager. He has known Bunches since he was a colt."

"His name, madam?" the manager asked, "I need to know all of this for the programs and maybe posters."

"John Chesser," Ben responded. "That's my father."

"Very good, then," he replied, "We have a horse by the name of Bunches running in the third card race on Saturday afternoon, managed by John Chesser."

"What about the jockey?" Ben asked. "When can I meet him?"

"I would prefer that you meet him on Wednesday, when we come and get the horse. A very experienced man he is. He has ridden wildcard horses before. He's a short little Irish man by the name of Fitzgerald."

"This is almost like a dream come true, like an answered prayer. I don't know what exactly to think or say. Do you know that I waited for nearly six weeks just to talk to you? Now, my horse is running in a betting race!" Ben exclaimed.

"Well, if your horse is as fast as you say he is, the jockey won't have any problems. I saw something in you, boy. There's something different and special. Everyone deserves a chance, and you are fortunate to get one. Not everyone that comes to me gets one. I believe you have a winner on your hands. I want to give him a chance. As a matter of fact, I'm ready to see tha race myself," Jean acknowledged.

"Well, I truly thank you sir!" Ben acknowledged.

"I've got to get back now. I need to promote the race on Saturday, but I thought about you and your horse and thought that you deserved a chance," he explained.

"We are most obliged, sir!" Amanda stated.

Ben tried to find some words of gratitude to say as Jean finished his tea, but his emotions overwhelmed him. Jean handed his empty glass back to Amanda and headed for the door. Turning about, he tipped his hat as Ben opened the door and watched him head for his beautiful, black buggy in the drive. Closing the door, Ben thought that perhaps he had died and gone to heaven. This was a dream come true.

"Can you believe that, mama?"

"Good thing you went over there when you did. Just wait 'til your father comes home and hears this. Won't he be surprised?" Amanda asked with a grin.

"Is Bunches really going to run in that race? Why, it's just like back home in Atlanta, except now it is for real betting money out in the open. People are going to bet that Bunches will win," Elizabeth added.

"Oh, I'm so happy for you, Ben!" his mother exclaimed as she clapped her hands together with exuberance.

"I just can't believe it," Ben responded, "Just out of the blue, the very manager that I waited six weeks to see comes knocking and wants Bunches to race? That makes all that waiting worth it."

"Well, that's one time that opportunity came knocking, and you did the right thing in letting a jockey ride him. Maybe someday, after he's proven himself to be fast, you can ride him," Elizabeth quipped.

"Oh, I'm just so happy and pleased," Amanda said again.

Ben couldn't wait until suppertime to tell his father of the surprise visit and reveal the fact that Bunches would run in next Saturday's race. Amanda wanted to make something really special in celebration of what had transpired, but she had to settle for hearty bowls of vegetable stew because they were completely out of meat. Ben didn't really care.   Before his father had even sat down, Ben blurted out excitedly, "Papa, Bunches is going to race in a race here! He's racing on Saturday!"

"Oh, papa," Elizabeth chimed in, "It's true. I was here when this all happened. I know it's something Ben really wants to do--"

"I really want to do it, But for now, a jockey has to ride Bunches," Ben cut in, and Elizabeth, who ignored the fact that she had been cut off because Ben was so excited, went on, "Papa, a man named Jean came by today. He owns the stables where the horses are kept and trained and so forth, from what I gather. He said that they are short a man for Saturday's race, and then he asked if Ben wanted to have Bunches in the race! Isn't it wonderful? Maybe someday, he will be a famous owner!"

"Now sweetie, I know you are excited, but let's take things one step at a time. First we have to get Bunches noticed," John said with a soft chuckle.

"Oh, Papa, it's so great!" Elizabeth squealed.

"Is all this true?" John asked Amanda with a skeptical glance.

"Yes, it is," Amanda said as she set the pot of stew before them.

"I'd like to say the blessing tonight," Ben stated, and John gave him the nod of approval.

"Amen," Elizabeth, Amanda and John said.

"I guess I know what we are doing on Saturday," Amanda said as she winked at Ben.

"But how did this happen so suddenly like this? I left for work this morning, and I came back to the news that Bunches is racing. Now, that is wonderful, but it is a surprise. What happened?" John asked a second time.

"Well, six weeks ago, I am sure you will recall that I went down to see that manager that stopped by today. I finally got to see him after more than a dozen attempts to do so. Apparently, I made quite an impression. He told me today that he wanted to give Bunches a chance to run. He said they were short a horse at the track because one of the owners or jockeys—I can't recall which, left him for the Confederates. They need nine horses. They can't run a race with just eight, so he asked me if I wanted Bunches in the race. Well, everyone has to start somewhere, so I said I'd like him to race," Ben explained.

"So, then Jean asked if Ben had a manager, and Ben said he didn't, and mama said you could do it...so that Bunches could race," Elizabeth added.

"So, I'm a manager now?" John chuckled.

"It was mama's notion," Elizabeth stated, "We had to have somebody and it couldn't be the manager or Ben, so mama choose you."

Amanda just smiled at the revelation and said, "I didn't think you'd mind, John. After all, there was no one else to be the manager."

"Well I guess I'm the chosen one, then," he laughed out loud.

"I guess so. What do you think of that, papa?" Ben asked, "Are you excited that Bunches will now have his chance?"

"I wish Bunches all the luck in the world, but he's up against the fastest horses now. This isn't some dirt road in Atlanta. We mustn't get our hopes too high." John said calmly.

Actually, John was delighted that the horse would run. It would further take Ben's mind off of Gabrielle Fontenot, or so John believed. Ben hadn't said a word about her since accepting the job at the railroad depot. Perhaps this opportunity to race Bunches would take care of thoughts of Gabrielle once and for all.

"Well, Ben," he reminded his son, "Need I remind you that you start work on Monday at the depot? Hopefully that jockey will ride Bunches a lot and they will get use to each other."

"I know, father," Ben replied, "Work comes first, and you always said that."

"I am not trying to rain on your parade. I think Bunches has just as much of a chance at winning as any other horse," John stated, "He's a fast runner, but he has never ran with several other horses. It has always been just one."

"So you think he should practice run with other horses, just to get use to them being there?" Ben asked.

"Yes, I do. Be sure and tell that to the manager, Jean Fournier, when they come and get him," John recommended, "I'm sure he'll be fine, though."

"See," Amanda added, "I knew you'd be a good manager. I chose the right one."

"Well," John replied, "We don't want to see another accident like that last one."

"I prayed that God would protect him, and He will. I just hope he wins," Ben added, "If he does, then there's a good chance that he'll be asked to run in the second card race tha next time."

"Here Ben," his mother said, "Finish up this stew. You are a growing boy."

Ben obliged and stuffed his mouth with the last scoop of his mother's delicious food. John looked at Ben as he ate and again was very appreciative of Mr. Fournier's visit and invitation to have Bunches run in the race. Getting Ben interested in something other than that bosomy French girl was something that he had been working on for quite some time now.

Ben went on and on about dirt racing in Atlanta. He could not believe that that's where Bunches had started, and now, he horse was running in a premiere race in New Orleans with some very high stakes involved. John just sat back and took it all in, knowing that Ben would have a plate full, and working at the depot would wear him out further. Ben would have little or no time for socializing with the beautiful daughter of a wealthy slave holder. It was just what John had wanted; he couldn't have planned it better if he wanted to.

That night Ben lay in bed and thought of the events of the day. It was overwhelming and felt like a dream come true. His horse would compete against others in an actual race that the public would bet on. It felt like a really good dream, but it wasn't a dream, it was reality.

Mr. Fournier had actually gone out of his way to seek him out. Bunches would be more than ready; he would look good, have new shoes and would be a fast runner.

Next, he thought of Gabrielle and the Fontenot stable. Would they be running a horse at the race circuit, as well? They ran Cajun King the last time, but he was involved in that ugly accident. Ben knew that he could run anymore, and that was too bad. He had been very fast.

Then Ben thought of Bunches. The horse would have to be groomed and made ready at the racing stable, although Ben had thought of the Fontenot stables. He couldn't take the chance with anything going wrong. Maybe it was better to have the racing stable take care of Bunches' needs. If anything did go wrong, it would be at the expense of the racing stable and not the Fontenot stable.

How could he tell Gabrielle of this? She was excited about horseracing as well. She surely would want to know, and she would be delighted to attend if she weren't going already. He had more confidence now, more ambition; he would either see her near the pond area or just walk right up to their massive doors and ask to see her. If she wasn't outside in her sun bonnet, then he would seek her out.

A slight rain had begun to fall, and it fell against his bedroom window panes just enough to keep him awake. He hadn't thought about the weather, or asked Mr. Fournier about it. What if it rained? Would Bunches still be qualified for another race? What if it rained during the race and the race got rained out? Would there be a winner by default, or would they reschedule the race for another time?

It was all too much for Ben to comprehend. In any event, he decided he would see Gabrielle the next day, or at least make a valiant effort to do as much. It was only a matter of three days before he started work at the railroad depot. His father had already told him not to expect any favors just because he was the boss, but Ben didn't. He would work as hard and be just as dedicated as the others.

The following Saturday would be the big race. He wanted to see Bunches win. He would have to get a good sleep that Friday night. His big hope was that beautiful Gabrielle would attend the horserace, as well.

The sun shone brightly upon Gabrielle's face. She opened her eyes and rubbed them gently. It was still early. The sun was not fully up. She watched the sun come up, and headed downstairs. It was so early that breakfast wasn't ready, so Gabrielle headed outside to inspect the pond's appearance.

Gabrielle was pleased with the landscaping of the old, forgotten pond area. It was beautiful and she found it was done exactly to her satisfaction. The water could not be seen from any angle. High manicured bushes, along with an inlaid stone fence, gave the area privacy. Several granite benches were appropriately positioned in several areas along the foliage and flowerbeds.

Pierre had spared no expense to please his daughter, supposing it would help her get over the loss of her mother. Gabrielle was pleased and that's all that mattered to him. Never-the-less, he was concerned that she was showing interest in the son of an interloping abolitionist family, a family that could in no way measure up to his own affluence and position in New Orleans. The boys' family was deemed 'outsiders' by many. Although they were treated with the expected social courtesies, they were not from the area and thought about things differently and everybody knew it.

He had hoped that she would show interest in Charles, and Charles was interested in her. He had even gone so far to have Charles strategically placed so that she might notice him and start a conversation. He had done everything that he could think of without being blatant, or letting her know that he had hoped that they might become acquainted. In an effort to increase Charles' chances of impressing Gabrielle without either of them knowing his real motive, Pierre had been teaching him about Cajun King, hoping that he would relay his knowledge to Gabrielle.

Gabrielle loved Cajun King and Pierre knew it. He gave into her tearful wishes to save him when he wanted to destroy the horse after the accident. Cajun King would never race again, but if it made Gabrielle happy to have him around, then so be it.

She had been working with the horse for sometime now, walking him about on the grounds and on the trial race track. She showed a genuine interest in his well being. It kept her busy, and everyday she had something to look forward to.

Besides, Pierre loved Cajun King, too. He wanted to see the horse improve, and he was. He was going to live after all. With few exceptions, he was worked with everyday. Unfortunately, it had rained recently, the ground would be muddy. Today wasn't the day to work Cajun King. Gabrielle didn't want to take any risks with him. One injury was enough. Instead, on this occasion, she visited the stall to pet him on the nose and stroke his back.

This was Charles' day off and she knew it. It gave her a peace knowing that he would not bother her or Cajun King. She didn't care to be around him. He was too forward with his mannerisms and not very tactful in his approach, but it was more than that. Although she could not place her finger on exactly what it was, there was something about Charles that made Gabrielle very uncomfortable.

"That horse likes that," a voice said from behind.

Gabrielle spun about to see who the voice belonged to. She thought she was alone with Cajun King in his stall. Apparently she was wrong. Well, she thought, at least it wasn't Charles. She would know his voice anywhere.

"Ben, you frightened the life right out of me!" she exclaimed.

"How are you? Figured I would find you here," he replied.

"I am fine, thanks," Gabrielle responded.

Gabrielle cued Ben with both a facial expression and head motion, trying to tell him that they weren't alone in the stable building. She was pretty sure her father was now working somewhere within earshot, or at least one of the stable hands. She cautioned him silently, letting him know that he should watch what he said. Ben caught that and responded with his own silent mannerisms, letting her see that he understood.

"I've come over here to see if I can get my horse shoed and groomed. I was going to do it myself, or have the racing stable's men do it, but then I decided otherwise. He is racing in a race on Saturday. They may groom him again before that anyway, but he should look nice when they come to get him," he announced most matter-of-factly.

Gabrielle stepped away from Cajun King and looked at his awaiting horse, standing just inside of the huge stable doorway. So, Bunches would finally have a chance to race. Gabrielle was so happy for Ben. She knew this was his dream, and Bunches truly was fast. Gabrielle wanted to say more, to at least ask questions just then, but she did not dare.

"I can get someone to help you," she responded, "I'll get one of our better stablemen. This must his first race, huh?" Gabrielle asked, pretending that she did not know the answer in the hopes that Ben would give her details. He knew what she was doing, so he said, "Yes. It is his first race. I had really wanted him to have the chance, so I had gone down to the stables that the racehorses are kept in and trained at and spoken with the manager. I guess I must have made quite the impression, because they were short a man for Saturday's race and the manager took the time to track me down and ask if I would be interested in racing my horse, Bunches, here."

"Well, that's great. It is rare in these parts to have a newcomer have a chance like that. You would certainly want him to look his best. I will get you our best stable hand," Gabrielle stated with a deceptively innocent grin.

"I would certainly most appreciate that," he replied with an all knowing mock bow.

Upon stepping further away from Cajun King and out into the open air, she was almost immediately seen by one of the stable attendants. Looking over at her inquisitive look, a wordless request for assistance, the available stableman stopped what he was doing and wiped his hands as he approached.

"Is there anything I can do for you, Miss Gabrielle?" he asked.

"Yes, Peter," She replied, "Could you take this horse to one of the back stalls and shoe and groom him, please?"

"Certainly, ma'am," he replied as he approached and took Bunches by the reins.

As Bunches was being led to the stall that was in a back corner, Ben remarked to himself that Gabrielle had the services that would befit a queen and her royal subjects.

"What do I owe for this service?" Ben asked.

"There is no charge for this, and you know better than to say something like that," she teasingly replied.

"Well," he replied, "Being the true gentleman that I am, I thought it was worth at least the asking."

"A gentleman! That you are sir! But our first grooming is always free when the patron will be racing," she replied, knowing fully well that she was lying, but making a mental note to slip her own three dollars and seventy-five cents in the money jar that night to make it appear as if she had charged Ben. She really wouldn't have, but if she did that, nobody would ever know any different. Besides, she had the money, and Ben had far less money than she ever had.

"Bunches is going to run in next Saturday's third card race," he explained in hushed tones, "Since I gotta start my new job soon, I thought maybe now is a good time to get him ready."

"Are you serious?" she asked, daring not to speak above a whisper, "Well, Ben that's just wonderful, but if you wanted to race over there, all you had to do was ask me and ah would have arranged it with Mr. Fournier. There's a good chance that I could've have gotten your horse in on the first card race."

"Well," he replied, "I didn't know, and besides, Mr. Fournier came to tha house looking for me. I think it is better that I work my way into racing myself without your help, anyway. To involve you at all could put our relationship in danger. I am not sure what your father would think. He doesn't like the fact that my father is an abolitionist," Ben replied.

"Forget my father and his feelings. Do I like slavery? No, and I am not my father and he is not me. Sometimes, love can't be explained or denied," Gabrielle stated with a fire of conviction in her eyes.

"I wish we lived in different times, like a time when the colored of someone's skin or their social status didn't matter so much," Ben said longingly.

"Who cares what society says? Folks don't want to have to be under the Church of England and all that, either. They wanted the right to have their own beliefs, so what did they do? They left and came here and started a nation where all men are created equal, with certain inalienable rights, including life, liberty and the pursuit of happiness, right?" Gabrielle asked.

"Sure, that's what the law says, but what does that have to do with us?" Ben asked.

"Well, if we have the right to be happy, that makes that what makes us happy is our right, correct? Well, I am happy with you. You care about me, too, right?" Gabrielle asked.

"I am madly in love with you," Ben confessed.

"Well, I am also madly in love with you, so let's just see where that leads and forget what everyone thinks. Does Bunches have a jockey?" Gabrielle asked, almost wishing that he didn't because she wanted to race him.

"Yes, he does. I wish I could have picked the jockey. I would have chosen you. He likes you, and I am sure you would have done well," Ben replied confidently.

"When's the jockey coming to get him? I am sure he wants to work with him before hand, doesn't he?" Gabrielle asked.

"Yes, he does, and he is coming on Wednesday," Ben responded.

"It's gonna take him awhile to get your horse ready," Gabrielle mentioned, "Let's step outside, but be quiet about it. I want to show you something."

Gabrielle led Ben away from the stable house and towards the restored pond area. It had been awhile since he had been there, but he had remembered it. He knew almost immediately where they were going, but the pond had been improved for more than he had imagined it would be.

"Lord Almighty, Gabrielle!" he gasped when he saw it, his mouth agape and his eyes bulging, "It's beautiful. Just look at this! Those bushes, that stone fence, that wrought iron gate, it's all new, and it's all hidden as far as I can see. I wouldn't have known the difference from the outside! Look how well covered this all is!"

"Do you really like it?" she asked.

"Oh, it's so nice," he replied, "I just can't get over it."

"Father has a colored attendant whose only job is to maintain the grounds here," she further explained.

"Well, he does his job. This must have cost a fortune!" he remarked as he took it all in, "It's changed so much that I'll bet those ducks and geese don't even know where they are anymore."

Taking Ben by the hand, she led him along the side of the pond area, a specially designated side.

"This is like the tall reeds at your house," she romantically whispered, "We can't be seen here."

Ben looked about just to justify and confirm it to himself. She was indeed correct. They were well hidden. Seeing that she was offering him her other hand, he took it and wrapped it around his waist and looked into her beautiful eyes.

"This is so beautiful Gabrielle," he whispered back, "You are beautiful as well."

"I did this for us," she confessed.

"I know. This is so beautiful, Gabrielle," he whispered back, "You are beautiful as well."

"It was at least I could do for us," she replied.

Considering the beautiful surroundings that he found himself in, Ben wondered if there was any end in sight of the affluence of the Fontenot family. Gabrielle had it all; beauty, poise, personality and wealth. She removed her sun bonnet and slightly shook her head, allowing her long, beautiful hair flow to her waist. It was a signal to Ben that she was ready; shaking her head like that to him symbolically represented shaking off the values of the past, and welcoming a new, more grown-up understanding.

It was much easier for Ben this time. She had extended her hand to him, and he had received it. He could sense that feeling in her, that same anticipation and passion they had shared before. Gabrielle had never felt this way before; her emotions were running much deeper. It was even unlike the incident in the tall reeds. This was exciting to her just to be with him by her gorgeous pond on this sunny day.

Once again, Ben placed his nose close to her neck and inhaled her sweet fragrance. Still, there was nothing that he could think of that compared. She always smelled good; it was the same as smelling a bouquet of flowers. Closing his eyes, he savored that precious smell and fragrance, if only for a moment in time.

Gabrielle felt deep, personal peace and acceptance in her beautiful habitat. Moving his head towards hers, he briefly scanned her beautiful face and saw that her eyes were closed. She was ready for his love.

Placing his lips on hers, he pulled her closer now, into a tightly locked embrace. She placed both hands behind his head and pulled him even closer than what they had been. Pulling him downward, he sensed that she no longer wanted to stand. He followed her cue and lay down with her in the hidden, grassy terrain. Rolling over and over in the hidden foliage, they moved about with carefree abandonment. It felt so good to Ben to be without worries once again, so unobstructed, to forget all formality, and to be so firm but gentle at the same time.

Gabrielle felt powerless to evade him, and didn't want to. She had never felt this way before. Somehow, this wasn't like the time they had done it in the tall reeds at his house. She sensed the impending movement from his body's unspoken communication, and didn't mind it at all as he reached toward her side and placed his hand under her left breast. Breaking the passionate kiss, she reached down with her lips and repeatedly kissed his neck from the front to the back again.

It felt so good to be alone with him in the hidden foliage, and not worry about being seen or interrupted. Moving his hand slightly upward, he now completely cupped her breast in his hand. It was soft and warm and tender. She didn't mind at all, and she moved more freely so that he could have better control because it felt so good. She slipped her arm out of her sleeve so that her left breast was now completely exposed.

He kissed her with more fervor and passion now, even stronger than before, and it felt so good to be carefree. As she moved from his chin down to his neck, Ben held his head as still as possible while she kissed and nudged him in the throat area. She was receptive as he pulled her toward him at the waist area.

It felt so good to be touched there, so natural. Communicating without words, they rolled over and over, seemingly not getting enough of each other's love.

In a moment her hands slid along his back, gently at first, then more aggressively. She rolled over and let him be on top. As he was on top of her, he closed his eyes and looked ever skyward as she gently stroked his chest and his stomach. It felt so good to be touched like that. He could hardly take it. They rolled over again, so that he was on the bottom.

Kissing her more passionately, he followed her example and kissed her neck from the front to the back. She, in turn, closed her eyes and craned her neck so that he could have better control. It felt so good to her; she had never experienced anything like this before. This was much better than the last time. The pond was secluded, and it was so secret and private to be with him like this. In that moment, all was wonderful, and nothing else mattered.

Turning on their sides now, she gently raked her fingernails across his stomach and upwards toward his chest. He unbuttoned his shirt to give her more freedom to do as much; it felt so good to be touched like that. She then kissed him and massaged his chest at the same time, mostly together, then alternately.

At that moment, she was in control and he loved every second of it. Her fingers felt so sensual on his skin and so soothing to the touch. It was a wonderful feeling, a feeling of absolute heavenly freedom. He gently ran his fingers through her hair, while kissing her more gently, and then more aggressively. She responded with the same eagerness, a wanting, and a driving passion that gave him the feeling that she wanted to please him.

Not at all caring and experimenting with their passions, they continued to kiss and hold and hug and touch in the privacy of the beautiful pond area. Gabrielle pulled him at the waist even closer now. Ben sensed that she wanted more, that she wanted to go beyond what they had experienced. He didn't even have to think about her unspoken request. He knew he wanted too, as well.

This was her beautiful, partially man-made and mostly natural habitat that she had envisioned and than had constructed. He couldn't ask for anything better than what she had provided for them. She was the queen here, and he was more than happy to oblige her. They decided that they wanted to go all the way into each other, and not just for two or three uncertain minutes. No, this time they were certain, and this time, they were not unsure how to do it.

She lay back and shuttered as she felt his thrusting against her movements. It felt so good, and yet painful, but this was a different kind of pain than she had ever felt. She took pride in that, knowing that there was always pressure to do so. She had never given into that pressure, knowing that she wanted to save herself for someone she really loved. Here he was, Mister Ben Chessser, and she knew that she wanted it. This passion was not just childish infatuation. He loved her, and she loved him.

Her whispering words only fed his drive, and he thrust himself against her body harder and faster, breathing heavily. The muscle in his chest that carried the blood to his cells was now pounding so hard that he thought it would explode. Though he loved her with all he was, he had never felt such a need to expend his energy.

Afterwards Ben gently rolled away from her and onto his back. He was suddenly left with no strength, and he felt weak and powerless. It was as if their passions had drained them both.

"You aren't going to pass out, are you?" she whispered.

"Oh, what was that?" he gasped, laying face up in the grass.

"I guess we now know what that feels like," Gabrielle responded, "I liked that, how about you? Isn't it really something?"

"I ain't never felt this way before, Gabrielle," he whispered back.

"I know, Ben. It was wonderful!" she whispered.

Ben staggered to his knees, and then his feet, as he looked down at her. She was outstandingly beautiful, even almost naked. They seemed to belong in her habitat, her pond, which was her royal kingdom. Her mangled hair still flowed to the left and right and down to her waist. Her flashing eyes told him that she thought it was a beautiful experience.

"Oh, Lord," He gasped once more, "I truly don't have any strength now."

Gabrielle ignored his comment and looked skyward, still reflecting on the moments of sweet romance. Almost gasping for breath now, Ben bent over and rested his hands on his knees to breathe better. He was coming around, and his strength was coming back.

"We need to get back, Ben," she whispered, "A moment like this should last forever, but it can't. We need to get back before I'm missed and they come looking for me."

She sat straight up and pulled her clothes up about her waist. Then, standing up completely, she, in a moment, realized how exhausted she was. It had been an exhilarating experience that had overwhelmed all her senses.

After being intimate with Gabrielle, Ben headed home. He was sore, but he was happy, too. In the back of his mind, the possibility that Gabrielle might be in the family way did surface. He immediately brushed the thought aside. They were young and that couldn't happen to them.

He started to think about his new job. Ben knew that he couldn't expect any special favors on the loading platform just because his father was the railroad's regional Deputy Commissioner. He would have to perform, just as everyone else had to at work. It just had to be that way; he would work just as hard as the others and be just as dedicated to getting the job done.

Chapter 29
First Days of Work

It was hard to believe that in just days, he would be working. He supposed everyone had to grow up, but he would have rather been with Bunches all day. Well, at least Bunches would have the chance to race, and at least the jockey wasn't paid up front. How Ben wanted Bunches to win. They had worked hard for this chance, and now Bunches had it. He just had to win. Well, the race was still several days away. Ben couldn't think about it too much or he would get even more nervous than he already was.

"You need a distraction. Are you still nervous about Bunches racing on Saturday?" Ben's father asked him when he came in the door.

"I am, but I am also happy. I really want him to do well. Do you think he will, papa?" Ben asked.

"He will do his best, I am sure. That is all anyone can ask, but you also need to give yourself some credit. You have trained him well," his father replied.

"I suppose you are right," Ben responded with a sigh.

"You look tired. Are you feeling alright? You better not be getting sick. You start work in two days, you know," John stated as he looked closely at his son. He did indeed look weary, and he was pale too.

"I am fine, pa. I am a little tired, though. I think I have been out in the sun too long. I am going to go rest for a few minutes," Ben replied.

"You better not be getting sick," John said again.

"I am just tired," Ben repeated as he closed his bedroom door.

John found it kind of curious that Ben needed a rest. He never rested. What had he done that had made him so tired? He had been gone for quite a long time. It was really warm out. He did not like the heat. John just could not figure out where he had been and why he had been gone so long. It did not make sense.

"Good thing that boy is starting work in less than forty-eight hours. Then I will know where he is and what he is doing at least some of the time," John grumbled to himself.

On Monday, Ben shuffled through the depot's halls. Every time that he had been there before, it was either as a traveler or to see his father. Now he was working. He was unsure of himself, but decided that only training would help that. He tried to smile and not show his apprehension.

"Just watch me and do what I do and say what I say. I am certainly not perfect, but I know how to do this job. I will teach you the best I know how," his experienced mentor, William, advised, "You just have to keep up a steady pace and keep going."

Ben felt different in a porter's uniform, so professional. It felt totally unlike anything he'd worn on the farm and in the stable. The cuffs were a little long, but he compensated for that by raising his sleeves and pretended that it fit just fine. He didn't want to complain on his first day. That would look really bad.

"Why so many cats?" asked Ben as he observed the pen from the rail platform. He had never noticed it before, but it contained almost a dozen cats.

"Well, Ben, it's like this: cats are a part of the railroad. They keep the rats, mice and snakes away. I might also add that they do a fine job. Any of these freight railcars that leave out of here will have no rats or nice. Others…well, I guess you are gonna find out!"

William went on to explain that the cats were not only welcomed members of the railroad industry, but mystique symbols as well. He added that engineers of the gulf coast preferred black, spotted cats because they brought good luck. East coast engineers thought gray cats would bring good luck. Northern engineers always thought white cats would settle the crew better. The few engineers of the west that visited always had a dozen cats about their railcars, just as an extra measure of good luck.

Expectant female cats were always revered above the males. Cats were mated and traded on a nod of a head or a wink of eye. For the new owners, a new cat was a prized possession. William told Ben proudly that his father's own bobtailed white cat was born in the pen out back. The father, a tom cat, belonged to a visiting gulf coast engineer, and the mother was a local domestic.

"We have a train in ten minutes," William said, "Just walk along beside me and help unload the baggage and the horses. The baggage goes to the left and the animals go to the right, in special pens. I will show you where those are if you don't already know."

Ben and several other new hires listened with intense interest as William, as well as other experienced porters, gave suggestions and directions about how to move parcels efficiently.

"The object is to get that train car unloaded and reloaded just as fast as you can without making a mistake," William stated, "If you make a mistake, then fess up to it. The worst thing that you can do is lie in front of a customer."

"Yeah, that's right, William," Another porter mused, "No smoking or chewing tobacco in front of the customers. I don't care if they do it or not!"

"You always say 'yes, sir' and 'yes ma'am,'" another added, "Here's another thing. You may be right, but don't ever disagree with a customer. You just be as nice as you can be."

Ben, as well as the other new hires, nodded to show that they understood the basic directions.

"You boys look right strong enough to handle it," William observed. "You don't have anything to worry about. When a train ain't here, then it's fine to go in the back room and smoke, chew or drink coffee, but when a train is arriving, you make sure that you are here, standing up against that wall and waiting for it to come to a stop."

Once again the new hires nodded that they understood.

"Now, all of you can see that train coming in the horizon," William said as he pointed at the train that had just appeared, approaching from the distance, "What are ye's gonna do about it?"

"Stand against the wall," Ben answered.

"Then so be it," William replied. "Let's all stand there and wait for the train to come to a stop."

Steam billowed from the train's stack as it slowed down and stopped directly in front of the reception area of the gated rail platform. Almost immediately, the doors opened for the arriving passengers and their cargo. William and the other experienced porters nudged the new ones to follow them as they proceeded to the baggage cars. Crate after crate spilled out. Suitcase after suitcase was taken off and placed on the platform, in alphabetical order, according the customers' last names. Animals were held in a separate pen, until the owners appeared to claim them.

William motioned for Ben to assist with a newly arrived racehorse. Another new hire was asked to assist with two goats.

The customers ranged from old to young, fat and skinny, well dressed and groomed to a poorly clothed, bearded, impoverished appearance. Still, each had bought a ticket on that train, so each would be treated with the same respect.

"Mr. and Mrs. Henley?" William inquired. "Do you require further assistance?"

"No, porter, I don't" he replied. "My father-in-law is waiting in that carriage," he stated, pointing as he added, "But thank you, anyway."

From observation alone, Ben learned quickly that this job wasn't like racing a horse. This required absolute teamwork; everybody had to work together to get the job done. The new hires soon figured out a system in which one new hire would take a parcel off the train and hand it to another newly hired individual, who would then pass it down a line of new porters until it reached the end. Each of the crates and suitcases were organized in groups on the platform.

For this train that just arrived, there were paying passengers in the depot, waiting to board when it departed. The only thing that prevented them from boarding was the fact that the train wasn't ready to be boarded because not all the previous passengers" luggage had been taken off. The arriving passengers were just as anxious to get their baggage and animals and depart in wagons, carriages or hired buggies. This was the final hurdle between them and their destinations.

"Hurry up!" William snarled under his breath, "Those folks in the depot have been waiting to board and some have little children."

"Miss Ledbetter," William smiled, as he greeted a young, attractively dressed lady with a parasol, "We can load your baggage in your hired buggy if you wish to have further assistance."

"If you would be so kind, sir, I would be most obliged," she responded.

William snapped his finger at a newly hired porter who was standing nearby. The young man sprang to life and helped the young lady with her parcels. Before long, the train was completely empty; it was now time to reload. The new porters reversed their newly developed system to load the train again. It worked just fine and everyone quickly learned to rely on each other.

"All aboard!" The chief train porter yelled up and down the platform, "All aboard!"

Patrons quickly boarded. Some of the young children squirmed or cried. The train belched steam as it started to slowly roll away from the depot. More steam flowed as the train sped faster, and within minutes, it had nearly disappeared into the horizon.

"All right all you new porters!" William yelled, "Let's gather about in the back room and discuss the arrival of the last train. A few things went wrong. You need to know that so that it won't happen again!"

The newly hired boys gathered in the back room. The meeting was for them, not the experienced porters. Most of them believed that they had done at least a fairly decent job, but they would listen to what William said and try to do better next time.

"I liked that system you boys devised. That seems to work well and fast for you. You may keep doing that. One thing, though. You boys need to smile at the customers. We are here for them. Judging from the looks of the few of you, it appears as if you'd rather be somewhere else. The paying customers pay your weekly wage, so smile and look livelier out there!"

Ben remarked to himself that William was so much different in front of the customers than he was when they weren't there. In front of them, he was relaxed and pleasant. Without them there, he was firm and business-like, although at least he had pointed out one positive thing. None-the-less, behind the scenes, it seemed like he was a different person.

"Another thing," he mentioned, "Offer your services to the passengers whenever the need arises. Don't just stand there and expect someone to do it for you. Be nice and always smile."

The new hires looked down, feeling rather ashamed. All that he said was true. They had been so focused on learning the ropes and how badly they wanted to do well that they had forgotten their manners. They had all been guilty of something, but now they knew the difference.

"That's the talk for today," William stated, "Smoke 'em or chew if you want to. Now is the time. Another train is expected in an hour."

Several of the new porters were relieved to hear that and produced cigars and chewing tobacco. They hated to admit it, but they were addicted to tobacco. Some of them had even craved it after only a half an hour of work. A few had been smoking for a several years, even though the oldest ones were only in their late teens and early twenties.

"Tomorrow we got six trains coming and going," William said as he read the schedule. "The day after that, there's eight. Today was one of those rare days with only two trains. It isn't always going to be like this, so don't get your hopes up!"

Later that afternoon, Ben felt sore and very tired. His legs and back hurt the most. Still, he had to admit that his first day on the job had not gone too badly. A sense of pride washed over him. There was something to be said for working hard. It made a man feel useful.

"See you tomorrow, Ben!" William said as Ben got out of his old buggy, "You did well today, and it will be a better day tomorrow."

"Good, I like it like that," he replied, "Always stay busy, tha day goes by faster like that."

William had another new hire in his buggy that didn't live too far way. He didn't mind giving him or anyone else a ride the first week or so, but after that they were on their own for transportation to and from work. They were not kids anymore. They had to learn independence.

Ben didn't want him to see that he was so sore that he could hardly walk up the La Rue St. Lazar drive, so he walked as upright as possible, enduring more discomfort as he went. The second train had heavy machine parts in nailed crates. The railcar was almost full of those crates and, to complicate matters, the depot was packed with departing passengers. It was hard work, the other boys were sore as well, but everybody just endured it all.

All he could think about was eating supper and going to bed, but that was an eternity away, or so it seemed. He still had to feed and water his horse. That would at least give him a chance to see Bunches, would help him to relax. Ben went to get a drink of water, then went to the barn to brush and feed Bunches.

Bunches whinnied and swished his tail as Ben entered the barn. Ben just smiled to himself. Bunches really was a great horse. He was so lucky and still elated that Bunches would have a chance to race.

"Hello, boy. How was your day today? Sorry I couldn't ride ya. Mine was really tiring and I sure am glad to see you."

Bunches whinnied again and Ben rubbed his nose and led him out of the stall to brush him. He had to be quick about it. He knew supper would soon be ready. Unfortunately, his coat was slightly matted and Ben only managed to finish about half of it before his sister hollered that supper was ready.

"I'll be back to finish brushing you later, and I'll feed you then, too," Ben told Bunches as he left the barn.

"So, how'd it go today?" his father asked at the supper table.

"It went good, father," Ben replied, "We got two trains in and I learned how to load and unload them with the rest of the boys. William taught us how."

"Ah yes, I know William. He's a hard worker," John recalled, "As long as he is there, that platform will run just fine. He should have retired two years ago but he just loves working there."

"Papa," Elizabeth asked, "Didn't you say you got your start doing the same thing?"

"Yes," her father replied, "During the off season with farming, several of the farmers did that. We needed to work year-round like that because we needed the money. Of course, during farming season, it was tough to make schedule sometimes, but we made it."

John could readily see that Ben was sore. He was tired, and looked it, as well. But that was exactly what he wanted, because it gave Ben much less idle time to think or talk about Gabrielle Fontenot. He would only have the weekends, and this weekend was the big race.

"Ah got a letter today from Thomas," Amanda mentioned, "He wrote and told us that we are to be grandparents!"

"Oh... my word!" John exclaimed.

"Really?" Elizabeth gasped.

Ben managed a wry smile, but otherwise didn't comment. He wanted nothing more than to finish his supper and brush his horse.

"When?" John asked.

"He said November, best as they figure. At least that's what the doctor told them."

"I'll have to schedule leave time for November then, so we can go back to Atlanta and see our new grandbaby," John mentioned.

"Oh, that would be so delightful, but Ben couldn't come with us," Amanda just remembered.

"Oh," Ben murmured, as he saw that he was now the center of attention, "I guess we'll just have to see what happens. That's a long way off."

"Here Ben," his mother said, "Why don't you finish that pork and them taters? I just hate to throw that out."

Ben obliged accordingly and ate even more, even though he wasn't in the eating mood. John was pleased with Ben's day at work. He had clearly worked hard. He was worn out, and looked it. He was pensive and quiet and moved his shoulders from side to side often to ease the discomfort. Eventually Ben excused himself from the table and went outside to feed and water his horse and finish brushing him.

"There you go, boy!" he said as he stroked his nose, "Have at it. This Saturday is our big day. I just know that you will do the best you can do."

Ben thought about his last visit with Gabrielle and realized that he had failed to ask her if her father would be running a horse in the race. Well, they had been kind of busy. That hadn't been at the forefront of his mind. Now there would be no time to ask her. He would just have to wait and see if a Pierre and one of his jockeys indeed was present. He petted his horse a few more times after Bunches had eaten, as he brushed him, and headed back to the house. A warm bed never felt so good.

Young men from New Orleans and the surrounding rural areas began to board.

Crowds began to appear on the platform as other young men arrived. All of them were volunteers for the Louisiana delegation to the War of Independence effort.

"We got the Yankees runnin' mama! Just one more fight an' it's over!" one young man could be heard saying as he spoke to his widowed mother. Fathers and mothers, kin and beaus all hugged the young men before them.

"Take care of yourself, Ted," One father could be heard saying to his son.

"I'll show 'em," said another, "I can shoot the eye out of a bird at fifty yards. I suppose I ain't a good shot for nothing. Them Yankees don't know who they're fooling with."

"We are gonna whip 'em. I'll be home in no time, mama," Another youthful and naive young future soldier could be overheard saying, "Pop, ya always taught me to stand up for what's right, and now I gotta do what's right!"

"I know, son, I know," he responded, "Ya know, Sarah Belle's going to be waiting for ya. I figure when you get back, you and her will get hitched."

"Oh, now pop!" the young man responded as he blushed and turned away.

"I guess the rumors of war aren't just rumors anymore," Ben told William.

"Tell me something I already knew and did not want to believe," William responded, his eyes glazed over with some sort of emotion that Ben could not quite identify.

"Are you alright?" Ben asked.

"Yeah…yeah….I am just…well…forget it," William said, his voice far away and the words detached. After awhile, the young military volunteers were all on their designated cars. Well wishers waved and smiled from the platform as the doors were closed.

"All aboard!" could be heard from the various areas of the platform.

A huge gust of steam belched from the gigantic coal engine as the train inched forward. Ladies on the platform waved handkerchiefs, and men waved their hats. Shouting and smiling, they bid goodbye to their sons, grandsons and nephews. Surging forward, the train picked up speed and traveled onward, away from the city and out into the surrounding farmlands. The porters relaxed for now, as another train had come and gone.

"Say William," Ben asked, "Is this war everything they say it is?"

"What ye mean, Chesser? Of course it is, and didn't you see those boys and all those people? There's a lot of fighting going on in Virginia. That's where they're all going, and I'm sure you saw how all the Union troops that were stationed here just up and left."

"Naw, didn't pay attention to that," Ben replied.

"Well, you better start paying attention. Half of the trains in the next few months will be carrying regular passengers while the other half will be transporting military personnel," he warned.

"More equipment, then," Ben muttered.

"You new boys are gonna get quite a workout, but that won't be the hard part," William mentioned as he bit off the end of a cigar. "So you better get use to it!"

"What's that mean?" Ben asked, not really knowing if he wanted to hear the answer.

"Now," William said, "We've got a train coming in three hours. It's a military hospital train. You just never mind what you are seeing, and try to keep that quiet. After all, the south is whaling it to the north, so you just keep still about it."

"Three hours, sir?" he asked, "What shall we do 'til then?"

"Why don't you and the others sweep that back room? It's a good something to do while we're waiting for the hospital train," William requested, "Move all of those barrels on the platform as well. We're gonna need all the room we can get."

"Very well, sir," Ben replied.

He left the office and ran into another recently hired porter, Carey, and said, "There's a train coming in three hours. It's a hospital train. William says we are not to draw attention to it when it comes. We are to do our jobs, never mind what we are saying, and be quiet about it."

"What? Why is it that we have to keep it so secret?" Carey asked, not knowing that he would soon know the answer, and unaware that he really didn't want to.

"Hey," Ben answered, "That's all William told me to tell you boys."

Two hours later, the depot was deserted. Both the back room and the platform had been swept and cleaned. William walked about and gave the work an approving nod.

"Wont be long now, boys. Just remember to do your jobs and forget what you are seeing," He said as he looked at his vest watch, "Go smoke and chew while you can, and there's a pot of coffee on the potbellied stove."

The porters appreciated the cool, shaded back room. It was their own little sanctuary, a place where the passengers weren't allowed. They would go back there to eat lunch when they had breaks, or rest briefly. There was also usually someone there to chat with, since their breaks usually were at relatively the same times.

"Hey boys, come take a look," one new porter said as he stepped in from the outside.

Several, along with Ben, stepped out of the back room and saw lines of military wagons waiting, along with carriages and buggies with families. Ben recognized several of them from church. There were also several funeral wagons and undertaker wagons on hand, parked right along side the others. It perplexed them all.

"What's that all about?" Ben asked.

"Like I said," William admonished, "Don't ask questions. Do your jobs. Try to forget what you see. You boys just keep your mouths shut. You didn't see nothing… you didn't hear nothing."

"There she comes yonder!" An experienced porter bellowed as he looked into the horizon. Ben, as well as the others, just gave each other inquisitive looks; they all silently wondered what made this train different from the other arrivals. It looked like any other train. It wasn't marked special, and it had no banners or flags.

The awaiting people from the wagons and buggies started to come to the depot. Many stood just out of loading reach of the porters. Pain could be seen on the faces of a few, while hope shone on more. The train belched and hissed steam as it slowed to a complete stop exactly where it should have at the platform.

All of the porters stood along the wall and waited for the doors to open. The steam subsided and the doors were opened from the inside by the porters inside the train. All the waiting porters had expected this to be just like any other train.

The first car to be opened contained the bodies of Confederate soldiers that were killed on the battle field, or worse, because they had endured slow and painful deaths, those that had died in transit to the depot. The new porters looked aghast and turned away. The stench was overwhelming. The bodies were wrapped in loose, bloodied blankets, some blown into pieces or otherwise mangled almost beyond recognition. They had nothing much to protect them from the heat of the day.

"You boys know what to do," William ordered in a low tone. "There are folks waiting for them. These are people's sons and daughters, so line the bodies up in the order they are taken out, right here on the platform."

The new porters held their breaths as they reluctantly went into the rail car that contained those killed in action. It was a horrible and heart wrenching scene. Many of the so-called 'men' were clearly very young; barely teenagers, and now they were dead.

"Lord Jesus, please have mercy on these men and those that are still living, and protect them. Please comfort those families that are now brokenhearted over these boys' deaths and encamp your angels around those that are fighting, and please don't let those that die leave this world without hearing of your love for them one last time. Thank You, Jesus, in your name, amen," Ben prayed as bodies were passed to him and he carried them out with the help of another porter.

The people in the depot now gathered nearby to claim their loved one. The other experienced porters were assigned to the hospital rail car, which contained the wounded, infected or diseased soldiers. Men bowed their heads and women screamed at the sight of their deceased loved ones, many of which still showed gunshot wounds about the head and shoulders. The wrapped blankets did little to hide the shot, mangled and bloodied corpses.

The new porters helped them load the bodies into the awaiting wagons, per specific directions. Preachers from several denominations were on hand at the wagon area and led dozens of people in a prayer. Each wagon then slowly disappeared, moving away from the train depot. Women cried and wailed in handkerchiefs and cursed the day that their loved ones signed up and left with great ambition and hope.

The rail car for the dead was unloaded quickly and efficiently. William then directed the new porters to assist with the regular hospital rail car. Many young soldiers could be seen hobbling about on crutches. Others were missing an arm, or were wrapped about the head, blind. This was more uplifting. Mothers and fathers, aunts and uncles hugged their wounded young soldiers. They had at least come back, not in whole, but alive.

"Oh Samuel," a mother cried. "We thought you were gone. We didn't hear anything for such a long time, until this morning… when we learned that you would be on the train, coming home from Virginia."

The wounded young man just looked down at his missing left leg, blown off from the knee down.

"I did the best I could, mama," he replied, "So many of the rest of the boys can't say that. They gave their lives. A Union boy shot me and I was in the infirmary for a long time."

"Well, God brought you back. That's what I prayed for. I am so proud of you. Come on, let's go home," his mother said as she kissed him on the cheek.

Walking slowly on homemade crutches that he had made himself because he wasn't going to allow himself to have a pity party, he unsteadily made his way with his mother and exited the platform. Another young soldier shook hands with his father with his left hand, because his entire right arm was missing. A huge bandage took its place.

"Tyler," the father said, "It's so good to have you home. Your mama is sick in bed, so I came by myself."

"What about Mary Ann?" the young, bearded, wounded soldier asked, "I haven't heard anything about her. We were supposed to up and get married."

"Son," his father explained, trying to be gentle in how he broke the news to his son, "Mary Ann cleaves to another man now. She married Nate Kincaid shortly after she learned you were wounded in action."

"Oh no!" the soldier gasped, "It just can't be! I thought she loved me! Oh, God, no. Oh, papa! No! But why? Did she think I could not provide for her?" he wailed as tears filled his eyes. Soon, sobs wracked his body, and all his father could do was let him cry on his shoulder.

One by one, the soldiers were reunited with their families and friends. Those that couldn't walk were carried out on gurneys and placed on the platform.

"All right, you new boys!" William said to the new porters, "Get some mops from the back room and good, strong lye soap! Then, mop out that railcar. There are people waiting to depart. Get those cats off there and put new ones on the rail cars."

"The hell if I will! This is terrible, and you seem to have no feelings about it!" a newly hired porter stated, "You know what you can do with this job? I am not cleaning up anybody's blood. You can just go find someone else. Besides, those cats haven't been fed, and I know what they have been eating!"

With that the young man stalked off and joined the last of the crowds leaving the depot.

"If anybody else wants to quit, then now is the time!" William snarled.

Nobody, including Ben, moved or batted an eye. Ben joined in with the work, but he didn't like it one bit. The rail car smelled of decay, disease and death. It was all that he could do to hold his breath while he worked, which he couldn't do all the time. He had to breathe. He just kept thinking about the race on Saturday. It was the only thing that kept him going. Somehow the work seemed easier if he thought while he worked. Winning the race was the only thing on his mind as he helped scrub the rail car that had once held the deceased young soldiers. William inspected the clean up and nodded with approval.

"Get it loaded up and that's it for today," he said as he walked away.

Having a lot of free time after loading spurned the new porters onward. They quickly formed a work line detail. They had almost forgotten about the wounded and deceased soldiers for the time being. They would have more time in the evenings to think about their work. They didn't know it, but they would never be the same again after seeing what they had.

"All aboard!" yelled the chief engineer.

The awaiting crowds in the depot quickly passed through the gate and boarded the train. The mess from the previous train's arrival had been so well cleaned up that not even the stench of blood remained. Nobody noticed anything unusual. They had not seen what the porters had seen. To them, this was just a paid ride on the train.

Steam hissed and belched from the train as it started to gain momentum and pick up speed. Within what seemed just like it a few minutes, it was gone in the horizon of the steel rails. The porters were then allowed to have a break. They went to the break room, but all of them remained in their own thoughts, and nobody had a cigar or even a cup of coffee.

The events of the day bothered Ben. He had not seen anything like that before, and prayed he never would again, though he sensed in his heart that he would. Several of the wounded and deceased were from his church, so he would see the wounded and disfigured every time he went to services. No wonder William had wanted them to keep their mouths shut. It was a horribly traumatic experience, one which would not be readily forgotten by him or the rest of the new porters.

The next morning, as usual, the porters waited on the platform when the arriving train could be seen approaching in the distance.

"Passengers this time, boys," William stated as he looked at his vest watch, "On time as well! Wonders never cease!"

"Passengers departing as well?" asked a porter nearby.

"No, take a look yonder. Can't ye see that it's all military? Look at the saddles, the barrels, caisson wheels, and parts of big guns," he replied.

The porters quickly looked at the area that he had mentioned and saw that there indeed were rows of wagons waiting to be unloaded. Some were still en route, and could be seen coming down the street.

"If we don't win the war with all that, then I don't rightly know what it would take!" One porter whispered to another. He just grimaced in response. War was ugly, no matter who won or lost.

The arriving train came nearer now. Steam started to belch from the front as it slowed down for a complete stop. The porters stepped back as huge billows of steam engulfed the front of the platform for just a few minutes. The train stopped and the passengers' doors were slowly opened. Well dressed couples stepped down onto the platform. Each person was dressed almost identically to the others in the group of the same gender and even carried the same type of luggage. There were no children among them.

"Church people," one porter quietly said to another, his tone one of displeasure, "Come down here to start up a new church, I'll just bet ya."

Church people or not, several of the porters sprang to life to assist them off the platform and give them directions to the buggies for hire. After their departure, people of all walks of life followed behind.

Ben reached over and opened the reception door so that waiting friends and relatives could greet them.

"Well, if it isn't little Charley!" an older woman remarked, "I haven't seen you since you were knee high to a grasshopper! I guess that wasn't exactly yesterday! Lord have mercy! You are a man now!"

"Oh now Aunt Claudia," the young man said as he hugged her, "It's good to see you again, as well. All I've got is six more months of law school here in New Orleans and I'll be done. Mama sends her regards for putting me up during that time. We all do."

Women hugged visiting sisters and men shook hands with old acquaintances and there were smiles all around. Ben smiled to himself; this was much different than the hospital train. This arrival was festive and cheerful and people were happy.

William walked about the platform as he visually inspected the efforts of all of the porters. If he had something to say, they would definitely know about it later. They noticed that he was there and became ever helpful to the arriving passengers, as they assisted with luggage, briefly held children, or gave directions to those passengers who were lost.

Within a short time the arriving train was ready for the military equipment. The porters knew that they were up against it that meant hard work.

"Alright boys, lets get with it!" William stated, "Good work with the passengers, now the boys in Virginia are waiting as well as all those wagons!"

He then went on to assign work for each of the cars, the new porters would work in pairs, the more experienced ones would work alone. Ben got matched with Andrew, he knew him as a son of local farmer, and as a quiet member of his church, but had never worked with him. William waved for the wagon drivers to approach the platform. Each wagon was unloaded in order of the cars, William had no control over the position of the rail cars, but he did have control over the distribution of the departing equipment.

"Wagon wheels next!" he yelled.

Another wagon pulled to the platform and was boarded by two rail porters, who commenced to roll wagon wheels by hand to the awaiting railcar. The others just stood by and watched as the two labored in the hot sun, they too would get their chance when it was their time to watch the others work. Other porters waited in the cool back room.

"Cannon barrels next!" he yelled after the wagon wheels were loaded and the doors closed.

Ben and Andrew were up this time; together they loaded loose barrels on wheeled wagons and towed each wagon by hand to the rail car. William instructed them on a specific stacking pattern inside of the railcar, alternate front and back.

Loading that railcar was hard work and tedious, both of them alternately took small breaks as they stretched their backs in the hot sun. At times William offered the both of them ladles of water, they were appreciative. What seemed like eternity was actually two hours or so, the last cannon barrel was now placed in the freight rail car, all of the barrels were then chained together.

"Barrels next!" he yelled.

Ben and Andrew, both dripping with perspiration ambled off to the coolness of the back room, another two new porters exited and headed for the wagons with the barrels.

"Hotter than the living hell out there!" Ben stated as the both passed by him.

"C'mon Jacob," one said, "Let's just get it over with."

Ben and Andrew drank water and sat on old crates, both sore from all that heavy lifting and tugging and pulling.

"Ah certainly hope this war is worth all of this," Ben stated, as he wiped his brow on his arm, "Damn, ah'm glad it's Friday!"

"Me too!" Andrew replied, "We don't have to work the weekend, another crew does that, but before long it'll be our turn, a lotta passengers trains on the weekends, so ah`m told."

Ben had never thought about weekend work, it just never entered his mind.

"Work weekends too?" he asked with wide eyed surprise.

"Where have you been Chesser, yes… we all take turns working…. we won't get a turn till prob`ly two er` three weeks from now."

Chapter 30
The Great Race

As promised, Mr. Fournier, as well as Mr. Fitzgerald, the Irish jockey, appeared at the La Rue St. Lazar estate that Wednesday night to get the horse and review the final details with the Chesser family, in particular, Ben. The jockey was most concerned about the horse's appearance. In his mind, Bunches' coat was dull; and other horses that he had ridden were shinier, glossier.

"This horse ain't sick, is he?" the jockey asked with a thick Irish accent.

"Oh, no sir, not at all!" Ben replied.

"He has always looked like that," John further explained, "He may not look like the best, but he is fast!"

Mr. Fournier gave the jockey an affirming nod to let him know that he had nothing to worry about. John was correct, the horse didn't look fast, but he was.

"We'll have him brushed out and looking good for the race," the jockey explained.

"As well, he'll be practice ridden… put through the paces if you will," Mr. Fournier added. "He'll have to get use to the other horses. He'll run alone, and then run with them. You'll get him back after the race in the same condition you see him now, whether he wins or loses."

"He looks strong," the jockey added, "Perhaps stronger than the Fontenot's horse that is running in the same race."

Mr. Fournier gave him a condescending look. It was improper to give out the names of other owners. The jockey caught himself and said nothing more as he looked Bunches over some more. Amanda and Elizabeth had heard what the jockey had said, but John and Ben did not. Now both of them knew that Bunches would run against a Fontenot horse in the third card race. Amanda motioned to her to keep it to herself.

But why would a Fontenot horse being running in a third card race? Amanda thought that it was unlike Pierre Fontenot to do that. He had enough money and resources to run a very fast horse in the first card race. He didn't need to run in the third race of the evening. From that point on, Amanda thought and knew that Gabrielle Fontenot would more than likely be there with her father. She had grown to greatly distain Pierre ever since her husband told her about the experience of selling slaves at the market.

"You say his name is Bunches," the jockey stated, "Would you consider another name just for the race, a track name, if you will?"

The Chesser family just looked at each other. They hadn't thought about that. A race name would perhaps be alright. It wasn't as if they were changing his name altogether.

"Ain't never thought about it," John replied, "What did you have in mind?"

"Well," Mr. Fournier explained, "Horses usually have race names just for the track, names like 'King Classic' or 'Excalibur,' or something like that."

"Or Cajun King," Amanda said under her breath.

"After all," the jockey explained in his thick Irish accent, "We all have a one third stake in this. I want the horse to win just as much as you do and Mr. Fournier does, because there's something in this for all of us."

"What about 'Road King?'" Elizabeth suggested.

"Sounds good to me," John added.

Ben nodded to show that he would go along with the racing name just for the race, but his horse would always be 'Bunches' to him off the track, win or lose. Ben felt bad about letting his horse go away for a few days, but he knew that Bunches, now also know as Road King, had to be made ready. Everybody had a stake in him winning.

"We are in agreement then," Mr. Fournier said, "I will use the name 'Road King' for the race on Saturday night. Gently, Ben stroked Bunches as he wished his good luck and said farewell to him. He had to admit that he had a good feeling about the whole thing. Even if Bunches didn't win, Ben had a six sense of sorts that told him something very good would come out of this.

The crowds were starting to fill the spectator seats; it was going to be a costly night for some because the stakes would run high. Everyone except for Ben and his family sat in high seats, mostly in the middle. The Chesser family had reserved free seats; after all, John Chesser was the registered manager of a fast race horse.

"Whoa there, boy!" Mr. Fournier announced as Ben walked passed him, "Where ya going?"

"To talk to the jockey for a minute," Ben responded. "Just wanna see if my horse is ready to run."

"Sorry kid," he responded as he bit off the end of a cigar. "The owners and managers can't see the jockeys before a race like this. There is too much of a fear of wrong doing and such. If you walk up to him now, you'll forfeit the race. Sorry kid, but that's the rules."

Ben stopped in his tracks when he heard the word forfeit. He most certainly didn't want that to happen. Not after all of this.

"Your horse is ready," Mr. Fournier assured him, knowing that he had just wanted to hear that, and it was the truth. Ben smiled as he heard, "They've been practice running since Thursday morning. Fitzgerald has taken quite a liking to him. Don't worry kid, he's fast. I've seen him run, and you are no liar. He's fast indeed, like you said. He's been eating good, as well."

"Alright, then," Ben responded as he shuffled about, "I'll just go back and sit with my folks and wait for the third card race. I am glad you folks have liked him and taken care of him. He'll make me proud no matter how he does, but I really hope he wins. This is his big chance to prove himself. I prayed he would win. Do you believe that prayer works?" Ben asked.

"Well, I guess we'll have to see," Mr. Fournier replied.

Mr. Fournier sensed that Ben was sincerely worried about his horse and put a reassuring hand on his shoulder, and said, "Nothing to worry about, kid. He'll do fine. After the race, you can take him home."

Ben sighed and tried to relax. He had to think positive. Bunches needed all the help he could get right then and horses were not dumb. If Ben was nervous, maybe Bunches would sense that, even though he was not with Ben. Ben turned and walked away, moving towards the spectators, but something caught his attention.

Someone or something was approaching him from the rear. It was Gabrielle. She sweaty and was almost breathless as she came up to him from behind. He never suspected it would be her at all.

"Ben...Ben!" she gasped out loud, "I've been looking all over for you!"

"Well, I'm glad to see you, too," he smiled.

"No...no," she gasped, "It isn't that. You don't understand. I'm so sorry... I had no notion that this would happen!"

"What in the world are you talking about?" he asked.

She looked about and regained her composure.

"My father has registered Cajun King to run in the third card race. It turns out that he wasn't so bad off after all and qualified with flying colors at the race trials."

"Does he know that my horse is running, as well?" Ben asked.

"Yes Ben, he does. They could have found someone else after that owner quit and joined the Confederate regiment, but my father had Mr. Fournier seek you out and convince you to run your horse. He's setting your horse up to lose. He really believes that you won't win, and he wants you to look bad. If you lose this race, your horse may never have another chance. You know that Cajun King is very fast, and my father has hired the best jockey to ride him."

"I can't believe it!" Ben said as he studied her face, waiting for further explanation.

"Ben, I had nothing to do with this. You got to believe me! I would never treat you like this! You know that! My father just doesn't like yours, so even though he knows your horse is fast and could win, he doesn't want that. He wants to ruin you before your horse has even had a chance to really race," Gabrielle stated, speaking very quickly.

"My father doesn't have much liking for your father either. Thought maybe you'd want to know. It's all over slavery. What a thing to fight over, huh? As if there isn't enough blood being shed on the battlefields, we have to fight here, too," Ben said sadly.

"I know Ben, I know," she responded, almost in a whisper, "I've known that my father and yours don't like each other for some time now, but it doesn't change tha way ah feel about you."

Suddenly, Ben and Gabrielle were almost pushed out of the way by the second wave of surging crowds coming in from the gate. Each attendee wanted a good seat and those wanted to bet still had to join in the wagering line.

"Get us a good seat!" a man said to his wife and children, "I'll be back in a moment. I want to place a bet. Tonight's gonna be a good night to bet!"

"Don't bet too much. We need to keep what money we have," his wife replied.

"I have to go, Ben, before my father misses me. I had nothing to do with this, but I wanted to warn you," Gabrielle said gently as she was almost pushed forward by three over zealous young men who had just come away from the wagering line.

"Thanks. I know you had nothing to do with it because I know you. You wouldn't be so cruel. When can I see you again?" Ben asked.

"I'll find a way, just trust me," she said as she further slipped away in the crowds. "Trust me!" she yelled this time, as she blew him a kiss with two fingers.

Ben was pushed, nudged and reminded to hurry it along by ensuing crowds of people who were ever so anxious to find seats. Ben felt different now. He believed Gabrielle because she had never lied to him and this was no exception.

He felt that a dark cloud was hanging over him because he had helped in Cajun King's rehabilitation. He knew that somewhere in the Bible, it did talk about evil men repaying good with evil. He had done something that was both good and right, and now this was his payment. He had been set up to fail. The injustice of the whole thing really enraged him. The more he thought about it, the more it angered him. Mr. Fournier had led him to believe something different.

Well, at least something good had come out of all of this. Pierre was aiming to humiliate Ben, but Bunches was in a true betting race, and who was to say that he was going to lose? Maybe he would win. Stranger things had happened. Besides, he was in a real race, and that's all that Ben had ever wanted.

All these things were flooding Ben's thoughts as he approached
the stands. His father had saved a seat for him. Ben told him of
the encounter with Mr. Fournier, but not of his meeting up with
Gabrielle.

"Well," John replied, "It's nothing personal that they have against
you. Rules are rules, and it seems reasonable that they would not
allow you to see Bunches. They just want to make sure that there's
nothing illegal going on, and I can't rightly blame them."

"I suppose," Ben mumbled.

"Watch what you say about racing, Ben," his father warned him,
"Brother Zachary and Ruby Lee are sitting right behind us."

Ben cringed at that thought. He did not like Ruby Lee as
anything more than just a church acquaintance. Re-thinking what his
father had just said, he thought it to be a huge coincidence that they
would be sitting right behind them. He didn't dare say anything, but
he thought his father may have orchestrated that arrangement behind
his back.

He looked back and instantly saw Ruby Lee's gaze. She smiled
all the while at his attempt to look back at her. She wanted to believe
that he liked her. Ben could sense that, and immediately turned
around to face the front. There was no way that she would be led to
believe that he was interested in her.

He did realize that their presence there wasn't just coincidence.
More than likely, his father had saved seats for them, just so he and
Ruby Lee might have chance to get acquainted in a public function.
His father's friend from church was not a gambling man, but had
envisioned Ben as an adventurous potential son-in-law.

Ben had wondered what would have motivated Mr. Fournier to
appear at the house and ask him to race his horse. He had previously
not been all enthusiastic. What Gabrielle had said made sense. Her
father was truly a man of influence within the community, and if
he had wanted to, he could have pulled off exactly what she said he

327

had done. Oh, well, now Ben would just have to see what happened, because nothing could be done about any of it.

The crowd roared at the start of the first card race. Ben watched, but had little interest as the local favorites easily out-distanced the other horses with little effort. Many applauded and some jeered, as a lot of money was won and lost on that first race. He looked across the crowds of people to find Gabrielle; she was nowhere to be seen. His greatest concern was that he didn't want to be seen cavorting with Ruby Lee. Although he didn't like her in that way, Gabrielle might think he had romantic feelings towards her, and he had nothing of the sort.

"Beautiful evening we're having, aye Brother Zachary?" John asked as he turned about. Ben could see right through that. His father wanted to start the conversation ruse, hoping that Ben and Ruby Lee would join in.

"Rightly so, Brother Chesser, beautiful night. That's quite a boy you got there!"

"Well, I think so. You know, he's a good boy, strong, with lots of goals and a strong faith, but he's single, and of course, being a couple is better than one person being alone all their life. I don't have to tell you that God created man and woman to be together," John replied.

The crowd roared again at the start at the start of the second card race. Ben tried to ignore his father's remarks. He wasn't interested in Ruby Lee, and that was that, so he watched the race. The horses were off and running and it was going to be a close race right to the finish. As the horses neared the finish line, the crowd shouted all the more. The winner won by only by less than a quarter of a length.

"Well, I chose the wrong one that time!" Zachary sighed, "What do you think, Ruby Lee?"

"Well, father," she replied, being fully aware of the ploy, "You just wait 'til Ben's horse runs. I've got all my money on him... and I'm expecting a hug from Ben, as well."

Ben didn't expect to hear something like that; it was the last thing that he wanted to hear. He really didn't want to hug Ruby Lee, but she could have asked for a kiss. That would have been worse. He cringed at the mere thought of that.

Leaning forward and paying closer attention, he realized that his dream was finally about to come true. In just a matter of minutes, Bunches would race. This was their big day. Ben had thought about this for a long time. Everything seemed so surreal. Ben didn't even see or hear who had won the second card race because he was in a semi-daze.

Once again the crowd roared as the line up for the third card race got under way. Looking across the track, he finally saw Gabrielle. She was sitting with her father, and if looks alone could talk, Ben sensed a foreboding energy of sorts radiating from Pierre Fontenot. Pierre looked as though he was the cat that had just swallowed the canary.

He was racing a horse against the horse that belonged to the young man that helped rehabilitate Cajun King. That wasn't the part that bothered him the most. Worst of all, the boy, who was nothing more than an incontinent worm in Pierre's eyes, was against slavery. What was so wrong about slavery? The coloreds were meant for work. To complicate matters all the more, he knew his daughter had spent some time with that boy, and if she ever tried to married him he would never consent to it. Pierre would disown her.

Ben finally saw his horse approach the starting gate. The jockey was poised and sitting low in the saddle. Bunches looked different. He was well groomed and a little slimmer. Ben could see Cajun King, the Fontenot sponsored horse, two horses away from his own. The other horses and their jockeys lined up, too.

The race starter waited for the crowd to settle down and then he raised his starting pistol high in the air. Upon the sound of the shot, the gate opened and the horses surged forward onto the track. Two unknown horses immediately took the lead. Almost neck and neck, they surged forward, just slightly ahead of the others. Ben watched as the jockey on his horse pressed down quickly on the horn of the saddle. Road King, as they were calling Bunches, inched forward ahead of Cajun King. The jockey did exactly what Ben had told him to do last Wednesday night; it was Road King's cue to get moving faster.

It was now Road King and Cajun King fighting it out for the finish. The crowd roared as they broke away from the pack. Closer and closer they came to the finish, as they ran neck to neck, bridle to bridle. Finally, Road King quickly surged forward and took the lead as they raced around the last oval and unto the final straightaway before the finish line. Cajun King was a third of a horse behind as Ben realized his ultimate dream.

Pierre glared at Ben as though he was a product at the bottom of the outhouse. He had set Ben up in the race thinking Ben's horse would lose. Instead, his horse had lost. Pierre felt absolutely humiliated. Ben didn't even look at him, though he was no fool. He knew that right then, Pierre was very angry.

Though her father would never know, right then, Gabrielle was glad that Cajun King had lost. She had wanted Ben's horse to win. After how Ben and his family had been treated by her father and other slave owners, they deserved to have a winning horse. Even Gabrielle knew that this could very well be a turning point for them all, but especially Ben.

Along with the people who bet on his horse, Ben leapt to his feet and jumped up and down, celebrating the triumph of Bunches, also known as Road King, over Cajun King. Ruby Lee screamed and jumped up and down, as well. She had bet every single dollar she had on Road King and had won a lot of money on Ben's horse. Ben was so excited that he forgot himself in the joy of the moment and hugged her after all. John was pleased. That was exactly what he had wanted to see.

Looking back across the track, to where Gabrielle and Pierre had been, Ben noticed that both of them were nowhere to be seen. It was as though they had up and vanished after witnessing Cajun King clearly losing an important come back race. Ben felt much different now. He had previously thought that perhaps Jean Fournier had set him up to lose and be humiliated, but Mr. Fournier had thoughts of his own, or so Ben now believed.

"We did it, kid!" Jean exclaimed as he slapped Ben on the back and handed over a fistful of money to John.

"We sure did!" John replied. "I knew he could win all along!"

"John" Amanda reminded him, "You did nothing to earn that money, and it rightfully belongs to Ben."

John had forgotten that himself, in all the excitement. He realized that what she said was true. He knew that he was a manager in name only. Ben was the one who had invested so much time and effort into training his horse.

"The money usually goes to the managers, anyway, but that's up to you. You do with it as you see fit. We got our cut," Jean replied.

John handed the money over to Ben. It amounted to more than what he would make in a month at the depot. Ben was delighted and smiled all the while. His horse had won. He truly believed that it was an answer to his prayers. Indeed, what Pierre had meant for his downfall had backfired.

"Here Fitzgerald comes now," Mr. Fournier observed, "He's happy, as well. Just look at him! He's glowing!"

"He's a fast runner, Mr. Chesser, fast indeed! Did you see that?" the jockey exclaimed in his thick Irish accent.

"I worked him hard to get where we are today, but I only met God half way. Really all the glory belongs to Him. He gave me a strong horse that runs fast, and I worked him hard, and God saw to it that he won," Ben replied jubilantly.

331

"You did very well!" Jean commented, speaking to Mr. Fitzgerald, "Was it you or the horse that won that race?" he teased.

"It was the horse," Fitzgerald replied.

He dismounted and gave the reins to Ben. Ben promptly petted his horse on the nose and nudged his ears. Bunches swished his tail and rubbed his warm nose against Ben's cheek. Ben just giggled, still savoring the joy of Bunches' victory.

"Was wondering if you would be interested in running in the second card race two weeks from now? Fitzgerald likes this horse and would ride him again, so how about it?" Jean asked John. Ben looked at his father, and his father looked back at him. Ben smiled and nodded, and John just winked at him.

"I don't see why not," John replied, "I think the horse can handle it."

"Very good then, Ben," Mr. Fournier said. "As usual, we'll be by several days before that to get Road King and work with him some more."

"Thank you for your business," Fitzgerald said, "Fast horse, and he won! Perhaps we can do better the next time."

"How much better is there than to win?" Ben asked.

"There isn't, but what I am saying is that maybe he will have even a better time next time," Fitzgerald replied. Ben just smiled; he understood that logic.

The crowds were departing from the viewing stands. It was now just as crowded with people exiting as it had been with people entering. Zachary and Ruby Lee caught up with the Chesser's just as Mr. Fournier and Fitzgerald shook hands with them and then stepped away into the crowds.

"Ben, Ben!" Zachary said, "I forgot to tell you. We're having a little get together after church tomorrow. We'd be delighted if you could attend, and it's just young folks is all it is."

Ben really didn't want to go because he thought this was just another setup to allow him more time around Ruby Lee, which he didn't want. His father had different ideas. That was just what John wanted to hear. It was another chance for Ben to get to know Ruby Lee. He smiled ever the more as he assured Zachary that Ben would be there. Ben had all he could do to keep from exploding at his father right then and there and Amanda could tell. Unfortunately, this was not the time or place to talk with him, and she also knew that if he wanted to talk, he would come to her. For the moment, she decided it was best to play along with the situation.

"That's nice, Zachary," Amanda said, as she, too, wanted Ben to get to know Ruby Lee. Maybe it was just the whole idea of girls that made him uneasy somehow. He was young, after all. Amanda really wanted Ben to give Ruby Lee a chance. Ruby Lee just stood there, twisted her parasol, and smiled.

"You might want to go, too," John said to Elizabeth, "You can both go together."

Elizabeth didn't mind at all. To her, it provided her with a chance to get out of the house and meet several boys from church. Ben wasn't interested in going, but felt that since she had bet on his winning horse, he could at least show some consideration in kind.

"Very well then! See you at church tomorrow, and we'll have a good time afterwards," Zachary stated.

Ben looked about again. He had been looking for Gabrielle, but she and her father were nowhere to be found. He hoped that Gabrielle wasn't too upset that Cajun King had lost. Now, after humiliating himself, perhaps Pierre would accept the fact that Cajun King would never again be the racehorse he once had been.

"I think its getting dark, father," Ben stated, "We need to get on home. It'll be dark when we get there, and you never bought oil for the buggy lanterns."

"Oh that's right," John remembered, "Perhaps we better be getting along, Zachary. Where's this thing at tomorrow?" John asked.

"I just thought we would have it at our place," Zachary answered.

"Fair enough, they'll be there after services tomorrow."

Ben was in no hurry to get home. He just wanted to get away from Zachary and Ruby Lee before he got any further involved with any discussion with her. As luck would have it, there was a big gap in the departing lines of the crowd. That was his chance to break away.

"See you tomorrow Ben," Ruby Lee stated as she smiled and then winked at him.

"That Ruby Lee sure is a sweet, wholesome girl," Amanda acknowledged, "It's such a shame that her mother passed away on her like that and all."

"Oh, I know," John stated. "Some sort of a lung complaint, from what I've heard, but that was a lot of years ago, and nobody ever really knew for certain what killed her. It's a good thing a lot of ladies from church helped old Zachary when he was raising her."

It was Ben's turn to read scripture that Sunday during services. In the moments when he glanced at the audience, he could sense Ruby Lees penetrating eyes. She was very interested in him; both sets of parents were interested in seeing them court, as well.

But he didn't react at all. He even went so far as to ignore her gazes. He wasn't having any of her subtle flirting and cavorting with his affections. He just wasn't interested; Gabrielle was the light of his life. But he would go to this young folks' get-together just as a favor to Ruby Lee. She had at least had enough faith in his horse to bet a considerable amount of money.

The preacher's sermon seemed endless, and church ladies fanned themselves against the hot, humid air. After what seemed like an eternity, the services were finally over. The leaders of the congregation congratulated the fiery gospel preacher on yet another soul- searching lesson on humility. The preacher thanked the powerful baritone song leader, and the song leader thanked Ben for his inspiring scripture reading. There were smiles and handshakes all around as the elders and deacons shook hands with the congregation's members as they exited through the front door, moving onto the pillar-supported, huge white porch.

"Here, Ben" his father said to him, "You and Elizabeth take the buggy over to Zachary's place. You drive carefully. Your mother and I will ride home with someone else."

Ben did not want to go to the event. He would have rather been in the barn working with his horse, or thinking up another way to be with Gabrielle. But he also had to respect his father's wishes that pleased both his father and God.

"Alright then, c'mon sis," he replied.

"Ruby Lee really likes you, Ben," his sister said as they pulled away in the buggy.

"I don't care if she does or not!" he snarled back.

"Oh, that's no way to be, Ben," she replied, "She talks about you all the time. You ought to hear what she says."

"Yeah, I can't wait," he replied sarcastically.

"To hear her say it, folks be thinking you two are pretty near beaus!" she said.

"Well sis, it aint the truth, that's for sure!"

"Well, say what you want, but I don't see Gabrielle going to church and trying to be a Christian girl! You like her, and worst of all, you are hiding it from mama and papa. Well, Ben, they ain't dumb. They know you like her!" she angrily snarled back.

Ben ignored her comment because he couldn't have cared less what she thought about Gabrielle. He didn't care if Gabrielle wasn't of the same faith. She really had a spirit, and she was definitely searching. She was beautiful, and had a pleasing personality to match her outer beauty. She was amazingly different, much more so than any frumpy church girl.

'Who are you to judge? Were you not also searching for God at one point?" Ben asked.

His sister did not know what to say, so she said nothing. He just kept driving. Finally, they arrived at the gathering. Ruby Lee had baked several pies and had sweet tea waiting as the church guests began to arrive.

"Nice to see you and Elizabeth," Ruby Lee said with a twinkle in her eye, as Ben walked past her.

Ben elected to be receptive and be a gentleman this one time only. After all, he was an invited guest. It was uncomfortable for him, and for awhile he thought that the get together might have been planned so that he and Ruby Lee could get better acquainted without being very obvious about it.

"Ben!" Nate greeted, another young man from church about Ben age, said, as he stood up to shake his hand. "Powerful scripture reading, you certainly made me feel inspired!"

"Well, thank you," Ben replied as he shook his hand as well as the hands of several other young church men.

It was obvious to Ben that they had been involved in a conversation about the Confederacy when he approached. They had immediately stopped and switched topics, discussing the weather instead. He didn't mean to interrupt but it just happened that way.

"Oh, I know you were talking about the Confederates," He stated. "Don't let me stop you."

"Not at all," One replied. "We were just discussing that the word is out that says that General Butler and his Yankee Army are going to stop the English and French frigates from arriving from the gulf. That means prices will go up because tha wares will be harder to get."

"You think he and his army can do that?" Ben asked innocently, as he knew nothing of it.

He honestly could not have cared less whether the frigates were turned away or not.

Ruby Lee interrupted the conversation by sitting next to Ben with an apple pie offering.

"Baked it myself," she said, "It's all for you."

Her teasing comment got a few chuckles and some knowing expressions from the young church men that were seated thereabouts.

"Got yourself a new beau, Ben?" one asked.

"Go ahead," tempted another, "Take some pie.

"She's got more to offer than just that," another teased.

Ruby Lee just looked over at them and gave them a nonchalant, uninterested look. Ben accepted the pie graciously because he had to. He did not dare to say anything. Ruby Lee did have feelings, and she was a sweet enough girl. Ben didn't want to hurt her feelings, especially since she wasn't mean or anything. He just wanted interested in courting her. He felt obligated to take the pie.

"Well thank you so much, Ruby Lee," he said in response, "I do appreciate it!"

"You can appreciate more than that!" another young man stated.

"Well," Ruby Lee finally stated, "Ben has something that you boys don't have!"

Her comment got a round of sneering laughs and subtle comments. Ben felt extremely uncomfortable. He was being out on the spot, and that wasn't what he wanted.

Chapter 31
Puppy Love

While Ben was getting teased about his supposed feelings for Ruby Lee, Elizabeth had found a friend in a church boy named Ethan. They had managed to strike up a good conversation. Ben saw that they were talking and wanted to join that conversation. His sister was typically very shy, and this was a good opportunity to determine what they were discussing. Maybe she had found a potential beau. Anyway, anything was better than sitting there getting teased about affections towards Ruby Lee, especially since there wasn't any truth to that assumption.

His mind was miles away. He didn't want to be there and didn't want to appear to be aloof and unappreciative. The discussions about The Confederate troops' movements defending New Orleans and other locations were barely heard. He just wasn't interested.

"So, Ben," one young man, James, said. "Are you going to enlist? Several of us are. The Yankees can't fight, so it will be over soon enough. We'll all be returning heroes!"

Ben hardly heard the word enlist, but he knew that the church boy was serious about joining up. Ben thought back to the train of wounded and deceased young soldiers. Ben knew that he would not willingly enlist, and if those boys that were with him and his sister had seen what he saw, they would think twice about enlisting. Men were dying in battle by the hundreds, if not the thousands. They didn't appear to be victorious at all.

"Yeah Ben, you ought to think about it," Another boy said, "The south is whipping the Yankees right and left. Everywhere you look, the south is victorious!"

"Well," Another mentioned. "Old General Butler and his Yankee boys won't get far if they decide to stay in the way of those incoming frigates. We'll have a fight right out there on the docks!"

"Got that right!" Another exclaimed as he raised a clenched fist.

"Oh, is that all you boys can talk about?" Ruby Lee mentioned. "Don't ya'll ever think about finding beaus?"

"I have a beau," one said.

"I don't have one, and I don't care to have one," another said.

The conversation wasn't going as Ruby Lee had planned. She had looked over to Ben and received no response. Ben was paying more attention to his sister now. Her church friend, Ethan, was the son of a blacksmith, and his conversation with her seemed interesting. What seemed like an eternity for Ben was actually just a few hours. The time was approaching for evening church services, so they would all need to get home and get ready.

"Reading scripture this evening, Ben?" James asked.

"No, he ain't," another replied for him, "I am, it's my turn."

About a half an hour later, all the invited guests thanked both Zachary and Ruby Lee for their hospitality. For Ben, it was nice to get out and visit someone, but he had been uncomfortable, and it was nice to leave as well.

On the way home, all Elizabeth could talk about was her new church friend, Ethan, and his hard work in his father's blacksmith shop.

"He seems like a right smart fella," Ben said, "I should stop by there sometime and see what they have for tools."

"He said they have tools, but those are a man's thing. We women cook and clean," she replied, "He also said that they shoe a lot of horses for the races. About half of the race horses go to the Fontenot's stable, though."

As they passed by the Chateau Villa, he could see Gabrielle near the pond area. She had seen him, as well, riding with his sister in the family buggy. Ben had remembered that she said that she would find a way for them to meet. She raised two fingers and waved them left to right, giving him a secret signal, and he responded back.

Elizabeth had no idea what the motions meant, and she didn't care. To her, it was just another ride past the Fontenot's Chateau. But Ben had a plan. After church that evening, he would take his horse out riding and meet with Gabrielle. Stolen moments with her were well planned, and he would see to it that it would remain like that.

Both Ben and his sister weren't hungry that evening. They'd had enough pie to quench any appetite that they may have had. None-the-less, they both sat at the dinner table and watched their parents eat and answered questions about the young church folks' get- together.

"That was mighty nice of Zachary to do that," Amanda mentioned.

"Ruby Lee needs to meet somebody away from the church building," John added as he eyed Ben.

"Well, John," Amanda mentioned. "They all do. It's just nice to get out and enjoy each other's company. We use to have those all tha time in Atlanta, if you do recall."

"Oh yes. Remember that party that I came to all dirty? I think your father was going to throw me out and not allow me to see you again when I attended all filthy and all," John chuckled.

"Well, he found out later that you had fallen off your horse and into a big hole just after it rained," she remembered.

"In my Sunday best clothes, no less. my papa would have whipped me a good one if I had been younger and it hadn't been accidental," he sighed. Both Ben and Elizabeth got a mild laugh from that recollection of times gone by.

"Ben," John said, changing the subject, "I think it's your turn to be one of tha usher boys tonight. You know that also includes holding the doors for folks when they come. Be sure and hold that door open longer for Zachary and Ruby Lee."

"It would be a nice gesture," his mother reminded him, "Be sure to shake his hand firmer and smile at Ruby Lee longer."

"I won't forget," Ben stated. Inside, he was nearly ready to explode. He didn't like Ruby Lee the way his parents and her father wanted him to, and he never would. He loved Gabrielle. They wanted to be with each other.

"I talked a long time with Ethan, that blonde haired boy from church whose father is a blacksmith," Elizabeth mentioned, "Oh, he has the bluest eyes I ever saw, and he looks so strong!"

Ben just rolled his eyes at her comment. She was infatuated with him. It wasn't really love that she was feeling, but she definitely was interested in him. Ben had to admit that he wasn't unattractive, and he seemed to have a good work ethic, but so what if he had nice blue eyes? Well, obviously Elizabeth cared. It sounded like something that she would say.

"Thought I would take Bunches out riding after church this evening," Ben mentioned, "I ain't been riding him for awhile now."

"It gets dark early," his mother mentioned, "Be careful. Remember, you have work tomorrow. William will be here bright and early."

"Have you been paying him for giving you rides to work and all?" John asked.

"We all pitch in and pay him for that. I remember when we first started working, he told us that after the first week, we couldn't ride with him anymore, but then we offered to pay him," Ben mentioned, "He's happy with what we give him, and we are always on time and ready for work."

"Can I sit with Ethan tonight at church?" Elizabeth asked.

"Elizabeth, that would be too forward," Her mother explained, "Let him make the decision to sit with you. Don't invite him, either."

"Yes Elizabeth," John added, "That would be best."

"Yes, papa," Elizabeth said in a disappointed tone of voice.

Ben did what he was told, holding the church door open wider for Zachary and Ruby Lee, but he just couldn't bring himself to smile any differently to her. She wasn't his beau, Gabrielle was. He had no feelings for Ruby Lee at all, although both sides of the family thought that he did. He would eventually have to tell them the truth, but he didn't know how.

Meanwhile, he had to allow himself to admit to his feelings. He loved Gabrielle, and she loved him. Their families could not know that yet, because if they did, they would be very angry. If it meant meeting Gabrielle secretly, then that's the way it would have to be. His mind was miles away throughout the service. He couldn't wait to get home and get on his horse's back.

"Don't forget, Ben," his mother stated as he exited through the back door of the house about an hour and a half later, "You have to work tomorrow, so don't be out riding that horse too long."

"I won't, mama, it's just that I haven't ridden him in a long time," He replied.

With that remark said, Ben made a hasty retreat to the barn
to saddle his horse. Riding his horse was a good feeling, but being
with Gabrielle would be even better. They were so happy and free
when they were together. Around one another, they could just be
themselves.

Ben mounted his horse and made his way out into the night
air. There was still a few minutes of daylight left. At first, Bunches
seemed like the same old horse, but once they were on the dirt road,
he reacted differently. He was sensitive to movement and ran faster. It
was obvious to Ben that he had been trained in a manner that he had
not taught him.

Ben wanted to see what he could do. He kicked him hard and
Bunches immediately broke into a graceful gallop. All that Ben could
do was lean into Bunches' movements, working with him in an
attempt to stay in the saddle. His long hair and shirt sleeves flowed in
the wind. Bunches sure was faster than he had been and Ben was so
proud of him.

He would have a nice, long dirt road to run on before he needed
to turn. Ben had purposely headed in the wrong direction; it was part
of the plan. He planned to ride away from the Fontenot Chateau and
back track along a parallel road about two miles ahead.

He had hoped that Gabrielle had not forgotten, that she
remembered that she had successfully signaled him and he had
returned the gesture. It was twilight now. The sun cast an orange
glow on the horizon as he rode parallel to it now. There was only
a half mile to go before he'd reach the backside of the pond area.
Slowing the horse down as he approached, he could see her in her sun
bonnet, waiting for him under the shade of a huge tree. The slow trot
then came to a halt as he dismounted and hid his horse under the
tree.

Gabrielle held her arms out for him. It was a signal to Ben that
she was ready. It was much easier for Ben this time, even easier than it

had been the first two times. This time, they were not only ready, but they had both waited for this moment like impatient children.

"Ben I'm so sorry about what happened at the race track. I am glad your horse won. That was downright evil of my father to do to you. It was very wrong of him to want to make a fool of you, and that was supposed to be a trap. It all makes me so mad. You have to believe me when I say that I had no idea that my father was going to run Cajun King," she whispered.

Ben put his index finger up to her lips. It was a gesture to let her know that he didn't care. His horse had won, and that's all that mattered. Gabrielle hugged him even harder.

He hadn't placed his index finger as a sign of intimacy. He wanted her to be aware of what he was sensing.

"Gabrielle," he whispered, "Defeating Cajun King was little to what ah'm about to tell you."

"What is it, Ben?" she asked.

"Look beyond the horizon there, far beyond those groves of trees, I know good and well that Union forces are encamped there, I have seen them out and about amidst the vicinity, before long they will react, they have specific orders, I overhead two Union officers at the rail depot."

"You can't be serious!" she exclaimed.

"They have orders, Gabrielle, just take my word for it," he replied.

She turned about quickly at Miss Prissy's beckoning call, she was needed at the Chateau. She gave Ben a condescending look that spoke of disappointment.

"I have to go, if ah don't go they will come looking for me," she muttered.

Chapter 32
A Special Night

John looked over the rail yard from his office window, feeling burdened. Many of his best yardmen had left the railroad to join the Confederacy. Replacing them was difficult. They had the experience and the knowledge to keep the rail yard traffic flowing and to a minimum. Unfortunately, pay increases and other incentives weren't enough to keep them there. They were determined to join their kin in the struggle for the cause of independence.

The colored men wanted nothing to do with the rail road. Their quitting started with the passenger depot, eventually crossing over into the yard itself. A handful of the older white men remained employed; they were just too old for fighting and had elected to help the cause by remaining in their present jobs.

The city of New Orleans, as well, was encouraging young men to join in the fight, thus making a contribution to the war effort, but that was to be expected. Enlistment posters were just about everywhere that anyone could look. His father knew that they only glamorized military service, but it worked. Ben had told him that many of the church boys were enlisting.

There would not be many workers to replace the ones that had left. Far more were leaving work at the railroad then applying for a job there. John suspected, whenever he heard anyone walking up to the steps to his office, that they had come to say they quit. He had grown so use to men quitting and enlisting that he could predict the intention of the caller.

Almost as if fate knew what he was thinking about, John heard someone approaching his office. Would someone else quit? This time was no different than any other time he had heard someone. Although he couldn't see the visitor, he prepared himself for the news that he had grown accustomed to hearing. A hard knock on his office door could be heard as the footsteps came to a stop.

"It's open!" he announced. The door slowly swung open. The caller wasn't anyone that John had expected. It was Frederick Bordot, his telegraph operator. He had a telegraph in his hand and seemed to be anxious to explain what the content was.

"Have you come up here to tell me you are enlisting?" John asked.

"Oh no, Mr. Chesser," he almost breathlessly explained, "Good men are still needed here back home, and I intend to stay here. I simply thought that maybe you would want to see this message that came across the wire about ten minutes ago."

John looked at the message and then looked back at him. He did indeed find the message of interest.

"The central office has approved the sponsorship of a ball for the returning soldiers, the ones either on leave or those that have been honorably discharged," he muttered as he read. "Why would they do that? These men deserve to be honored, true, but they will be humiliated. Will they be in the mood to be celebrated? Why would the railroad want to do that?"

"Don't quite know, sir," Frederick responded.

"The railroad employees have been invited, and Governor Watkins, as well as Mayor Hoyt, will be there as well," John continued as he read more.

"Sounds like a big, formal dance," Frederick replied.

"All of the big wigs in New Orleans, as well," John continued as he read more, "I never knew anything about tha railroad doing this. I wonder why," he wondered out loud.

"Mr. Chesser, perhaps it is a way to please the south so that they won't split the railroad in half, like what we have been hearing all this time."

"That's some good thinking, Frederick," John replied.

The unexpected, festive event was the talk of New Orleans as word got around about the dignitaries that would be there, as well as other high society people. All of the railroad employees, as well as their spouses and families, were invited. Many wondered about the real reasoning behind the seemingly bizarre invitation.

The guest list was as unusual as the invite. It was a blend of wealthy politicians and well-to-do society people from New Orleans. Oddly, common people from every walk of life were also invited. The two groups rarely spoke to each other.

Elizabeth was delighted when Ethan appeared at the door and personally invited her. She would have gone anyway, by virtue of being the Deputy Commissioner's daughter, but being invited by Ethan himself was elating. Ben wondered if Gabrielle would be there. Well, he thought, of course she would because her father was very wealthy and politically connected. But he was in a bind; he didn't dare invite her like

How Ben wanted to invite someone, a special someone like Gabrielle. Ethan had invited his sister. Sadly, Ben could not invite Gabrielle. They had vowed to keep their relationship a secret from their families. But still, there would be an orchestra and dancing. If he danced with other girls, she would know. If he danced with

Gabrielle, then both families would know, and if he didn't dance at all, then he would miss out on a good time. This was a really difficult position to be in. He was between a rock and a hard place.

The day before the huge ball had arrived. The city of New Orleans was prepared. Hotel rooms had long been reserved, and finding a regular carriage for hire was impossible. Visitors came from miles around, some traveling hours or even days to attend the gala and hear Governor Watkins speak. The governor, the mayor, and Pierre Fontenot, along with the governor's and mayor's wives, toured New Orleans in a beautiful, white carriage, stopping at points of interest along the way.

Pierre, being a widower, drove the beautiful carriage and shared information that he thought they may find interesting along the way. The carriage stopped at the entrance to the Chateau Villa. Pierre had gone through great lengths to have the property prepared for their visit, though he knew it would be brief.

"This is my house. Just my daughter and I and our slaves live here now," Pierre said.

"Splendid, Mr. Fontenot, jus' splendid!" the governor exclaimed. His wife said nothing, but admired the Chateau Villa with wide eyes and a dropped jaw. Pierre flashed a big smile and a hasty salute to his uniformed property manager, who had done an outstanding job.

When the carriage was out of sight, Miss Prissy and her crew of house matrons breathed a sigh of relief. They were told to be ready in the event that the guests had wanted to visit and stay for dinner. Nobody was really too comfortable with that idea; none-the-less, she and her staff had the mansion in tip-top shape.

Pierre had previously told Miss Prissy that if the guests didn't have time to visit, then the elaborate feast of roast pheasant could be eaten by the kitchen staff. Gabrielle had immediately spoken, proclaiming, "Papa, I'd like some if that's alright!"

"Oh, yes, that's right, you like this pheasant meat, don't you? Well, they'll be plenty. You are welcome to have some. So, Gabrielle ate with the kitchen staff that night. She had told them that she would serve herself so they could have a break. They had smiled at her kindness; deep down inside she was very considerate.

The carriage passed by the Chateau, the grounds crew was nowhere to be found. They had done their work exceptionally well the day before, so that the grounds were groomed and beautiful. Pierre had given them the day off if they did a splendid job the previous day, which they had. Actually, he didn't mind the kitchen matrons being present; they had to be, but not the grounds crew. Giving the grounds crew the day off with pay was a treat to them, but to him it was a way of getting rid of them. He didn't want anyone there that day that didn't have to absolutely be there.

While Pierre was giving a tour to the governor and mayor, Ben was hard at work at the railroad. All day, he kept thinking about the ball. Oh, how he hoped that Gabrielle would be there. He would consider himself lucky to dance even one dance with her. They would have to be careful not to attract any unwanted attention to themselves.

"Alright, boys, we got a train a comin' in here later today. Maybe it'll this evening, matter a fact... there's two of them. It's an easy load, though," William explained when the porters were gathered together and listened to him in the back room.

"Any word on hiring anymore boys?" asked a voice from the crowd. William was perturbed that the boy had blurted out the question, but quickly forgave him. Everyone else had the same question, anyway, and they did have a tight to know.

"Some," he replied, "With so many boys leaving to join to militia, the railroad is offering a good job deal to keep some of the best here. It's true that the Confederacy needs good men on the front lines, but we need some here, as well."

Several of the newer porters leaned forward to listen better to what he had to say. Ben wondered if, as part of this deal, he might get some sort of raise. That sure would be nice. He had no plans of leaving. He wouldn't fight for the cause of slavery under any circumstances.

"I am hereby vested to tell all of you about a contract with tha railroad. It's a generous, damn good offer to stay here and work for us. Any of the newest boys won't be offered contracts for awhile, maybe a month or better. You still gotta prove yourselves."

"What about the contract, William?" Andrew asked, "How is it better for us to stay here and work instead of joining the militia?"

William had expected to hear such a question at some point. All eyes were upon him, and that was fine. He had to tell them of this anyway, but he hadn't expected a question like that so soon. Looking them over, he continued to explain the main terms of the contract and the impact it would have on their employment at the depot.

"The railroad is offering a contract, if you will. They don't want you to quit because we need you, so any time that you spend working here will triple when tha war is over. That means that if you stay for six months, then you not only get full pay and benefits, but we count that six months as eighteen months. Then, since we do that, that's a year seniority that no one else has, and besides, it means an extra twenty dollars a month for all who stay. There's another benefit that starts right away."

"What would that be?" Ben asked, as he had never heard of any contract deal from his father, and he most certainly would have told him about it. William looked about to see if there were any others nearby that might hear him, except for his crew, then replied, in a lower tone, "Boys, sometimes passengers come in this depot that aren't taxed. I'm talking about special passengers. They arrive and get loaded off right away, in the moonlight," he explained.

"So?" Ben asked, "Is it for the ball tomorrow night?"

William dodged his question and continued, "Any of ye's that want to make a hundred dollars in cash can be here at ten o'clock this evening, 'cause the last scheduled train is tha special passengers. Get 'em off and into the wagons and carriages just as fast as you can. It pays a hundred dollars a man, in cash, payable when tha train is empty."

The porters just looked at each other in amazement. Was William serious? Could they really make a hundred dollars? It was a king's ransom, and it was just for a little work on the side.

"In cash, sir?" one porter asked in utter surprise, "Payable tonight?"

"Yep, any takers?" he quickly responded.

All of the porters, new and experienced jumped at the opportunity to make that kind of money in such a short time frame. It seemed especially important to do just that because the war was going on, and the future remained uncertain. They did have families to provide for. Transferring special passengers out of a train car and into the awaiting carriages and buggies for that kind of money seemed too good to be true.

"Hell, yes!" Ben responded. "I'll do it. I'll be here!"

The day at the train depot wore on after that. A passenger train carrying rich potentate people to the ball had arrived and was long gone. The evening train that William predicted was nowhere in sight. The entire depot crew had appeared for this one time event. They had gone home, had supper, some had taken naps, and had all come back for the promised train that would result in a huge bounty for just a little work. Several had thought that he was just having fun with them, but the railroad contract part of it sounded very good, so maybe this was true, as well.

Ben had made it a point to discuss the contract with his father at suppertime. It was true; the railroad was indeed offering healthy stay-at-home contracts to those young men that would choose not to enlist. Also, John didn't have any problem with Ben going back to work that night because an extra transit of incoming passenger trains was on the schedule.

"Oh, where is it?" William asked nervously as he paced the platform while looking at his vest's attached watch, "We don't have all night, and no work means no pay, boys!"

"Think I see her, sir!" James said as he peered into the horizon of darkened steel rails.

Several happily looked in the same direction and saw the first glimpses of steam.

Ben happened to look in the other direction and saw rows of old, boarded up wagons. Did they have something they were trying to conceal? He had expected plush carriages and buggies. Something felt very wrong, though he dared not ask any questions then.

Directly behind the old wagons, scattered groups of men held torches to provide light in the darkness of the night. The torches cast an eerie glow in the near horizon as the nocturnal crowds saw the train as well, and inched toward the receiving platform, seeming to move almost in one movement. William looked back at them and gave them a gesture to stay back until the train was in the station and had completely stopped.

"Easy money tonight boys, easy money," William said, "Easy load. This won't take long at all."

"Not a lot of heavy crates?" Ben asked.

"No crates, Ben no crates at all," William responded. The train made its way to the station platform, with a billow of steam being released as it stopped.

"No cargo at all?" asked James.

"No cargo. Jus' count passengers. Each of ye will be assigned twenty. Take turns countin'. Uh, just in case you forgot, I may wanna add that it's worth a hundred dollars a piece for the each of ye's. There are three hundred and sixty passengers in all, or that is what I'm told," William replied.

"A hundred dollars jus' for a little work?" Ben asked in amazement.

"Hell yes!" Andrew said, "Weren't you listening earlier today? He said it earlier. Let's get those doors open!"

"Chesser, take this and come with me," William ordered as he handed him something in the darkness. Ben did as he was told, unsure what he had been handed. In the darkness he thought that William had handed him a piece of rope, but actually, it was a whip.

"Chesser, use it like this!" William yelled as he cracked his own whip. Only then did Ben realize, to his horror, what it was, and what he was about to use it for, in all likelihood. The mere thought of that made him feel sick to his stomach. As the tip recoiled, it sounded like a revolver going off.

"Use it as ye will. Remember to unload twenty, and then get off!" William ordered.

From his higher, moonlit vantage point on the platform, Ben observed William conferring with one of the wagon masters. He could clearly see William open an old suitcase and reveal rows and rows of paper currency. There was so much currency that William had to close it quickly to avoid drawing attention to them.

"Nah, I gotta make a livin' too, so eight fifty five each!" Ben could hear William say to the man in the shadows.

Alright then...done," came the response, "Cash, no bank receipts."

The voice was distinctive, and Ben knew it immediately. With its heavy French accent it, he would know that voice anywhere. It was none other than Pierre Fontenot himself.

"I want to be paid in cash right now!" William said, "That's tha deal"

"Alright then," Pierre's French voice said again, "It's all here. Here's your cut for the deal and for arranging all of this."

They were unaware that Ben could hear them. Was he the only one? No, he was not. He had to remind himself that although he was perhaps the only human being that heard them, God could hear them. In the end, either in this world or the next, there would be some form of justice for the crime they had committed.

"Alright Chesser, you're up first. Get 'em outta there!" William yelled back to the platform.

Numbly, Ben walked up to the train just as the doors were opened. This was a train full of nigger slaves, much as he had feared, and the stench from the inside of the cars was almost unbearable. A hunched over, boney, gaunt black man emerged from the railcar as Ben pointed to the platform. He really did not want to use the whip in his hand. The man understood to proceed to the plank, but he could hardly walk. William, who had put the suitcase in an undisclosed location in the back room, had been watching and leapt aboard the platform with his whip in his hand.

"Here, Chesser, give him this!" William ordered as he cracked his whip across the black man's back. The man shrieked in pain as a ribbon of red appeared on his back. With waves of pain throbbing through his back, he had to force himself to take steps as his knees nearly buckled. He hauntingly made his way across the platform as quickly as he could, stumbling as he went. The man was quickly placed into an awaiting, open wagon.

Looking at him, Ben's heart just ached. He wanted to say something, but didn't know what to say. The man was old and frail, yet he had never known freedom. Ben wanted him to know what freedom was, but because he had more pigment in his skin than Ben, he never would. As that reality sank in, Ben almost wanted to cry.

"Is this right in your eyes, William? Did God not create that man in His image, just as He created you and me? Can't you see that he is old and frail?" Ben asked.

"I don't care what he is! Now he is merchandise! He's for sale! Soon he will be someone's slave!" William hissed his tone so indifferently cold that Ben nearly threw up.

"But, sir, I thought this train carried arriving passengers for the ball," Ben helplessly objected, his heart feeling so heavy it almost hurt physically.

"Think again, boy!" William said as he turned his back and left, bellowing over his shoulder, "I don't care what you believe! If you wanna keep your job, you will keep your mouth shut!"

A line of slaves had emerged from the train car. Ben looked at them menacing, trying to look colder than he was. The truth was, as he pointed to the platform with one hand and held his whip in the other, he was glad they all moved quickly. He did not want to have to use it.

"That's it...that's it.......get em in there!" William shouted from the rows of wagons.

"Sixteen, seventeen, eighteen, nineteen and twenty. That's it, sir!" Ben yelled down to the pier. Never in all his life had he been more relieved to have completed a job.

"You're up next, Billy!" William shouted to the next porter in line who was standing nearby. Ben stepped down from the platform and handed over the whip to his replacement. Billy just shot Ben a dirty look. He knew that Ben and all of his family were abolitionists. Nearly everyone in town seemed to know by then.

Actually, Ben felt alright about everyone knowing that he was against slavery. Sure, it caused his family difficulties, but it was better to suffer for being against injustice than to suffer because one had committed injustice. Slavery, as Ben saw it, was utterly brutally and totally unjustified.

"Thatta boy!" William yelled up to the platform as Billy took over and whipped the first slave as he came within reach. The man wailed and winced. Billy just laughed as if he had no compassion at all.

Pierre was almost astonished to see Ben there helping with the unloading. He supposed Ben thought the pay was attractive, but wondered if Ben knew what this extra, after-hours work consisted of. He really hadn't thought Ben would be there, yet there he was. Ben's eyes met Pierre's, and then Pierre could see his utter indignation with what was taken place.

In a matter of minutes, the job was done. When Ben wasn't working, he was watching his co-workers. He hadn't liked being there, but the more he thought about it, the more he realized how evil Pierre was and how Gabrielle was so different.

William handed Ben the promised one hundred dollars, but Ben felt bad about taking it. Yes, the Bible said that a worker was worthy of his wages, but was that true when human suffering was involved? Was it justified in God's eyes to mistreat humans like that to earn money? Ben didn't think so, and to Ben it was a fortune to be made at once. If he didn't take it, he would have to explain why to his family, and that would be next to impossible without getting everyone in serious trouble.

Well, it wasn't as if Ben had condoned what had been done. He had no idea that getting that enormous amount of money meant helping to unload arriving nigger slaves in the darkness. Ben glanced at Pierre in the torchlight as he passed by, but said nothing. He was just to hurt and angry to say anything nice to anyone, so he opted to say nothing at to Pierre.

"You're free to go home, Ben. You did your part," William said. Hanging his head, he added, "I can't give you a ride home, so find a ride with someone else."

"I can wait for Andrew," Ben replied, knowing full well that it was best that he didn't ride home with William. He was too mad at

William at that point for the fact that he had lied and deceived Ben and had whipped that old black man and others that were feeble.

"Thanks for your help, Ben" William mumbled, his voice seeped with guilt.

Ben just shrugged and forced a smile. He wasn't happy with what he had just done. It felt so wrong to him that he couldn't even force himself to say 'you're welcome' to William, mostly because he was so ashamed that he had partaken in anything that night. Now he wished he had just stayed home.

"Does my father know what goes on here?" Ben finally asked his voice barely audible.

"What, boy?" William demanded sharply.

"Does my father know about what goes on here when these night trains come in?" Ben repeated.

"Well, I hope not. I don't think so. We keep it a secret. That's why it's done under the cover of darkness," William said slowly. Then, almost barking the order, he snapped, "Don't you go telling him either, or I will have you drafted into the Confederates!"

William continued to watch the scene that unfolded as he slowly drove away. Scores of stench laden, filthy, colored slaves were now out of the train cars and crammed into rickety buggies or carriages. Looking back on the scene, he saw Pierre conducting his own private auction. Each slave would be sold for more than what he had paid, and as long as he made a profit, that was all that mattered to him. He just wanted to auction off some of the slaves that he no longer had used for, who were just extra mouths to feed.

After the train was emptied and had left the station, the porters reassembled in the back room. Ben had watched William leave, but he must have only pretended to leave, because there he was amongst them. That led Ben to wonder why he would have pretended to leave. It seemed he had more of a hand in this whole very suspicious scenario than he was letting anyone know of. William still carried his bloody whip around the crook of his left elbow. A wad of money protruded from his pocket. He tossed the blood stained whip on the wooden floor and then paid the last of the men the money that they were promised.

"Damn…. a hundred dollars for jus' a little work," exclaimed one of the younger porters, who had just received his money.

"Hell, yes!" exclaimed another as he smacked his fist into his left palm.

"We've gotta do this again sometime, sir!" Andrew said as he accepted his hundred dollars.

All of the depot porters that had not been paid yet received the promised reward. Many requested another night job, to take place under the cover of darkness on another night.

"There are no trains coming in tomorrow. Now then, go home, sleep, get baths, shave and get ready for the ball tomorrow night. Remember boys; don't make trouble at the ball. Listen to the mayor and governor talk, eat and drink and dance, but no trouble out of any of ya's," William reminded.

"Ain't gonna be no trouble from any of us," One responded, "We all know better than that."

Ben kept his money in his back pocket, but felt strange about it, almost as if there was blood on his hands. He had no idea that he would be participating in unloading a slave train. He knew that if his father knew about it, he would pitch a fit and possibly confront Pierre Fontenot about conducting a slave auction on railroad property by torch light. At the same time, Ben thought about the ball and about Gabrielle. She would be there and he could hardly wait to see her again.

It was remarkable to Ben that Pierre was fifty percent responsible for Gabrielle's very existence. She and her father were as different as night and day. She was quiet, sweet gentle and intelligent. He was a money hungry, seemingly cold hearted business man. Ben had to wonder what Gabrielle's mama had been like. Maybe Gabrielle had inherited much of her gentleness from her mother.

Little did he know that Gabrielle couldn't wait to see him again either. She had spent most of the day fretting over what dress she would wear, how she would look and constantly changing her mind about her appearance. She normally didn't change clothes fifteen times in three hours. Who would? That was crazy, but without her mother there to offer suggestions, Gabrielle felt very unsure if she really looked attractive.

"Oh, now Miss Gabrielle," Miss Prissy said somewhere around the twelfth dress, "You look beautiful in anything you wear, but that dress just ain't the one for you. You can wear it in a couple years if you really want to, but right now, you just can't show your bosom like that."

"But it's so beautiful, and it's the last one that I got when mama was alive," she sighed.

"Well, that may be so, but it ain't right for a girl of the Fontenot family to wear," Miss Prissy replied.

"What do you think tha rest of the girls will be wearing?" she asked.

"Well, I can't quite answer that question, but I know good and well that any respectable girl won't show her bosom in all them crowds a people," Miss Prissy replied.

Gabrielle looked over her rows of dresses for a more suitable dress. Miss Prissy could see that she was dismayed over why she couldn't wear the dress that was too revealing.

"Now Gabrielle," she said. "You just can't go a looking like that poor white trash girl, Tori. She ain't nothin' but a hussy."

"Their family ain't poor white trash," Gabrielle responded as she shifted through final selections of possible dresses that she could wear, "They have plenty of money."

"She's poor white trash in my book! Just look at how she dresses. No respectable girl should be dressing that way. You certainly won't be dressing that way. If she wants to look the part of a white trash girl, then she is one!" Miss Prissy replied, as she was starting to visually approve Gabrielle's dress selections now.

"And if you feel that way, that's fine with me. You are entitled to your opinion, but she is my friend, so if you would keep your mouth shut, I would appreciate it!" Gabrielle growled through clenched teeth. Miss Prissy decided to be quiet. Gabrielle was a teenager, after all, and she wanted to believe she knew everything. Of course she didn't, but this was not a battle Miss Prissy could win.

Pierre had his best carriage polished to a luster for that evening's ball. The brass lanterns glistened with prisms of light. This was his day to show his wealth and he wasn't about to be out done by any of the other affluent families in New Orleans.

"Excellent!" He commented to his stable house manager, "Beautiful indeed," he said again as he walked about the carriage.

"The two horses are being groomed now, Mr. Fontenot," the manager replied as he swelled with pride over the appearance of the beautiful carriage. He and two others had spent nearly three hours polishing the outside and cleaning the inside. Pierre's approval was much appreciated.

"Very good, then!" Pierre replied.

Pierre then left to check with Miss Prissy and see what she had accomplished. He had requested that his best tuck and tail suit be cleaned and pressed, as well. His pleated white shirt and collar tie had to look perfect. The suit hung in his wardrobe valet in his bedroom. It was right where he had requested her to leave it, and it was indeed immaculate.

Not even a mile away, the Chesser family dressed up for the occasion, but not to the extent that befitted the Fontenot's. It was their Sunday finest, but that was the best they could do. That meant suits for the men, and dresses for the ladies. Both Amanda and Elizabeth had gone through a great deal of effort making sure that it all looked good. This was the finest event that they had ever been invited to, and they would all present themselves in a manner that they were not accustomed to.

Elizabeth fretted over every detail. Ethan would be there soon to take her to the ball.

John and Amanda were both delighted that a local church boy had invited her, and they wished that Ben would have invited Ruby Lee. In their eyes, he had no escort, no date and it just didn't seem right. He could have his choice of any of the girls in church.

But Ben was happy; he knew that Gabrielle would be there. He would get to see her again. At some point, they would have to tell their family. Oh, how Ben loved Gabrielle, but he felt so guilty about keeping their relationship a secret. Pretty soon, he would have to tell someone or it would drive him insane. Why should he be ashamed that he loved Gabrielle? Was love ever wrong?

Elizabeth was ready when Ethan knocked on the door. Opening it, she invited him in for a moment. He looked better than any church service attendee. He was so different in her eyes. Elizabeth was impressed. Ethan looked like quite the young gentleman.

"How do I look, mama?" Elizabeth asked, as she turned around and waited for one final word of approval from her mother.

"You look fine. You look like a beautiful, young lady. I would be proud to dance with you!" Her father answered. Everyone in the room chuckled. Elizabeth felt herself relax.

"You really do look absolutely stunning, Elizabeth. Why, the only time you look even half that beautiful, at least that I have ever seen, is when we are in church!" Ethan exclaimed.

"Why, thank you," Elizabeth responded as she blushed slightly.

"Should we go? I have the carriage outside," Ethan said.

"Ethan, aren't you just a little young to drive a carriage?" Amanda asked, sounding concerned.

"Oh, my father has taught me well. I am quite a fine driver. Don't you worry, ma'am. Elizabeth will be fine with me. If I injure her, you can take me to court, I promise!" Ethan stated with conviction.

"Nah, there will be no need for that. I have prayed for both Ben and Elizabeth since they were in Amanda's womb. I am sure that the Lord will watch over both of you," John said, his tone one of reassurance for everyone within earshot. Ethan wouldn't admit it to anyone, but he was nervous about having Elizabeth with him in the carriage. He didn't want either of them getting hurt or killed anymore than Amanda did.

"Well, we'll see you there, Elizabeth. You and Ethan have a good time," John said as they left.

"Thanks, we will," they responded in unison.

"Ethan?" Amanda called after him and Ethan looked back, "You take care of my daughter."

For a minute, John and Ben just looked at her in surprise. Although she did tend to get emotional, she very seldom cried in front of anyone. She had only cried in front of John a few times in all the years they had been married, and Ben had only ever seen her cry twice that he could recall.

"My little girl is going on a date," Amanda sobbed, "And the next thing I know, she will be getting married."

"Oh, now, mama," Ben said, trying to comfort her, "That's a ways off yet. Don't move too fast. She's still a kid."

"I have prayed for her all her life. That's all we can do, honey," John said tenderly, "All we can do as parents is teach our children good values, about God's love for them, and help them along in the world the best we can. Then, all we can do is hope that it all works out, and they go far in life. That's it, honey, and the rest… we just have to leave in God's hands."

"I know what you are saying is the truth," Amanda said, trying to compose herself again, "But this still isn't easy."

"I know, mama. Change is hard. But, just because she's growing up doesn't mean she loves you any less. The fact is, when you are old and frail, maybe you will need us, just like we needed you when we were children. We'll always be here for you the best that we can, and we won't leave you and pa to face this world alone," Ben reassured her.

"Thanks, I do appreciate that," Amanda replied.

New Orleans' streets were packed with overwhelming crowds. Lines of well dressed people took to the brick streets for passage because the wooden boardwalks were not accessible due to the numbers of people, most of which were going to the same place. Carriages' coachmen helped their passengers onto the brick street; visiting wagons with waiting, black mammies crowded the narrow side streets.

"Lord, this is pretty incredible! I have never seen these streets more packed," Elizabeth said to Ethan.

"It is pretty amazing," he agreed.

They pulled into the parking lot of the hall where the ball would be held. Ethan struggled to find a parking place and offered to drop Elizabeth off at the door. She said she wanted to stay with him. They finally found a spot and parked, but then they had to walk quite a distance before they reached the doors.

There was shoulder-to-shoulder people, with standing room only, as an usher opened the massive double doors made of oak doors for the dignitaries and invited guests. Inside, the ballroom was more crowded than the outside. Uniformed Confederate officers, local dignitaries, elderly gentlemen and matron ladies were ushered in by invitation only.

"Tori thinks she is just the queen, as usual," Mary murmured under her breath, speaking to Gabrielle, "Just because she is spoiled rotten doesn't give her tha right to look and act like that!'

Victoria, better known as Tori, emerged from the carriage first, which was once again a slight violation of proper etiquette. The other girls almost gasped at her risqué appearance. This dress was even more risky than others they had seen her in. Her low cut dress revealed much more cleavage than what theirs did, and it barely came down past her ankles. Her hat was tilted at a tempting angle, which was considered by several of them to be unfeminine-like. Georgette's jaw dropped at the slight of Tori as she strutted about with her parasol, obviously seeking attention from the unmarried Confederate regulars that had their own reception area. Mr. and Mrs. Boyer were both graciously received by the awaiting reception line and joined them. There were handshakes, hugs and compliments all around.

Other carriages began to arrive as well. Each party was received and carriages were parked. The reception continued until there were no more quests on the invitation list that had not shown up. The ballroom overflowed with people, to the point that hardly anyone else could fit in. Many wanna-be guests that were not on the list had to be turned away at the door.

The crowd positioned themselves and struggled against one another in an attempt to get the best view of the podium. Shoulders bumped shoulders as gentlemen nodded for pardon. Several rows of tables were all taken; members of the orchestra stood in their pit with instruments in hand, or those that played the larger instruments stood next to their instruments.

The governor and the mayor, along with their wives, sat in a secluded, elevated box seat. As William looked about, he caught the mayor's gaze and gave a top of the head salute, indicating that the events of the railroad slave sale had gone well. The mayor smiled and returned the gesture. The nocturnal slave deal had made tens of thousands of non-taxable dollars.

Then Pierre, who sat behind the mayor, leaned forward and whispered the success of the sale in the mayor's ear. The mayor would get his percentage from Pierre Fontenot later. The money guaranteed that the mayor's office would look the other way. Sure, they knew that what was happening was wrong, but the money made the risk and any consequences their actions might bring about worth it.

The railroad porters had arrived separately, and were looking to find each other and stand as a group. They were completely mixed in with the hundreds, so they only achieved their goal to some extent. Before long, the mayor arose, straightened his collar and stood at the podium. The audience sensed his presence and came to order.

"Ladies and gentlemen, distinguished guests…it is with pleasure that I introduce the speaker of the hour, a man of honor and grace. Please welcome the governor of the great state of Louisiana, the honorable governor Henry W. Watkins!"

The audience roared with applause as Governor Watkins arose from his seat and took his place at the podium. The mayor slightly bowed at him, then sat down.

"My many thanks, Mayor Hoyt. It is with pleasure that I attend this evening's events. My wife and ah both extend our gratitude for the invitation. I must say that the wonderful folks here in New Orleans have been so very good to us. We had a wonderful tour yesterday, and the food and hospitality of everyone has been so appreciated."

Once again the crowd applauded. The governor waited for the clapping to subside.

"My gratitude to your own citizen, Mr. Pierre Fontenot who has been most gracious, as well as all the fine citizens of this beautiful city!"

The governor took a drink of water as he waited once again for the applause to calm down. Ben looked about at the mention of the Fontenot name. Gabrielle was nowhere to be found in the hundreds of people who were there, at least not that he could see. But she had to be there, didn't she? He looked about once again, but still did not spot her.

"Divine providence has blessed our great land with plenty, and with good fortune," The governor started, "The northern enemy has been driven out of the Attakapas parishes, as well as away from the Atchafalaya. Although our farmers have suffered from drought and from the late invasion by Yankee troops, we have corn enough for two years subsistence. I know who rules the destiny of the south. We do, and if we unite, we will be fine, for we have plenty in this land!"

The audience again broke out in thunderous applause, with "Here, Here!" heard in shouts. The governor waited even longer this time for the thunderous applause to quiet down.

The governors' fiery speech for reform continued as Ben, shoulder-to-shoulder with an elderly gentleman, began to look about at the ballroom. Its high, red, velvet drapes and rows of chandeliers were indeed quite impressive.

A group of young ladies in hooped dresses and tie-down hats congregated together in an isolated corner. Some sat in arm chairs and some on couches. All eyes were on the governor, whose speech had enthralled all who listened.

"Yes, my good friends, the northern states don't have seaports like New Orleans has, and they delight in telling us how to run our markets. This treachery will cease!"

Ben noticed Andrew about ten feet away, in the same situation, wedged between a Confederate gunnery officer and a fat, gray-headed, local gentleman. By slowly shifting and moving his feet, Ben was able to move the ten feet towards Andrew. The short journey seemed like an eternity, as Ben did not want draw attention to himself. The gentleman noticed him coming in, and traded places so Ben was now standing next to Andrew.

"The nigger markets...who has any right to tell us that the niggers have any rights at all? I'm a telling ye's, ladies and gentlemen, the niggers are states' rights for us. We have the rights... and always have!"

"This is treason!" shouted a man with long white hair and a cane.

"Yes it is, and that's all it is!" the governor shouted back. The governor again wiped his forehead with a handkerchief.

"Thank you for listening. I know this was a short talk, but I hope it was worth your time. My wife and I shall be in the main lobby for all those that wish to converse with us about this matter or anything else. Now, a speakin' of taking your money, I now introduce Mr. Pierre Fontenot!"

The audience chuckled softly at the governor's remark and welcomed Pierre to the spotlight with a warm round of applause.

"Thank ye, Governor Watkins. I'm sure that, like others, I agree with what you said. We are all at your service to defend our God given rights. I had no idea of the tyrannous strife of the north, and I remain your devoted servant, sir!"

The governor nodded from his box seat as Mayor Hoyt patted him on the back for his fine oration. Looking across the audience, at first Pierre said nothing as he surveyed the massive ballroom.

"Now, ladies and gentlemen, Governor Watkins, Mayor Hoyt... let the festivities begin!" He finally stated.

The audience applauded briefly and quickly settled down. Many of the older audience members moved through the huge oak doors, as those wishing to visit with the governor moved forward and out. The twenty seven orchestra members took their seats and had their instruments at the ready. Confederate regulars in dress uniform congregated together, and so did the railroad porters.

From a nearby service door, colored matrons carted in huge, sculptured crystal bowls of sweet drinks and plates piled high with pastries. Ben noticed that his parents had chosen not to attend the dance portion of the festivities, but had joined other older couples in the huge lobby to hear the governor speak some more.

Later, when the governor was through, the same audience would move to the ballroom. There just wasn't enough room to have a combined dance. Ben also noticed that Elizabeth and Ethan, along with other couples, had found a table and were enjoying the sweet drinks and pastries. The Confederate regulars offered poured crystal goblets and delivered them to the group of young ladies that were nearby. The railroad porters, following their cue, also dispensed drinks to another group of stunningly dressed young ladies seated nearby. Andrew ended his rounds with an extra goblet in his hand and, being curious of the taste of the contents, drank it quickly without anyone noticing. It was nothing more than sweetened, strained strawberry juice. The railroad porters were all dispersed as they struck up conversations with the young ladies.

"Drink, Miss?" Andrew asked as he noticed a pretty girl with no goblet in her hand.

The young lady wryly smiled, turned away from his gaze and walked away giggling.

"Care for a sweet drink?" He asked another, and once again, the young lady swept away without a word.

"Strawberry nectar?" he asked the next, who once again gave him a smirk, and made a quick exit.

It was then that Andrew caught Ben's gaze, and Ben gestured across his lips with his hand to let Andrew know that his quick drink had left a red, upward semi circle stain on his mouth, giving him the appearance of a perpetual red smile. Andrew didn't understand what Ben was trying to tell him at first. Ben pointed to his mouth, as he was too far away to speak. Andrew finally got the cue and wiped away the red stain with a handkerchief. Ben smiled at Andrew to let him know the stain was gone.

Meanwhile, Tori had a large group of Confederate regulars crowded about her, waiting on her every need for drinks and pastries. She teased and cajoled each and every one about who would get her a treat from the matrons. Giggling and chuckling, they were spell bound by her sensual teasing and her low-cut frilly cuffed dress. Ethan almost immediately caught Tori's eye gaze, but preferred the mannerisms of another girl, namely Elizabeth. Ben looked for, and finally spotted, Gabrielle. She was stunningly beautiful, and she was sitting with her friend.

Pierre Fontenot stood behind the podium once again, cleared his throat, then said, "Uh, ladies and gentlemen, it's now time for the necklace auction. Gentlemen if ye would, form two lines face to face, and ladies, ye know what to do!" he said as he passed his hat to the young ladies.

Each young lady would remove her necklace, and it would be auctioned off to the highest bidder. The reward would be that the highest bidder of them all would win the hand of the necklace's owner for the opening dance. The necklace would later be returned.

"Bid generously, gentleman. Proceeds help to pay for Governor Watkins visit, and I'm sure that we should do anything to assist the governor in the legislature. Let me be the first to give, although I don't need to bid on any of your fine necklaces, ladies!" He announced as he walked over and placed several bills in the hat.

Each young lady removed her necklace and placed it in the hat. The Confederate regulars and the railroad porters all craned their necks to determine what necklace belonged to what girl.

"Now, now, gentlemen!" Pierre half-heartedly admonished them as he curtly smiled. Heads and shoulders quickly turned straight again. Pierre then took the hat and handed it to the other group. With the hat now full of necklaces, the young ladies waited in nervous anticipation, each one hoping that her necklace would bring the highest bid. From their point of view, the girls could not see what necklace was up for auction. Pierre stood before the assembled two lines, each line facing each other.

"Alright, boys, one bid per necklace. If and when ye don't want to bid, then pass it along. All ye's understand?"

Pierre's instructions were interrupted by the governor's fiery speech, which was still going on in the lobby across the hall. Muffled shouts and exhortations of law reform could be heard.

"Boys, now what ye say, ye pay, whether or not you have the winning bid. Boys, every dollar collected here is one more dollar against the northern treachery," Pierre said. They all nodded to show that they understood the bidding rules.

Ethan stood next to Ben and tried hard to remember what Elizabeth's necklace had looked like. He had not paid much attention to it. Ben noticed Gabrielle near the seated groups of girls. He would have no problem remembering her necklace because it was the same one she usually wore. Other boys struggled within themselves, wishing to dance with a certain girl and trying to remember what necklace belonged to what girl.

Pierre gave the first necklace to the first man, a Confederate regular.

"Dollar," He said in a thick and heavy southern accent, as he passed it to the next man.

"Dollar and a half," came the response as the necklace was passed along, Pierre kept a bid record as he walked along and witnessed the line of bidding men. Man-to-man and hand-to-hand the necklace passed. The bid stopped at seven dollars. The next necklace came out. There was a pass, another pass and then a bid, "Four dollars." Then the next man said, "Five dollars." Necklaces were arranged in order on a table according to their bid value.

The young ladies, who could not see the ranked necklaces, were ever more anxious as the bidding went quickly and necklaces went from hand-to-hand. Three, four, seven and ten dollar bids could be heard. Squeals of delight, along with the muffled, emotional crowd's exhortations of the governors' speech attendees could be heard. The bidding continued fast and furious.

The orchestra members had taken a personal interest, and they stood to watch the proceedings. Ben had handed over so many necklaces that his wrist was getting sore with monotony. He waited for the right one to come along.

"Eight, nine, nine-fifty, twelve dollars!" exclaimed the railroad porters, against the Confederate regulars, as a necklace was passed down. This was the one he had waited for. Ben recognized the necklace and exclaimed, "Hundred dollars!"

A few men looked at him as though he had lost his mind. That was a lot of money, no doubt about it, but he knew that it would be worth every penny. There were still quite a few necklaces left, but Ben passed on every single one. He was only interested in one girl. Bid after bid was placed. Some necklaces ranked high, others low; the end was near and bidding was almost over.

"Last one, boys!" Pierre said as he dropped it in the hand of the same Confederate regular.

"Dollar, three dollars, three fifty, five dollars, ten dollars, fourteen dollars, fourteen and a half," came the quick shouts, "sixteen .. seventeen .. seventeen and a half," then nothing. The last man gave it back to Pierre, who grouped it on the table.

Pierre took a few minutes to tally up the fund raising auction's totals, adding rows across, and then rows down.

"Three thousand nine hundred and ninety-two dollars for the governor!" He said.

The men applauded the efforts of the successful auction, but were more interested in the winning necklace.

"The winning necklace is this one. The highest bid is one hundred dollars. Will the gentleman from the railroad depot please come forward?" Pierre asked.

Ben was astonished at the fact that the bid had actually won. He had only said it to spend the money that he earned the night before and despised having. To him, it was slave money, ill gotten and earned only because he didn't know what he was getting into. Had he known what he had to do to get paid, he would have turned the job down.

Pierre was astonished and his jaw dropped when Ben stepped forward. He didn't know that it was his high bid that had won. He regarded him as a country bumpkin from Atlanta, the son of an outsider and abolitionist, a young man that he believed would never succeed, that just happened to have a lucky day at the racetrack one night.

Pierre was dismayed that Cajun King had lost to a common, country road horse and had not forgotten about it. Pierre pretended not to know Ben in the presence of the others gathered there, deciding that he would play it safe. The male audience hooted and howled at Ben teasingly, and he smiled all the while.

Pierre placed the winning necklace in his hand as they went off to find the owner. The Confederate regulars, as well as the railroad porters, continued to give Ben teasing, whooping shouts. Ben turned and smiled, accepting their ruckus simply because he did not anticipate that the bid would win. Pierre dangled the necklace in front of the faces of the anxious girls; each face fell as she realized that it didn't belong to her.

"It is mine!" shouted Gabrielle as she adjusted her tie down hat.

Pierre's face fell, his eyes widened and his jaw dropped. He was caught in a difficult moment. He couldn't tell Gabrielle she could not dance with Ben. Ben had paid a huge sum of money to dance with her, and the more Pierre thought about it, the more the fact that he had had won enraged him. It was fair and Ben had won the first dance with her.

"But, ah... ah.." Pierre stammered. Gabrielle just smiled at him, knowing he was irritated. That fact just made this whole occurrence all the more enjoyable for her. He never finished his sentence, as the orchestra leader turned to the orchestra and mumbled..... "Minuet in C, a one an' a two and a..."

The ballroom floor cleared away as Ben took his prize and swept her forward in a slow waltz. Round and round the couple went, her dress twirling as Ben spun her around. The second highest bid was determined, and that couple also joined the waltz, and then the third and the fourth highest bids were determined, and before long the floor was filled with couples.

Ben noticed that the couple next to them had abruptly stopped. The girl suddenly broke away with a defiant gesture, turned about, clenched her fist and returned with a right hand round house swing. The blow caught the Confederate regular on the right side of his jaw as he reeled backward, stumbling across two chairs and into the outstretched arms of his commanding officer.

"Why... you! If you were a man...I'd!" he said through clenched teeth, his face contorted in anger.

"You, sir, are no gentleman!" the girl shot back as she twirled around and left.

"I paid twelve dollars to get punched after two minutes on the dance floor? I expect more for twelve dollars," he muttered to himself as he quickly composed himself.

"That's Annie for you!" Gabrielle whispered as Ben looked at the soldier who was now on his feet.

"You know her?" Ben asked, "That soldier was mighty forward with her."

"Yes, we use to go to harp lessons together, but she gave it up."

"Virginia reel!" yelled the orchestra leader.

"Know how to reel?" Gabrielle asked as her face lit up.

"Well, uh, no, but I can catch on fast!" Ben replied.

"Nothing to it. Jus' follow along, and you'll be fine. Just do what I do," she replied.

Two lines formed. Ladies were on one side and gentlemen were on the other. After slight bows and curtsies, the orchestra broke into a fast tempo song. Arm in arm, round and round the couples twirled. Feet danced a shuffle; the handclapping coincided with the fast music, and each couple took a turn dancing through the middle as the others clapped in unison. The orchestra held the last note, and then abruptly stopped. That signaled the end of the reel. Couples applauded themselves and the audience then retreated to the tables or stayed on the floor for the next dance. The hours went by quickly as Ben and Gabrielle danced, talked and drank nectar at the tables.

"Well well!" Tori teased as she noticed Gabrielle with Ben, "Aren't we cozy?"

Gabrielle disdained Tori, but had no choice but to speak with her.

"Cozy enough Tori, but at least I only have one man to get cozy with! You are just a big slut that has a future with the whores of New Orleans, and all the money in the world won't change that!" she shot back.

Tori ignored Gabrielle's insult and turned her attention to Ben.

"Well big boy," she hissed in a lower tone, "I heard you got a fast horse and you actually beat a Fontenot racer, so don't even think about running against my horse!"

"I wouldn't dream of it," Ben responded in a flat tone with a blank face.

"Don't you have somewhere to go, Tori? You certainly have your share of gentleman callers from the Confederacy," Gabrielle said sarcastically, "Go be with them!"

Tori ignored Gabrielle's slur once again and turned her attention to Ben once more.

"You can do a lot better than to run with a slut like Gabrielle Fontenot!" she hissed under her breath so that Gabrielle would not hear her.

"If you were a man, I'd knock you senseless for saying that!" Ben replied indignantly.

"Why don't you just run along, Tori?" said Mary, who was standing nearby, "You seem to have a line of men waiting for you, and they all seem to be on furlough."

Tori shot her a long and devious stare, and then said, "I'd rather be with a line of real men, instead of socializing with a group of whores like you girls are!"

With that, she turned and joined a line of men, who were more than eager to wait on her every need and listen to her sensual mutterings. Ben just rolled his eyes. In his opinion, Gabrielle was right about Tori; she was a whore. She was not a young lady. What Ben did not yet realize was that Gabrielle had not meant what she said. She was just trying to get Tori to go away.

"Is she always so rudely forward?" Ben asked Gabrielle.

"She is the way she is, I suppose. I cannot change her. Pretty much as long as I have known Tori, she has been kind of..." Gabrielle paused, trying to think of the right adjective.

"Disgustingly straight forward, even when it's not proper?" Ben suggested.

"Yes, yes, that's it," Gabrielle agreed, and Ben laughed heartily.

"I've had a wonderful time, Ben, but it's time for me to leave. My father is having the governor spend the night at tha Chateau, and asked me to help out and be the hostess because my mama isn't around anymore. I'm sure you understand."

"Well, uh, when can I see you again?" he asked.

"This next weekend should work. Let's quickly plan on something," she whispered.

Ben and Gabrielle quickly formulated a secret time and place, as well as a new secret signal; it was perfect.

As they talked, the ballroom emptied out as buggies and carriages were kept busy picking up departing, well-dressed couples. The governor and his entourage had been afforded the privilege of being the first to leave to avoid the crowds. Both he and his wife smiled and waved as the white carriage headed away.

"No chance for a carriage," Ben whispered back to her, "Besides, I have to go home with my folks. I'll see you this weekend."

"Damn, my feet are killing me!" Andrew said as he approached Ben, who was now standing alone at the exit, "Ain't use to all this dancing."

"Well, I'm not either, but I had a good time," Ben replied.

"So did I, I saw you dancing with a really pretty young lady. Are you and her smitten?" Andrew asked.

"That's not any of your business!" Ben snapped.

Chapter 33
Confrontations and
Political Issues

The governor's speech left a profoundly impacted the townspeople, and several groups were still discussing the implications of war news and southern occupation. A heavy set man adjusted his top hat to a different angle as he listened to another man express his concerns.

"The hell if I'll pay extra! For what? Should I pay for them northern potentates to make up more and more tax laws?"

The heavy set man interrupted his friend and exclaimed, "Keep on and on and they'll be charging sales tax on our house niggers! I agree wit' the governor. The northerners won't be happy wit' just a war. What do you railroad depot boys think?"

"Well sir, we just unload the depot's railcars. We have nothing to say about the new policies," Ben replied, "But I did enjoy seeing Governor Watkins."

"Well, I'd think about it. You better get an opinion and starting saying what you think! Costs will get so high that the railroad just might let all ye's go an' fill the depot with nigger labor like they had before. You ever think about it like that? Men that don't work don't eat! That's what the Bible says. Don't you believe God's Word, boy, or do you think He is a liar?"

"I believe in God," Ben responded simply.

"Ah, George," the man's friend cut in, "Leave those boys alone. I am sure they would rather dance!"

"The dancing is over," George shot back.

Andrew thought about what the man had to say. He suddenly realized that these days, people were coming and going at the railroad all the time. It seemed like everyone wanted to fight in the war. It was possible that slaves had worked the platform before, and the thought that he might lose his job scared him. He did have bills to pay, and he certainly did not want to go hungry. He was clueless as to whom he had replaced on the depot platform.

"Ben," he asked, "Did niggers have our jobs before we did?"

"I guess I never thought of that, and I am unsure. I'll have to ask my father about that one," Ben replied. "But what's the difference? We both are making good money, aren't we?"

"You made very good money unloading the train last night," a man's French accented voice said from behind them. Ben turned about to see Pierre Fontenot standing directly behind him. He apparently had heard every word that Ben had said to Andrew.

"I don't know how you bid on my daughter for tha first dance, but I do know that you spent your hundred dollars on her. Just let that be the last time you spend any money on her!" he said with a stern expression.

Ben was speechless. He didn't know how to respond to that, and turned to Andrew. Andrew looked just as shocked by the whole episode as Ben was. When Ben turned back to respond to Pierre, he observed that he had walked away and mingled with the exiting crowd.

"Do you know him?" Andrew asked.

"Yes," Ben responded, "That's Gabrielle's father. She's the girl that ah danced and sat with tonight."

"Oh, yes, I saw you two together. She's really pretty. She's definitely a keeper!" Andrew exclaimed.

"She has the winning personality to go with her looks. Well, to me that's more important, but hey...there's nothing wrong with having both, so we'll maybe see what happens between us. I don't know. She's rich, and I am not," Ben said softly, so that only Andrew would hear.

"Do you think money is everything?" Andrew asked, "Money can't buy love or happiness."

"Well, it can do lots of things, and to her father, I think it's everything. Boy, I really don't like him. I don't know why he would say something like that. I ain't never had no quarrel with him over nothing."

"Well," Andrew responded, "If you spend anymore on her, then he can't know about it."

"Got that right!" Ben shot back, "He can't know!"

Along with several Confederate regulars, the remaining railroad porters lagged behind the exiting crowds. Well dressed gentlemen and southern belles continued to discuss the fiery speech from the governor. The colored matrons went about their business in the ballroom, organizing chairs and picking up hundreds of goblets and remnants of sweet breads left behind by the younger, dancing audience. Ben had long lost his parents in the emerging, exiting crowds, but he had remembered that the carriage valet would bring the family carriage up to the cobblestone drive.

"I'll see you tomorrow," he said to Andrew, "Better get while the gettin's good!"

Finally, he saw a chance to get through the crowds, and accomplished the small feat with friendly smiles and cordial head nods. The last thing that he wanted was to be enjoined in a discussion about the speech of the evening. He felt differently about slavery and the war then probably over ninety percent of the people. He didn't want to get in any arguments or become the object of ridicule.

The scene outside was almost as chaotic as it had been on the inside. A long line of carriages waited amidst the crowds. Men stood up in the carriages to get a better view and draw attention to themselves, mostly for the sake of those who were looking for them. Ben walked along the line of carriages as best he could. Surely, his parents' carriage would be nearby.

"Well, what a strong and handsome man I do see!" said a female's admiring voice as he passed by her. Ben turned about to notice who had spoken to him, as he had not paid attention in his haste to find his parents' carriage. A southern belle stood next to an oil driveway lamp, dressed in pink and twirling a parasol. She was unusual in appearance because all of the rest of the women were attired in white or beige.

"Why surely you remember me, Sugar!" She said with a seductive gaze, "Ah'm Louisa Lovejoy!"

"I don't know you!" Ben stammered back at the unusually dressed woman.

"It makes no difference to me. We can have just as much fun!" she replied.

"Ah don't know you and ah don't want to know you," he said with a sour facial expression.

"Well Ben," she replied with an ear to ear smile, "Whatever you get from Gabrielle Fontenot, you can get from me!"

"How did you know my name when I didn't tell you?" he asked.

"You know where my balcony is, Mr. Chesser. Anytime you want something better than that Fontenot white trash, why, you just come and see me!" she laughed.

Ben was shocked and for a moment, he didn't know what to say or how to respond. Finally, he heard himself say, "Go to hell you crazy bitch!"

He turned away as she still laughed at him. As he disappeared in the crowds, he could still hear her sensual beckoning and pleading tease calling for him. He passed by an elegant carriage that Tori was sitting in. She simply gave him a smirk and then a knowing, despising glare. He ignored her completely. Looking into the horizon of carriages, he finally spotted his father, who had noticed him in the boardwalk crowd. Almost running now, and dodging pedestrian traffic, he arrived almost breathless at the family carriage.

"Get in quickly!" his father said, "I see an opening, so we can beat it out of here real fast!"

Ben did what he was told and jumped into the back seat. Never had he been so glad to get away from a crowd. That girl, whoever she was, wanted passion and he had no desire to do that. He loved Gabrielle. She was the only one.

"Where's Elizabeth?" he asked, almost breathlessly.

"She told us that Ethan's folks were taking her home," his mother replied.

Ben wiped his sweaty face on his cuff just as they passed by the same southern belle dressed in pink. He noticed that she blew him a kiss as their carriage passed by. John jiggled the reins and the carriage quickly mainstreamed into the cobblestone street traffic.

"What did you think of the governor's speech?" Ben asked, because any conversation was better than riding in silence. He had expected to hear rave reviews, or anything similar to what he had heard from other people.

"You know my views on slavery, so we needn't go there, and we won't. The speech was basically a chance for the governor to get the people worked up, and he sure did that. It was nothing more than a fund raising event for the Confederacy," John commented, "But I can see the railroad's point of view. They want to please the south and not split the company with the north."

"You really think that's what it was?" Ben asked, rather bewildered.

"Well, Ben," his mother further explained, "You weren't present for the vast majority of the speech portion of the governor's visit. All of the big bosses in the southern half of the railroad were there, and their wives were, as well."

"The war isn't going well for the Confederacy, Ben," John said, "The early victories were only because the south was better prepared at the time, but not anymore. Too many boys are enlisting and not coming back. The south just doesn't have the substance to continue much longer."

"Did you say this at the meeting with the railroad bosses?" Ben asked.

"I didn't have to say it. They said it to me!" he replied.

A group of church boys and others that Ben had known as acquaintances were walking home; they didn't live far away. The carriage stopped at an intersection to allow several others to pass in front of it. Both the boardwalk and the road were congested.

"I'm enlisting!" Ben could hear one say to another, "So is mah brother and cousin."

"I'm going in next Thursday!" another said proudly.

"Tell me where to sign up and I'll go too!" another voice said.

It was obvious that the governor's visit had spurned a wave of young men to enlist to fight for the Confederacy. Never had there been so many boys vowing to sign up and whip the Yankees. Ben thought that he recognized one of the voices, but couldn't see who it was because the groups of boys were walking away.

John smiled and waved to several of his railroad employees. His telegraph operator smiled and tipped his hat as he passed him by, then turned left. The volume of the conversations from the well-dressed people on the boardwalks was difficult to talk over. It was going to be a noisy ride through the French Quarter. The oil lights of the cobblestone street finally gave way to subdued darkness.

John saw an opportunity and stopped the carriage in a remote spot to light the side lanterns. Amanda was just beside herself. She had wanted to say something ever since they had left. The events of the evening had an effect on her, as well, and she couldn't wait to say something about it.

"Oh!" Amanda sighed, hoping to generate conversation after such a long ride. "Did you see that Tori Boyer?"

"Yes mama, I did," Ben sighed back, with a roll of his eyes.

"Oh, it was such a disgrace. Did you see all those young soldier boys around her like that, and tha way she was dressed and carried on that way? Why, if I had done that, my daddy would have worn me out with a switch!"

"With the money that those people have, they can do pretty much of anything," John replied. "It didn't surprise me at all."

"We heard ya won tha first dance, Ben," his mother stated, "Didn't hear who you won it with, though. Would you mind telling us? Was it with Ruby Lee?"

"No, mama, it wasn't," he replied.

"We heard that Zachary and Ruby Lee arrived late and she was looking for you, Ben," His father stated, "I even heard that she wanted that first dance with you. Now, if that ain't somebody likin' ya, I don't know what is!"

"No, I didn't see her," Ben muttered under his breath, when actually he had, and had deliberately dodged her presence.

"Whoever it was, her necklace would have been worth remembering," John mused.

"She was just such a sweet darling. Why, Miss Emma told me that Ruby Lee made a white dress herself, just for a chance to win that first dance with Ben. Can you imagine that?" Amanda asked. Ben had all he could do to not burst into either a fit of rage or yell right there. He decided that he had to talk to someone—preferably his mother—about his true feelings soon.

"Zachary looked very good himself, if I can say," John recalled, "Why, he looked like he was ready to give his daughter away, if ya know what I mean!"

Ben tried to change the subject, but it was no use. His parents were adamant. They wanted to know which girl he had won the dance with, and they weren't backing down. Ben knew that he couldn't lie. There were too many witnesses.

"Gabrielle Fontenot," he finally admitted.

He had expected that there would be a shouting match between the three of them right then and there. That did not happen, but he could tell they were not pleased. Both of his parents pretended that he just wasn't there and didn't speak to him for the remainder of the ride back to La Rue St. Lazar. It was obvious to him that his response wasn't what they had wanted to hear, and he could feel the coldness.

Ben lay in bed that night and thought about the events of the evening. He felt so bad about having kept his relationship with Gabrielle a secret. His parents were not stupid, so perhaps they already knew he was courting her. Worst of all, she and him were intimate, and he knew that was a sin. Sure it was a sin, but he loved her, and he knew he wanted to marry her. He wanted to marry her, and yet he knew that his parents would be so angry with him for that.

He loved her so much that he would have given his life for her. Didn't that count for anything? Should he be ashamed of his feeling? He needed to talk to someone before he went crazy. Perhaps his mother would listen. He decided for certain right then and there that he would talk to her.

Perhaps this internal turmoil he was facing was just part of growing up. He wasn't a child anymore. It was almost overwhelming.

He hadn't planned on winning the first dance with Gabrielle, it just happened. It wasn't the money it had cost him that kept him up. He was glad to give it up because he had been conned into unloading that slave train anyway.

He thought of the encounter with Tori. As dreadful as it was, it angered him even then. She had no right to say what she did; it was uncalled for and unacceptable remarks for a public setting. Sure, Gabrielle had told her off, but that was understandable. Tori was being outright disrespectful.

Then he thought of the lady of the evening that was dressed in pink, wondering again how she knew his name and was aware of his relationship with Gabrielle. She had obviously laid in wait for him to appear. His parents wanted to believe that he was through with Gabrielle, but of course he wasn't. Maybe now, they knew that.

He could hear the reveling from the Chateau Villa as far away as three quarters of a mile away. Pierre must have had several hundred people over there. Amateur horse races up and down the dirt road from the Chateau could be heard for several hours. When the horses ran their course, then it was buggy races with, by this time, drunken riders.

Ben had not forgotten the secret signal that he and Gabrielle had agreed on. He could not wait until he would have the chance to do it. He would be ready to see her again.

The slave cabins on the back property of he La Rue St. Lazar estate were vacant, and he thought they could use them. In particular he was considering the furthest one back. It would be perfect.

She would be riding Samson on the dirt road, and then turn left. From there, the path was hidden by trees and foliage. The cabin could not be seen from any angle from the old mansion. He would meet her by the old tree, and direct her to the cabin this one time. The horse would be hidden for a time in the overgrown foliage. The door to the cabin faced away from the house, so it was perfect. It would look as though she was just out riding her horse, just like he had been.

The next day, he would personally walk the path and eliminate any obstacles along the way. It had been such a long time to him since he had seen her in private. The distant noise of the reveling from the Chateau didn't bother him anymore. He had a plan that would work; now all he had to do was work out the plan. It was going to be a long week before he could see her again. But he would have plenty of chances to give her the secret signal as she knew, like when he would come down the road after work and would watch for him. Then, on the given day, they would meet in that old slave cabin, the one that nobody would see them enter.

The next day, Ben couldn't conceal his secret anymore. He did his chores earlier so that he would have a chance to speak with his mother before supper. He was not sure that he really wanted to, but the sooner he told her, the sooner he wouldn't have to hide his feelings anymore. She could then tell his father. His father would take this all better if he heard it from his mother.

She was in the kitchen, working on supper, which smelled really good. He just stared at her for a second, and then cleared his throat. She looked up.

"I could sense you were watching me," she said.

"Are we having chicken and dumplings, mama?" Ben asked.

"Yes, it has been a long time since we had chicken," she replied. Ben then cleared his throat again.

"What is it?" his mother asked compassionately, her eyes filled with concern. She looked at him in such a gentle way that Ben relaxed a little.

"Mama, I don't like Ruby Lee the way that you and papa want me to. I am in love with someone else," Ben began slowly.

"I was afraid of this," Amanda said softly. She looked down as she added, "It's Gabrielle, isn't it?"

Ben only stared at her in disbelief. He felt as if his heart had stopped. So, she did know. He wondered if she knew the rest. Well, if she didn't, she would.

He had to tell her. He knew if he didn't, he would feel guilty for years to come, and maybe for the rest of his life.

"Mama, I am so sorry," Ben stammered out. He swallowed, but didn't make much of an effort to fight back the lump in his throat. He knew that she was his mother after all, and everyone needed to confide sometimes.

"Ben, love is never something to be sorry for. You can't help the way you feel, and I know that. It's kind of silly, at least in my opinion that your father is trying to set you up with Ruby Lee. Well, he is doing what he knows to do," she said.

"You can't be forced to love anybody," Ben replied.

"I know, and your father's blessing would be nice, and so would her fathers, but you'll marry her without them or with them, I am almost sure. Am I right?" Amanda asked.

"Mama, I don't know how to feel!" Ben replied. "I want my father's blessing, and her father's, but if we don't have it, does that make our feelings any less real?" he asked in agony.

"No, no, sweetie, and God knows your heart. He also knows hers. He knows that you love each other, and I suspected it. I have to admit, I am disappointed, but that's fine. I know that you weren't trying to hurt us or Ruby Lee. You remember what the Bible says about the human heart? Only God can really know it, remember? Sometimes, we don't even know how or why we feel the way that we do. Fine, Ben. I appreciate your honesty," Amanda said, as she held him in a soft hug.

387

"Mama, I love her...and we have been intimate," he said haltingly, almost forcing the words out. He felt so ashamed. Well, if she was going to condemn him, this was her chance. But, her reaction surprised him.

He glad nobody else was in the house. Elizabeth was outside doing something and John was working in the barn. So, they both stared at each other for a few minutes. As he looked at her face, Ben could feel a weight lifting off his heart. Well, at least now, his mother knew his secret.

"I want you to know that I love you," she whispered in his ear, her chin on his shoulder and her arms still wrapped around him, "I want you to know that God loves you, too. I also want you to know that if Gabrielle is in the family way, I will still love you. No matter what happens, I will still love you. I want you to know that you did the right thing in telling me, and that you are still my son. I will not tell your father, because he may not be as gentle with you, and right now, that could really hurt you. You are so young, Ben, but you are a good man and I know that Gabrielle will be happy with you. I want to tell you right here and now that even if your father doesn't approve of you courting her, I am fine with that."

Hearing those words, Ben began to feel relief. His mother wasn't about to reject him. He needed her support, and if his father was actually angry, he would need it twice as badly.

"Mama, I never wanted to disobey you, dad or God. I just love her, and yes, I believe we will get married. We didn't plan on being intimate. I know that you always said that was for marriage only, and I am so sorry. I guess my feelings got the best of me. It just happened, but I won't lie; I like it when we do it," Ben confessed.

"Thanks for your honesty. Yes, it is beautiful, especially when it is with someone that you really love. But outside of marriage is a sin. Ben, if you love Gabrielle as much as I believe you do, you need to marry her," his mother advised.

"But papa won't approve, and she isn't a Christian," Ben said.

"Has she asked you questions about God? Does she seem to be searching for Him? Have you shared God's love with her?" Amanda asked.

"Oh, yes, mama, and I think she's really searching for something right now. Her heart was absolutely broken when she lost her mother, and she is looking for answers and meaning to it all. She's really hurting and running from God on one hand, but on the other, she is looking for Him. Well, call it a hunch, but I think she will find Him soon. She already knows that all her wealth and comfort isn't filling the void in her heart," Ben responded happily.

"Well, that is definitely a start, Ben. You just be patient and see where God leads. I do appreciate your honesty, as I said," Amanda said as Elizabeth entered the house and asked, "Is supper almost ready? Something smells good. Is it chicken tonight?"

Several days later the family was settled down at the supper table. His parents had seemingly forgotten about his bidding the first dance with Gabrielle Fontenot, although he knew his mother knew the whole truth now. However, his father continued onward with interest in Ruby Lee every chance he got. Ben wasn't having any of it; it just wasn't going to work with him. He was too obvious in his approach, too eager to see them get together.

Ben really had to bite his tongue. Obviously, his mother hadn't told his father of their conversation yet. Ben just looked helplessly at his mother, who looked him and smiled. He knew she understood. However, that didn't stop his father from continuing with the conversation.

"Ben," his mother asked, trying to ease the situation a bit, "Be a dear and eat the rest of that pork roast. It's just too good to throw out."

Ben gladly dished himself up another helping of pork roast. There was just enough left over for one helping. Pork roast was his favorite, and his mother prepared it just the way he liked it. But his mother knew that, and had prepared it special for tonight. It was meant to put him in a likable mood to perhaps to discuss Ruby Lee. After all, the way to his heart was through his stomach. She, of course, knew that he liked Gabrielle, but she wanted to make it appear that she didn't for just a few more hours. That night, in bed, she would break the news to her husband, or so she planned to. That might not happen.

Amanda waited until he had a mouthful and then continued her mild rave of Ruby Lee, talking about how pretty she was and how her father worked so hard in that sundry store. At that point, Ben understood that she was playing so sort of game to make his father happy, and decided to relax and play along.

"Oh, Ben, he's so lonesome there. He's there all alone working. If you marry Ruby Lee, you could work there with him. He could really use a hardworking man like you," Amanda said, apparently sounding genuine enough, because John was about to say something as several hard knocks was heard on the door,

"Who could that be at this hour?" John wondered.

Removing his dinner napkin from his lap, he stood up and went to answer the door. Ethan stood on the big porch. His horse was in appropriately tied to one of the porch banister railings.

"Well Ethan, what brings you out here at this time of night? Do come in, do come in," John invited. A stylishly dressed Ethan silently stepped in the vestibule and removed his hat and held it to his chest.

"Thank you, sir." he stated politely as he bowed slightly.

"Why, Ethan," Amanda said as she approached, "How nice to see you."

Elizabeth was surprised more than any of them. Her jaw dropped and her face broke into a bubbly, almost childish, smile.

"Mr. and Mrs. Chesser," he said, in a gentlemanly tone, "I've come to tell you that I've enlisted and I am leaving for Virginia in a month."

"Oh my word!" Amanda gasped, "Aren't you a little young to be fighting? Did you talk this over with your folks?"

"Oh, yes madam," he replied, "Both my cousins and I am signing up together. That way, we'll be in tha same regiment."

"Well, isn't that a surprise?" John said, almost not knowing what to say.

"Well, sir...ma'am," he continued, "I didn't come over here just to tell you that we had enlisted and would be leaving. I have also come over here to ask for Elizabeth's hand before I do have to leave!"

John's and Amanda's jaws dropped a mile. They were caught in a supreme moment of surprise, as they didn't expect that. Ben was shocked, as well; he didn't expect to have a brother-in-law so soon. John looked at his wife, and then looked at Elizabeth. She seemed a little young to be getting married. She had barely turned fourteen. But, that wasn't so young if she was ready. Elizabeth wasn't looking at anyone. She had her hands folded against her chest and was looking upward in an almost prayerful attitude.

"Well, I just don't know what to say, Ethan. She is a little young to be married," John stammered.

"I'll be good to her, sir," Ethan asserted, "You won't ever have any problems out of me. You know my family real well and know that I'm a Christian man."

Elizabeth was overhearing the whole thing, and praying her father would say yes. She wanted to be with Ethan. She was so kind to her. Amanda kept her silence; Ethan was looking directly at John for a response.

"Alright Ethan, Elizabeth is fourteen, and that's a little young, but soon enough happens to be now, I guess. God's will be done. This is not a time of peace, and if you want her hand, this may be your last chance to have it for years. So, yes, you may have my daughter's hand. Don't you ever take her far away and don't you ever hit her, and you be sure that when you have children, they are raised going to church and hearing about God's love. Other than that, I don't have any concern."

Elizabeth relaxed and approached Ethan with a hug. She was so happy. Amanda was just shocked. Her youngest daughter, whom she believed she had at least a couple more years with, was going to be getting married. Not even Ben was married, and he was older.

Two weeks later, Ethan and Elizabeth were married in a small ceremony at the Church of Christ, where they both had attended. Both sides of the family were in attendance and blessed the union as fellow Christian families.

Ethan never had second thoughts about joining the Confederacy. He didn't even question his decision when a local New Orleans major newspaper featured columns of war news. Casualties were mounting in the mid-southern states. Fewer hometown boys were coming back home on furlough, and those that did described horrendous hand-to-hand fighting, and more retreats on the southern side than advances.

General Grant and his army had control of the Mississippi River as far south as Memphis, Tennessee, and they were pressing further south, almost without resistance. Men were being killed everyday, sometimes by the thousands. A huge portion of the southern side of the railroad was captured by union troops, as well. Trains were stopped and searched for artillery and weapons.

Mercifully, as if to prove that even in war not all sense of humanity was lost between so-called 'enemies,' trains that were transporting wounded Confederate soldiers home were allowed to continue southward. Regular paying passengers were searched, along with their luggage. Each train arriving from as far north as Memphis was expected to be at least five hours late. The north had stopped all medical supplies, weapons, equipment and food from reaching southern military command centers. In some cases, paying passengers were detained and not allowed to continue.

General Butler patrolled the roads leading in and out of the east and northern part of the city, miles away from population. Supplies for the people of New Orleans were getting difficult to come by, as a blockade of the gulf was successful. Foreign frigates that were charted for southern ports were boarded, and the cargo was seized. Union clippers could be seen in the horizon off shore, armed and waiting for any approaching vessels.

Foreign captains soon grew wise and sailed for the west shores, along the swamp lands adjacent to Point Chevreuil and Atchafalaya Bay. New Orleans was under a cold siege. Seemingly overnight, the cost of food more then doubled, and wages did not increase to compensate for that. The economic and political conditions in the country as a whole did not allow for wages to increase.

"My lands!" Juneau exclaimed, "Only a millionaire can afford to eat anymore!"

Miss Prissy gave her a short, contemptible stare. Nobody was doing too well, especially not the field slaves. As house servants, they had fared much better than those working the fields or tending to the grounds of the estate.

"Let's just fix what we do have and be grateful," Miss Prissy responded.

"Father will be home soon," Gabrielle added, "I trust everything is prepared?"

"Rightly so," Miss Prissy responded, "He ain't been the same since the governor visited, if I can say as much. Maybe you didn't notice, but I have."

"I know what they talked about, Miss Prissy," she replied, "The south isn't doing well in the struggle for independence. They may have talked behind closed doors, but I heard it way out here."

"I'm afraid for our kind," Miss Prissy said, almost under her breath, but Gabrielle heard her.

"We've always treated you right. Even the field slaves we have eat well enough. Nobody here goes hungry. That would not be right at all. You colored folks are still people. We treat you the best we can. You have no fears with us," Gabrielle replied, "I just hope tha Yankees can be stopped before they reach New Orleans."

"I know," Miss Prissy answered, "But I'm really afraid for our kind in general. I know you have been good to us, but if tha north abolishes slavery, then what is to become of us? Slavery is all we have even known in this land. The change will be hard, and I am not sure how we will handle it. Also, what if we are forced to fight? They could force coloreds to fight if and when they run out of white boys."

"It doesn't look good for the south right about now," Gabrielle answered. But she saw Miss Prissy's point. They didn't want to go back to the fields, but they didn't want to work for the Yankees or the Confederates, either.

"Can you talk to Mr. Fontenot for us?" Miss Prissy asked.

Gabrielle noticed the whole kitchen staff was looking directly at her. Well, this was technically her place now that her mother was dead, but she suddenly felt so grown-up and important. It was as if they all recognized that she was no longer a child, and she understood more than her father wanted to give her credit for.

"I'll talk to him tonight," she answered to inquisitive faces.

Miss Prissy gave Gabrielle an appreciative look, and for the time being, they all breathed a sigh of relief.

"I'll speak with him tonight in the study," Gabrielle further explained, as she looked out of the window, "I'll have something for all of you tomorrow."

No sooner than she said that when Pierre's buggy could be heard approaching the stable. She watched as he dismounted and handed the buggy over to Charles. Turning about, she was pleased to find that the table was set, and the supper meal was ready.

The matrons were all standing against the wall waiting for the evening blessing on the food. Pierre offered the evening blessing as he usually did, but was pensive and quiet at the supper table. Gabrielle could sense this and waited for the right time to start a conversation.

Miss Prissy had been correct, he wasn't the same after the governor's visit, and something changed. She didn't know quite what to say.

"The pond area looks beautiful, father!" she finally said with a brilliant smile. He needed to relax. She had hoped that some flattery would work.

"Are you happy with that?" he replied, "It's a beautiful memorial to your mother."

"Yes, I am so happy with it, and I do appreciate it all," she replied.

"I'm glad I spent the money when I did," he replied, "I have assigned a dedicated groundskeeper to maintain it, and yes, he has been doing a good job."

"Why would you say that?" she asked.

"Say what?" he asked, as he reached for more apple strudel.

"That you were glad that you spent the money when you did?"

He thought for a moment, and then looked about. The kitchen matrons were gone now. He had to be sure they were out of ear shot. He didn't need any rumors spreading amongst his slaves.

"Are you alright, papa?" Gabrielle asked.

"The currency is almost worthless, Gabrielle," He said seriously, "The northern dollar can buy much more. Our money is so inflated that people are starving. Goods are difficult to get. I've heard that hungry raiders are looting the better farms at night, stealing food and whatever they can get."

"Are you worried about Chateau Villa?" she asked, surprised by what she was hearing. They were well off, and she knew it. She wouldn't have imagined that her father would be telling her the things he now had to.

"I am not too worried, but some changes might have to be made. I really don't think we will starve, if that's what you are asking. It's just good that I bought that newest slave when I did. He does a nice job keeping the grounds around here clean and well kept up. But, it might be awhile until I can even buy another slave, so we will try to keep him around," Pierre said.

Gabrielle knew who he was referring to. The slave was named Israel, and he was the latest addition to their household. Pierre had purchased him at the slave market a while back.

"He does quite a fine job indeed, and he even smiles while he works. Sometimes, I even hear him singing. He isn't a bad singer," Gabrielle remarked.

Pierre was more receptive now, and he was starting to relax more. It had been a stressful day and it weighed heavy on his mind.

"Are we ever going to be homeless or have to sell any of our slaves? That would be bad, because not all white people treat their colored folks well. We won't have to sell any of ours, will we?" Gabrielle inquired.

Pierre didn't answer her question, but gave her a rather condescending look. It was starting to come together as Gabrielle thought about it. He did have reason to worry. They had much acreage, and he just couldn't afford to pay night watchmen because the money that he had was no good. So, at some point, their crops would likely be taken in the night, and maybe some of the slaves they owned would be taken, or other things they had.

Eventually, it was either going to be the approaching Yankee army, or starving townspeople, who would stage quiet, nocturnal raids for food and whatever else they could get. Pierre didn't have to say anything, as it didn't take much to figure out where he was going with this discussion.

He wasn't hungry anymore, and neither was Gabrielle. They both stared at their plates, only partially eaten, on the table. He reached in his vest pocket for a cigar and pushed his chair backwards. Even though they had not finished their meals, he was fine with that. It was time for a smoke in the study.

"May I speak with you, father?" Gabrielle asked.

He responded with a nod, and they both entered the study and closed the door.

Although he did not know it, some of the kitchen matrons had overheard his comment about the deflated value of southern currency, and felt even more anxious about the future of their jobs.

They all stood in a circle, held hands and prayed as they waited for Gabrielle to emerge from the study and tell them something. Though many of them could not read, they had heard the stories of Moses and the children of Israel at church, and they knew what the Bible said about God's miracle working hand. Now, they needed Him to intervene in the current situation.

After what seemed like an eternity, Gabrielle emerged from the study. She cleared her throat as she approached the kitchen area. They all turned to face her and hear what she had to say.

"I guess it's no surprise to all of you that the south isn't doing well," she began, feeling both a tension and a divine peace lingering in the very air, "The north has munitions factories. We don't. They have thousands of more soldiers and equipment, which will enable them to keep the war up for a longer time than the south can."

The kitchen matrons looked about, waiting for her to tell them what they wanted to hear. They had no control over what the north had and what the south didn't have, so it made to difference to them. They just wanted to know what the Fontenot's were going to do about their employ in the household. Gabrielle could sense their unease, and got right to the point.

"Since mama and grandma passed away, all of you have directly worked for me, and I don't want to see any of you go, but things are rough now, so father and I have worked some things out. Father is going to make some changes, and they will be effective tomorrow, and you all need to know about it."

"Yes, Madam," Miss Prissy murmured, expecting the worst.

"Almost all of the field workers will be released tomorrow, as we don't want the Yankees to find us with any slaves. Those we keep, or those that want to stay, will not work the field. They will stay in the house at night. Some of you will perhaps need to share your rooms with more people then you have been. I hope that is alright. We know that you already share your room with one other person, but you might end up having to share with one or two more. We believe in treating slaves right, but not all white people do. We don't want to see anyone taken by a Yankee, and the only way to make certain that doesn't happen is to free our slaves. So, freed they shall be. Papa will give those that want to go their freedom papers, and they can simply walk away," Gabrielle announced.

The kitchen staff's mouths all fell open. Gabrielle just smiled. She could see both disbelief and joy in their faces as she said, "Those that want to stay will be considered free as of tomorrow, and will be offered pay for their services. No kitchen help will be fired, but come tomorrow, all of you will be offered regular pay for your services. You can either accept or leave, that decision is yours, but you are no longer our slaves. You will be paid fairly if you choose to stay," Gabrielle announced, as she felt a feeling of satisfaction and peace wash over her.

A sigh of relief filled the room. Most of the colored folks that worked the kitchen didn't want to be anywhere else. They'd thought that they would be fired and sold, and they didn't want that. Many of them had been owned by several masters throughout their lives, and all of them had been whipped, for all of them had come from the fields at one time or another. All were hand-picked to serve in the Chateau. Several were fluent in French, having been trained to speak the language by French tutors.

"It's all about changing, isn't it?" Juneau asked.

"Yes," Gabrielle replied, "We don't want the Chateau, or its grounds, raided by the Yankees. My father feels that if they think there are no slaves here, they will leave us alone."

"If I can say something here, Miss Gabrielle?" Juneau requested.

"Sure, what is it?" Gabrielle asked.

"I feel that the Chateau is just as much my home as it is yours. I'm certain that Mr. Fontenot is making the right decision, as hard as it may have been," Juneau said.

"Amen to that sister!" Miss Prissy responded.

"For those of you that want to leave tomorrow, this will be your last day. I wish you good luck, and you are free, so make sure to get your papers from my father. For those that want to stay, then it's welcome again, I suppose," Gabrielle replied.

"I ain't leaving! You folks treat me well. I have never gone hungry here, or been beaten until I bled. In fact, in all the years that I have worked here, I have even been allowed to have my opinions and voice them. Now, that really is unusual. I like that. I am staying. I'm not going anywhere," Miss Prissy affirmed.

"Me neither!" Juneau said as well. Gabrielle beamed. She had hoped Miss Prissy, especially, would not leave. One by one, all of the kitchen matrons affirmed that they would not be leaving. They had been treated kindly, so they would stay with the Fontenot's, for better or for worse.

"Well now," Gabrielle replied, still beaming, "I'm glad that's over."

"We all are, Miss Gabrielle," Miss Prissy responded. "We all are!"

To her surprise, they surrounded Gabrielle and bombarded her with questions about the war, the nearness of the potentially invading Yankees, and what they would do if New Orleans were to be occupied. She knew so little herself, but she tried to answer the questions she could. They all knew that the war was now in full swing and the deflated Confederate currency was almost useless, as well.

That night, Gabrielle lay awake for a long time. She couldn't help but wonder what was happening on the front lines. Would the Yankees really invade the Chateau? Well, she would find out soon enough, if that really did happen. She didn't want it to. She had such a beautiful home, and things seemed so ideal. Sure, she had been through quite a bit, but she had always come out on top. She always would, wouldn't she? This time, the thought that she might not scared her.

She wasn't one to pray, but she saw that she had no other choice at that point. She really hoped that Ben was right, and that God was indeed able to hear her prayer. She knelt by her bed, only because that is what she had seen church people do, and she slowly began.

"I am not one to pray," she confessed, "But if you are up there listening, God, I want You to protect us and this land and our workers. God, I know that I have never really prayed before, but Ben seems to think that you are real. He says that you care about me, and even love me, so I pray that you would hear this prayer and answer," Gabrielle said.

When she stood up, her first thought was how foolish that had sounded. She had no idea if she had said the right words. She was almost certain that if there was a God, He was laughing at her right then. Little did she realize, but she was very wrong. God wasn't laughing at her at all.

What she also didn't realize was that the Yankees were getting very close. If she had known, she would have been very frightened. But, as it were, she was unaware of that, and forced herself to go to sleep.

Chapter 34
From the Front Lines to the Home Front

"Well, the way I see it is that the rebels will fight for New Orleans," Union General Mansfield Lovell observed as he studied his map early the next morning, "There's a lot of back roads, but I do think we'll meet and engage somewhere outside of the city."

"That may be all true and well, sir" replied his fellow officer, "As it stands right now, we have them outnumbered and outgunned. Judging from the prisoners we've been taking it seems that the rebels are down on their luck for provisions, so ah… won't be much of a fight."

"Could be, but we've been wrong before, and we got licked. They had us on the run, but this time is different. We have to whip em' this time…plan is to push east toward the right and left sides of the city, flank left and right," he responded as he gestured with his fingers in two sweeping motions.

"Surely you don't mean to take the prisoners and the wounded behind our lines, sir?" his fellow officer asked.

"No, no, all wounded and weak rebel prisoners will stay behind in New Orleans, and only the more stout men would go to behind our lines. General Norwell and his units will travel from the north, and end up right here," he replied as he pointed at the map again.

"Well then, we have them blocked from the west and from the north. Put the squeeze on them and force them to the gulf, is that it? Onward to New Orleans then!" he replied as he took a puff on his pipe.

"Hmmm…the city will be left with no rebel defenders. I think I know what General Sherman would do, and he's jus' the man to do it," the general said.

"And what would that be?"

"Burn it all to the ground. Spare nothing. Burn all of it, if they don't surrender, which we don't think that they will."

"I think that taking Richmond is just a matter of time after New Orleans, but we first have to conquer these little towns along the way. It won't be hard. They won't be guarded, so no heavy guns there."

"Battery Second Division of Illinois and Michigan Federal Division will be joining the fight… if New Orleans chooses to fight," he explained.

"Excellent plan, sir!" his fellow officer exclaimed with approval.

"Well, that's the plan, in a matter of speaking. It's not firmed up just yet, but that's what we been talking about. We'll talk later on this as the runners come in with news. Thing is, some of the boys from other regiments have never been in a fight. We just had a bunch of new boys join, and most of them are just kids, really. I mean, like thirteen and fourteen…but, there's a first time for everything."

General Lovell folded up the map and looked outside at the flickering campfires. Around just a dozen or so fires, hundreds of men slept almost back-to-back. Very few of them had decent blankets, because the blankets they had been given were dirty and worn by then.

"It's a shame those boys have to sleep like that. Next time we invade some place we'll take several farms and let them spread out a little."

"Aw...don't hurt them none. We are old and they're young. Just 'cause we can't handle that anymore doesn't mean they can't. They're fine. Why, if I were to sleep on the field like that, my back would ache for a month, and so would yours."

"Rightly so, and well stated. We're not young men anymore, but I'm proud of all of them. They give it everything they got without complaining. We don't hear nothing out of nobody, except sometimes they go too much on the whiskey."

"I've known for a while now that they have a whiskey wagon, but who am I to judge? As long as they do their duty, I don't care what they drink."

"Well, still, I'm glad to get on with the conflict an' all. This is all wearing on me. I hate to see all these boys dying and crippled for life. I know its all part of war and all, but the soldiers that are volunteering are getting younger and younger. I don't know what their poor parents must be thinking. I would be worried sick and heartbroken. I bet you didn't know that I almost hired a substitute to serve in my place."

"Why, no sir, I did not," The other officer said to the older general.

"Well, just keep it to yourself. I still have all the money that I would have paid him, and once the other units get here, we're going to have a big poker game."

"I don't play, sir, but I sure as hell can watch."

"Yes, well, these boys need a break from the bloodshed. I know it has to be hard on them, and we all have to relax sometimes," The general stated.

Rows of covered wagons, along with a greater number of tents, formed the Union encampment. The night air smelled of firewood.

Smoke encircled the camp as damp wood, still not dry from a rain the night before, sat in mud. Soldiers in standard blue uniforms mingled among the campfires, visiting and sharing provisions with others.

"Hey boy, pour me some more of that brew!" exclaimed a heavyset soldier as he held his cup out to a water boy.

"Ain't water sir, it's Chattanooga brew, and it got captured from the rebels near Chattanooga," the boy muttered as he poured the cup full, "I heard we have three wagons of it."

"I don't give a damn where it came from."

"Here, here boy!" said another, "Hell, why don't you jus' walk around and pour everybody some?"

"Now then," the heavy set soldier said, "Lets get back to the campfire an' tell some more stories."

Laughter swelled from a campfire as the newer regiment recruits reacted to a particular funny story.

"Yeah that's it boys... laugh while you can. Soon you'll be facing all them rebels from New Orleans, and you won't be laughing then!" he commented as he gestured with his cup to the south.

"Ah... you are drunk!" a young, laughing voice reply from the group.

The soldier did not respond as he walked away from the group. Taking a sip from the cup, he wiped his mouth on his sleeve and looked back to observe the young recruits returning to their laughter. While most soldiers sat outside, about the fires, some took to the wagons to write letters by candlelight. Still others, weary from all of their marching, sat with their pant legs rolled up to the knees and massaged the calves of their legs.

"Damn, plum forgot about how big the mosquitoes get down here!" one commented to another.

"I know," his friend said, "Put some lard on your skin. That'll keep them away."

"Heard we might get heavy rain tomorrow," one said as he looked skyward.

"I don't know, but those clouds in the northeast there look they could open up."

"They say we're going meet the rebels tomorrow in New Orleans, and we're going to join up with other boys and get after them."

"Yeah, I heard that too. Heard it's regiments from Illinois, but you know, you just don't know what to believe."

"Well, you can believe this," said the soldier with the cup, "You boys better get some rest, because tomorrow there won't be any time for any rest."

"Will do, sir!" replied the young soldier as he finished rubbing his leg.

"Don't try to win the war by yourselves. There is strength in numbers, so don't get caught out there by yourselves. Stand by each other, and by the will of God this will be over soon and we can go home," the experienced soldier stated as he held his cup out, his eyes solemn.

"Is it going to be a big fight tomorrow?" asked another young soldier as he yawned.

"That's what we expect. We are going bring the fight to them. But I would think there will be big kills on both sides. None of those rebels like it 'cause we're here. I heard it is going to be a shooting fight!"

One young Union soldier emerged from a wagon that he had been writing a letter in. Looking about, he spotted his artillery mate at the campfire and motioned for him.

"I wrote a letter to my mama," he explained, "I want you to read it to see if it sounds about right, and then tell me what you think."

"I can do that," his friend responded as he stood there with his arms folded.

"Or would you prefer if I read it?" the soldier asked.

"Whatever you want to do is fine," his friend replied.

"I can read it," the soldier said.

"Read it out loud to me, then," came the response.

April 24th, 1862

Near St. Bernard Parish, Louisiana

Dear Mama,

I take my pen in hand to let you know that I am well at the present. I hope that when these few lines come to your hand, they arrive to find you and father well.

I received your letter with news of last month; it gave me great satisfaction to hear from you once more.

I got paid today, twenty-three dollars, and I send you all I can spare. We will be paid again the first of every month.

Direct your letter to the first regiment, as we deemed before.

I remain your dear son, until death,

Nathaniel

"Nothing wrong with that," his friend stated, "I still have my twenty-three dollars. A lot of boys are broke already, from a playing poker by candlelight."

"I'm keeping my money, as well," Nathaniel replied, "I'll put this in the post first thing in the morning, then."

As the night passed, the campfires dwindled, embers died out, and the camp fell silent, except for an occasional cough or sneeze from the rows and rows of tents. Sergeant Smith and the general and other Union officers rode between the rows of artillery and tents, pointing here and there to formulate an organized offensive. Pausing along the way, they exhaled cigar smoke and hoped for the best, but they also knew that for some of these men, this would be their last night on earth.

Chapter 35
Can A House Divided... Stand?

As he had promised his daughter, Pierre made a pact with his slave work force. They were each given a small settlement and the option to remain at the Chateau as paid workers. Their other option was that they could take the settlement and leave. The deal included all of the former field slaves who lived in the back shanty cottages, and all of the colored slaves who worked in the stable. All other non-colored, non-slave workers were given pay increases to stay on.

To his dismay, almost all of the former field slaves took the settlement and left the Chateau. Those that stayed were promised the better, more recent, cottages, and told that when conditions warranted it, they would sleep in the house. All of the former stable building slaves left; all regularly paid, non-colored workers stayed.

Pierre was worried about the approaching Yankees and wanted to make the best impression, should they occupy New Orleans and happen to pay him a visit. There would be no slaves there now. They were all hired help. There would be no reason to think of him as a slave holder; he had heard that affluent, slave-holding plantations were being looted by invading Yankee troops.

One of the former slaves that elected to take a settlement and stay was a more recent purchase that Pierre had called Israel. He had assigned the pond area to Israel and had never been disappointed with the upkeep. Israel spoke English better than most of the former slaves did and paid greater attention to detail. Pierre had hoped that he would stay on.

In a worst case scenario, Pierre reasoned, the local militias would engage the enemy just north of New Orleans. Both Pierre and his upper-crust plantation owners had hoped that this wouldn't happen. There would be nowhere to escape to, as New Orleans was land bound by the gulf to the south. Perhaps the city would be surrendered without much destruction and the Yankees would leave the plantations alone after all.

Well, Pierre had freed his slaves. That would certainly make a good impression on the Yankees, wouldn't it? It wasn't as if Pierre mistreated his slaves. He treated them well, and he was sure they would tell the Yankees that.

But, just because they were free didn't mean they knew what to do or even where to go. The kitchen staff didn't know how to quite handle their news. If they acted jubilant, then Pierre might think that they thought they were better than the former field slaves. If they acted solemn, he might think that they were not appreciative of his kindness to let them stay on. However, in the end, they all thanked him and acted as though nothing had happened. All of the wealthy folks of New Orleans were worried, and even the slaves and the middle class were concerned about the approaching Yankees. They had never experienced anything like this before.

Some packed their valuables and jewelry in cases and buried them in flowerbeds along the side their mansions. Others buried items in marked pastures and rice fields. They thought that the Yankees would have no way of knowing about the buried riches, and would simply take what they wanted, if the city was to be occupied at all.

"They'll never get into New Orleans," Marcel said to Pierre one afternoon when they were visiting, "Our boys are doing a fine job out there. The Yankees will turn and leave."

Pierre looked at him in earnest and hoped that he would be correct. After a momentary pause, he said, "I let my nigger slaves go, save a few," he responded in a French whisper.

"That's not all that uncommon anymore," Marcel answered in English, "Many of the freed niggers are leaving the city in droves, but there's a problem with the east part of the city, over by the racetrack."

"What would that be?" Pierre asked as he switched back to English.

"There are big shanty towns of freed blacks there who are staying to see if the Yankees take over. They are looking for a chance to have a voice in the occupied government, and you know what that means."

"Vengeance on former masters," Pierre muttered, "Betrayal to the Yankees, as well."

"Got that right, my friend," Marcel responded as billows of cigar smoke poured from his nostrils, "There is a resolution, if you would like to get involved," he whispered.

The populace of New Orleans certainly had reason to worry. The cost of everyday items had soared outlandish high, and no longer did cash guarantee anyone a purchase. The sea and land blockades had proven to be very successful in blocking the transport of general goods to New Orleans.

People were hungry and sick at alarming rates. Even the money that the formerly wealthy people used bought them relatively little. Most of the people would have readily agreed to surrender the city to the Yankees if it meant lifting the blockade for food and medical provisions. The blockade affected everybody, the rich and the poor, the simple dirt plow sharecropping farmer and the affluent plantations' owners alike.

The people were divided in their opinions about what to do about it all. Many wanted to surrender, but others called for a citizen's militia to meet the Yankees just north of the city.

Any thoughts about the Yankees' intentions were intensified when the first of the hurling cannon shots reached within the cities limits.

The shots had been aimed to destroy small businesses and put fear into the hearts and minds of the populace. To destroy a business at random meant that the Yankees knew where to aim. Without being from the city itself, and since it was general knowledge that they did not know the city's layout, the act of destroying a business would prove to everyone that they had somehow become familiar with the city. There were spies working with them to pinpoint the key businesses. They aimed to hit the businesses that were just enough of a loss to either force surrender or lead the general populace into a fight.

Word had reached Union encampments that there was a mass exodus going on, an exodus of citizenry that neither wanted to fight, nor surrender, to the aggressive north. They were leaving in wagon and carriages, in lines that were often two and three miles long, everyday. Even though the railroad was still open, it wasn't an option because so many soldiers were using it, and neither was leaving by sea. Both options meant being stopped and turned back, or even robbed of their belongings by militant Yankee troops. New Orleans now belonged to the stubborn wealthy, mostly plantation owners who refused to leave, as well as the elderly who were too old to travel.

Ben watched in amazement at the long wagon lines of the populace exiting the city.

Wagons, carriages, and buggies of every type went past the Chateau, along the now rutted dirt road, and soon passed in front of the La Rue St. Lazar Mansion.

Amanda and Ben kept busy one Saturday, filling up jars and other containers with cold well water for them, as many had asked for cold water on such a hot, blistering day.

Amanda recognized several church families leaving and wished them well. Ben saw several of the stable hands and jockeys from the racetrack with their families. They were also leaving.

"Don't worry, Ben!" one shouted from the road, "There are many folks at the track that won't leave!"

"Glad to hear it," he shouted back, "Good luck to all of you."

One by one, the wagons and carriages disappeared in the roads horizon. Wagons of new people that he didn't know passed by and waved. He waved back as a sign of courtesy.

Well, he thought, Gabrielle wouldn't be leaving. That would break his heart. But, he knew she would stay because her father wouldn't leave. He was the wealthiest man in town. He had too much to lose, and Ben knew it. They wouldn't be going anywhere, and Ben was very glad.

His choice of the former slave cabin hideaway for him and Gabrielle had been successful several times. They were well concealed behind the thick foliage and the line of sight by other cabins. It was their getaway, a love nest. The facilities weren't the best, rustic and primitive to say the least, but for the time that they were together, it didn't matter.

Tonight was the night that he would see her again, and he could hardly wait. The exiting wagon lines would not travel by night, and always stopped just before twilight.

"That's it," Amanda announced as she looked down the road, "No more water for tonight."

"I think I'll ride Bunches tonight...after supper," Ben replied as he wiped his brow. His arms ached and he was exhausted after a whole afternoon of fetching water.

"Oh, you deserve to go. You did well," she added.

They both turned about and were about to leave the dusty roadside when another old buggy could be heard approaching quickly. From the sound of it, the driver wasn't in need of water. The buggy showed no indication of slowing down. Amanda looked backward, and then her mouth fell in surprise and she cried, "Elizabeth!"

Ben watched as his sister quickly pulled the buggy into the drive at collapsed in a heap across the empty seat next to her. Both Amanda and Ben came running to see what was wrong. Elizabeth was almost inconsolable as she cried and pounded the seat with her fist.

"What's wrong?" Amanda asked as she put her hand on her daughter's shoulder.

Elizabeth sensed her comforting hand and calmed down enough to speak.

"Ethan," she cried, "We all read the casualty list in town. He… and others… were wounded and taken prisoner. From what it said, they were all going to a place called Rock Island, because he got captured. All of the boys were wounded in one way or another and are all going."

"Oh my!" Amanda gasped, as she covered her mouth with her hand.

Ben just stood there in complete surprise. He had heard stories of acquaintances of his being killed or wounded, and even captured, but this was different. Ethan was a part of the family.

John had witnessed what had occurred, and came running out of the house to see what had happened for himself. He arrived breathing heavily and was, by then, perspiring.

"Ethan got wounded and captured," Amanda said softly as he approached her.

"Oh Lord!" John exclaimed, "That's not good."

Amanda looked at him and then gave her daughter a sympathetic look. She felt awful as well. They all wanted to offer words of comfort, but nothing they could say would ease her pain.

"Elizabeth, just come on in the house and stay with us for awhile," Amanda suggested.

Elizabeth wailed for what seemed like an eternity. She finally composed herself long enough to straighten up and ease out of the seat. Her heart was so heavy she could literally feel the pain of it breaking. Ben took the reins of the buggy, and then helped his sister get down. Once her feet were on the ground, Elizabeth took several deep breaths and wiped the tears away from her pasty face.

"C'mon in Elizabeth," her father said, "I'm so sorry to hear that Ethan was captured. We haven't had supper. You are welcome to join us. Ethan would want you to be strong. Come on in and at least eat a little something. You'll feel better after you eat something."

"We all feel bad," Amanda added.

Ben took her buggy to the barn. He was very burdened by the news. The very thought that Ethan may be dead almost sickened him. Well, at least Ethan was a Christian, so Ben knew where he was if he was actually dead. Still, Ben hoped that he was alive.

"Oh, Lord have mercy," Ben sighed as he entered the barn.

Her horse looked like he could use a good watering and a feeding, so Ben fed Elizabeth's horse and gave him some water. While he was there, he saddled Bunches and got him ready for that evening's ride. Deep down, he felt bad about his brother-in-law getting wounded and taken prisoner, but it was better than being dead, so Ben hoped that that's what had really happened.

"Good boy!" Ben muttered as he patted his horse on the nose, "Be back for you after supper."

With that he closed the barn doors and headed to the back porch. When he entered the house, the smell of vegetables filled the air. They were having carrots, broccoli and potatoes that night. It had been a while since Elizabeth or any of them had eaten meat. The last time she had had meat had been the night that her mother had made chicken and dumplings. That seemed almost as if it had been a different time and place.

Elizabeth explained, after supper, that she and other young, married ladies from church had been in New Orleans on a shopping trip. A Confederate ordinance officer had a crowd about him, as he was distributing casualty lists from a recent battle. Lydia, one of the young ladies of their group, went to get one and brought it back to them. It was then that they learned that several of the area's early enlistees had been wounded and were being held captive, and would be taken to Rock Island for the duration of the war.

"Did it mention anything about the seriousness of the wound?" John asked.

"It just simply said the Ethan had been wounded in the line of duty. There was no other information. No nothing of anything else," she replied.

"Were there any other young boys that we would know?" Amanda asked.

Elizabeth thought that she might become emotional again, but gathered herself enough to answer her mother's question.

"Claude Mallenet, from the race track, and Peter Allen Marshall from church and Harold Jones from the carpenter shop outside of the French Quarter. There were many others involved, but those are a few that I knew, and you might know them, as well," she replied.

Ben had a particular interest in Claude. He had met him at the race track before the race with the Fontenot horse. Out of respect for his brother-in-law, Ben didn't mention that he knew Claude, but did indeed feel bad that he was wounded and taken prisoner.

"Peter Marshall, hm? He's the boy that read scripture a lot in church services," John mentioned, "I do remember him."

"Yes," Elizabeth added, "Ethan told me before he left that they had signed up together. They grew up right across the road from each other."

414

"Damn shame… this war is," John muttered, "Nothing will come out of it for the boys that get wounded or captured."

"Sorry to hear about Ethan, sis," Ben said, as he patted his sister on the hand.

"I do appreciate it, Ben," She responded, and somehow his involvement made her feel better.

"What is this place, Rock Island?" Amanda asked.

"It's an internment camp for captured Confederate soldiers and it's between Illinois and Iowa on the Mississippi River," John responded.

"Oh, Lord," Amanda sighed out loud, "It's very cold up there and that's such a long ways to go after being wounded and all."

"Well, Elizabeth," John mentioned, "If it's any comfort at all, the war won't last much longer now. It's just a matter of time. The southern independence cause just won't last, and Ethan, as well as the rest of the boys, will be home soon enough."

Elizabeth felt much better now. She's couldn't do anything for Ethan but pray, and she certainly would do that. Her father's comment had soothed her. She had her confidence back now, and acted like the same Elizabeth that everyone knew.

"I might go riding Bunches," Ben said, "I won't be out too long."

John nodded in approval. Amanda already knew that he would go out riding that evening.

"Elizabeth," Amanda asked, "Why don't you just come live with us until we know better? It's no good for you to be living over there in that rooming house by yourself. Just tell that landlord of your situation, come back and be with us."

"Your mother is right, Elizabeth," John added, "Your old room is still upstairs."

Ben had waited all week for the opportunity to be with Gabrielle again; however, hearing of his brother-in law's plight put a slight damper on his mood. It was just dreadful news that he hated to hear.

"Well Elizabeth, Ethan is in God's hands, and you are in my prayers, as well as him," Ben said.

"Thanks, Ben, I do appreciate it. I need all the prayers I can get right now, and so does Ethan. You have a good time riding Bunches," Elizabeth responded.

"C'mon boy," he said to his horse, "We're gonna go for a little ride and then take a rest, if you know what I mean!"

Mounting his horse, he firmly commanded, "Walk on," and moved the reins lightly to the left. The horse obliged, and almost trotted forward. As they passed the huge dining room window, he waved to his father, who just happened to be looking out. Nearing the rutted, dusty road, Ben tugged the reins to the left and got an immediate response. He knew what he was going to do. This was what he always did; make it appear that he was going on a long ride with his prized horse.

"Haw boy, haw!" he yelled.

The horse took off in wondrous speed; it was all that Ben could do to hold onto the reins. The wind whipped his hair back about his shoulders, so that it was almost all he could do to stay in the saddle. But Ben didn't know what he savored the most, the fast ride or another opportunity to be with Gabrielle. For the moment, he had them both.

For several miles, the horse kept up an exhilarating pace of speed. Looking ahead in the horizon, Ben could see the turn coming up and pulled on the reins, decreasing his speed to a canter and then a trot.

Turning left, he looked to the left and right and then behind to see if anyone was following him. No one was. After another small run, he knew exactly where to direct the horse. It was to the left and along an old path that they had been down before.

A slow walk along the path, among dense foliage, soon had them concealed from view. The old cabin was just ahead, exactly as they had left it. He stopped and dismounted, then tied Bunches to an old hitching post. He looked at the cabin and smiled knowing that he and Gabrielle would soon be sharing some very precious moments.

The hideaway was far from luxurious. He had made a crude bed of straw and taken advantage of two chairs that head been left behind. As usual, he waited for the sound of Gabrielle's horse. He knew that nobody else had been at the cabin as he had made his own little tell-tale booby trap. An old tin can placed on top of the door was still there from last time.

Finally, he heard the sound of her horse. She was earlier than usual. Upon her arrival, he flashed a wide smile and assisted her with dismounting her horse.

"Oh, it's so nice to be with you again!" she said as they embraced.

"The week has been to long," he replied as he broke their embrace and helped hide her horse in the foliage.

"You didn't have any problems getting here, did you?" she asked.

"No," Be replied, "Thought that wagon train out of the city would never stop, though, and I received word that my brother-in-law has been wounded and taken prisoner."

"Oh, that's terrible!" she replied.

"Not exactly the right news for the moment, but how is everything at the Chateau?"

"My father let the slaves go free, but offered full-time jobs to those that wanted to stay. Some did, and some didn't, but the kitchen staff remains," she replied.

"I suppose that right now, he's scared. I suppose he thinks he could lose everything. Well, not to concern you, but he actually could. I hope that he doesn't, if only for your sake," Ben said.

Leading her by the hand, they both entered the old cabin, with Ben leading. While Gabrielle was certainly interested in being intimate with him, she had other questions in her heart and on her mind. They were questions she needed to ask or she was going to go insane. What scared her most was that she didn't know if she would have another chance to ask them.

"Ben," Gabrielle confessed, "Nothing makes any sense anymore. I have lost my mother and my grandmother, and now I may lose my house. If the Yankees come, they will take everything we have. I am scared, and I am not sure whether they'll throw my papa in prison. I did nothing, Ben. I am just a young lady. I realize that my father is not the best person in the world," she said, and then lowering her voice a little, she whispered, "Sometimes, there seems to be something that is down-right evil using him as a means to accomplish whatever it wants."

"Gabrielle, that is very perceptive of you, and I believe that, too," Ben responded in a whisper so quiet that she barely heard him.

"Well, not necessarily, but the scripture does say to give no place to the devil. Let me ask you, have you ever used the word nigger?"

"Of course, but who hasn't?" Gabrielle asked.

Ben couldn't help but chuckle at her last comment.

Chapter 36
A Meeting of the Minds

Pierre didn't know quite what to make of Marcel's invitation to a private business meeting. Curiosity was more of the motivation that led him to go as it was a meeting that he and several other higher affluent society men were invited to. Marcel had advised him not to bring his usual buggy and horse, but to ride something different, something that he would not be recognized with. Pierre chose his daughters' horse, Samson. He had never been seen with Samson. Whenever he did ride him, it was always on the grounds.

Turning his collar up to the cool night air and pulling a wide brimmed hat almost over his face, he turned the horse eastward and trotted along the dirt road. Farm dogs barked and as he trotted by, but no one otherwise paid attention.

The scheduled meeting was to be held at Marcel's barn across town. All of the participants were asked to bring their horses and buggies inside. The meeting would commence after the double door was closed.

Pierre had thought that perhaps Marcel was ready to accept the new racing saddle and organize the financing and profits. Perhaps he had called this meeting with Pierre and other businessmen to discuss things regarding the saddle amongst them. He had criticized the new racing saddle in times past; he felt that too much time was spent on adjustments. He had mentioned improvement ideas, but had never discussed them in detail.

The secrecy of this meeting had Pierre perplexed. It wasn't like they had competitors. Why would Marcel want Pierre not to be recognized? It wasn't that secretive, was it? Besides, it wasn't as if a great many people were out at that time, anyway. Except for a few buggies and carriages, the roads were deserted. Businesses had closed for the night, and some had closed forever because the owners had left New Orleans.

Marcel was waiting behind his barn when Pierre arrived. Other participants had already arrived. Pierre turned his horse into the big barn, as Marcel directed, and dismounted.

"Well, if it isn't Pierre Fontenot!" one observed.

Pierre did not immediately respond. Pierre's flimsy disguise had fooled several of the men gathered there. He indeed didn't appear as they had seen him in public, on occasion. He laughed as he removed his hat and straightened his collar; he could see the surprised look on their faces.

"That's quite a horse you got there, and I have never seen him before," another observed.

"Well," Pierre answered, "He's my hideaway horse!"

"Cognac… Pierre?" Marcel suggested, as he held a bottle and several goblets.

"Not for me, Marcel," he hoarsely replied, "Doesn't agree with me, so I'll be up half of the night if I drink that."

Marcel ignored him and led the group to a crude table behind huge bales of hay.

"Gentleman!" he said, addressing them in French, "I do appreciate your attendance. There are some matters at hand, and they are matters that concern us all, matters that need to be taken care of."

Pierre just knew that he would begin a conversation about the new racing saddle, which had almost been forgotten, for the most part. He decided he would definitely hear him out. He may or may not agree or disagree with Marcel about improvements that were never discussed in detail. Marcel looked about at his guests, trying to study their faces and to get a feel for how he would present his ideas.

"All of you know Pierre Fontenot; of course," he muttered in subdued English, "I do have to say that if it wasn't for him, this very barn wouldn't be here. Pierre is certainly a generous benefactor to many in New Orleans, and indeed a close friend."

Pierre curtly smiled at the surprise introduction. He just knew that at any moment, the racing saddle would be brought up. He wanted Marcel to make a nice sales pitch, and he was ready to do his part to make that happen.

"That's Jacque," Marcel said, motioning with his hand to his left, "Of course, everybody knows him. He's the owner and proprietor of the saddle shop," Marcel continued, "A very skilled man and a valuable asset to this group."

Likewise Jacque wryly smiled and looked at Marcel, waiting for him to continue.

"Jake Kelehey," Marcel continued, "Quite the horseman, I should say, and quite the gentleman, as well."

Mr. Kelehey nodded in appreciation for the considerate and kind introduction.

"Lastly, there's John Rufus," Marcel went on, "Owner of Rufus Stables. He's certainly an appreciative and supportive man, whose participation in the recent ball was certainly a contributing influence to its success."

John smiled and nodded as he sipped a goblet of cognac. Pierre was just waiting for the moment when Marcel would discuss the new saddle. After all, that introduction and the fact that all the right people seemed to be there to discuss a new saddle only seemed to confirm that that's what this meeting was about.

All eyes now turned to Marcel. He sensed that, and lit several more oil lanterns as a sign of the sincerity of his proposed discussion. He knew all of his guests well; at least well enough to know that flattery worked with them. Compliments and kind words worked on the racetrack, at the stables, and now in a private meeting with his most trusted colleagues.

"Gentleman," he said in a tone of authority, "I do recall that a famous patriot once said, 'These are the times that try men's souls.' We certainly are about to have in our midst a lot of unwelcome company, if we just sit here and do nothing."

Pierre, and most everyone else, leaned forward to better hear what was being said.

"I have brought you all to this meeting because we are indeed the leaders and representatives of our local southern rights."

Pierre's high hopes tumbled as soon as he heard that. This wasn't going to be a discussion about the new saddle at all. This was some sort of private, nocturnal political meeting.

"Gentleman," Marcel continued, in a stern manner now, "It's up to us to preserve our lifestyles, our southern dignity and our rights. Many have left New Orleans. Even several members of my family have left, and some of my friends have, as well. Oh, well, I say let them run! They are mere cowards in the face of adversary!"

"They most certainly are cowards!" John reaffirmed, "I lost half of my stablemen to the exodus, and they most certainly cannot have their jobs back... if and when they return!"

Marcel knew that he was striking an emotional chord with his plea. Others would soon comment on their situations. He would turn up the heat and get more responses. But before he could say anything more, someone else spoke.

"My own son-in-law, whom I treated as my own son, just up and joined the Union army!" Mr. Kelehey added, "After all I did for him, he wants to turn against the south! The bastard said he dislikes slavery. He said something about slaves being enslaved against their will…and that being in violation of God's plan for man, or such self righteous thing like that."

"Jake it is so dreadful to hear something like that!" John interjected, "I can truly sympathize with you. I have lost a son, two brothers, and a cousin on the field of battle, and nothing in the world can bring them back. The truth is, having anyone you love fighting is a nightmare. My family is forever scarred by their absence."

"What I can't believe is that he is fighting with the Union! It's hard enough that he is fighting, but not only did he go into battle, but he went into battle against us. I just can't believe this war is dividing my family," Jake said as he forced himself to swallow his emotion.

Each of the participants, except Pierre, shared their own emotional, heart wrenching stories and feelings about the war and the profound effect it had already had on their families. Pierre just sat there and listened with interest, as he had no son or any other male descendant to lose in the war. He only had his daughter Gabrielle, and for the first time, he was grateful that he had no son.

'God help the Yankees if they capture Gabrielle,' he mused to himself in thought. But Marcel had a psychological edge; he wanted to bring out the real purpose of this meeting, but his tactics were working. First, he'd used flattery, and now sentiment. Pierre continued to say nothing in response to the personal losses that the others were discussing.

"Say Pierre, you're mighty quiet," Marcel noted.

"I don't have any sons," he muttered.

"But surely you have suffered. If in no other way, then much more so financially than the rest of us have. We may have the sons and the men folk who enlisted and died, but you have released more slaves than anyone else I can think of," Jacque noted in his French accent.

"Yes, I have," he stated, after a moment of deep thought.

"Those slaves cost a lot of money, Pierre, and you can never get it back," John quipped.

"I know that," Pierre responded, "But my reasoning for letting them go is that the Yankees, should they arrive in New Orleans, will eventually discover the Chateau and will see that there are no slaves, so there would be no reason for them to invade my land and destroy my property."

"Maybe that's good logic... and maybe not," Jacque responded, "I still have my slaves, but because I built saddles for the cavalry, I'm trusting that they won't destroy my shop."

"Gentleman," Marcel said, "My purpose for bringing you here is that we all have suffered losses due to the War of Independence. We all have a high stake in keeping what we have and grieving over what we have lost. We are the most affluent, but war knows nothing about classes, and the rich and poor alike suffer."

"Go on," John muttered.

"Now, we find that the Yankees are almost in out midst, just north and northwest of the city, in tent encampments and caissons of cannons that remind us of their presence everyday," he continued.

"We all know that," Jacque added.

"To form a public militia would be devastating. We would not win, and worse, it would lead to further loss of life. I do propose that we deal with them and let the enemy drive out our own enemy."

"Who would that be?" Jake asked.

"I do hate to say this Pierre, but the freed slaves and liberated blacks will rise up and be a thorn in our side if we don't take care of this soon," Marcel advised.

"What do you have in mind?" John asked as he leaned forward.

"All that I'm trying to say to that the "Cause," as it is sometimes called, is worthless now. The north will win. We don't stand a chance, and if we at least give the slaves something… at least we won't be fighting two enemies at once. Let's admit one thing to ourselves. Our slaves that we have freed, if they are given the chance, may tell the Yankees who owned them and some of the things we did, and we may get in serious trouble," Marcel further explained.

"I concur with John," Mr. Kelehey added, "What is your point here?"

"We can't fight the Yankees, with their caissons of cannons, we would be slaughtered, as well as lose most of New Orleans. Perhaps a deal could be struck with them, as well as the freed blacks," he said.

"What kind of a deal?" Pierre asked, as he leaned forward even further to understand better.

"Who doesn't love horseracing? We could talk to the blacks about being caretakers of the grounds, substitute jockeys and gate attendants at the racetrack. All they are doing now is occupying the track with their filthy, lust infested shanty town. Besides, we are due for a good race."

"What about the Yankees?" Pierre asked.

"The Yankees would provide the horses. As you know, almost all of our good, blue blood racers are gone, caught up in the exodus. It would be like it was years ago when the track was first built and those mares ran, long before the ball," he explained.

"So, what you are saying, Marcel, is that to please the blacks and keep the peace, we should let them have an active role in the races?" John asked.

"I am afraid, gentleman. I am afraid of what is going to happen if they are left there by themselves in those shanty shacks and tents. Not only will they tell the Yankees about their former lives as slaves, but they might join them and turn on us. I don't just mean us….the townspeople, I mean."

"I don't like it!" Mr. Kelehey replied abruptly.

"I think what Jake is trying to say is that there is no guarantee that if they would have given tasks and roles at the track, they would not turn on us. They could have paid work and still turn on us. Some of them were not good slaves…and needed to be handled accordingly. I have whipped a few in my time, as a matter of principle. I always made sure that Gabrielle, my daughter, did not see. She thinks that I have never been cruel to our slaves, and I'd like to keep it that way. I feed them and let them speak their minds. That's more than most white masters do. Some former slaves, though, might turn on us just because they can. What makes you think that giving them duties at the track will change that? We have no foundation for that," Pierre explained.

"Some of those freed nigger slaves are just out for vengeance," John Rufus stated, "They can't be trusted to do the right thing."

"It's worth looking into," Pierre added, "Some of them were mine, and they have a worse life now, in freedom, than they did being slaves. They are hungry and lack any really nutritious food. Well, everyone has to eat, and I don't believe they should starve. Men and their families don't eat if they don't work. No one wants to hire them or have anything to do with them."

Marcel's discussion hit a sentimental chord with Pierre, or so he was led to believe. True, Pierre was thinking about the future of the city. But as well, Pierre thought of the new racing saddle. If he got in trouble with the Yankees and ended up in jail, he would be broke, homeless and separated from his daughter. He didn't want that. He loved Gabrielle dearly.

John seemed to relax as Pierre spoke. Pierre was thinking very logically. But then again, Pierre just had a way of seeming calm and collected around others. Inside, he was petrified. He was so fearful of losing all he held dear, not just his daughter, but his land, his reputation and his workers.

"Does anyone else have any suggestions? Does anyone have a better resolution than the one I offered?" Marcel asked the group.

"This would have to be handled carefully," John said, "I've never heard of nigger jockeys, but that doesn't mean it can't happen as a means of saving ourselves."

"Perhaps something could happen here," Jacque added, "Everybody loves horseracing, even the Yankees."

"Maybe pit their best against our best?" Mr. Kelehey thought aloud.

"Well, that might work," Marcel said as he took another sip of cognac, "But what I have in mind is racing our best horses against the best Yankee horses. As a huge race opener, perhaps Mr. Boyer's horse could run against someone else. You all know that he has the fastest horse, and that is meant with no disrespect to you Pierre, but he does."

Pierre just nodded. He didn't take offence to it, and it was the truth. None of his prized racehorses ever beat a Boyer horse.

"Well then, who would the Boyer horse run against?" Jacque asked.

"There is only one horse locally that could qualify," Pierre added, "That horse belongs to that abolitionist family that lives down the road from me. I don't care for the family, but the horse is fast. I do have to give him credit, because he beat my horse fair and square."

"I saw that race," Mr. Kelehey mentioned, "They brought that horse here from Atlanta. He was a dirt road racer, from what I'm told."

"I heard that too," John added, "I certainly don't have a horse to beat him, that's for sure."

"The Yankees will certainly like that abolitionist angle," Marcel thought out loud, "Even though those people are from the south, they own no slaves. The Yankees will surely play up to that. We could too!"

"This could be the race of the century. Posters could advertise it as such!" John said as he almost laughed.

"The Boyer horse against that abolitionist horse," Mr. Kelehey mused, "Come to think of it, it would be a good race. Those horses never met."

"Mr. Fournier is still around," John mentioned, "He paired your horse against their horse, didn't he Pierre?"

Pierre just nodded to acknowledge that indeed, Mr. Fournier had been responsible for that match up.

"All that needs to happen now is that we contact Mr. Fournier and see what he thinks," Pierre suggested, "I know for a fact that he is still here. His Irish jockey is gone. He left with the exodus, beat it out of here and headed back to Ireland, from what I'm told."

"Didn't know that," John muttered.

"First, we have to sell this idea to the coloreds who occupy that track area with their shanty town," Mr. Kelehey mentioned.

"They would have to be a part of this to make it happen," Pierre added, "Have to be."

"Well Pierre," Jacque said, "Didn't you say that some of them were yours at one time? You treated them well, and certainly they would vouch for you."

"They would... if there was something in it for them," He replied.

"What would that something be?" Mr. Kelehey asked.

"Pierre, could you meet with them on friendly terms and describe what we propose?"

Jacque asked, "There seems to be something in this for all of us."

"I can do that." Pierre replied.

"Well, we have to do something, or soon we will all go broke. The trains are all for the military now, with very few passengers. They just don't bring in the revenue that this city needs," Jake remarked.

"And if we don't earn money somehow, we will all go hungry," John commented with a frown.

Passenger service at the depot was almost nil, at best. The Yankees now controlled so much of the railroad property north of New Orleans that the liked to think they could control everything, including the trains, so very few passengers were allowed to proceed southward. Freight cars were confiscated, and their contents removed. Any equipment to aid the Confederacy never made it to its destination; it had all been re-directed northward.

Several of the depot new hires had left to join the last stand northward to defend New Orleans from occupation. Business at the depot was dismal. William was no less concerned than he ever had been as he stood before his scant crowd of workers in the back room.

"Boys," he said hesitantly, as he looked about, "I'm sure you all know why I'm here to speak to you. I haven't stood before you in a long time, only because there has been nothing to say, but today I do have something to say. In light of the economic conditions, I'm letting most of you go today. I am truly sorry to have to do that. I know some of you have families to take care of, and I wish you the best of luck. I am only doing this because I have no other choice. We just are not bringing in the money that we once did. Those of you that have been here less than ten years no longer work here."

A slight murmur surprise came over the boys as they all looked about in shock. They all had pretty much guessed this might happen, but never thought that all of them, with the exception of only a few, would be laid off at once.

"It wasn't a difficult decision at all," William continued, "You only have to look about to see what is happening out there. The north will soon control the railroad. The only boys that will remain will be the ones that are needed to service the few cars that are still in service."

"Will we get a chance to come back?" One asked.

"That's highly doubtful," he responded, "I do wish there was a better way to do this, but there just isn't. All you boys did a good job while it lasted, and I'm damn proud of all of you!"

The boys just stood there for a moment, many almost in shock. To them, this job meant the world. It meant the difference between having food on the table or not.

"You are all free to leave now," William said, "Just take your belongings with you."

With that, he turned about and exited, leaving them to deal with the reality of being let go.

"I'm surprised he kept us as long as he did," Ben said.

"Damn," another said, "It's just me and Sarah and little Billy. I can't work. My boy has to eat. If I have to, I will go hungry so he can eat, but he has to eat. Where am I going to find another job?"

His question was the same one that everyone was asking themselves. They had to live, and now they were without work. Nobody had any answers for him or themselves. One by one, they shuffled out of the back room, shook hands and went their ways.

There was no ride home today; William's transportation service had just ended.

Throwing his coat over his shoulder, Ben stepped down off of the platform steps one last time and headed home. It was going to be a long walk, but he didn't mind it. It would give him time to think and pray. Besides, he had to think of how to break the news to his family that he no longer had a job. Well, maybe his father already knew this was going to happen, and simply didn't have the heart to tell him.

The cobblestone streets were almost deserted. For those that remained in New Orleans, there was hardly anything to get out and see anymore. The nicer shops were closed, and the windows were boarded up. The owners had been part of exodus.

It seemed so unreal to him without the hustle and bustle of everyday street traffic.

On that windy day, several boys could be seen flying a kite along a long stretch of a grassy plain. They were the only ones that were seemingly having a good time, totally oblivious to the world around them. They laughed with glee as their kite sailed higher and higher. It made Ben want to be a kid again just watching them.

Moving along the sides of, and in between, several buildings, now Ben could see the abandoned slave auction block. With a sick feeling in his stomach, he recalled a time when he and his father had witnessed the awful scene that must have taken place there several thousand times. There was nothing there now; it was purposefully abandoned to please the soon-to-be, northern occupants.

"I'd know you anywhere!" a female's voice yelled from a balcony. He looked up and saw the same southern belle in the pink dress that had blown him a kiss.

"Who are you?" he asked.

"It's not a question of who I am, it's a question of what I am," she yelled back.

"Why do you keep speaking to me when I want no part of you?" he asked of her.

She laughed, and then hesitantly spoke again, "There is no need to be ashamed of me. I am what I am, but I could tell you a lot of things!"

"What could you tell me that I don't already know?" he inquired, almost curious now.

In a teasing manner, she put her index fingertip against her cheek in a flirty, inquisitive way, and then rolled her eyes to further emphasize whatever she was about to say.

"Well, well, let me see. I bet I know why Pierre Fontenot let all those slaves go, in particularly, the younger females. Oh, I could tell you a lot of things about the Chateau and what went on there, behind his wife's back. May God rest her sweet soul and all. She was a kind woman, a fine wife and mother."

Ben held his hand up horizontally to his forehead to shield his eyes from the glare of the sunlight. He could not believe what he was hearing. How could this woman know anything about Pierre, and what did she know? Furthermore, was what she claimed to know the real truth?

"What did you say?" he asked, almost dumbfounded.

"You heard me well enough, and should you not believe me, we have several of his former slave girls working for us now," she replied, almost sarcastically.

"Well," Ben stammered, "That has nothing to do with me. I certainly could not care less what happens at the Chateau anyway."

"Perhaps not," she responded in a lower tone, "But I do know something that does concern you. I would be surprised if you didn't know."

"Oh?" Ben asked, returning her almost sarcastic response of earlier.

"The word is out, mister, that people have been looking for you and that horse of yours. You are to race Tori Boyer's horse in a grand exhibition to please the Yankees, and to take their money, as well."

"People are looking for me?" he asked, almost forgetting himself.

"New Orleans will be surrendered," she said, "When that happens, all of us girls are going to dump our chamber pots on the heads of the northern invaders as they march along this street."

"You're just asking for trouble," he replied.

"I'll tell you something else. I'm not worried about it… because Gabrielle Fontenot and I have something in common," she said, with an all-knowing look.

"What would that be?" Ben asked as he shielded his eyes from the glaring son.

The flirtatious girl was about to answer when an older woman appeared in the window and beckoned her back inside of the room. Ben watched as they both disappeared behind a curtain, and an ornate shade was promptly pulled down. He turned away, heading down the empty street once again.

This was the first time that Ben had needed to walk home from the depot. It was more tiring than what he had expected. Eventually, after what seemed like hours, the dirt road came into view, a welcome relief at last.

As he walked past the Chateau, he noticed Gabrielle waving and motioning from an upstairs bed room window. Judging from her actions and pointing, he could clearly surmise that she wanted to speak to him.

He chose a huge shade tree, slightly out of sight from her point of view, and pointed to it as he responded to her inquiry. She motioned to show that she understood, and quickly disappeared from the window. Ben wiped his brow with his shirt sleeve and sat under the tree. It provided him with a much needed rest. Any shade looked good at this point.

Eventually, Gabrielle appeared in a beautiful sun dress and matching parasol. Smiling all the while she seemed happy and in an upbeat mood.

"Ben, so good to see you again!" she exclaimed as she quickly gave him a hug.

"Nice to see you again, Gabrielle," he replied with equal enthusiasm, "I look a mess. It's mighty hot out here, and I am sweating like a pig. I am so ashamed to be seen like this. Look at me. It looks like somebody threw a bucket of water on me."

"Oh Ben," she replied, "You fret about the smallest things."

433

"Well, I lost my job today. We all got let go. Only the ones that have been there for awhile will be allowed to continue working there. Some of those folks have kids. Heck, there ain't no jobs anywhere!"

"Well Ben, here's a good money making opportunity. I don't know whether you know this or not, but the word is out that your horse will be in a big race soon. As a matter-of-fact, the race is against Tori Boyer's horse!"

"Say what?" Ben asked, "How do you know this?"

Ben did not tell her that he had heard that from the flirtatious girl in the window as he walked home.

"Everybody knows Ben, everybody!" she replied with wide eyes and a dropped jaw.

"I am the last one to know that my horse is to run against the best? How can this be?" Ben asked in response.

"Well, there's more to it than that, sir. You are being called the 'son of the abolitionist' because you don't have any slaves, and, well, the Boyers' have lots of them, and all this is done to please the Yankees, to let them know that there indeed people who live in New Orleans that don't have any slaves," she explained with a bright smile.

"So it's a political thing?" he inquired.

"Ben, the object is to stop the Yankees from burning the city or destroying property. Everybody likes horseracing. Everybody likes to bet and see a championship race," she further explained as she adjusted her sun bonnet.

"I knew it all along, Gabrielle. The war is lost. The south will not win, despite everything that we have done, and it's just a matter of time," Ben said in a woeful lower tone.

"You have a winning horse, Ben, so take advantage of the moment. There will never be another opportunity like this. I know for a fact that Mr. Fournier is looking for you so that your horse can get better training. This is a chance of a lifetime, Ben; don't let it pass you by."

"So it's slavery versus no slavery in a horserace?" Ben asked.

"Well, Yankees like races, too. I need to go, Ben. We'll see each other soon. Remember, all the race will ever be is a political rivalry, played out in a contest of wills," she acknowledged.

Ben could clearly see that Miss Prissy was waving her onward. Obviously, she was needed back in the Chateau and there was little time to waste.

"Bye for now, Ben," Gabrielle said as she stepped past him and headed for the main drive.

"I guess there's nothing like being in a hurry, but good day for now," Ben said.

He turned to walk the remaining three quarter mile to his own house. The short break from the unbearable sun felt refreshing. He would feel much better once he got back to the house and splashed cold well water in his face. The long walk from the depot had been strenuous, and something that he wasn't accustomed to.

"Here Ben, let me pump some cold water for you," his father said as Ben came into sight.

"It's hotter than the living hell out here!" Ben barely gasped through parched lips.

The cold well water felt like medicine on his dry throat, and to Ben, it had never tasted as good as that moment.

"Take it easy now. Don't drink too much at once," his father advised, "You just might get sick over it. It's a shock to your body at first."

Ben drank three more ladles of cold well water and splashed the fourth one on his face. Regaining his composure, Ben stood upright and then shook the water from his face.

"There you go. Now I know you'll feel better."

"What are you doing home, father?" Ben asked, suddenly realizing that at this time of day his father was normally at work.

"I'm here for the same reason you are," John answered, "I know good and well that you don't have a job anymore, and I don't, either!"

"Say what?" Ben gasped, "They let you go, too?"

"Very few remain now, son," he replied, "I know all those Yankees are using the rails now, and the slaves need to be free. I hope they win. The railroad wanted me to stay, I think. They gave me a nice offer, but it was still considerably less than we need to be able to live. They told me I could choose to walk, or take a pay cut, and I chose to walk."

"Good for you!" Ben said. "There is no need to work for less. I would have done the same thing, but somehow I didn't get an offer to walk. They fired all of us!"

"Well, anyway," John answered, "The railroad won't get back on its feet again until the war is over. I don't know what we will do now to make money. Now is the time that I guess we will just have to trust God to provide our needs."

"I walked all the way back," Ben recounted.

"I can see that," John smiled, "I also know that your horse will be involved in the biggest race that New Orleans has seen for years!"

"Why is it that I don't know any of this?" Ben asked.

"Well, now you do," John replied. "I have heard that there is off-track betting in your favor. People have faith in your horse, Ben. They really think he can win. Do you? Are you going to allow him to run? He's a winner, so are you going to let him run?" John asked.

"I knew it all along!" Ben smiled, "I knew it all along!"

"You just said that you didn't know! Now you are saying you did know," John said.

"I knew all along that I have a winning horse!" Ben proudly proclaimed.

"C'mon, let's go and get something to eat," John recommended.

His mother had a huge roast beef supper in the making. The house smelled of baked bread and cinnamon. Elizabeth hugged a letter to her chest and slowly danced about the parlor. Spinning and almost whirling as she went, she was in unusually good spirits. She had every reason to be. She had good news. Her husband had not been severely wounded after all, as she had thought.

What she danced with was a letter from him. It was true that he had been taken prisoner and was held at Rock Island, along with many others. Fortunately, the rumor that he had been hurt seriously was false. He was fine and in good health. Ben was glad to hear it. John had already known about it for awhile by the time Ben heard. To all of them, it was an answer to prayer to hear that Ethan was uninjured.

"John, we had a letter from Thomas, as well," Amanda mentioned, "It's on the mantle."

"I'll read it after supper," John replied, "Everything sure smells good! Where did you get meat?"

"I bought it. I had to save up, but we needed meat. Well, it's a special day. With the both of you out of work, it's about time some work got done around here!" she teased.

"That may be true," he replied as cigar smoke billowed from his nostrils. "But this house isn't ours, either! I got it when I started working for the railroad. So, does that mean we are homeless? I guess I hadn't thought about that until just now. Oh, dear Lord!" John exclaimed as the colored drained from his face.

"Dad, doesn't the Bible say that God counts even the hairs on our heads and even watches over the sparrows? He knows what we need. If we do lose this house, he'll give us a better one somehow," Ben said.

"Elizabeth," her mother called, "We have two hungry men here that need to be fed!"

Elizabeth stopped her prancing about and helped her mother set the table.

"Must be a special occasion with this huge meal and all," Ben said.

"Let's go wash our hands," his father reminded him.

Chapter 37
Mansions of Fire

A young Union courier stopped and tied his horse in front of the captain's quarters. It was a welcome relief from the sweltering heat. He had an important change of orders in his saddlebag for the captain, who had held his troops, pending further word. The courier opened the door to an impatient captain.

"Well, it's about time!" the captain exclaimed as he stood up from behind his makeshift desk.

"Sorry, sir!" the courier replied as he handed over the document, "I had horse trouble near Baton Rouge. He had to have a new shoe put on, and I was delayed, but I got here as fast as I could."

"Very well, then," the captain replied as he accepted the document. "You could use some water. Help yourself to the barrel."

It was a merciful word to the sweaty courier, who had long ago, ran out of canteen water. He had brought extra water with him when he left, but it wasn't apparently enough. He was so thirsty that his

438

head hurt. The captain read the document with interest, but kept his eye on the thirsty courier.

"Don't drink it all so fast like that, son. You'll get sick. Take that ladle and drink slow and easy!"

"Yes, sir!" the young man gulped between swallows.

The captain read the orders with greater interest now. His direct order wasn't what he had expected.

"Go see the quartermaster. He'll give you some supper and put you up for the night," the captain said as he folded the order. The young courier thanked the captain for the water and the generosity and left.

The captain had been ordered to take his battalions and enter New Orleans from the west and stage a surprise, night raid of pilferage to strike fear into the hearts and minds of the inhabitants. It wasn't what he had expected, but he had his official orders. The Union had wanted a complete surrender. The captain would assemble and organize his battalion that very night. The order weighed heavy on his mind.

Summoning his subordinates at almost twilight, he quickly detailed the plan. They didn't have any time to waste, and there would be no sleep for any of them that night. They had to get moving. Each of the battalion's soldiers had a lit, wooden torch in their hands as they followed their respective leaders on horseback.

"Alright, boys!" the captain hollered out to the troops, "It's time to teach these rebels a lesson. Let's show them that we mean business!"

With an almost eerie glow about them, the army moved forward in rows of two abreast. They would travel about twenty miles down the packed dirt road and start the tirade of burning, then loop back and burn on their way back.

Buildings and fields were of the utmost importance. The starving former slaves residing in shacks were to be left alone. The fiery intimidation was meant to strike an awesome fear into the white, middle and upper class citizens, causing them to surrender and pledge allegiance to the Union.

Ben awoke to the resounding thunder of horses' hooves in the distance. Peering out of his window and beyond the tree line, he could see a huge multitude of Union soldiers with lit, wooden torches. For him, getting dressed seemed an eternity; all the while he kept thinking over and over that they were up to no good.

Scrambling towards his parents' bedroom door, he yelled that there was an invading army on the road with torches in hand. His father immediately sprang out of the bedroom to see for himself. Elizabeth and Amanda both appeared in the upstairs hallway at about the same time. Each held a candle holder and a lit candle. They had also heard, and been awakened by, the thunderous noise

"Damn it all!" John cursed, "What do they want?"

"Look at all of them, father. There must be two hundred of them, and they aren't here on a social call. What are we going to do?" Ben asked in wide-eyed horror.

"Those men are Yankee soldiers!" Elizabeth muttered under her breath.

"We never see Yankee soldiers at this edge of New Orleans," Amanda answered back, "What do you suppose they are doing here?"

Knowing that his family was safe, Ben immediately thought about Gabrielle and her well-being, but didn't reveal his concern to the family. The invading army moved on down the road. As the last of the horsemen passed the house, Ben had already made his way downstairs in the darkness to further investigate the mysterious appearance of Union soldiers with lit torches in the middle of the night.

Opening the front door, he could smell the dirt that the horses had kicked up on the dusty road. Stepping out onto the lawn, he could see the last of the riders, far ahead, way down the road and almost past the Chateau. To his horror, he watched helplessly as one of the last Yankees threw his torch toward an abandoned out building on the Chateau's property. His father fully dressed by now and concerned for his safety, finally arrived on the lawn.

"What are they doing?" he asked.

Ben didn't answer for a split second, and finally surmised what they were up to.

"One of the last of them threw his torch at a building near the Chateau," he answered with squinted eyes.

His father said nothing. There was nothing he could say or do at that point. Ben watched in utter horror as the building caught fire, and then another torch was thrown at other out buildings on the other side of the road. John watched as the horizon down the road turned into an eerie, orange glow.

"Oh my Lord!" John gasped, "They'll be here next, when they double back," he said.

"Do you think so, father?" Ben asked.

"We had best better gather up all of the things that we want to keep and load up the wagon. I am sure they will be coming back."

Ben could see several darkened, shadowy figures near the dusty road but none seemed to be Gabrielle. He wondered if she knew what was happening or if she was asleep and didn't know about the fire.

John looked back for a moment at his own house, and then looked toward Ben. Ben wasn't there; he was sprinting towards the Chateau as fast as he could.

John watched in disbelief as Ben disappeared into the darkness of the night. Eventually, his shadow could be seen mingling with the others. There was no way for John to know which one his son was. He feared for Ben. His son had always been impulsive, even to the point of being somewhat rude and abrasive.

Amanda appeared and asked of Ben's whereabouts. John just sighed and nodded toward the Chateau. She then realized that Ben was so concerned about Gabrielle's safety that he was willing to leave his own family behind.

"Oh, dear Lord, have mercy," Amanda whispered, saying it as more of a prayer than anything else.

"They seem to be burning and destroying everything. Before Ben took off running, I told him that we should pack up the wagon and leave. When I looked about, he was gone!" John hollered in horror.

"He loves that girl, John," she muttered, as she stared down the road.

"I'm afraid that they will double back and throw torches at our place. We'll be left out in the cold with nothing but the shirts on our backs," he sighed.

"You stay here in case Ben comes back, or something happens to him. I'll get Elizabeth and we'll start packing up as fast as we can!" she recommended.

"Alright then, that will have to do. Once that's done, we can leave and turn left down Sugar Haven Road. The troops didn't take that way in, and they don't know that it's there. It will lead us away from New Orleans," he replied.

John didn't quite notice as his wife slipped away and set off on her mission. His mind was racing. Should he wait for Ben or hurry and retrieve the wagon and get the horses? Should something happen to Ben he could never forgive himself for not being there. Looking back at the house, he could see both his wife's and daughter's shadows scurrying against the candle lights that they held. They were packing clothes and family papers just as fast as they could. They worked quietly and efficiently. Obviously, Elizabeth understood the severity of the situation. He could sense that.

From Ben's vantage point, the distance to the Chateau seemed longer on foot than what Ben had remembered on horseback. He was almost breathless now, as he hid behind a huge tree. Turning his head, he could barely make out the outline of his own house. The Chateau was much closer at that point.

The Union's horsemen were indeed burning everything that their torches could reach. Outbuildings and parched grass lines were blazing. The emitting fire light only served to provide more illumination for them. It had been a dry year and foliage burned quickly.

Ben crouched and watched as the fires crept towards nearby, country houses and out buildings. Many of the houses had been vacated during the exodus. The invaders didn't seem to notice, as they continued their burning rage that no occupants were leaving their properties. It would be just a short time before the fire would creep closer to the Chateau.

He watched as the ground burned and trees cracked as they caught the wind, which was fanning the merciless flames. He wondered if the Chateau was empty. No activity could be seen. There was no candlelight from inside, and no stablemen, no nothing; it was completely darkened.

As he in watched in grief and horror, windswept embers from a burning tree settled onto the roof of the mansion. Still, there was no movement from inside of the mansion. Ben began to think that maybe they really weren't there.

The Union troops said nothing as they pitched their burning torches here and there, with random, guiltless abandonment. Several entered the paved drive of the Chateau and pitched their torches at anything that they could see that would burn. Ben watched in horror as the foliage of the pond where he and Gabrielle had met and talked slowly become engulfed in flames.

Finally, a shadowy figure appeared, emerging from the mansion's side door, and then another followed. Moving away from his sanctuary provided by his hiding place, he could see that there was an aura of confusion around the darkened shadows. They apparently didn't know what to do. The Union horsemen galloped away, as their sickening deeds caught hold.

Gathering up all of his will, and clearly seeing that there was no one but him near, and nothing between him and the Chateau, he ran toward it. Gabrielle had just emerged from the side kitchen door, and just by coincidence, he happened to meet her.

"Gabrielle!" he screamed from a short distance, "Yankee horsemen are setting fire to just about everything!"

"Ben, Ben!" she replied through her tears, "I know! My father is ill and in bed. He has been sick since last Monday sometime!"

Finally reaching her in the misty, smoky, steamy, night he hugged her and stood in a tight embrace for what seemed like an eternity, though it was a mere second.

"Can your father walk?" Ben asked.

"Not on his own," she replied as she looked nervously about.

"Where is he? I will help you with him, how's that?" He asked.

"Come on! I will quickly show you! The mansion will burn, so we must hurry! The fire cannot be stopped," she hastily explained with a French accent. Ben had only known her to accentuate a French accent only in times of personal despair and defeat. This certainly was one of those.

She quickly led Ben by the hand into the mansion and up the winding, massive stairwell. From there, she opened her father's bedroom door, and Ben saw that Pierre was in an almost paralyzed state. He could obviously see that Pierre was so sick that he couldn't hardly move or whisper. An orange, shadowy glow could be seen from the ornate bedroom curtains, and still Pierre didn't seem to know what was happening.

"There is a buggy in the stable," she said. "Let me run and get it, Samson is the only horse that is still here."

"What happened to the other horses?" Ben asked.

"They were taken to the other stable or stolen by renegades," she replied.

"We don't have much time. I have to move him as soon as possible. Go, then. I will carry him downstairs. We have to be quick about this. The fire is licking at the window panes!"

Gabrielle disappeared from the bedroom. Ben could hear her running down the stairs.

Ben looked at Pierre, and saw not a slave trader, or a man with too much money and a shadowy, even dark, past, but a man he had known before.

This was the same man that he had once admired in a painting. He was a man that people saw as a man of wealth and character, a champion of the poor, and someone who had once been nothing, but rose above his own impoverished childhood.

It was obvious that now, he was so sickly that he could die. Noticing that Pierre had no shoes on his feet, he found a pair of house slippers and quickly put them on his feet. If Pierre knew that Ben was at his bedside, he didn't show it. He was just too sick.

Ben picked him up in his arms and immediately realized that he wasn't as heavy as what he had imagined. Making his way down the hallway, he stopped at the top of the stairs momentarily to reposition Pierre so he wouldn't be hurt, then proceeded down. The orange, glowing shadow was becoming more intense now. From a gaze at a parlor window, he realized that it was just a matter of minutes until this very house he now stood in would be ashes.

Making a wrong turn, and then correcting himself, he continued on. Finally, he found a side door and slipped out. It had seemed like an eternity. The night air was actually much hotter now. At least they were safe. Ben ran away from the house as quickly as he could. Within a matter of seconds, Gabrielle led Samson to the door. He was attached to a buggy. Walking around back, Ben placed Pierre in the back and turned his head so that he could breathe better. Ben noticed that Gabrielle had a packed suitcase in the back, as well.

"I need to tell you something Ben," she said as she hurried to the back of the buggy.

"You can tell me later. We don't have much time, Gabrielle. The flames are closer than you think," he explained as he hurried along with her.

"You drive," she commanded, "Let's leave quickly then!"

Gabrielle climbed in back with her father. Ben sat behind the reins and jiggled then once. Samson trotted forward. Another jiggle and he trotted just a little faster.

"There you go. Just keep doing that," she said, "He's an easy horse to control. He knows who you are, anyway."

As the buggy approached the front of the mansion, the severity and magnitude of the fires fury was quickly realized. They both knew that they would be in trouble if they didn't get away as fast as possible. As they turned away from the cobble stoned drive, they both noticed that there were people in the road now. Many of then just had their night clothes on, and nothing else with them.

"Gabrielle! Gabrielle!" yelled a neighbor woman, "I summoned a doctor just like you said. I was coming over there to look for you. The doctor is at my summer place, and the fire won't reach there 'cause its across the pond. He got there late and I put him up for the night. There are only a few places that the fire can't get to, and that's one of them. Your father needs a doctor. You need to bring him over to my place."

"Best to do what you are told, Gabrielle," her husband acknowledged.

"He'll be fine with us. You need to get to safety. The good doctor is asleep right now," The woman continued.

Gabrielle looked about. The dirt road was becoming crowded with people who lived further northward. She then looked at Ben for reassurance. Ben sensed her anxiety and nodded with approval. Her father did need a doctor, and it was the right thing to do.

The fire was ever raging. Looking back over her shoulder, she could clearly see that the mansion's roof had caught fire.

"Well, I hate to just leave him," Gabrielle said.

"If your father could understand what is going on right now, he would want you to get somewhere safe," the lady said.

"She's right, Gabrielle," Ben stated.

"Lead us there, then," Gabrielle said.

Both the neighbor lady and her husband walked ahead. Ben slowly guided the buggy past the rows of townspeople who had lost their homes. It wasn't the scene of chaos and confusion that he had expected. People moved out their way as they passed by. These were the people who had waited it out. Those that refused to leave during the first exodus out of New Orleans were now leaving because they had to.

"I hope Mr. Fontenot gets better," a young woman said as, hastily, she walked past the buggy, "I hope you find what you want after all, Ben!"

Ben did a double take. He had seen her before. She was the same one that had hollered to him from a window, and the same one that said she had something to tell him about Gabrielle. Gabrielle gave her a wry smile, but the young woman gave her a look of disgust.

Many people passed by the buggy. Some were in carriages and buggies, but most walked. Ben paid attention to every movement that the couple in front of him made. When they tuned left, he turned left. He was led to a dirt road that he didn't know of. As predicted, there was a huge pond just beyond.

Gabrielle seemed to relax more now. She knew that her father would be in good hands. It was true what the neighbor lady had said. The fire would not reach there. The Yankees had no way of knowing that the secluded house existed. A barren field with a huge pond next

447

to it served as a buffer. The neighbor lady had been an angel in a time of crisis. Slowly but surely, Ben guided the buggy along the drive and then stopped.

"I've got him," the man said as he lifted Pierre from the back of the buggy.

The neighbor lady had been walking ahead, and opened doors as he walked forward.

"I'll get some towels soaked in cold well water," she said as he passed by.

Ben held Gabrielle's hand as they slowly followed the man to a nearby bedroom.

"Pierre has a fever. That much I can tell you just by looking at him. I think there's more to it. He is a sick man, and he needs bed rest," the man mentioned. The woman appeared with dampened towels and placed then across his forehead.

"He'll be fine until the morning. The doctor will be awake and will tend to him. This sickness is wicked, and there is a lot of it going around," she said as she placed the last towel about his head. Gabrielle felt much better now. Although her father was unresponsive, she knew that the woman and her husband would help him the best they could.

"I need to go check on my own family," Ben said.

"Ah yes, you are kin to that Chesser family, come to think of it," the man said.

"I'm Ben Chesser," he replied.

"I need to go with you," Gabrielle said, "I'm sure my father will be fine while I am gone."

"Go, then," the woman said, "I can just about think that the Yankees have doubled back by now."

"Don't worry about your father," the man assured her.

"Thank you so much for all you have done to help us," Gabrielle replied.

As they exited, Ben noticed an orange reddish glow reflecting in the pond's surface. Looking far ahead, they both could see huge crowds, much more than before. It seemed to Ben that the whole world was exiting down that road. This time, they would be traveling in the direction of traffic. A portion of the crowd stopped to let them merge into the line of traffic.

Ben looked over at Gabrielle. He was pleased that she had wanted to come with him.

It wasn't her family that they were going to see. He perceived that she was just returning a favor in kind. He had helped her, and now she was offering to help him and to be there in a time of crisis.

Gabrielle had her own thoughts. But, they were very private, and she wanted them to stay that way. She waited for a time when hardly anyone would pass by their carriage.

"Ben," she said firmly, without any shame when they were alone, "I hope you really do want to marry me. I want to marry you. In my heart, I married you long ago. I am with child. I'm going to have your baby."

"Oh, my Lord!" Ben exclaimed, "Oh my Lord! Gabrielle that is a true miracle. Children are a gift from God."

"I have known for two months now. I just never had a chance to tell you."

"Oh, I'm just the happiest man alive! Yes, I want to marry you. I wasn't being intimate with you just because I wanted to. I really do love you. I know that love is supposed to be for marriage, but God has a way of working things out for the best. Now, we will have to get married, or it will look bad for both of our families."

"I wanted to tell you before, I really did, but I had to wait until now. I haven't seen you in so long, and there was no way for me to tell you."

"Oh Gabrielle, that is just wonderful news. Oh, I just can't believe it!"

As they came into view of the house, it was clear to Ben that it was on fire. Thankfully, there was nobody near it, no family members, and no living soul. From his vantage point, he could see that the barn doors were open and that the family wagon and horses were missing. He was so relieved and happy that he almost cried. They had escaped safely.

He understood that they could not wait for him anymore. There was no sense or safety in stopping. As he continued along past the house, the glow of the fire illuminated a horse tied to a tree far away from the burning house. For a minute, the sight seemed so odd to Ben that his heart skipped a beat. Then, the pieces of the puzzle that was being constructed in his mind fell into place.

"It's my horse, Gabrielle!" he cried joyously.

"Yes, it is, and he is saddled. Stop the buggy and get him."

Ben immediately stopped and approached. He could tell that the horse was agitated and nervous. He noticed a note protruding from the saddle bag. He untied his horse and led him to the back of the buggy, then retied him.

Quickly retrieving the note, he gave it to Gabrielle as he again sat down in the driver's seat. Moving forward again, he took one last look back over his shoulder. The elegant, old house and the slave quarters out back were engulfed in flames.

Ben knew that he would never see that house or that land again. A part of him was saddened, yet another part rejoiced. The railroad's offer had brought him here with his family, and the wrongs committed here had finally exiled him. He had never been wanted here, though he had learned to like the place. Well, change was a part of life, and this would simply be another change. God had been with him so far, and He would not leave him or Gabrielle now. The best part was that she now shared his faith.

"Our meeting place is gone," he whispered as the buggy surged forward.

"This child was conceived there. I know it was," she whispered back.

"I'm glad, Gabrielle, I truly am! God has richly blessed us indeed."

"He sure has, and I am so glad it happened this way," Gabrielle asked.

"Yes, I would have married you long ago if I could have without upsetting my family so badly," Ben confessed.

"Well, now they have to let us get married or it would look really bad. I'm sorry that I could not have told you before all of this happened. I just never had that chance to be alone with you," Gabrielle stated apologetically.

"Don't fret about that. We are alone now!" Ben exclaimed compassionately.

"Yes, Ben we are."

"What does the message say?" he asked.

Gabrielle opened the folded note and read, holding it out against the glow of the moonlight and the fire, "*Sugar Haven Road. Do what you need to do. Love you. God bless you.*"

"They couldn't wait for me anymore and left my horse with the message to tell me where they went," he said.

"Yes, Ben, that's exactly what they did. Did they know that you were in love with me?" she asked.

"I told my mother. My mother said she would tell my father. I never actually heard if she did or not. But, I suppose when I started running toward your house, he may have figured that out, and still he wrote for God to bless me…and if God blesses me, that means you will be blessed, too. For now, I need to get you back to the neighbor lady's house," he said as he looked about for a place to turn around. He was just testing her.

"I'm not going back, Ben. I love you, I am carrying the child that we have conceived together, which God created, and He wants this child to have a father. You will make a fine papa. My father can live without me. There is nothing left. I have nothing to go back to. I don't want to go back. I want to be with you. Back there, there are only burning houses and mansions of fire."

Ben had hoped that she would say that. He turned the buggy onto Sugar Haven Road.

They would have a life together, far from the burning houses and mansions of fire.

About The Author

The acclaimed author's themed genre of another work of historical fiction strives to a triumphed cause with cleverly mingled sub-themes. With overwhelming challenges, a cast of common and affluent parents will approach a major set of controversial circumstances that involves their son and daughter.

A believable resolution is only possible with the creative portrayal of clever and yet compelling approaches of problem solving. Overcoming traditional obstacles with careful tact and wit will eventually result in change in this historical yet compelling steamy southern novel.

Other novels by the same author include *Isle of the Wind, The Treehouse Society* and the soon to be published *Bullknuckle Inn,*

Cemetery Road, The House of Arla Roe and Winds of the Isle, all by the same publisher.

In addition to creating challenging themed novels with ever-changing plot twists the author enjoys cooking, camping and fishing.

CPSIA information can be obtained at www.ICGtesting.com
Printed in the USA
LVOW07s2303230415

435909LV00003B/223/P